ALL THE

SEAS

OF THE

WORLD

ALL THE SEAS

of the

WORLD

GUY GAVRIEL KAY

BERKLEY
NEW YORK

BERKLEY
An imprint of Penguin Random House LLC
penguinrandomhouse.com

Copyright © 2022 by Guy Gavriel Kay
Penguin Random House supports copyright. Copyright fuels creativity, encourages diverse
voices, promotes free speech, and creates a vibrant culture. Thank you for buying an authorized
edition of this book and for complying with copyright laws by not reproducing, scanning, or
distributing any part of it in any form without permission. You are supporting writers and
allowing Penguin Random House to continue to publish books for every reader.

BERKLEY and the BERKLEY & B colophon are registered
trademarks of Penguin Random House LLC.

Map copyright © 2022 by Martin Springett

Library of Congress Cataloging-in-Publication Data

Names: Kay, Guy Gavriel, author.
Title: All the seas of the world / Guy Gavriel Kay.
Description: New York : Berkley, [2022]
Identifiers: LCCN 2022008050 (print) | LCCN 2022008051 (ebook) |
ISBN 9780593441046 (hardcover) | ISBN 9780593441060 (ebook)
Subjects: LCGFT: Novels.
Classification: LCC PR9199.3.K39 A78 2022 (print) | LCC PR9199.3.K39 (ebook) |
DDC 813/.54—dc23/eng/20220224
LC record available at https://lccn.loc.gov/2022008050
LC ebook record available at https://lccn.loc.gov/2022008051

Printed in the United States of America
1 3 5 7 9 10 8 6 4 2

Book design by Lisa Jager

This is a work of fiction. Names, characters, places, and incidents either are the product of
the author's imagination or are used fictitiously, and any resemblance to actual persons,
living or dead, business establishments, events, or locales is entirely coincidental.

Dedicated, with love, to the memory of
SYBIL KAY

Swallow's heart,
have mercy on them.

—WISŁAWA SZYMBORSKA

ORANE

FERRIERES

MARSENA

ESPERAÑA

CARTADA

SILVENES

ALJAIS

ALMASSAR

ABENEVEN

THE MAJRITI

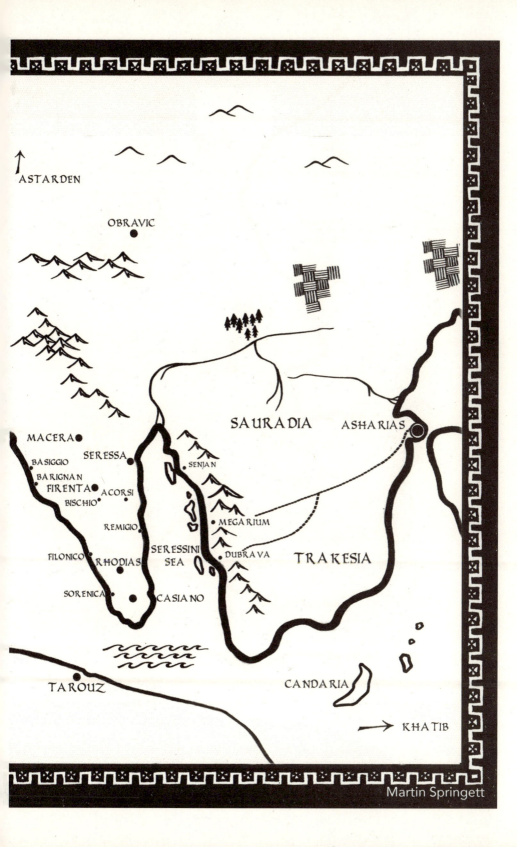

ASTARDEN

OBRAVIC

MACERA

BASIGGIO

BARIGNAN

FIRENTA

BISCHIO

ACORSI

REMIGIO

FILONICO

RHODIAS

SORENICA

CASIANO

SERESSA

SENJAN

SERESSINI
SEA

SAURADIA

ASHARIAS

MEGARIUM

DUBRAVA

TRAKESIA

TAROUZ

CANDARIA

KHATIB

Martin Springett

PRINCIPAL CHARACTERS

(a partial list)

Aboard the Silver Wake

Rafel ben Natan, a Kindath merchant and corsair, born in
    Esperaña, sometime envoy for the khalif of the city of Almassar,
    principal owner of the _Silver Wake_
Nadia bint Dhiyan (so-called), his associate, originally from Batiara
Elie ben Hafai, Rafel's childhood friend, helmsman of the _Silver
    Wake_
Ghazzali al-Siyab of Almassar, engaged on a task with them

In Abeneven

Keram al-Faradi, khalif of that city
Nisim ibn Zukar, his vizier

In Tarouz

Zariq and Ziyar ibn Tihon, brothers, khalifs of that city, notorious/
    celebrated corsairs
Farai Alfasi, their most powerful commander at sea
Ayaash, his young son

In Sorenica

Raina Vidal, called "the queen of the Kindath," widow of Ellias Vidal
Tamir, her sister-in-law
Folco Cino d'Acorsi, encountered here, lord of Acorsi, notorious/celebrated mercenary commander
Caterina Ripoli, his wife, in Acorsi
Gian and Leone, two of his principal men

In Rhodias

Scarsone Sardi, the High Patriarch of Jad
Count Anselmi di Vigano, an aristocrat
Kurafi ibn Rusad, a captured Asharite diplomat, employed by di Vigano
Arsenius Kallinikos, a scholar from Sarantium, also working for di Vigano

In Seressa

Ricci, acting duke
Guidanio Cerra, a principal adviser to Ricci
Brunetto Duso, guard to Cerra
Branco Ciotto, a member of the Council of Twelve
Tazio, a relative of Ciotto
Bentina di Gemisto, First Daughter at a religious retreat near the city

In Firenta

Piero Sardi, banker, acknowledged leader of Firenta
Versano and Antenami, his sons
Saranios della Baiana, a high cleric of Jad
Pelachi, a physician

In Bischio

Leora Sacchetti, a precocious child
Carlo Serrana, a breeder of horses
Anni, his wife
Strani and Aura, his children

In Macera

Duke Arimanno Ripoli
Corinna, his wife

In Ferrieres

Gaelle, a Kindath woman in the port city of Marsena
Isacar, her brother
King Émery of Ferrieres
Hamadi ibn Hayyan, an Asharite envoy to his court
Camilo Rabanez, another envoy, from Esperaña

Others

Gurçu, named "the Conqueror" or "the Destroyer," khalif of Asharias
Ban Rasca Tripon, now called Skandir, a rebel against Gurçu and
    Asharias
Itanios and Ilija, brothers, two of his fighters
Duke Ersani of Casiano, in the south of Batiara
Querida de Carvajal, an Esperañan naval commander
Ibn Udad, deceased, author of the *Prologue to Knowledge*

ALL THE

SEAS

OF THE

WORLD

PART ONE

CHAPTER I

The memory of home can be too far away, in time, in distance across the vastness of the earth, or of the sea.

It can fade or blur for us as the years pass. And there is often pain in that, too. In their dreams some travel back to remembered voices, sounds, scents, images. But many do not dream, or not of the place they came from. Too much loss, too old and hard a sorrow. And some who have such dreams forget them in the morning's light where they find themselves. That can be a blessing.

There will be others who cannot forget. Who wrap themselves in memories as in a heavy cloak. They will walk a street in a far city at twilight and hear a stringed instrument down a laneway, and it takes them back. They might decide to go up that lane, towards where a spill of light suggests a tavern, or perhaps someone's home with a courtyard where music is being offered at day's end.

Most often they do not. They do not do that. Perhaps it isn't, as they listen, the remembered instrument from their childhood. Nor the tune of a song their mother sang to them at bedtime after prayers. There are no orange blossoms here. No oleanders, mimosas, no jacaranda trees with blue-purple flowers. There might be fountains in this distant city, but not like the ones remembered from that time before they were forced to go away, uprooted like a tree torn from its earth.

For someone else, their memories, or the dreams pushed away at sunrise, might be very different, but just as hard. From a time, say, before they were stolen as a child from a place with other sorts of trees and flowers, but home.

There are many different ways for a home to be lost, and for the world to become defined by that loss.

THERE ARE ALSO many different ways into a tale.

Whose voice, whose life will start it off? (Whose death?) Where are we when the ship of our story moves from shore towards open water, past rocks that need careful navigating? Or, where are we when someone *does* decide to walk up a darkening laneway towards the pull of music, and listens at an open doorway? And finds . . .

These things matter for the reader or the listener—and so for the teller. They matter, whether it is being written down on a creamy parchment bought in a canal-side bookshop in Seressa, to be set in type and printed and bound one day, or if it is being told to a smaller or larger crowd in the storytellers' quarter by the marketplace of some city, between the morning and the midday summoning to prayer.

There are women and men here, ready to step forward into what light we have. There are others circling them, with affection or malice (or doubt as to which of these will prevail). We might even go back, start with people expelled from their beloved Esperaña. Or to a girl taken by raiders from her family home far to the east of that land. Or to the man who—

But see. Look now. Even as we speak of these things, as we consider the differences shaped by choosing one opening note or another to play, there is a ship in the night, sailing without lights along a coast, the last lantern just now doused by order of the captain.

They are laying into a shallow bay on the long coast of the Majriti. Not far from the city of Abeneven, but it should be far enough.

They are alone here, under stars and the white moon, before the rising of the other one. Being unseen is imperative for what they are here to do.

It seems as good a place as any to begin. The night sea, this bay, stars, moon, remembered music. We will act as if this is so. We will not set out to sea, after all. We will lower a small boat and send it ashore, instead, to a stony beach. Three men, one woman, a light breeze, spring night. Men waiting for them on that strand.

Nadia watched as Ghazzali al-Siyab rode off with those who had met them, as Rafel had arranged. Rafel was good at these things; she had learned that in three years.

Al-Siyab would head south for two days, then turn east, avoiding villages, and after two more days, on camels by that point, start back north, to enter Abeneven through the landward gates.

He was arrogant, young, too aware of how handsome he was, but he'd come to them specifically for this undertaking, and he was greedy and ambitious—which was good for their purposes. He was to be paid only when they were done. He wasn't going to run off. It was possible he'd betray them, but unlikely.

Neither she nor Rafel knew al-Siyab, but the men who had hired them had also hired him for this, and if you trusted no one you couldn't do very much in the world, and they were doing something significant now, or hoping to.

Well, yes. Assassinations did tend to be significant, she thought, amusing herself. She didn't laugh (she didn't laugh much) but she smiled in the dark.

She was glad to be ashore. She'd spent a great deal of time at sea since killing someone herself and escaping, but she was happier on land. It was simply a truth. She had been born inland, well away from the coast. That ought to have offered protection against what had happened to her.

You didn't necessarily live your life in the ways that made you happiest, of course. She hadn't been *happy* killing Dhiyan ibn Anash, but it had occurred to her that she'd been a slave for longer than she'd been free, and that had come to seem . . . unacceptable. A kind man who had bought you at a slave market and had taught you skill with words and numbers, then had you trained with weapons to guard him, was still a man who owned you and made you do things he wanted done, whenever he wanted that.

Really, what did *happiness* have to do with anything? Rafel might propose an answer. He had an answer for most such questions, had read a great deal. Sometimes (not always) she thought what he said was wise. He could make her smile sometimes.

He also annoyed her, drove her nearly mad at other times, but they worked well together, had done so since he had accepted her on board the *Silver Wake* and hidden her. A real risk for him, and she'd known it. She'd acted as a guard, gradually took on other roles. She did know numbers, though he was better with them. But she was useful for certain things: Jaddite-born, and so better for some tasks on the northern side of the Middle Sea where they worshipped the sun god. She was a partner now, with a share in the ship and their profits. Small at first, it had grown, because she was even more clever than she was good with knives, and Rafel ben Natan of the Kindath was the sort of man who could see that, even in a woman. That wasn't a thing she would ever forget.

They had survived, made some money with the *Silver Wake*. They traded along both coasts, north and south. Rafel was an occasional emissary of the khalif of the city of Almassar in the far west, at the gateway to the wide, wilder sea. The Kindath often played that sort of role among the Asharites. They were trusted, in part because they had few paths to success beyond trade and diplomacy. Well, perhaps piracy, in their case licensed by that same khalif, who urgently needed money and claimed a share of whatever they took in raids.

Whether you called yourself a corsair or a merchant or a smuggler or an emissary, or moved back and forth between all of these as opportunities arose, you could do well enough if you were shrewd (and fortunate) along this part of the Middle Sea, with the Majriti coastline to the south and Esperaña or Ferrieres north.

Not Batiara, however, not for her. She had made that clear from the start. If Rafel proposed going there for any reason, she'd disembark somewhere first. They could pick her up on their way back. It had happened twice.

After so long a time there was no going home for her, Nadia had decided.

There was no home to go back to. Only memories and the dead. There was no *her* to go back, she'd told Rafel once when he'd asked about Batiara. He asked many questions, answered only few about himself. He'd started a reply, she remembered, a disagreement, of course—about needing to put the past behind you, build your life forward—but he'd stopped himself. He was not an insensitive man, and had losses of his own, she knew. She wondered if he'd done it himself: put the past behind him. She didn't ask.

So they'd raided and traded, sometimes using the small ports and bays that were havens for corsairs, and for smugglers avoiding customs officers and duties. They sailed into larger city harbours when they had legal goods to trade. They had people on both coastlines with whom they banked some of their profits. Rafel looked after that, using his Kindath brethren or a Seressini bank. She let him do this for her, as well.

Other than the khalif of Almassar, who provided them with some protection, they'd kept a careful distance from major figures who could be dangerous.

Until now. Until this task, this night landing. Because two of those major figures had found them, and had made a proposition one evening back in Almassar. She had dressed as a man for that encounter. It was unlikely anyone in Almassar would recognize an escaped slave girl in a woman from a merchant ship, but better to be safer when you could. Rafel was always saying that.

They might, he had said when they were alone again after that meeting at someone's home (they never knew whose), be able to just about retire on what they'd earn from this. No longer live on the sea. Or become entirely respectable merchants if they wanted, no piracy. He among the Kindath, she wherever she wished, back in Jaddite lands. She could get married. Let others brave the wind and waters for them, he'd said. Or she could let him buy out her share of the *Wake*, pursue whatever path she wanted in the world.

He had been staked to the ship by Almassar's khalif and some older Kindath merchants originally, but over years he'd made enough to buy it from them. It was his ship now, and she was the one staked to a part-owner's share, and expanding it with their profits. She wasn't far from having a quarter share after three years.

It was a life. It was not a home. There *was* no home, but she was free.

"Is that what you'd do?" she'd asked. "Stay ashore?" She'd ignored the part about her marrying.

He'd shrugged. She hadn't expected a reply.

He was a few years older than her, had two sons, it was said. Maybe three. No one was certain as to Rafel ben Natan's life. He sent money to Sillina, the Kindath quarter outside the walls of Almassar. His parents were there, she knew that much. It was remarkable to her that she didn't even know if he had a wife. But a discreet man was more likely to be a trustworthy partner. And Rafel was discreet, and clever. So was she. He knew it, to be fair.

One of the three men who had come to the beach with her was now rowing the small boat back to the ship alone. Al-Siyab had gone inland. The remaining man would join her, riding on the mules that had been brought for them, heading to Abeneven.

She disguised herself in the moonlit night, soft red wool cap, over-tunic, hooded cloak, Muwardi mouth veil. Her hair was short and tucked under the cap. She was wearing leather boots. She had bound her breasts before leaving the ship. She was slim-hipped, and tall for a woman. They'd be joining the main road along the coast before day-light, and it was better to be disguised ahead of the need for it.

With her smooth cheeks, she could pass for a boy on the edge of manhood. She'd done it before.

What would follow in Abeneven, if all went as planned, they had never done.

But she didn't mind killing Asharites.

∾

Watching from the railing, Rafel lost sight of the small boat before it reached shore. He wasn't worried. It was good that the night was dark. He worried about many things, it was his nature, but not, as it hap-pened, about Nadia. Or at least not as to her getting to the strand, dividing the party as planned, and making her way into Abeneven.

When the boat returned and was made fast again, he ordered Elie to weigh anchor and lay a course to the east. No point lingering, some slight danger in doing so. (Why was a trading ship at anchor here? Were they smuggling something on or off? Were they worth raiding?) Without being told, Elie had the lamps lit again. He knew this coast better than Rafel, who knew it well. They kept a respectful distance from the rocky shoreline as they went.

The lights were lit because they were not hiding. The *Silver Wake* was a merchant vessel, based in Almassar, headed for Abeneven to trade in that city, and perhaps conduct some diplomatic affairs for the city's khalif. The ship's owner, the well-known Kindath merchant Rafel ben Natan, would call at the palace, as usual, with gifts. It was what they did.

It *was* what they did. Mostly.

He'd had no great ambitions in the world. That was not generally possible for one of the Kindath. He wanted to be able to support his parents, and two children he was responsible for, and save enough money to sell this ship one day and retire somewhere. Possibly back in Sillina, where his parents were. For reasons, Marsena in Ferrieres was another possibility. He wasn't committed to any place. Reasons for that, too. His parents had been forced to take him, very young, his brother not yet born, from Esperaña, in the accursed time of the Expulsion.

A child, but old enough to remember both that home and the losing of it. Perhaps carry down to the coastline and exile, through the days and years of a life, the feeling one *must* not grow too attached to any place, or perhaps any person. Whatever you had, whatever you thought you had, could be taken away, by careful planning on someone's part, by caprice, by random chance.

We are marked by what we have experienced young, some of us more than others.

He still remembered (not a thing you forgot) the lamentations among those gathered on the coast back then. His father paying the predatory fees being charged to take Kindath across the water to the Majriti and exile—to find a place they might dwell. Because the clerics of Esperaña had fulfilled a long-held desire and the king and queen there had expelled both Asharites and Kindath.

The Jad-denying infidels would live no more among the children of the sun god, to sully his golden brightness with their pernicious doctrines and secret blood, with the seductive beauty of their women and bold men.

His father had not been among those lamenting aloud, Rafel remembered. Still remembered. Mouth firm, eyes cold, he had bargained for passage for three, then hired a guard for them and their belongings, payment to be made after they landed safely on the southern shore. There were wars among khalifs and their rivals in that new land, he told his young son on the ship. They'd have to deal with those, too, in order to begin a new existence in a new place. "It will be hard," he'd told Rafel, "but we will do it."

What had really been in his father's heart all those years ago, Rafel ben Natan often thought, remained a mystery to him—decades ago, and now, on the deck of his own ship in a spring night.

There were mysteries everywhere. That was all right. You didn't need to solve them all. Only the ones that affected you: the challenges to survival, to making enough money to claim *some* safety in a rootless, warring, divided world.

If he lived long enough to settle somewhere, he imagined texts of Kindath liturgy and philosophy. A place, perhaps, where one could buy or even make good wine, grow fresh grapes, figs. He pictured, sometimes, a small garden with a pond, a few fruit trees, places of both light and shade, a quiet life. He didn't see companions or women with him in those reveries. Well, one woman, sometimes. But that was too hard to envisage from where he was now, and where she was. He was often restless at night.

The possibility of any of this lay far into the future, in any case, and not necessarily along a path he expected to find. Who knew what paths one might walk? Those who cast fortunes and futures by the moons or the bones of sheep? But . . . if he and Nadia did what they were approaching Abeneven to do, that imagining, that choosing, might not be so far off.

For now, for tonight, Elic and their mariners needed to get the *Silver Wake* to Abeneven by morning. They'd tie up at the harbour, greet people they knew, and Rafel would begin the part of this plan that established him as an emissary carrying gifts from one city's khalif to another, and also as a merchant doing his customary business in the market, with the desert caravans now arriving through the mountains as spring came to the Majriti.

He would take those gifts to the palace to proclaim the return of the genial Kindath merchant ben Natan, sometime envoy of the khalif of Almassar. He had a pretty young boy on board to carry it there with him. He always made sure he did in Abeneven. Keram al-Faradi was one khalif whose tastes were not hidden. He knew this, though he'd only once met the khalif himself. Normally, Rafel spoke with al-Faradi's vizier—or the vizier's subordinates. He wasn't important at all. A minor diplomat, though somewhat protected by that status, even as a Kindath.

Nadia and her escort would arrive on mules overland. She didn't need to rush, and wouldn't. People in the market knew her as well, but she wouldn't look like herself when she entered the city. Not this time.

Ghazzali al-Siyab, that celebrated philosopher and storyteller, would reach Abeneven five or six days from now, coming up on a camel from a lengthy sojourn among the tribes beyond the southern mountains, bearded and burnt by the sun above his mouth veil. Nadia would contrive to come upon him in the marketplace.

He wasn't really a storyteller or a philosopher. Nor was he celebrated, nor had he been in the south, but there were ways to seed rumours of a man of repute arriving in any city.

Then they'd see. It was not a perfect plan. Rafel had said that several times to both of them on the ship, but perfect plans existed only in dreams.

∽

There were too many khalifs in the cities strung out on the coastline of the Majriti, and inland towards the mountains, and beyond them. It made for unstable, often violent conditions.

That was the considered view of Nisim ibn Zukar, vizier to one of those khalifs, in the prosperous port of Abeneven. Too many people asserting a holy title diminished it, he had long thought (though was not so foolish as to say).

Historians taught that in the years before the terrible fall of Al-Rassan to the Jaddites, under the accursed Fernan Belmonte, centuries ago, there had been a proclaimed king or khalif in just about every town with falling-down baked-clay walls and a weekly food market. It was not a thing that could ever have lasted, however glorious the memories and legends might be.

Ibn Zukar had never seen any of the gardens or temples or palace ruins in what was now entirely Esperaña. The Asharites were not welcome there any more. The Jaddite conquest had been long ago, but the final expulsion had come in their own days. For centuries they had been permitted to stay, paying a tax to keep their faith, with laws curtailing what they could do and be, but that had now changed.

Only the sun-worshippers dwelled in Esperaña now—and some who pretended to be so. There were Asharites (and Kindath, for that matter) who simulated worship of the sun god, in order to stay in that land. He wasn't sure why anyone would do that, living a daily lie, risking zealous clerics hunting them down for a pyre. Also risking their souls, of course. But people varied greatly, in Nisim ibn Zukar's experience.

He preferred living in an important city ruled by those who worshipped, as he did, Ashar's god and the holy stars. Yes, there were divisions of tribe and doctrine, and conflicts from this. How not? Some of the khalifs were from tribes that had always been here in the Majriti. Others owed their position (and their allegiance) to Gurçu the Conqueror, lord of the Osmanlis of the east, ruling now in Asharias: the man who had thunderously taken the golden city of Sarantium four years ago and renamed it to Ashar's glory (and his own), changing the world. *He* deserved the title and honour of khalif! Those governing here in the west did not. That was ibn Zukar's view. Those swearing allegiance to Gurçu were just governors ruling at his sufferance, acting in his name. Able to be dismissed with cause or on a whim—or killed, for that matter. Their best soldiers were djannis, the feared tall-hat infantry *sent* to them from Asharias. And those men would take their ultimate orders from the east.

Keram al-Faradi, khalif of Abeneven, was not one of those mere governors, however. Al-Faradi was not a servant of the Conqueror. This city, and its Palace of the Pearl, remained independent of the east. So far. There were storm clouds, however. There were always those.

Keram was fortunate in his city's location: at the end of a major caravan route from the south, and with a deep harbour along this mostly exposed southern coastline of the Middle Sea. Taxes and duties coming in were reliable; he could afford soldiers and could stock his granaries for his people against times of need. He was outwardly pious, so the wadjis preaching in the temples and the streets accepted generous donations and kept relatively silent about decadence in the palace, in its various forms.

Of course, reliable revenues also made you a target. It was a precarious world in which they all lived: the poor, the uprooted, the urgently striving, those of power and rank. Who would, as a vivid example, ever have imagined triple-walled Sarantium falling a few years ago?

Ibn Zukar had never seen the golden city. He hoped to sail there one day. No, he *intended* to. He was still young enough, still tasting the sweet, seductive wine of ambition. His loyalties and devisings were aimed like an arrow at one thing: the great khalif in the east learning his name. In a good way, of course. He often dreamed of performing the obeisance before Gurçu, rising to be greeted formally, welcomed. A dream that could wake him, aroused.

At this moment, however, on a spring morning in Abeneven, the greater likelihood was that Gurçu might learn of him in a lamentably bad way. Or that he might be dead by orders from the palace right here before that happened, despite his rank. *Because* of his rank, really.

The errors and negligence of the vizier, one ibn Zukar, came shockingly close to causing the death of Abeneven's beloved ruler! Only by Ashar's grace and goodness, and the infinite mercy of the stars that watch over us, did Khalif Keram, may he be ever blessed, survive this treachery. The wretched vizier was decapitated in the marketplace.

He couldn't stop framing this letter in his mind! It was terrible!

Herewith, lord, and only should the thought somehow find the least favour in your illustrious eyes, are two names proposed to the grand khalif—loyal, capable, pious men—offered as replacements for the treacherous vizier and the reckless khalif here, if it is judged a propitious time, amid current disruption, to send more soldiers to Abeneven to save us from chaos—and assert your rightful claim to the city.

That could indeed be how his name was carried east, sent by some other man seduced by ambition. He knew several who would do that. It could happen. It could happen now!

He looked down again at the figure of his khalif. Keram al-Faradi lay upon one of his elegant divans in this reception room. Thank Ashar and the stars his purple robe, discarded, had been draped over his body, hiding a shocking nakedness. The khalif's unwrapped turban lay on the carpet.

There was little enough ibn Zukar could do now, but finding the man who had just left this room was utterly necessary. He should never have been allowed to leave! The fact that it was ibn Zukar who had permitted that, in a moment of confusion, was not a good thing.

He'd issued a number of death threats of his own, with details, should the guards fail to locate that wretched man. And this had been done *before* a servant, going to build the dying fire back up, saw a gold chain gleaming on the back wall behind it, and brought it to him, and the vizier realized, with horror, what was missing. What had happened here.

They did find the man, relatively quickly. It was not satisfactory, however.

⚬〰⚬

Abeneven was easily large enough for Nadia—disguised as a boy with her red wool hat and mouth veil—to disappear into its crooked lanes and warrens for a few days, waiting. Her escort would make his way back to the ship, discreetly.

There was a man Rafel knew and trusted here, another of the Kindath, and she stayed with him in their quarter. Asharite travellers weren't supposed to live among the moon-worshippers, of course, but for the poor it wasn't uncommon. People saved money as they could.

It was interesting, really, how reliable the Kindath tended to be in protecting and aiding each other. What happened when there weren't many of you. When you had no true home, and when much of the world was prepared to hate you on the slightest provocation. Or without any at all. She didn't envy them this necessary loyalty of faith, but she admired it.

Rafel was versed in the beliefs of his people, but she had doubts about the intensity of his devotion to the sister moons and the god. He had always seemed more a thinker than a believer. He was rarely in one of their houses of prayer. Perhaps after calamities on a certain level you might lose some of your faith? She had done so, hadn't she, and her calamity had been entirely personal. Jad of the sun, she had decided long ago, didn't care nearly as much about his suffering children as the clerics and devout believed. She wouldn't deny his existence, his power, but she wouldn't *rely* on him. You relied on yourself, and stayed alert.

Rafel was like that. He had two other names he used, one Jaddite, one Asharite, as dictated by circumstance. His skin colouring allowed it, and he was good with languages and accents. Another adaptation to what life had offered him, or imposed.

She wasn't without these skills herself. Born in Batiara, down south, she was dark-haired, dark-eyed, olive-skinned. It let her pass as Asharite. Her Asharic was fluent after all these years; she had a western Majriti accent, which was not a problem. She spoke only a handful of Kindath words, mostly insults. It was a good language for insults. Her Batiaran was perfect, of course.

She never used her name from home. No one knew it.

On the third morning after her arrival, white-bright in the dusty streets but not yet as hot as it would be later, she did her walk through the crowded, noisy marketplace filled with stalls of vividly varied goods amid a striking array of foods on offer. A man played a small pipe while his trained monkey danced. Another was juggling objects, one a flaming torch. She watched him for a moment.

Entering one of the larger squares, she saw that Ghazzali al-Siyab had arrived.

Which meant this could now begin.

A speeding up of her heartbeat. The danger was considerable. The reward, too, or they wouldn't be trying to do this, would they?

She had seen Rafel and others from the ship on her first day here. The ship would have arrived before her. He'd have been to the palace already in his role as an emissary of the khalif of Almassar. He was buying goods, she saw, arranging for delivery to the *Silver Wake*. The first two caravans of the season had arrived. Buying goods was what they did here. That, and selling items from farther west or north across the water in Ferrieres, depending on the season.

They'd given no hint of knowing each other. They were not beginners at this. She had needed to wait for the storyteller to arrive.

And now he had. In a corner of the square Ghazzali al-Siyab had spread out a large red-and-blue carpet, woven in the style of the people south of the mountains. His turban was tied in the southern manner, she saw. He knew what he was doing, too, it appeared. She eyed the other storytellers around him, keeping her distance, standing at a stall that sold hummus and lamb. She looked like a boy, she knew.

Sometimes there was tension, the tellers of tales fighting to make a few coins doing the same thing, but it appeared to be civil, just now.

"They are artists, aren't they?" Rafel had said last year, here, as they'd paused to listen to one and then another weave their stories. "And that makes them peaceful?" she had replied.

He'd laughed. Rafel ben Natan had an easy enough laugh, though it was sometimes hard to tell if he was truly amused or just suggesting that he was, for some purpose. She didn't think that applied when they were together. Three years gave you confidence you knew a man, at least something of him. She owed him a great deal. He'd had no need at all to accept her in the first place, on a night in Almassar, a woman on the run from something. She'd arrived with stolen jewels, yes. She gave him those, they were valuable, and she had useful skills, some unexpected, but even so . . .

Ghazzali al-Siyab they didn't know at all. She needed to become joined to him this morning. She listened to the story he was telling. He had a good voice—carrying, not harsh—and a manner that included both jests and promises. People were lingering, she saw. He was telling of a mountain tribesman's youngest daughter herding their goats on the slopes and encountering a djinn and then a Trickster, one of the Clever Fools of the old tales. She even found herself caught up in it a little, which was wrong, but harmless at this point. It was useful that he was good at this.

It was necessary.

When al-Siyab finished, and lifted an earthenware bowl in front of him, tilting it one way and the other, inviting donations, Nadia stepped forward, as if forcing boldness, and took it from him with an ingratiating smile. "Permit me, lord!" she said. She began walking the half-circle of those who had been listening.

"Here is a master tale-teller!" she cried. "You can hear it, gracious people! Honour him with a coin or two, in Ashar's name! He who loved the stories of our people, who shared his holy visions as tales and prophecies! Let this man have enough to feed himself and tell us more." Her own voice was naturally deep for a woman, she didn't need to alter it. A good thing: people trying to change their register could forget, and be exposed. She had seen it happen.

People dropped coppers, and one or two small, square silver coins were tossed in the bowl. She bowed at each of these, praised the givers for their assistance to one practising an ancient, honoured trade. She took the bowl back to al-Siyab. "Lord," she said, "people have been generous."

"And you want me to be so now?" he said loudly, in a tone of exaggerated outrage. People laughed.

"I am hungry," she said. "I would gladly work for you, lord, and I need little beyond something to eat."

"Can you sing? Can you dance?" he asked, playing with tone and expression to simulate suspicion. Onlookers were registering it, still amused. A larger crowd had gathered.

"Not well," she said. "I can fetch a meal and wash clothes, and move through the market telling people that the great . . . whatever your honoured name might be . . . that you are here!"

"My name is Ghazzali al-Siyab," he said, still loudly. "This is my first visit to your city of Abeneven. I come from Almassar, but I have sojourned south of the mountains for two years learning their tales, speaking with the wise among the tribes. I have stories and secrets and can shape foretelling magic, for those who wish to know what lies ahead of them—and have coins to pay. I do encounters in private, can answer urgent questions, or discuss and teach the wisdom of the sages of old, and of now." He smiled, a well-built, handsome man with a full black beard. He turned back to her. "And you, my young friend? What do you need to know? Are you in love? Is there a girl you wish would see you and love your eyes?"

"Not yet," she said. "Not here, anyhow."

"Or another boy?" someone called from the crowd.

Laughter again.

"Let it be so, in Ashar's name. I will take an assistant. Carry yourself through the market," Ghazzali said to her. "Tell them the celebrated al-Siyab is in Abeneven for the first time. If you are of use, I'll not let you starve."

"Thank you, lord!" she exclaimed.

"Your name?"

"Enbilcar, lord," she said, as arranged.

He laughed. "A warrior's name from long ago." He looked around. "Does anyone remember it? Does anyone know his story?"

Two people lifted their hands. They were smiling.

"Very well, to celebrate my brave new assistant, I will tell you, my friends, my darlings, the tale of Enbilcar of the Zuhrites and his war in Axartes against those who came before the Jaddites, before Ashar and his visions. It is a tale with both darkness and light in it, deeds of courage, and blackest treachery. Gather, and I will share it. It will be worth the listening before it ends, my loves . . ."

He told it well, broken cleverly into segments so she could pass around the bowl he was using for donations. People would need to pay for what they'd already heard to learn what came next.

Nadia didn't stay nearby for all of it, she was doing her job, roaming the marketplace, among stalls selling many things one might desire: clothing, jewellery, household goods, books, religious objects, weapons, amulets against evil, food. Someone had pigeons grilled with honey. There were dates and figs, mutton, couscous with chickpeas. She was hungry, she realized. That could wait.

No wine or other spirits were to be seen, not in a public market among the Asharites. They'd drink in private, though, many of them. Or sometimes among the Jaddites or Kindath, in their inns and taverns here, forbidden though it was. Forbidding things could make them appealing, she'd often thought. A hint of danger with your wine, like spices.

Whenever she looped back, as if herding those she'd urged to come hear the newly arrived storyteller from the south, she paused long enough to listen and confirm: the man knew how to tell a tale, and to seductively promise more in the intervals when the collection vessel was going around. He called people *my darlings* and *my loves*, drawing them in, as tale-tellers did.

There were a number of women among those around him now, of all ages. He was a handsome man; she imagined some of the women lingering hoped his eyes might linger on them. They were unveiled if they were from the Muwardi tribes, had their faces carefully covered if they were from the east or owed allegiance there. They were all Asharite, worshipping the stars of his vision, but there were differences. Just as there were differences among her own Jaddite people, east and west.

There had been an Eastern Patriarch in Sarantium until a few years ago. Sarantium was no more; neither was that holy man, whatever his name had been, and there was no successor. The world had changed with that fall. It mattered and it didn't, Nadia thought. You still needed to feed and shelter yourself, try to achieve—on your own, or with friends if you found any to trust—whatever you decided your destiny and desires were. That remained unchanged for ordinary people, whether a golden city far away was claimed by one army or another. One faith or another.

Neither the Eastern Patriarch nor the one in Rhodias, so near their home, had been able to stop corsairs from raiding her family's farm, killing her father as she watched, taking her away screaming, selling her as a slave. They hadn't raped her on the ship. Virgins were worth more.

No Patriarch would protect her now, either. No one would. She was a woman dealing with life on her own. Anyone, she thought, who lived by trusting in prayers, or too readily accepting others, was not living in the world as it was given to them.

Bells began to sound throughout the city, the temples summoning the faithful to midday prayer. She took the earthenware bowl around a last time, quickly, before the crowd left. Donations were good; people liked being generous before going to ask mercy of their god and the stars.

She carried it back to al-Siyab. "It is a goodly sum, my lord," she said, as if excited. He hadn't stopped her from calling him "lord."

"It is a start," he said dismissively. "Never worry, I will feed you. I keep my promises." He met her eyes for a moment. Probably too long a moment, but it was all right. She did file away, as if in a coffret in her mind, the idea that he might be reckless as well as arrogant. They *did* go together, those traits. Rafel would have said that; she could hear his voice saying so. Was she beginning to think like him?

She and al-Siyab also went to a temple, one of many near the market, following a crowd. A man offering sight of the future, or protection against the evil intent of others, or secret words to elicit love . . . such a man *needed* to be seen praying, honouring the visions of Ashar. The wadjis were everywhere, watching, anxious to preserve their own influence in a city with a notably dissolute khalif and traders from all over the world coming in and out by land and sea.

There were many things, Rafel was always saying, that a prudent merchant needed to be aware of, let alone a smuggler, in order to find a profit, stay alive. Which made it, of course, even more unexpected that he'd said yes to the offer presented to them that night in Almassar, the proposal that had brought them here.

She'd said yes, too, hadn't she? There was that.

CHAPTER II

It took five days for him to be summoned to the palace, but he had thought it would be longer, so this was good.

Ghazzali al-Siyab, born in Almassar to a family expelled with all the Asharites (and the Kindath) from Esperaña, had, accordingly, no memories of a family home there, no sense of loss or absence—that was his father's calamity, and his mother's, not his.

Once settled in Almassar, the family had flourished. He knew only that. He had benefitted from his father's erudition and his own quickness. Also, perhaps, as the years passed, from a willingness to deviate from a strict observance of laws and codes. His father said he was shaming their name in those years; Ghazzali became skilled at ignoring this. It was complicated by loving his father. A reason he moved from their house, quite young.

He had come into contact with similar young men as he passed into adulthood, and through them, eventually, his particular talents became known to more powerful figures in the world of smuggled goods. In Almassar at first, and then beyond. And because of this, later still, he came to the attention of some who worked for two extremely prominent men. They had recruited him for a small, testing task, then another, then a third one, more dangerous. And now this, in Abeneven, which might make his fortune, but involved killing someone.

He'd never done that. He was trying not to think about it too much. He told his stories in the market in the afternoons, with the Jaddite woman, disguised as a boy, moving among the crowds, crying his praise, bringing him listeners. She interested him. He was certain she'd been enslaved, though no one had talked about that on the ship, let alone how she'd become free, if he was right. Her role in finding listeners for him became less necessary as the days went by. He was good at storytelling, enjoyed it, had a range of tales, and some *were* from the mountain tribes and even farther south.

He'd never been beyond the mountains. That was a lie. He'd just listened, carefully, to storytellers in the marketplace at home. A young man with time on his hands. Good listeners learned a lot, even those who preferred the sound of their own voice. He was a vain but not a foolish person.

The last three mornings here, he'd welcomed paying students into the courtyard of the small, comfortable place where he was staying (it had been booked for him; their two patrons were well-connected). He taught the work and thoughts of revered scholars. Also some less admired, or even condemned, but nonetheless in his view (his father's view, being honest) deserving of discussion and reflection. He really did know what he was talking about. It was a part of why he'd been chosen to do this with the Kindath man and the Jaddite woman and their ship.

He wondered about their partnership, those two, how that had come to be. They weren't lovers, he was certain of that.

They controlled his payment. He didn't like that part at all. He'd spent a lot of time on the ship trying to devise a way to change this, and had failed. He was not, after all, in a position to negotiate, and the amount he would receive if they did this was colossal. He wasn't entirely trusted—by the two who'd hired them, or the two on the ship. He supposed he wouldn't have entirely trusted himself.

But one of the people who'd attended his morning discussion two days ago (he'd been putting forth a part of the thinking of the very great ibn Udad on the fall of empires) had come from the palace. A manner, a way of standing, then assuming a sitting position when he invited them all to do so. Those from a court were . . . different. Even in how they moved. Ghazzali hoped, one day, to be one of them, be different in that way.

In the event, he was unsurprised to receive a visitor the next morning, before he was due to begin teaching. He had told the woman, Nadia—she was staying with him now, in her guise as a boy—that this was likely to happen. Perhaps he really was a magician, tapping the half-world to foretell what was to come. Perhaps a djinn, or an angel with a hundred eyes, would appear to serve and defend him . . .

Perhaps. But for now he was in a complex state of mind as he walked with an escort and his disguised boy-servant, passing through Abeneven towards the palace on a bright, windy morning. Scents and sounds, fruit trees flowering, the fragrant arrival of springtime along the coast.

They went up the hill, away from the harbour and the market, eventually arriving at the city's great temple. There was a crowd in the forecourt there. Looking to his left, back down, al-Siyab could see the sea, choppy with whitecaps, and the boats moored at the docks beneath the fortifications and the city's cannon there. He could see their own boat.

They climbed farther, walking towards the sunrise. A stronger breeze up here. They came to the massive entrance gate in the palace walls. The Palace of the Pearl. No one knew where the name had come from. Some pearls, probably, he thought, amusing himself. He had arrived. The walls were formidable, warlike. Defences were always needed, the world being what it was.

They were eyed carefully, searched, and waved in. Passing through those stern, high gates, and then an open courtyard, he saw gardens.

They entered the first of these. Gazelles and peacocks, orange and lemon trees in tidy rows amid the riotous flowers of spring. Perhaps *riotous* was the wrong word, al-Siyab thought, if one was going to be diplomatic at a court. He smiled to himself. He was tense, focused, alert.

A second garden beyond a two-toned horseshoe arch, made in imitation of Al-Rassan. A fountain here, stone lions guarding it in the light—also modelled on those of Al-Rassan the beloved, the long lost. Another nod to vanished glory. Himself, he told stories of the past but preferred to look forward to what might come in the time in which they lived. Or what might be caused to come, by a man clever and brave enough. The fountain was handsome, though. There were more gazelles.

They approached a shaded arcade. He saw yet another garden beyond it, through another arch, but they turned here, walked a distance on stone, their steps loud. It was cooler in the shade. They climbed an exterior flight of stone stairs. That was good, he thought, he was being welcomed to the more private level of the palace. Another corridor. Finally, his escorts stopped outside a heavy wood-and-metal door. It was here, evidently, that he was to meet and converse with the khalif of Abeneven, who had learned of his presence here. As they'd intended.

The boy, Enbilcar, stood quietly behind him—the woman, Nadia, really. He didn't know the rest of her name. She'd never told him. He could find out, of course. Her presence in the room was part of their first plan today, if it could happen. If it didn't, there was another plan. He'd been told she was skilled with knives and small swords. He didn't ask how this had come to be. She wouldn't have told him. He knew that much by now.

She would not have been able to carry a knife into the palace. Unless she knew how to hide a blade so that guards could not find it. Unlikely. Perhaps she had ways to kill that did not require a weapon. On reflection, that might be so.

It was not to be, in any case. The guards at this last doorway were clear, and in a manner not admitting of discussion. Only the teacher was permitted to enter. He was searched again for weapons. He carried no weapons.

Only a vial. It was not found. Al-Siyab had some experience in hiding things, but it had been the Kindath merchant, ben Natan, who had shown him this concealment. A long-time smuggler, versed in such matters, it seemed. Ghazzali had been pleased; he liked learning useful things.

Nadia made no objection outside the door, of course. There was no possible way for her to do so—a boy who'd met him in the marketplace and run around with his bowl collecting coins? She'd be beaten for opening her mouth here. Nor could al-Siyab object. He had no plausible reason, and they had anticipated this would happen.

Briskly, he told the boy to return to their quarters and await him. "If I appear likely to be late for the marketplace, go to where we always are and tell them I have been summoned to an audience with the khalif. It will be a good thing for people to know this."

It would have been, if a storyteller's reputation and coins in the market were what they had come here for. She turned and left, back the way they'd come. A man escorted her. This was not a careless place, it seemed. He said a quick prayer under his breath. He wasn't above doing that (you never knew, in this life). He entered the room as the door was opened for him.

It was large, expensively furnished. This was a palace, and this would be a room where only selected guests were received. He was being treated with respect. It was good.

Handsome eastern carpets on the floor. Tables inset with mother of pearl, leather-covered divans, stools with animal furs covering the seats, multicoloured fabrics hanging on the walls. Three tall, standing candelabras, many candles burning in each. A large fireplace with a large fire burning, even in springtime. The shutters on the window overlooking the garden were closed. The ceiling, he saw, was blue-black, painted with Ashar's stars.

A tall, plump man in a severe dark robe awaited him. There was a servant or slave by an inner door. Another guard, with a short, curved sword and an unexpectedly malevolent glance. Al-Siyab wondered if such glances, the capacity to deploy them, were a part of being posted here. He knew the tall man wasn't the khalif. He assumed he knew who it was.

He felt a surge of excitement, a wave in the blood. Moments like this, he thought, were what a bold man lived for. He was anxious, though. You'd be a fool and a half not to be.

"For the khalif and this court, I bid you welcome, Ghazzali al-Siyab," said the tall man. He did not bow, which confirmed the guess as to his identity.

Ghazzali did bow. Once only, but in full. "I am honoured beyond my worth by the invitation," he said. He smiled—it was brief, professional. "Would I be correct in thinking that I have the great privilege of addressing the celebrated vizier of his excellency the khalif?"

The man nodded slightly. No visible reaction to *celebrated*. He wore a turban—as did Ghazzali in this city; his was wound differently. He had his reasons. The vizier had a neatly trimmed beard (vanity?) and wore three rings, one of them a large ruby (also vanity?).

The vizier said, "We will converse here when the illustrious khalif is gracious enough to join us. You will be permitted to sit if he does, and will remain until he signals an end to the discourse. You will then leave the same way you entered, bearing this reward." He spoke with exaggerated precision, enunciating each word with such care that Ghazzali wondered if he'd had a speech difficulty as a child. He knew people like that.

The vizier held out a small, crimson-dyed leather pouch. Ghazzali bowed again, stepped forward and accepted it, tucked it into a pocket of his robe. Bowed yet again. It was heavy enough. Not that it mattered, with what was at stake here. He saw a silver tray bearing a flask of wine on a lacquered table beside one of the divans. Another tray held candied citrus peels. A number of intricately patterned cushions were scattered on the carpets. For his use, clearly. Sitting at the feet of the mighty. The wine mattered. There were three glasses, he noted. A problem. Not insurmountable, they'd discussed this, too, on the ship.

They had been counting on wine, even in the morning. The khalif of Abeneven had a reputation.

The khalif of Abeneven entered the room. No announcement or ceremony. An inner door was opened and a slight man entered. A waft of scent accompanied him. Sandalwood. The door closed behind him, softly.

His turban was green, Ghazzali saw, for royalty and power. His robe was purple, rippling shades of it, gold-trimmed down the sides and across the bottom. The Jaddites in the east had used purple to symbolize imperial rank, before the fall of Sarantium. No one else was to wear it. Al-Siyab wondered if a khalif in a western Asharite city knew that, or if he just liked the opulence of the colour. The robe was open-necked, which was decadent and unusual. Even more decadent was the necklace he wore. Or, more particularly, the absurdly large, arrestingly green diamond that hung from it.

He knew that diamond. Knew about it, at any rate. Everyone did.

Seeing it now, *worn* by this khalif, not sequestered in some treasury, caused Ghazzali al-Siyab to begin rapidly amending the plans for this morning—while dealing with an accelerating pulse.

He hoped, if anyone noticed his disarray, they'd attribute it to awe.

It *was* awe, in fact.

You needed to be able to do this, he thought. Amend plans. Circumstances altered, you reacted to them. This . . . was a circumstance.

He knelt and made obeisance twice, both times with his head touching the elegant carpet. He drew a few breaths, trying to steady himself. He sat up straight but did not stand, remaining upon his knees. He smiled up at Keram al-Faradi, who had reigned here for almost ten years now, from his earliest entry into adulthood, when his father had died and he'd had his younger brothers strangled, as was usually the case.

This time the smile was his best one. One handsome man greeting another appreciatively with his eyes. He was *good* at this, Ghazzali reminded himself. The khalif stopped beside a divan and registered the smile, registered Ghazzali al-Siyab, kneeling prettily before him. You wanted to appear in such moments like a honeyed pastry, irresistible. That diamond, however. That *stupefying* object . . .

"This is the philosopher?" the khalif asked. His voice was light, appealing.

"It is, excellency," said the vizier. "Here in response to your summons. Shall I pour wine for the three of us?"

There was a pause. Brief, but it was there.

"No. No. Conversations of this sort are best shared between one thinker and another. You may leave us, my vizier. Take the guard as well. I do not fear a philosopher," said the khalif of Abeneven.

Mistake, thought Ghazzali al-Siyab. He felt his heartbeat slowing towards normal.

He said, with a self-deprecating gesture, "Ah, I fear that title honours me too greatly, excellence. I am a teller of tales and somewhat versed in the writings of thinkers. I can teach some of their thought. I would never proclaim myself a sage, or learned. I . . . I suppose I enjoy wine, and other pleasures of life, too much for that."

"So," said the khalif, smiling a little, "did many of those thinkers. You may go, Nisim. I will call if you are required."

"Excellency—" the vizier began.

The khalif looked at him. No more than that.

"Excellency," the vizier said, in a different tone.

The vizier, the guard, the slave, all left through that inner doorway. It closed behind them.

"Why," asked the khalif of Abeneven, without preamble, "are you wearing a turban? They told me you are from Almassar, a Muwardi. Of the Zuhrite tribe. No green or red cap?"

Ghazzali was surprised, and impressed. The palace hadn't had a lot of time to have him investigated. He searched backwards, a memory came: a women stopping with her slave to listen to his stories three days ago. She had lingered, after, asked questions eagerly. She wore no veil. Her eyes had been remarkable, her questions and gaze flattering. An appealing mouth. The vizier, Ghazzali thought, was good at his tasks.

To a point.

He said, "Excellence, I will confess, only to you, that I wear the turban to present myself, for those who come to me in the marketplace, as having crossed the mountains from the south, which is true! I have returned with stories and teachings from there, where turbans are more often worn than the head coverings of our Muwardi tribes. I have even wrapped mine in the southern fashion, as you see. My lord, appearance matters when one is in a marketplace, competing with others for attention." He allowed himself another smile.

It was returned. "You are not in the marketplace now," said the khalif. "You have . . . my attention."

There was no real way to miss the implication. Ghazzali nodded, said nothing. Silence was useful sometimes.

"You may remove the turban while we are alone. No one will disturb us. No wadjis to censure, I promise. Not here."

You'd have to be an ignorant youth from some mountain slope, herding your goats, not to take the meaning here, Ghazzali thought. He nodded acquiescence and slowly unwrapped his pale-coloured turban. He kissed it and set it down, then shook out his long, thick, black hair. The khalif watched him closely. Then smiled again.

"Better. You may stand. I have something to show you. Let me find it." He turned to a low table by the wall behind him.

It became, accordingly, almost too easy. "Should I pour us wine, excellence?" Ghazzali asked, rising.

"You should," the khalif of Abeneven said, busy at the table, which held several texts and coffers.

There had been much practice aboard the ship with the glass vial tucked into a fold inside his sleeve. A full portion of what it contained would kill, he'd been told.

Ghazzali made the quick bending-up-then-straight-down motion of his left arm that freed the vial to fall into his cupped, waiting palm. He removed the stopper of the wine flask. He poured a glass mostly full with wine, opened the vial quickly, and dropped some of what was in it into that glass, his body screening the motion, should the khalif turn around.

Only some, however. Only about half.

Circumstances. They changed, you responded. He poured a second glass for himself. Waited a moment, watching the contents of the vial disappear in the first glass. He put the re-stoppered vial back inside his sleeve.

He had just altered all their plans. Made the decision himself. There was no one to talk it over with, was there? He couldn't call a meeting! The woman had been ordered to leave. The Kindath was on the ship or in the market, pretending to be here to trade. His partners would simply have to adapt with him. When they saw what he brought, if he succeeded, they would agree with what he'd done and celebrate, setting sail. He would play fairly with them, he *would* bring it back to the ship. They'd decide together where to take it. And they really didn't want too many people hunting them down across the world. Why he'd used only a part of the vial.

Might be an error. You could always make errors.

He was standing by the table, waiting attentively, bare-headed, when the khalif straightened, turned, crossed the room. He gestured for Ghazzali to examine the book he held.

Ghazzali bowed again and accepted it. He looked at a stained, dark-brown cover. A very old book, worn leather, frayed binding. Not in good condition at all. He wondered. He read the title. Knew it, of course.

A premonitory shiver. He opened the book, carefully.

He saw the name, beautifully written, on the first page, realized it was a signature, and that the text was in the same handwriting, and . . .

And his mouth fell open. Not, this time, a contrived expression.

He swallowed hard. He reached, a little desperately, for words. He said, surprising himself, "My father would have fallen to his knees. This is . . . the original text, lord?"

The khalif smiled. "It is. His own handwriting. He copied it out himself. It was bound in this leather at that time, or shortly after. It is inscribed by ibn Udad for the khalif of Khatib, where the writing was finished in exile in the east, two hundred years ago. Your father was a scholar?"

"He was, he is, excellence. Much of what I know, I know from him."

"You remain close, then? Commendable."

This was not where he wanted the conversation to go.

"Distance has an impact, as always, excellence. May I ask . . . is it permitted . . . how is this here? This is . . . it is . . ." He seemed to have become inarticulate. "This is the hand of ibn Udad? And the text of the *Prologue to Knowledge*?"

"It is," the khalif said again. "The original. In his hand." It seemed to give him pleasure, repeating this.

Only the first copy of the most famed work in the Asharite world.

Even Jaddite and Kindath scholars knew of ibn Udad, honoured him, studied him. This book, the masterwork of a great man's life, was no less than an effort to explain the forces of time and history, the rise and fall of kingdoms and empires. Nothing like it before. And in the two hundred years since? Mostly other men grappling with this text as best they could.

The khalif of Abeneven looked immensely satisfied with himself, and with Ghazzali's dazed response. He glanced over at the wine, meaningfully. Ghazzali put the book down with extreme care, and took the two glasses. A narrow, *narrow* escape. Carelessness! If the other man had reached out himself, taken the wrong glass . . .

He couldn't allow himself to remain as overwhelmed as he was feeling just now. He had a task here.

He extended the necessary glass. It was claimed. The khalif took a sip. The contents (the partial contents) of the vial were odourless and tasteless, he'd been told. A poison that went back to Al-Rassan. He didn't care about its origins. He did care whether or not he'd judged rightly, doing so at speed, without knowledge as to the amount he'd poured.

The khalif of Abeneven set down his glass unfinished, which worried Ghazzali a moment, but then the other man reached up with slender arms and began unwinding his own turban. When this was done he dropped it on the carpet, carelessly, and ran a hand through his hair. He was still a young man, of an age with Ghazzali. The scent of sandalwood lingered, in a carefully judged degree.

"The book, lord, please. How . . . ?"

"I had it stolen for me," said Keram al-Faradi, khalif of Abeneven. Another cheerful smile. "From the palace library in Khatib. Three years ago. You might remember hearing of it? They were . . . distressed."

Distressed. Word of that theft had raced across the Asharite world, right to the western edge of it in Almassar. Ghazzali's father, learning of it, had rained down imprecations against the barbarians who would steal such a glorious text. The *original*, in the great man's own hand? This book was, for the right person, as valuable as the impossibly green diamond the khalif wore.

Which meant, right now, *now*, further adjustments to this morning, which was changing by the moment as the sun rose outside.

"You understand, of course," said the khalif, carelessly, "that if the least breath of a word that it is here slips out, you will be killed?"

Ghazzali said, "I would never do that, lord. I would happily spend days reading and discussing this with you, excellence. I am . . . I am ravished to be looking at it."

"Ravished?" said the khalif.

Ghazzali lifted his glass. "I salute you, my lord, for having been so bold as to want it here and cause it to be so. Ibn Udad was one of us, from the Majriti, surely his book belongs here in the west. Let Khatib have its own scholars! He has written in these pages that civilizations may rise and fall on the boldness of their leaders. Or its absence. As much so as their piety, he says, important as that is." He sipped his wine.

"Sometimes," he added, "we must be brave in pursuing the desire for knowledge that Ashar places in our hearts. Or . . . any other desires. In our hearts." He seemed to have regained his control of words.

The khalif laughed aloud. He had a pleasant laugh. Their eyes met and held. Ghazzali lowered his, as was proper. The other man picked up his wineglass, and this time he drained it. "Shall we now," he said lightly, "discourse together upon the teachings of ibn Udad?"

But what he did, after saying this, was set the glass down, step forward, and kiss Ghazzali on the mouth, displaying no inclination at all towards haste, or philosophical discourse.

Ghazzali wondered for a frightened moment about any poison that might be on the other's lips, or his tongue, but then inwardly shrugged. There was nothing for it. He looped his hands around the khalif's waist and kept him close. The kiss lingered, shifted, grew intense.

"What would please you, excellence?" Ghazzali asked at length, drawing his head back a little.

"This does," the khalif said.

"I am happy to hear it. I have other thoughts, as well. Perhaps your robe feels . . . superfluous? Just now?"

That appealing laugh. They moved towards the largest of the divans. It had almost certainly been used in this way before, Ghazzali thought. Keram al-Faradi lifted his robe slowly over his head and let it fall beside the divan. He had a slender, beautiful body. He put his arms up, crossed upon his head, a picture, posed. Ghazzali glanced down along the length of the other man's body. Saw that he was aroused, and . . .

"Oh my," he said sincerely.

The khalif sat down and then lay back on the dark-brown leather of the divan. "What other thoughts did you have?" he asked, his words languorous now.

More than languorous. Slurred, in fact.

Ghazzali, taking his time, knelt on the carpet beside him. "I have many thoughts, exalted lord. Shall I tell you some of them? One might involve your nether garment here, if that is not too bold on my part."

"Bold? Yes. Boldness would . . . that would be . . ."

It would probably have been a pleasing encounter, also a lucrative one, had a greater opportunity not already presented itself, Ghazzali al-Siyab thought. The khalif happened to be extravagantly endowed. Ghazzali's exclamation of surprise when he'd glanced down had been real. It was not the important thing here, however.

Rather more so was that the khalif was now unconscious. He was breathing slowly, but steadily. His erection had not subsided, which was mildly of interest.

Ghazzali began moving quickly. He stood, bent forward, unclasped the golden chain from around the other man's neck. The Diamond of the South was in his hands. Famed enough to have a name. He was holding it, this dazzling magnificence. The world was a remarkable place, he thought. The gem was heavy, especially on the thick chain. It was shockingly green. An enchantment. Unique in the world.

As was the book. He removed the diamond from the golden chain. Walked over and tossed the chain so it hit the back wall and fell down behind the fire. A moment's thought and he freed the vial from his sleeve again, and tossed it into the flames. It shattered with a small sound. It was a small vial. The diamond . . . he picked up his turban and began winding it back on his head, tucking the diamond securely within. It was too big, too heavy to go inside the sleeve of his robe or a pocket. You adjusted, adapted. You might grow impossibly rich, with great good fortune.

The book next. A larger challenge, but he'd worn loose, belted linen trousers under a tunic today, by the grace of Ashar. An accident, a random choice. Such things could save you or destroy you. He fitted the book inside the trousers at his waist, tightened his belt over his tunic, over where the book sat. It stayed. It would have to, for long enough. He reminded himself not to bow too deeply. To anyone.

He might be dead in moments, of course. He'd die, if so, with two of the great things of the world on his person. Boldness was not only the province of leaders of civilizations, leading to their rise or ending. A single, ordinary life could rise—or end—because of it as well.

He looked around the room. Only a little time had passed, but it felt as if a chasm lay between now and moments ago. The khalif on the divan was still breathing. Ghazzali seemed to have made that decision, too: he was not going to kill the other man. An assassination on top of these thefts? There would be nowhere on earth they could ever go, he'd decided. He was aware it was not necessarily a perfect thought, and that his innocence in the matter of murder might be guiding him here.

So be it, if so. Men could make mistakes. Or do exactly the right thing for unlikely reasons. Time ran and showed you which it had been. Only afterwards could you look back and smile and shake your head—or be beheaded and disembowelled in the white sunlight of the same marketplace where you'd been telling stories.

On impulse, partly mischievous but partly not, Ghazzali walked over and pulled the other man's silk undergarment down to his knees, exposing his continuing erection. It really was exceptional.

He straightened. He was ready. He was even ready to die, but he wasn't going to leave these two things behind. And he wasn't a murderer. Truths found and known. As simple as that, if anything was simple in a man's life. He had a sudden, unexpected image of his father, back home, holding the book he now carried tucked into his trousers.

He'd be weeping, Ghazzali thought. He'd be trying to keep his tears from falling on the book.

He walked to the inner door. Took a steadying breath.

"My lord vizier!" he called, anxious but not frightened, and not too loudly. That was the needed tone and level. "Please be so good as to enter. I know not what to do."

The door opened quickly. They hadn't been far.

What was to happen next would now happen.

CHAPTER III

The vizier of the court and khalif of Abeneven would stand at the very precipice of a violent death later that morning. At the moment, however, alive and agitated, he strode back into the room where the khalif lay, followed by the guard.

In his view, he should never have been asked to leave it. And it is true that much would have unfolded differently had he not. For himself, for many others in the world. Lives changed because the khalif had instructed him to leave.

The Muwardi storyteller, looking uneasy but not especially disturbed—more of a disconcerted expression, the vizier would decide later—held a finger to his lips for quiet, and pointed at the largest divan. Upon it, asleep, disturbingly unclothed and displaying an enormously large, very much erect organ of procreation, lay the khalif.

Their guest appeared to belatedly notice that last.

"In Ashar's holy name!" he exclaimed, but under his breath.

The storyteller moved swiftly, claimed the khalif's purple robe from the carpet beside the divan, and draped it over him, covering Keram al-Faradi carefully from chin to lower legs. An improvement. The erection beneath the robe did still cause a dissonant distension, but it was no longer so . . . assertively present. And it wasn't as if they could *do* anything about it!

The vizier would not, himself, have invoked Ashar's name in that particular context, but that wasn't the important thing here. Profoundly disturbed by the sight that greeted him, Nisim ibn Zukar whispered fiercely, "*What happened here?*"

A heartbeat later he realized that he mostly knew—and didn't want it said aloud. He held up both hands abruptly, palms out. "*Never mind!*" he said quickly, as the man opened his mouth, appearing much too eager to explain how the khalif happened to be unclothed and . . . excited.

"This," Ghazzali al-Siyab said intensely, but keeping his voice blessedly low, "has *never* happened to me!" The guard, ibn Zukar noted, looked murderous. He felt somewhat so himself.

The vizier had a good idea what the guest meant by those words and a very good idea that he didn't want details. Whatever had been in progress in this chamber had not had much to do with the writings of the learned. Nor, based on evidence still presented through the covering robe, had it reached a conclusion.

Not that he wanted to know.

"Get out," he said, setting in motion his own destiny. "You have your purse," he added. "It is more than generous. Leave the palace, go back to the marketplace. Do what you do there." He made his gaze hard and cold, a thing he knew how to do. "If anything, *anything* of this morning becomes known in the city, or anywhere else in the world, you will be found and flayed and gelded before dying. Is it understood?"

The other man stared at him. "But . . . but, my lord vizier, it was, we did not—"

"*Silence!*" the vizier snapped. Too loudly. He glanced instinctively at the divan. The khalif showed no reaction at all. He lay on his back. He breathed quietly, covered by his robe. The bulging of that robe remained, midway along his recumbent form, one's gaze helplessly drawn to it. It really was, the vizier thought . . . well, he didn't choose to apply a word or phrase to what it really was.

"Go," he repeated. "You have done nothing worthy of punishment, but must not remain here. If . . . should the illustrious khalif have further desire, er, further *wish*, um . . . have any need for your presence, you will be summoned."

Words could be such awkward things, the vizier thought.

Before leaving, the storyteller turned at the door. "Does he . . . has the blessed khalif ever shown an inclination to fall asleep like . . . in this fashion before?"

The man was impossible! Why had they ever invited him?

The vizier declined to answer. He pushed past, opened the door himself. The guards were outside, as they were required to be. He said, "Take this man to the gates. Escort him with courtesy."

He was careful to keep his body positioned so neither guard could see into the room. The sunlight beyond the arcade was very white; they couldn't have seen much, thanks be to Ashar and the stars.

The storyteller finally performed his bow—not as deeply as upon entering, the vizier noted sourly—and left. Ibn Zukar quickly closed the door. He looked back at the khalif, where he lay, as he lay. He sighed. He set himself to thinking.

What he did not think about until later—after the slave, going to build the fire back up as the khalif slept on, found the gold chain behind it—was how carefully the storyteller had brought the robe right to the khalif's chin, hiding his chest.

The vizier walked over then and gently pulled down the robe. No diamond. Of course no diamond. He'd known from the moment the chain was lifted out of the fireplace. Ruin stared him in the face, an executioner's sword loomed like a curved blackness blotting the bright sun.

He summoned the leader of the palace guards. "Find that man!" he ordered. "Find him at peril of your life! Call everyone on duty! Say the same to them! *Go!*"

He felt as if he could still say things like that, about risk to *their* lives, rather than his, but not for much longer if they failed. He didn't offer an explanation. They were merely guards. He was the vizier of Abeneven. But he had invited the man to the palace. He had left him alone with the khalif!

And then, later in the day, calamity was piled upon calamity, as a mountain might be laid upon a mountain by the god. Never by a mortal man; some things were beyond the power of mortal men.

Still, the vizier thought, a little desperately, holding the necklace chain, aware that he was perspiring heavily, you had your life as long as . . . as long as you still had it. And you did whatever it was that you could do to survive.

GHAZZALI WALKED AWAY briskly but with no sign of haste. He had done this before, though never with thefts on this scale. There was nothing on this scale, he thought. Someone greeted him, he was the new, engaging storyteller in the market, he was known in the city now, it seemed. He smiled benignly as he went by, but didn't slow. He had no idea how long it would take for an alarm to be raised in the palace, but he thought he had some time. He kept an eye out for Nadia, either still in disguise or having changed back to female clothing. He didn't expect to see her, though. They had a meeting place. Not the rooms he'd taken, nor the Kindath home she'd used before he came.

She and Rafel had been precise in planning this. Even to branching paths if possibilities closed off: such as her not being allowed in the palace room. He'd taken mental notes all along as they'd talked on the ship. There was much he could learn from these two. He hoped to continue doing so, until they sold the two treasures he was carrying and were all impossibly rich.

First, however, he'd have to persuade them he'd done the right thing, switching from assassination to theft.

A branching possibility, he'd call it! And not just *any* thefts, he'd say, and then show them what he had taken. He'd explain about the book, and why it was surely better that they not also be hunted across the whole of the Middle Sea by those seeking the assassins of a khalif. He thought that was true, he was persuading himself it was with every step he took through the market noises and smells. But *surely better* was overstating things and he knew it. He'd say *likely better*. These were shrewd partners he had.

A sudden thought. It was even possible al-Faradi, when he woke, would keep the thefts quiet, out of shame. Unlikely, but possible! Ghazzali had made a decision at speed, in the midst of changing circumstances. He'd say that, too. And here he was, he'd say, bringing them two of the most valuable objects in the world . . .

Here, initially, was a shop at the back of a smaller market off the main one. The shop was empty, boarded up, no wares on display, no sign of what it had once been used for. You couldn't see in. He looked around. No one. It was quiet here. Not, of course, an accident. He opened the low door, left unlocked, as promised. He ducked his head and went in.

Nadia was waiting for him.

She was back in woman's clothing, wearing an eastern face veil now, pulled down to her neck at the moment, out of the way. He was to trim his beard here and put on a mouth veil to walk back to the ship. On a small table he saw the green Muwardi hat he'd exchange his turban for. His own change of clothing was laid out. They wouldn't walk together. She had lit two lamps, there was little light entering, slivers of sunlight through cracks in the wall. Also on the table was a pair of long scissors. No mirror. The beard didn't have to be tidy, just short. The veil would cover most of it.

She nodded. "Good. You are here. Now tell me he is dead."

"Wait," he said.

"No. Is he dead?"

"Wait," he repeated, and began unwinding his turban. Her expression was not a pleasant one, but she waited.

He was careful with the turban, reached up and in before it was fully unwound, claimed the thing of glory inside, the object that would, if carefully dealt with, change their lives.

He showed it to her, smiling; the Diamond of the South. In this small space it looked even more stupendously large. The lamplight was reflected by it, though some of the light seemed to penetrate the green depths of the stone. It was heavy again in his hand. It was a wonder of the world.

"You know what this is?" he asked.

"A large diamond," she said. "Valuable. Is he dead?"

"It is the largest diamond of its kind in the world, Nadia! It is unique, famed. It is worth more money than we could ever have dreamed of! All we need do is work out who can buy it, where they are, perhaps create a competition among wealthy men for it!"

"He is not dead," said Nadia. Her tone was flat.

"*Are you even looking?*" Ghazzali exclaimed. He was more than a little outraged. "I should hold back and not even show you the other thing I have!"

She said nothing. She had, he decided, a cold face when she was angry. It was hard, unyielding. Like a diamond, he thought, sourly.

He lifted his robe, undid his belt, let it fall to the dirt floor. He claimed the book from within his trousers. "And . . . he had *this*, too! He showed it to me, so proudly. Had it stolen for him, from Khatib. Three years ago. The theft was notorious, no one ever knew who had it! Look!" He was talking too much, he thought. She'd made him nervous.

"What book is it?" she said quietly. She didn't move to examine it.

"The first copy, the very first copy, of ibn Udad's *Prologue*! In his own hand! This . . . for the right buyer this will be worth as much as the diamond! Nadia, I have brought treasures from that palace!"

"And the khalif is not dead."

He sighed. "Nadia, I made a decision quickly when I saw he was wearing this diamond. I didn't want to have them pursuing us even *more* ferociously! I only used half the vial. He's asleep, or he was when I left. The rest went exactly as planned! The vizier actually ordered me to leave, had me courteously escorted to the gates. We need to move. Can we please discuss this on the ship?"

She was still another moment, then nodded, expressionless. "Do your beard, get changed."

He gave her his best smile. "Good," he said. "This is all good!" He turned, picked up the long scissors, more like shears, really, from the table where he'd laid the book and diamond down.

Died.

SHE WAS GENUINELY good with knives and smaller swords and other lethal things. Had been trained as a bodyguard, some years after she'd grown into womanhood, by the man who'd owned her. There had been civil war, chaos, violent unrest within and around Almassar. Ibn Anash, an ally of the khalif, had thought it prudent for his own safety to have her learn these things. It also amused him, a woman guard, something others hadn't done, didn't have. He liked doing that.

Not wise, in the event, though he'd been an intelligent man. First person she'd killed. She did it with a knife. Letting him see her do it. Looking into his eyes.

She *really* did not mind killing Asharites.

For this one now, she used a knife again; thin, slender handle, sheathed on her right calf, under her boot. She hadn't worn it to the palace. She stabbed Ghazzali al-Siyab at the base of the skull, as she'd been taught, the blade turned sideways to slide in better. A silent death. She moved to the left as she drove it in. There should be little blood if done right, but you needed to be careful. She couldn't walk out of here bloodstained.

Nor, she had decided, could they risk letting him live. Al-Siyab was simply too accustomed to working alone, making his own decisions, ignoring plans, partnership. They'd taken an *assignment* here! Were being extremely well paid for a killing. But no, the half-dose of the poison, reckless thefts instead of the assassination that a pair of fiercely dangerous men had hired them to do. And if he was being pursued right now . . . ?

She was already thinking of the lies they'd have to tell as to why the assassination had not happened. It had always been possible al-Faradi would keep his guards, that Ghazzali would not have a chance to put the contents of the vial in the wine. That there might *be* no wine in a morning encounter. They might have to say that was what had happened, she thought. But this was a problem, depending on what was reported, or even known in the palace and not reported . . . because the people who had hired them would have extremely good information.

They could pay back the money they'd been advanced. They would probably have to do that, she thought. Rafel had insisted they not spend any of it; she hadn't disagreed. This task was so much beyond their usual.

It was not remotely the same as, say, smuggling gold sun disks from Esperaña into the port of Marsena using wine casks with false bottoms to avoid the duty on religious objects. Or bribing a man they knew there, a bribe being much less than the duties charged. *That* they knew all about. This? This represented uncharted waters, with whirlpools, as if they'd left the Middle Sea for the far west and were sailing north in the vast, open ocean.

Al-Siyab lay dead at her feet. She'd done it neatly. There was little blood. If she were a better person, Nadia thought, she'd feel more regret that this had happened. Correction: that she had *caused* this to happen. She didn't feel regret. Some anger.

That was what happened if Asharite corsairs had raided your farm and killed your father and taken you away, screaming and punching and scratching until you were clubbed unconscious with the hilt of a sword, to wake on board a galley.

She had no idea, to this morning in Abeneven, if her mother and brother were alive. They'd been sent away when word of an inland raiding party had reached the farm. Her father wouldn't leave. He'd told her to go too, and she'd refused. There were animals to be brought in, and she had a hiding place they'd devised long ago, in case the warning (there were many false warnings) was true this time.

Not a good enough hiding place. Not a false warning. The girl whose name had been Lenia then had been pulled from the covered pit behind the pigsty and dragged through the yard in triumph. Her father had been lying in the dirt, wounded, dying but not yet dead. So she had seen the sword stroke that ended his days. Heard the exultant cry behind the thrust.

Remembered it, still, always.

She was aware that the man lying here now had been clever and charming. That he had a father of distinction in the world of scholars and judges. And even that al-Siyab had—as he'd noted—brought two treasures to her, to them. As his partners.

Even so. Not a virtuous, loyal thing. A necessary one for him. He'd have known he couldn't escape alone. Not from them, and not from those who'd hired them. He needed the ship. The palace would be hunting for him, possibly right now, and also looking for the boy who'd been his companion in the marketplace.

No. Ghazzali al-Siyab had not been reliable. Not safe. He hadn't done what they'd come here to do. Not because he couldn't. Because he'd chosen not to. He'd placed them in immense, immediate peril. For a jewel. For a book. You could die in the world if you did things like that.

She did take them both before she left. And she also took the purse in his robe. There was a chance this might look, when the man was found, as if someone had killed him for that purse.

She cleaned and sheathed her knife. Back outside, walking to the main marketplace, joining the stream of people there, she appeared to be a woman, veiled, carrying a book for her husband, father, brother. Women didn't read. The diamond was in her robe. She had a sudden mental image of wearing it about her neck on a chain.

Absurd thought. Not like her. She was more shaken than she'd realized, clearly. But they hadn't anticipated this at all. It had never been a perfect plan, there was no such thing for an assassination like this. They'd done the best they could to have alternatives. The vizier, the palace guards, might have stayed in the room when the khalif came to meet the storyteller. If that had happened, Ghazzali was to talk (he was good at that) and leave. The hope was that he'd be appealing enough, one way or another, to be invited back. And be alone that next time. Rafel had said they could plausibly remain in the harbour for two weeks, perhaps a little longer, if rumour arrived of another caravan on the way. They'd claim they were waiting for that.

But now? Now, this stay in Abeneven was over. A hunt would be on. If the guards had found Ghazzali alive, and did the things they did to make people talk, he *would* have talked. His death might slow the pursuit when they found him, at least for a time. They'd be looking for the boy, yes, but Enbilcar didn't exist.

Two people she'd killed now. Both men she'd known. One for a long time, mostly kind, educating her. He'd had her brought to his bed, from the very start, young as she'd been. When he wanted. He'd done that.

Two *Asharites* killed, she amended the thought.

Nadia took a deeper breath and kept moving. No one looked at her. It was nearing the time for midday prayer, but if she walked briskly she'd make the ship before the bells.

There was no hint yet of any disturbance in the city. It was a bright spring day in Abeneven. A breeze. She was still thinking about her father. Not a good thing at this moment. Memories of him alive, then that last image of a sword spitting him where he lay, though he was already bleeding out his life on the ground. Their own ground. Home.

Home could be what you'd lost, she thought.

Halfway to the docks she walked away again from the crowd, moving to the right down a winding street with laundry hung overhead, then she turned along a very narrow lane. When she was certain no one was about, she stepped into another small merchant's stall they'd paid for. Again, an unlocked door. Inside, she changed her clothing a second time into what was waiting for her there, including a different hat. She removed and discarded the veil. She didn't wear one on the ship, or trading from it.

Rafel was extremely careful in his planning; so was she, after three years. They were very different in some ways, not in this. She'd be known now when she walked back out, but the *Silver Wake* was visible in the harbour, and she and Rafel were expected to be about and trading. She wanted to be recognized, in this part of the city.

She remembered to transfer the diamond to the new robe, a handsome blue one, as befitted a merchant woman of some success. How amusing it would have been, she thought, had she forgotten to take it. Or not. Really, not. She wasn't a forgetful person, though.

The diamond was heavy. It was enormous. She hadn't known diamonds could be green. This time she put the book out of sight, as well, in the large inner pocket of the robe. If someone she knew stopped to talk, they might easily ask what book she had bought for Rafel, request to see it. On impulse, she left the red leather purse, for the Kindath friend who would come now to take away her clothing. Loyalty deserved reward, and rewards ensured future loyalty.

He was the same one who'd given her a room for the first nights. He would collect what was left behind in both locations, then burn the clothing. He'd find a dead man in the first of those places, and a leather purse here. She hoped he'd keep his composure. There were risks when you needed to trust someone, but there were risks to being alive. Every day, until you weren't.

Two now, Papa. Jad keep you in light, she said to the ghost in her mind.

"THERE'S SOMETHING YOU need to know," Rafel said.

No one had stopped her to talk on the way to the ship. An uneventful last stage of a dangerous walk. Still no sign of unrest. Not by the harbour, at any rate. She'd lifted a hand to two merchants they knew, but they were busy in front of warehouses, and only waved back.

Standing on deck, desperately relieved to be there, she had briefed Rafel tersely about the partial dose of poison. Also, of course, that Ghazzali al-Siyab, their partner, was dead. Only that, no details, though her eyes, when she looked at him, said she had done it.

"You, too," she said. "Something else you need to know. Let's go down."

They went below at the stern to where they each had a cabin and a cot. He led her into his. Closed the door, his expression grave but calm.

She locked it, sliding the iron bolt. She turned back and, wordlessly, showed him the diamond. He looked at it, eyes very wide. Calm now quite gone. He took off his hat and pushed a hand through his hair. She put the diamond down. Then she took out and gave him the book.

Ben Natan opened it. He made an involuntary sound, a gasp more than anything else, and sat down, abruptly, on his narrow cot. The small round window at the stern of the ship was open to allow air and some light. She could see his face clearly. It frightened her.

"*This?*" Rafel ben Natan said, barely above a whisper. His hands were trembling. She had never seen that in him before.

The book, she thought. Not the diamond, which seemed larger on the small table by his bed than a diamond should ever be. And so much more green.

"No one knew where it was!" His voice wavered.

It seemed Ghazzali al-Siyab had not exaggerated the importance of this second treasure.

Rafel wiped his forehead with a hand.

"He stole them both," she said quietly. "Said he left the khalif alive, seeming asleep, so that there'd be less of an outcry when he woke and the thefts became known."

"That makes . . . no sense," her partner said. His voice was still unsteady.

"It might. Possibly. Obviously, there could be no holding back the search for an assassin. But say the khalif doesn't want it known he had the book. Ghazzali said he'd admitted stealing it."

Rafel looked at her. Nodded. "Perhaps. Yes. It was a notorious theft, from Khatib. He might not want that known. But they'd still *hunt* for it. And the diamond. No?"

"Hard to do that discreetly. And they might not want to disclose the loss of the gem . . . or the circumstances surrounding its theft. Is it truly valuable, the book?"

"I can't even put a price on it, Nadia."

Her turn to nod. "All right. Now you," she said, in her most level voice. "You said you had something to tell me."

He made a face she knew. Then he told her.

Nadia blinked. She drew what seemed to be her twentieth deep breath of the day. She sat down beside him on the cot. She felt weak, suddenly. Realized her hands were trembling this time. She didn't like that. She clasped them together.

They looked at each other. Outside and above, the ordinary morning noises of a ship in a harbour. Sounds from that harbour through a small window. Someone laughing in a high-pitched tone. Someone else coughing for a long time. In here, their quiet breathing. She leaned against his shoulder. Couldn't remember ever doing that, with anyone, since home. She straightened, on the thought. He leaned on her, then, also for just a moment.

She said, "You are certain?"

Rafel nodded. "I didn't want him to slow down to measure. And I also had a thought he might be afraid, try to avoid his task, use too small a dose, claim after that it didn't work. He told me he'd never killed anyone. Killing can be hard. So I told him he needed the full vial."

"He didn't? Need the full vial?"

"No," said Rafel. "He didn't."

∽

The illustrious Keram al-Faradi, son of a great khalif, himself khalif of Abeneven for a decade, still a man in his lion-years, drew his last breath that same afternoon.

He had never awakened on the divan where he lay.

There had been signs before the end. The doctors had noted an increasing shallowness to the khalif's breathing and a slowing of his heart when they checked with an ear to his naked chest. They were still unable to say what the cause might be. Or to propose an effective remedy, more importantly. Bleeding the khalif was not going to help with this, it was agreed. They applied cold to his forehead and feet, then changed to heated cloths. One physician suggested, hesitantly, that it was possible the storyteller had used magic on him, invoked a djinn—an act of unspeakable evil, if so. There were no signs of poison on the khalif's breath, but it was noted that two glasses of wine had been poured, and one had been drained.

The vizier, resolute ibn Zukar, had already ordered a hunt throughout the city for the morning's visitor. It was unclear why at first. At that time the khalif had merely appeared to be resting (perhaps fatigued from exertions on the divan, although *no* one said that). And the storyteller had been permitted to leave—by the vizier himself. But doctors did not interfere with matters of the court. And they also did not know what ibn Zukar knew: that the khalif had worn his beloved green Diamond of the South that morning.

There was no explanation for that order to find the man. Or none offered by the vizier, who believed he knew what had been done by a thief he himself had arranged to have escorted here, left alone with the khalif, then permitted to depart. This was not . . . it was not a sequence of events that suggested he'd live past the evening prayers, or whenever the khalif woke.

But the khalif did not wake. And then the khalif died.

The doctors, in abject fear, reported as much to him, kneeling, foreheads to the carpet. And so a moment arrived for the vizier of Abeneven—as moments do sometimes arrive in a life—when one needed to be swiftly decisive.

That, or be executed by whatever decisive person came to power here, with ibn Zukar the vizier proclaimed as the traitor responsible for a calamity.

The palace guard were already seeking Ghazzali al-Siyab. The vizier didn't have many guards assigned directly to his personal service—to claim more would have been overly bold, showing too much ambition—but he did trust them, to a point. More than the palace ones, at any rate. Now, in the presence of a terrible death, he ordered the doctors from the room. He watched them scurry out, pathetically glad to be left alive, and he summoned the commander of his guard, a certain Bakiri, who came from south of the mountains.

He instructed him that the slave who had been in the room earlier, and had found the necklace, and who would not now be far from here, was to be taken away and his throat slit and his body disposed of outside the palace grounds.

He further instructed that the khalif's most-favoured guardsman, who had also been here when the storyteller arrived, be similarly executed. Bakiri asked no questions. Which was only proper.

That favoured guard, it turned out, had fled the palace as soon as the necklace was found behind the fire. He was, evidently, no fool. And he'd have seen the khalif wearing his diamond, ibn Zukar realized. Blame for such things fell where it fell, and not always where it belonged.

But the man wasn't quite swift enough, alas for him. The vizier's guardsmen found him negotiating for a camel by the southern gate, with obvious intent to leave the city. He was seized, duly killed, and left in an alley not far from that gate. The vizier's men came back to the palace and Bakiri reported these things to the vizier.

Ibn Zukar took thought. He needed to be quick, but also precise! That slain guardsman was a useful person now that he was dead. He ordered Bakiri to have men go back to the southern gate and bring the body to the palace. The vizier was thinking as fast as he ever had in his life, trying to react to events. Trying, really, to remain alive, and perhaps—just perhaps—more than that. The sour-faced guard had been responsible for protecting the blessed khalif this morning, hadn't he? He had failed, hadn't he? Why had he failed? Why had he been seeking to flee the city?

It was a sign of a desperate, guilty man, wasn't it?

After taking even deeper thought in an *extremely* challenging time, the vizier sent Bakiri and three other men out again with significantly more demanding tasks. These to be done swiftly, before news of what had happened here spread. As it would spread. Again, Bakiri said nothing, only nodded. No expression could be discerned in the chief guardsman's face. A good thing, ibn Zukar decided—if he was loyal.

The khalif of Abeneven had left no heirs. His harem had been much neglected. There would be, the vizier judged, two obvious rivals to himself once word emerged in the city of this shocking death.

Better there were none.

He stayed in the room where the khalif lay. He needed to control access here. He kept four of his guards with him: two at the inner door, two replacing the palace guards outside. He might be slain here himself, it was entirely possible, but you seized certain moments like you seized a woman by the hair when you wanted to take her to your bed and compel actions you found pleasing.

That was what he was doing now, while invoking the blessings of Ashar and the stars.

Next thing: two of the first set of guards, the khalif's men, not his own, came to report. Ibn Zukar allowed one to enter. He was told that the storyteller had been found.

"Good," said the vizier. "Bring him."

"He has been brought to the palace, lord. He is dead. We found him in an empty shop in the Murtash side-market. He was stabbed in the neck."

Ibn Zukar paused, thinking urgently. "Was he searched? Was anything found?"

"He was searched, lord. Nothing was found. But there were footprints in the dust. Someone had been there."

"Well yes, fool. You just said he was stabbed! Of course someone was there!"

The guard looked down.

"If this is not the truth," said the vizier grimly, "you will be dead before sunset."

Harsh words; he was not known for them.

"I do not speak untruths, lord! Before you, before Ashar, before the stars and the god."

The largest green diamond known might induce an untruth or two, thought Nisim ibn Zukar, but he elected to reserve judgment, and stay watchful. He now had a story taking shape: the khalif's guard of this morning and the storyteller, acting together. Poisoning the beloved khalif, fleeing with the diamond. The guard killing the other man, then caught by the vizier's men while attempting to leave the city.

It needed the diamond to have been found on that fleeing man at the southern gate to be a perfect tale. But it hadn't been. Or, they *said* it hadn't been.

Perhaps, the vizier had a sudden thought, perhaps no one need even learn the Diamond of the South was missing? Yes! The slave and the guard of this morning were both dead! And now so was the storyteller! And he himself hadn't mentioned the diamond to anyone. The slave who had dressed the khalif would need to die now, quietly, but there was a very good chance no one knew the diamond was gone! The necklace . . . the necklace had been thrown away for . . . for some reason. He'd work out an explanation. Or claim to be mystified and angry. They could discover the diamond's absence some time later, weeks, *months*, institute a hopeless search . . . this was all possible, suddenly. He needed only to survive the coming days!

He was not aware that the *Prologue to Knowledge* was also missing.

Full knowledge can be hard to come by. We live, we make decisions, without it all the time.

A PALACE IN turmoil is not an ideal place for the keeping of secrets.

It was widely known by late afternoon that some men had been killed by the palace guard, and others by the vizier's personal guard. In the second group were two figures of the very highest importance. One, in fact, was the city's military commander. Not a man much liked in Abeneven, but even so . . .

Another of the dead, apparently, was the handsome storyteller who had visited with the khalif, privately, in the morning. *Privately*, for Keram al-Faradi, had always had a particular meaning in his palace. The storyteller had been escorted to the khalif in an upstairs room, had gone on his way after, and was now dead. He had not, it was said, been killed by any of the guards. That might or might not be true, of course. Some people in the market had apparently seen a body being carried out of an abandoned shop by guards, back up towards the palace.

Finally, and worst of all, it began to be said—first as wild rumour, then with increasing conviction—that the khalif himself was dead on a divan in that same reception room. The source of this information, it was claimed, was one of the palace physicians.

It was a great deal. It was overwhelming. Panic seemed the proper response. And this loud confusion of rumours did not remain, of course, within the palace buildings or gardens. It could never have been contained there.

In the military barracks soldiers began arming themselves. No one had specifically ordered this, but it seemed the thing to do. Abeneven was a prize. The khalif had no heir. Their own commander had been killed. There was going to be trouble. They might even choose to be the trouble.

It was said that the vizier, ibn Zukar, was working to enforce calm. He wasn't hated any more than viziers were customarily hated, but the fact that it was said to have been *his* guards who had murdered the military commander and the court's principal taxation adviser . . . well, that told a tale, didn't it? An old sort of tale.

Who was next in line for power? Was Nisim ibn Zukar trying to ensure it could *only* be him? Good luck to the vizier if he believed it would be smooth sailing in calm waters, if so.

As to actual sailing, in the harbour where more than thirty merchant ships and galleys of all sizes were currently moored, many of these began leaving with the evening tide, and the tidings. The ones that remained were owned by merchants of Abeneven, for whom this was their home harbour. The prudent owners and captains among this group did have their sailors summoned back on board from the city, with instructions to arm themselves. Violence was entirely possible.

The city would not be a place for anyone to be trading goods, or waiting for caravans, if any of the stories now spreading were true. And some of them were going to be. In the Kindath quarter the inhabitants closed the iron gates early, well before sundown, and began to take their own too-familiar precautions. The Jaddite warehouses by the harbour were being bolted up and guards posted there, too. A few of those guards decided they weren't paid enough to do this, and quietly slipped away.

Departing galleys could row their way out from the docks. Sailing ships, which meant most of the merchant vessels, needed to manoeuvre, of course. Fortunately, the wind, as the sun westered on a beautiful day, became agreeable. There were near misses as they all laboured to get out to sea and away, but no actual collisions. Something of a miracle, in the circumstances.

"IT IS A MIRACLE," Rafel whispered. They were standing together at the prow. Elie had worked them free of a wild tangle of ships and they were headed out. The white-capped waves of the Middle Sea had never looked so enticing, Nadia thought. She knew Rafel didn't believe in miracles. She wasn't sure if Kindath usually did. Jaddites like her were supposed to: the intervention of the god in times of dire need, invoked by prayer and virtue.

She didn't believe in them either, herself. This was a result they could have predicted. Chaos in the city with word of the khalif's death. Other deaths after. A coup would be suspected now. The duties of the harbour officers: checking holds of ships for unrecorded items, enforcing payment of duties and harbour fees—these were not going to be at the top of anyone's list of tasks. Not this evening.

They'd hidden the diamond and the book, one in his cabin, one in hers. Though it really didn't mean anything, dividing them. She'd said to Rafel that if either was found they were dead in an extremely bad way. He had smiled thinly.

But they weren't going to be searched, it seemed. Nor, now, would their departure be noteworthy. Looking about her, a twilight wind whipping at her hair, Nadia saw that the last of the ships trading at Abeneven were working to get out from the harbour.

She shook her head. They had two wildly valuable stolen objects, and had assassinated a khalif, and they were sails up and headed for open sea. She looked at Rafel, standing beside her.

"It might be," she said, against every instinct in her life. "It might be a miracle."

SHE WAS IN her cot later, the ship rising and falling in choppy seas, when he tapped on her door. She'd heard his footsteps in the narrow space outside.

"It is open," Nadia called. She said it softly, though there was no one else down there. She pulled the sheet to her chin and sat up on the cot. Her hair was loose, of course. It was short now, just touching her shoulders. Rafel entered with a ship's lantern, set it on the heavy hook. He closed the door.

"You should probably be locking this now."

She shook her head. She hadn't been asleep, felt alert. "The crew know we never do that. Shouldn't make a change. I trust our hiding places."

"I trust nothing on earth or on the sea." A thing he said all the time.

She granted him a half-smile. "What is it, Rafel?" He didn't do this often. She'd need time to try to recall the last occasion.

She had a square-seat stool in the cabin. He pulled it from by the wall and sat down, didn't answer immediately. When he spoke, it was something unexpected.

"I feel old tonight," he said.

"It was a challenging day. You aren't old."

He shook his head. "Older than everyone on this ship."

"Even Elie?"

"Perhaps not Elie. We grew up together."

"You don't look old. You look like a bold, handsome corsair."

He laughed at that. "Do you know, no one has ever called me handsome in my life?"

"Indeed? Shall I do so again? Would that make you happy?"

"I am never happy, Nadia. But . . . yes. Do so. But on deck, so the others hear it."

Her turn to laugh. "May I look amused while doing it?"

"No. We wouldn't want it thought you were insincere."

HE HEARD HER laughter. It made him realize, again, how seldom one did hear that. Nadia hadn't lived a life, he thought, conducive to laughter. Perhaps that might happen now, finally? If they succeeded? Danger didn't balk laughter; not the way slavery did. Or was that untrue? Perhaps it could. Her face was serious again, already, within the framing of her hair.

"Am I to believe this really matters to you?" she asked. "As it happens, it has rarely been said of me, either, since I was a girl." She never talked about her childhood. "Why are you here so late?"

He approached the matter indirectly. He almost always did that. Old habits, a chance to observe the listeners. "Not handsome? You are, of course, but much more than that. You are terribly *capable*. Blades, words, numbers, you have learned how to handle a ship. Hmm. What else? Can you ride?"

"Not at all. Though I grew up in riding country. We didn't have horses. It was just a farm."

He hadn't known that. He didn't even know where in Batiara she'd been born. Only that she'd sworn never to go back. Which was why he was in her cabin tonight, in fact.

He said, still angling towards that, "Nadia, you must know by now that most men will find you desirable, if a little frightening."

"Oh? Do you?"

He hadn't expected that.

He cleared his throat. "Frightening? Only when I intend to suggest something you won't like." There was a pause. She was looking at him. He knew that wasn't what she'd asked. "I would never," he said, "act so as to offend you, ever."

"Fearing my knives?" Her voice had gone soft, for a jest.

He shook his head. "Fearing to risk your friendship. I haven't many friends. Not in my nature."

Her turn to clear her throat. "Nor mine. Thank you. Now tell me why you're here, so I can go to sleep."

So he said, with less preparation than he'd have preferred, "I think we do need to go to Batiara."

A silence. She didn't look frightening. She looked afraid, he thought.

She said, slowly, thinking it through, "To sell what we now have?"

He nodded. "I think it needs to be there. I have ideas for each, the diamond and the book."

"And both ideas are . . . both are in Batiara?"

He nodded again. "You can disembark at Marsena when we stop to be paid for . . . for the khalif. We'll pick you up on our way back. If you trust me."

"Of course I trust you," she said, shaking her head. "Though almost no one else, to be honest."

"I know," he said. "Thank you. So that is a possibility. If you . . ." He said it: "If you don't want to go home."

Another stillness. Creaking of the ship, wind, slap of waves. The lantern swaying on its hook.

"I wouldn't go home, no," she said. "But it is a large place, Batiara. Where do you plan to go?"

He told her.

She looked at him a long time. He couldn't read her expression. She said, "That's close to my home, as it happens." She took a breath, so did he. Her mouth crooked, not quite a smile. "You are, in fact, an acceptably handsome man, Rafel ben Natan. So you know. And my friend. I think you'll need me. Selling those things will be very dangerous. I'll come. I have just now . . . I have decided I don't like the idea of the past *preventing* me from doing things."

"Just now?"

"This very moment."

"Good," he said. He was surprised at how relieved he felt. "Very good. I'll see you on deck in the morning. Remember to say how attractive I am." He stood, unhooked the lamp, pushed the stool neatly back against the wall, unbolted the door, and went out.

SHE DIDN'T SLEEP for a long time.

For no good reason she found herself thinking about *desire*, and being desirable. She knew she could appeal to men, had done it with intent if it was useful in a negotiation. But feeling desire herself? That was different. She had no clear memory of that feeling.

It had been, she thought, taken from her. Stolen. When she was stolen. She'd certainly been old enough to think about, to want such things, before being taken from home, but she had no real recollection of *what* she'd been. That girl on a farm. What she had thought and felt about anything. It was lost. She believed she had kissed someone once, but it wasn't a *clear* memory. As if there was a wall, or a dividing sea, and she lived on the other side of it, the other shore.

When she did sleep, she dreamed of horses, which was new, and very strange. She was riding on a plain at night under both moons, her hair (which had grown long) blowing back.

Outside, above, the moons, waxing, shone on the Middle Sea, and the wind in the sails took them north in the night.

∽

Rafel was nowhere close to sleep either. He blew out the lamp, hung it on its hook outside their two cabins, then went up on deck. Elie was at the wheel. He never slept, that was the jest. It wasn't far from truth, Rafel thought. He walked towards him under stars and the moons his people worshipped as sisters of the god.

His thoughts kept sliding to the past, which he was normally able to avoid. Nadia wasn't the only one, he thought.

"Anything I need to know?"

Elie shook his head. "Easy running. I think this wind should hold all night." He looked at Rafel. "You all right?"

Ben Natan shrugged. "I will be, my friend. Thoughts crowding."

"You're always like this when go to Marsena."

"What? I am? Really?"

The other man nodded. "Every time. Stands to reason, I'd say."

"I don't like being predictable."

Elie laughed. "Of course you don't, Rafel. You live your life trying to avoid it."

"Damn you, Elie," he said, which seemed appropriate.

Elie laughed again. "Want a drink? I have a flask."

Rafel said, "I don't think so. I'll just stay here for a bit, then try to sleep."

"Sleep," said the other man, "is a waste of time."

"No it isn't," he said.

He walked forward to the prow. They had a figurehead there, a sea creature, a woman with a fish's tail. The tail had a hidden latch around to the front; they hid things inside sometimes.

He stood beside it, remembering the most recent of those occasions, then his thoughts went further back, to when Marsena on the coast of Ferrieres, in its wide bay, had become an important place in his life. Elie was probably right. He did feel the past coming back whenever they went there. And an odd sense of the present, too— after they docked and he went ashore.

How not? Truly?

In the salt spray and the wind, feeling sorrow trying to claim him, he spoke a prayer for his father and mother, and then another—he always did—for his brother, wherever he was in this night's world. If he still *was* in the world somewhere.

⁓

It would be some time, not until summer, before word of the violent death of young Ghazzali al-Siyab reached Almassar, where he had grown up and where his family lived. They went into mourning, led by his grieving father.

Ghazzali, eldest son, born not long after they'd fled Esperaña into exile, had not been the most virtuous of young men, but he'd been a sweet-faced, sweet-natured child, an appealing boy, and startlingly quick-witted. He'd memorized, when still youthful, stories his father told him, or that he heard in the marketplace, and also, when his father had challenged him at ten years of age to do it, the first difficult pages of ibn Udad's great text.

Siyab al-Aram had never surrendered the hope that his son would turn back to Ashar's path and a life of wisdom and study, to attain the rank and stature the father had, or even surpass him. Since the murder some years before, by an unknown assailant, of Dhiyan ibn Anash, Siyab had been the chief judge of Almassar, admired and respected for both rigour and fairness. Learning that his son had been stabbed (also by someone unknown) in the market of Abeneven, and that it had happened months before, took all peace away from that good man.

The death of a loved child can do that. What follows will vary widely. For Siyab al-Aram, what followed was yearning. A helpless longing to see his boy again, to let the hard words that had passed between them towards the end, like lashes of two whips, have been courteous and affectionate instead, not the ones with which they had parted.

He wept, often, even in court. It was said that he was never really the same. He died himself less than two years after; not young, but hardly an old man. Only broken.

Keram al-Faradi, the murdered khalif of Abeneven, was not greatly mourned, possibly because there was so much chaos in the period that followed his death.

He ought to have been. He had not been the most pious of leaders but had never oppressed the virtuous. He had led Abeneven through a decade of stable prosperity in a world that had seen the fall of Sarantium and vicious civil wars nearer home. It ought to have been enough for him to be remembered gently, affectionately, in his city. With sorrow, commended to Ashar and the watching stars. He was not.

Alas, this happens. We do not always receive kindness in life. Or in the memories carried of us after our dying. Unless it is from the god we worship, which is a matter of longing and desire, never certainty.

CHAPTER IV

It was an uneventful passage to Marsena. No weather, no corsairs. They were corsairs themselves, of course, under licence to the khalif of Almassar. Some protection in that. Not much, however, and not at all from Esperañan pirates, or royal ships.

They were ahead of any tidings from Abeneven. They'd *be* those tidings. He'd wanted that. He'd had Elie do all he could to make speed. They would be carrying the news to the two men waiting for them. Rafel didn't fear them in any immediate way just now: they had done what they'd been hired to do. But these two were wildly unpredictable. The younger brother, in particular, could kill on a whim, in a mood. It was known that he had.

Marsena was safe for Asharites, notoriously so. The war for supremacy in the Jaddite world between the king of Ferrieres and the king and queen of Esperaña had led to complex alliances, and flirting with the forbidden. Although to *forbid* a king was a challenge, even for the High Patriarch. Scarsone Sardi had tried, mind you, thundering his imprecations from Rhodias, threatening to deny all rites of Jad—and therefore any hope of finding the god's light after death—to the whole of Ferrieres for its king's accommodations with accursed Gurçu.

He'd been a frivolous man, the still-young High Patriarch, placed in his exalted position by a shrewd, wealthy uncle governing Firenta in all but the title. Scarsone had been seen purely as an instrument of the Sardi family in their ascent from local bankers to a great force in the world. But he had changed, and everyone knew it was the fall of Sarantium that had caused that.

No man would want to be known forever as the Patriarch who had let it happen. No Jaddite would want to go to his god after dying, seeking shelter and light, with that blackness to his soul and name.

So the High Patriarch was still aggressively summoning every Jaddite monarch and city aristocrat to war to reclaim the golden city. He wasn't just an instrument of his family any more. Which is not to say he was *achieving* the holy war he sought. There were conflicts and hatreds nearer home, and there was profit to be pursued by city-states like Seressa, which had smoothly resumed trading within a year of Sarantium's fall, dealing with Gurçu the Destroyer in what was now called Asharias.

The High Patriarch had, famously, forbidden the very word Asharias to be uttered in his presence. That didn't change the city's name, of course. You needed an army for that, and he didn't have one.

In the meantime, King Émery of Ferrieres allowed Asharite corsairs and merchants to repair their ships, take on water and food, and trade (with duties paid) in his deep-water port of Marsena. In exchange, the raiders of the Majriti left his merchant vessels alone, and levied steady, deadly attacks on those of Esperaña, his enemy. In their pursuit of Jaddites—for galleys, for household slaves, for children to be turned into court eunuchs or into soldiers—they never touched the coastal cities of Ferrieres.

Esperaña, yes. Batiara, where the loud, empty Patriarch tried to thunder a war into existence, yes, indeed. Jaddite lands farther east, nearer Asharias, absolutely. Galleys, after all, didn't row themselves. They needed slaves to row them, then die.

And Jad's pirates did exactly the same to the Majriti towns and cities. And Esperaña's royal ship commanders attacked to the south whenever they could, looking to take ships, claim harbours on that coastline. Or simply kill the deniers of the sun god's glory.

It was not what anyone would have called a safe time to be sailing on, or living beside, or anywhere near the reaches of the Middle Sea.

Which, of course, is how Nadia, a female slave of Dhiyan ibn Anash of Almassar, had come to be owned by him. Until she'd used a blade to end that. And him.

Rafel, living on the outskirts of Almassar, in the Kindath community beyond the city walls, had actually known of the man who'd bought his partner as a young girl long ago. He had seen him, at a distance. Not so unusual: he was a prominent judge, a scholar, a *distinguished* figure in the city, Dhiyan ibn Anash. No one knew who had killed him. Would any decent soul condemn the girl who'd become the woman who'd done that, if they did know? Well, many would, yes. Almost all, in truth. Rhetoric had its limits, even in your thoughts.

He didn't condemn it at all, not since the night she'd made her way to the docks, and the *Silver Wake*, and taken a chance he might let her join them, and he had. She'd told him some—only some—of her story.

He forced his thoughts back to what he was on deck this morning to do, which was pay his crew. They would dock at Marsena's harbour later today. The wind had stayed benign right across in a chancy time of year. They'd been extremely fortunate so far. Rafel ben Natan didn't trust fortune. *If you laugh too much today*, his mother used to say, *you'll cry tomorrow.*

He also didn't trust crewmen who made sour jokes about payment as they lined up before him, where he had a table and his ledger and their coins waiting. It was the big, slope-shouldered Esperañan, Bastiao. Again.

"And I expect he'll short-pay us now, because we had to leave Abeneven before they finished buying. Watch for it!" He said it to two men behind him, as they neared the desk. He didn't do so quietly.

"I don't think so," said one of them.

"Watch," Bastiao repeated confidently. "He's a Kindath, remember?"

"*Don't react!*" Rafel said quietly to Nadia, standing behind him. Elie was at the wheel, giving instructions just now to the men handling the ropes.

Bastiao reached the front of the line. "My lord," he said, bowing obsequiously. He was a good-looking man.

Rafel looked up at him. "Full payment, always," he said. "No man on my ship suffers for events we can't control. You can apologize."

Bastiao glanced past Rafel, and it was obvious he saw Nadia's expression. It would not be benevolent. "But jesting, captain. You know that! It's my way!" He smiled.

"Perhaps amend your ways in this?"

Rafel counted out the coins, ticked off the payment in his ledger, placed the money on the far side of the table, towards the sailor.

"Surely will!" Bastiao said. "Thanks, captain!"

"No thanks needed. Agreed-upon payment. Report to Elie."

He worked his way through the crew, then made the usual payment of a coin at the end, tossing one overboard as the men watched, for the lords and ladies of the sea. Pagan gods and spirits; no one was supposed to believe in them, not in any of the faiths. It was heresy, but not a sailor anywhere didn't appreciate it if their ship's captain or owner performed this ritual.

He finished with the ledger, doing final calculations, happy to find that it balanced. He was good with numbers, a small thing in which he took pride. Nadia waited until he was done. He looked back at her, finally.

"Don't like him," she said quietly. They were alone now.

"Nor I. Don't bring him back on board when we've finished."

She nodded. "Can I have him killed?"

He made a face. "No, you cannot. Stop it."

"You take away all my pleasures in life."

He snorted. "Not all of them, I trust."

She grinned. "Just because you are such a handsome man, don't think I'll agree with everything you say."

"Saying it now doesn't count. No one heard. You are coming to meet the brothers tonight?"

"Would not miss it for my hope of light with Jad after dying," Nadia said.

ELIE AND THE CREW finished securing the ship. Rafel and Nadia arranged for the first guards on board while everyone else went ashore, and for their replacements to take over. Then they made their way, greeting people they knew on the docks, towards the inn where they'd been told to find their employers. Some anxiety as they walked, how could there not be? It was late afternoon, not yet dark.

Zariq and Ziyar ibn Tihon were already there, waiting for them. They had chosen this port as the place to meet. He was not in a position to make suggestions. It suited him, though, for a few reasons. The brothers were seated at a table towards the back. There wasn't much light there. They'd prefer shadows. Ferrieres was currently safe for Asharites, but they were . . . not ordinary Asharites.

Rafel would have preferred to arrive first, do them that courtesy: be found awaiting the most feared corsairs of the Middle Sea. Men who also ruled the city of Tarouz now, east of Abeneven along the coastline. They governed as khalifs, but in the name of Gurçu, conqueror of Asharias. They had hundreds of his djannis sent west to them as infantry—a symbol of his support, but they still ruled with a considerable degree of licence, so far away. And one of them was almost always at sea, usually the younger.

They were, after all, also Gurçu's naval commanders in the west.

They were wealthy, unpredictable, more than a little terrifying. They used that fear as a weapon. Cultivated it as a farmer cultivated his fields. They burned villages simply to burn them, permitting their men free rein within before the fires began. They let the panic shaped by even a rumour of their presence cause chaos among the Jaddites on or near the coasts.

They were also, still, vastly ambitious. Tarouz was not enough, it seemed. Which is why they'd had an obscure Kindath merchant and his associate coordinate the assassination of the khalif of Abeneven for them. Rafel's obscurity was a part of it, of course.

They *could* have besieged the other city, launched an assault by land and sea, but Abeneven would be hard to take, harder to encircle and starve, and the appearance of doing either would not be good: too naked an attack on fellow star-worshippers. Too much about themselves.

Gurçu might not like that.

Some campaigns were better done quietly, some ambitions explored that way. Let one of the wretched, wandering Kindath prepare it for you. Arrange an assassination, then arrive as star-blessed rescuers to a city in chaos. The Kindath merchant? He could be torn apart or gutted if the plot was found out—along with whoever had been working with him. Little lost, if so. Nothing lost, in fact.

Rafel knew all this. So did Nadia, he was certain, although they hadn't discussed it. She was too clever not to know. And she also knew how to keep quiet.

As now. They had only met the brothers the one time, that home in Almassar, the owner absent, corsairs for guards. Two very large men sitting in a courtyard at twilight as the fireflies began. The elder, Zariq, had a notorious red beard and blue eyes; the younger, Ziyar, was also bearded, but darker. He was the more dangerous one in moments like this. Maybe.

You could measure danger in different ways, Rafel thought. The brothers had been born Jaddite in the east, on one of the fishing islands north of Candaria. Captured with other boys in a raid. Meant for slaves, or djannis, perhaps. But they'd seized that boat in the night. Killed the men who'd taken them. Thrown the bodies into the sea. That was how it had started. So the story went.

They might indeed have become djannis, had they been strong enough, and sold to the right person. The djannis were almost always Jaddite, owing everything to the court and army, loyal because they had nothing else to be loyal to, having been taken from their homes.

The brothers hadn't become djannis. They'd become pirates, with the one ship, then another, then a fleet, other raiders coming to follow them, the one brilliant, the other savage. Eventually the ibn Tihons claimed a city for themselves, Tarouz, near the ancient ruins of Axartes.

Small things can have large effects. Everyone knows this.

Rafel ben Natan bowed to them in the shadows at the back of an inn in Marsena. He had the good sense to be afraid. He hoped Nadia was.

These men were rulers, and had left their city—both of them—to come here for this meeting. That was significant. He hoped Nadia would also be bowing, staying properly behind him. He didn't look back to see. A woman might be allowed to be part of this, but needed to show she knew her place.

"My lord Zariq, my lord Ziyar. My most humble respects to both of you."

He spoke Asharic. The tables around them were empty, he saw. No one wanted to be close to this. At least six Asharite guards stood not far away, blocking the sight of them. The inn, towards the door and the street, was a tense, uneasy place. Men were walking out, Rafel saw, allowing himself a glance over his shoulder. Not surprising. People in Marsena knew of these two. People everywhere along the Middle Sea knew them.

He turned back to the table and looked closely, trying not to be obvious about it.

He didn't think they were drunk. Asharites were not supposed to drink, but . . .

"Report, Kindath," said Zariq ibn Tihon, crisply but not disturbingly so. He hadn't greeted them. Nor was it a question. He'd spoken a command.

"A good report," said his younger brother lightly. "Or I'll fuck the woman on the table, and then my brother will kill you. He only needs to scratch a man with his blade."

"Stop it, Ziyar," his brother said. "No cause. We offered an arrangement and they accepted. This is a proper meeting."

Ziyar grinned. Rafel could see white teeth in the dim light. "A proper meeting!" He might be drunk, after all.

With his dark, unruly beard, the lamps and shadows made the younger brother look like a demon, a half-world spirit. Rafel was surprised to discover he was now more angry than afraid. He did have anger in him. He didn't like it, but it was there.

"Thank you," he said calmly to the older one.

He turned to the younger and included him. It was notoriously easy to offend this man. "We undertook to do a thing you desired. We all agreed it would be difficult and delicate."

"Delicate," Ziyar mocked again. He *was* drunk, Rafel was sure of it now.

"Yes," his older brother said. "We did agree as to that. I remember the courtyard. I remember telling you of Ghazzali al-Siyab. Results, ben Natan?"

His name, at least, this time. And framed as a question.

He said, "The khalif of Abeneven, Keram al-Faradi, has gone to his place among the stars, sadly before his time."

"This is certain?" Again, it was the older brother, but with a quickening in his voice now. Excitement. This was the one people did not think was insane.

They were both such *large* men, Rafel thought.

"Every ship in Abeneven harbour left the same evening, with the tide. The military commander and the minister of palace revenues were also both reported killed that day."

"Not by you?" said Zariq quickly.

"No. No. Most probably by the vizier's guards."

Ziyar let out a shout of laughter. "Hah! You *said* that would happen, brother!"

Zariq allowed himself a small smile. He sipped his wine. "Well done, then," he said to Rafel, and he let his gaze shift briefly to where Nadia would be. "And Ghazzali al-Siyab?"

"Is dead, my lords," she said. Rafel became nervous again, she really wasn't supposed to speak here.

A change of expression on Zariq's features. "You know this how?"

"Because I killed him, lords," said Nadia.

Rafel had known she was going to say that. He kept his expression grave, earnest. He waited, anxiety back, edging towards dread.

"Because?" Zariq ibn Tihon's voice was quiet.

"Because he was reckless, and known to have been in the palace that morning, and if captured that day he'd have talked. He'd have named you both. I couldn't risk it, for you."

A silence. Then the younger brother's laughter again, loud, heavy. He banged the table with an open palm. He would laugh this way while killing someone, Rafel thought. Ziyar clapped his older brother on the back. "Ashar in the desert never prophesied so well as you!" he cried. "You said they would do this, too!"

"Heresy," his brother said, shaking his head. "You must repent for it at prayer. But yes, I did think it likely these two would kill him. Out of greed, or caution. I thought it would be on the ship, though."

"It wasn't, and it wasn't greed," Rafel said. "His share may be kept back, offered to the poor or the pious, or whatever you see fit, my lords. He was a danger to you, not just to us. He knew who had hired him."

"So," said the younger brother, "do you."

"Of course we do. Will you kill us now, or pay us honourably? I have never heard of the ibn Tihon brothers not being honourable to someone who did them good service."

"True. But I haven't fucked either of you yet," Ziyar said, but he was smiling now.

Rafel didn't allowed himself a smile in return. He was a Kindath, after all. Barely tolerated in the world.

He said, "You may wait for word from other ships to confirm what we say. I'm sure some are making their way here. We were fast, with this meeting ahead of us."

"And your payment."

"And our payment."

Zariq asked, with what seemed genuine curiosity, "The poison, the Esperañan vial. That did it?"

"It did, lord. Ghazzali told me so," Nadia said. He was still nervous about her speaking.

"And then you killed him. How?"

"A knife to the back of his neck. Held flat, to ensure there was little blood. I didn't want to walk out with blood on my clothing."

"I see. You are familiar with ways to kill, Nadia bint Dhiyan?"

Rafel hadn't thought a khalif of Tarouz would remember her name. Zariq was not to be underestimated, he reminded himself.

"I have had to learn, yes, my lord."

He prayed she'd not say more and, blessedly, she didn't.

"It is a hard time we live in, is it not."

"It is, lord."

"Do you pray, Nadia bint Dhiyan?"

"I do."

"Where do you pray?"

Rafel didn't like where this was going.

"In the temples of Ashar and the stars, lord. Or by myself, seeking mercy and forgiveness for sins."

"Not in Jaddite sanctuaries?"

Rafel swallowed. He heard Nadia say, "Not since I, like you, was taken as a child, lord."

Rafel held his breath. A frozen moment in a barely lamplit space in a tavern in Marsena, early in the spring of that year.

Then, by grace of the sister moons, there came laughter again, this time from both brothers. It went on for some time. But it might easily not have come at all, Rafel knew. His partner, he thought, was magnificent, and could get them killed. Both things felt true.

Zariq ibn Tihon lifted a hand. One of the guards came over, out of shadow. Quick apprehension, then something else. Ibn Tihon extended the same hand, palm up, and the guard placed a sealed envelope in it. "We use the Carraza Bank of Seressa for dealings in Jaddite lands," the elder khalif of Tarouz said. "I trust payment drawn upon them is acceptable? They have branches in many places. Including here, of course."

This was half a courtesy, half a mockery of it, Rafel thought. What was he going to say?

He nodded. "Of course it is acceptable, lord. Thank you."

"You did what you contracted to do, and one of you sadly died doing so. You are receiving full payment, and can do whatever seems proper to you with respect to al-Siyab's share. We are grateful, we will employ you again if a proper task arises. You may leave."

He knew better, he knew *infinitely* better, than to unseal the document and check the amount.

They bowed. They left. People parted to make way for them.

It had grown dark. On a windy street near the harbour, both moons rising, clouds moving overhead, stars, it seemed to Rafel that he was finally able to breathe properly again. It felt as if it had been some time since he'd done that.

"I thought you handled it well enough," Nadia said. "For someone inexperienced in these matters."

He turned on her, beginning a string of curses, then saw that she was smiling. "Well done," she said. "I'm sorry for baiting them. I seem to be careless that way."

"Very," was all he could manage.

"Also, you looked handsome inside. Must have been the lighting."

This time he did swear at her.

Rafel insisted she leave him there. He had a right to *some* private life, didn't he? He reminded her he knew Marsena well, had been coming here for years, well before he'd allowed a certain Jaddite fugitive on his ship.

There was a Kindath quarter here. Ferrieres was not the most welcoming Jaddite country for his people—he had worn a blue-and-white cap when they came ashore, as required by law—but they hadn't been exiled from here, and the clerics leading inquisitions in Ferrieres were less indulged and feared than in Esperaña.

"You have to have a guard, Rafel. You can't deal with a thief by debating ethical principles with him, and you aren't even supposed to be outside the quarter after dark."

"I've done that," he said. "Debated ethical principles. But it's all right. I'm not going far and—"

"Let me walk you there and wait outside the gates. Unless it's a whore you're going to and you need all night, in which case I'll walk with you and come back in the morning."

He made a face. "I am not going to a whore." It was paining him a little, not being able to tell her the truth. This wasn't entirely his story, however, or even mostly his.

She wasn't smiling.

"It isn't a whore, Nadia." It *was* a woman, but he didn't have to tell her that. "We're only in Marsena, by the sisters and the god, I'll be all right."

"Marsena is a port, with everything that means after dark."

She was so accursedly stubborn.

"You are accursedly stubborn," he said.

"Makes it a good thing you are so pliant and agreeable, doesn't it? I'm walking you to the Kindath quarter, Rafel. Or wherever you are going."

Pliant and agreeable? The very *idea* offended him. Nonetheless he let her come with him. She could take him to the gates. Easier than arguing in a cold wind, and he was in a complex state of mind. Always was, in Marsena.

Near to where Gaelle lived, at the edge of the quarter, they were accosted. Five men.

SHE HAD NO weapons, not even her boot knife. You couldn't go to a meeting with the ibn Tihon brothers with a hidden blade. She wasn't a fool. Well, perhaps she was. Perhaps they both were. *What a stupid way to die*, was her first thought.

Her second was that this *was* the brothers. But that made no sense. Those two wouldn't need to do this in secrecy. They killed openly, sometimes randomly. To remind the world that they could, whenever they chose. Yes, they were on Jaddite soil, but Ferrieres needed the brothers and their ships raiding Esperaña. If they killed a Kindath man and some unknown woman who had been a slave . . . who would even care? A phrase used earlier snagged in her mind: *He only needs to scratch a man with his blade.*

But no, it wasn't the brothers. In addition, this was an oddly slow-moving attack.

They were on a narrow street with no inns to send light into the night. Only moonlight and the stars, scudding clouds. She couldn't see the men clearly, couldn't tell what weapons they carried. They were motionless, as if waiting. Nor, she abruptly realized, did Rafel seem panicked. Alert, and . . . irritated. Irritated? What in the god's name did *that* mean?

"I have no weapon," she muttered to him. She had positioned herself beside him.

"I know," he said. "Never mind."

"*Never mind?* What—"

"I know them," he said.

"Oh, good," Nadia snapped. "I much prefer being attacked in the dark by people you know."

"How did you learn I was in the city, Isacar?" Rafel lifted his voice to ask the question.

"Don't be an idiot," came the reply. "We know your ship. Why were you meeting those Asharite scum?"

An angry voice. Not local. And she realized something else. What sort of a name Isacar was.

"Careful tongue, you," Rafel said. "They might have sent guards to protect me. They like me."

"There are no guards. I'm not surprised you are liked by murderers."

"Isacar, truly, lower your voice. Be cautious."

"*You* are going to give me instructions?"

"To save your life, yes."

"No," said the man named, evidently, Isacar. "Here is what happens now. You do not go through the gates to her. You do not enter the quarter. You go back to your ship. You will be watched, and stopped here every night, every day, until you sail."

Rafel sighed. He didn't seem afraid. It did calm her.

"She is her own person, Isacar. In life, if not formally by our laws yet. She can make her own—"

"She can indeed make her own choices, and she will," said a woman's voice from behind the men blocking the laneway. "Brother, if you and your extremely stupid friends remain here another moment I will scream for the quarter's guards and accuse you of attacking a Kindath merchant—outside the gates, after nightfall. And I will name the ibn Tihon brothers and a meeting, to show Rafel's importance. You know what will happen to you then. I am *finished* with this! You humiliate yourself, and me. Get away from here, Isacar!"

"Gaelle, this is not your decision to make! There is family and—"

A scream tore through the night. "*Guards!*" cried the woman, who was obviously named Gaelle, and a sister to this Isacar, and was Kindath. They were all Kindath, Nadia realized.

"Oh, fuck, Isacar!" cried another of the men. He turned and fled up the lane, past the woman. A heartbeat later so did all three of the others, a clattering of sound, fading. Leaving the man named Isacar alone in front of Rafel, with the woman who appeared to be his sister and, Nadia now assumed, Rafel's lover.

A silence, loud after the scream. "Shall I do it again?" this woman asked.

"Gaelle!" It was Rafel this time. "Please don't. It—"

"Quiet, Rafel ben Natan! It is not your time to speak," Gaelle said.

She was only a shape in the darkness beyond her brother, who had also turned to her now. There had not yet been any response to her cry. It was possible there might not be. People didn't charge out of doors and down lanes at night just because a woman screamed in a port city. And who knew where Marsena's civic guard was right now?

The woman in the darkness softened her voice. "Isacar, he is almost certainly dead. For years, most likely. In any case he is *gone.* I will not let you control my life. In this, or in anything. Go home, brother."

"How . . . how did you know we were doing this?"

"That is your reply? Brother, you are a fool of a fool. How are we even of the same blood? We will talk tomorrow. If I feel inclined. Now go. I *will* scream again. I enjoyed it."

Nadia was sorry now that she was here. She was an intruder. Rafel had been right to ask her to go back to the ship. She heard him breathing beside her. She wondered what he was thinking, how many things he might be thinking. Finally, the man named Isacar moved. He walked away from them, past his sister. She heard him say, low and fierce, "You shame us in your bed."

"Curse your narrow, rotting soul, Isacar," she said fiercely. "With what I do in my own house? Look at you! You bring four others out here? To do *this*? Who brings us shame, brother? If I wake in the morning and decide not to kill you, consider yourself fortunate."

Nadia took a step forward, fearing violence from the brother. Rafel gripped her quickly by the upper arm. She stopped. Isacar said nothing more. She had really thought he might strike his sister. He walked on, however, was lost to sight in darkness.

"Sorry," Rafel muttered to her, letting go. "I knew he wouldn't do anything."

"Should I leave now?" she asked quietly.

"Should you have come at all?"

"I know. I'm sorry. I'll see you in the morning."

She turned to go.

"Wait," said the woman named Gaelle. Nadia saw her come forward. "Rafel, I believe an introduction is in order. This is another of your women?"

"I am not—" Nadia began.

"Stop it, Gaelle," said Rafel. "You know better. This is my partner on the ship and in trade. Her name—"

Everyone seemed to be interrupting everyone else tonight, Nadia thought. So she said, "My name is Lenia Serrana, from Batiara. I was captured by Asharite raiders and taken as a slave a long time ago. You don't like allegations about you, neither do I about me. In my case, they happen to be untrue. Good night."

She turned and walked away, back along the empty street, her boots the only sound.

Why in Jad's name did I say that? she asked herself, striding towards a hint of tavern lights, with the harbour a distance beyond. Some danger now, a woman alone, and she was unarmed. She wasn't afraid. Probably would have been wiser to be, but you couldn't always be wise, could you? Not every single moment of your life. She didn't know what had just happened, what this story was.

She didn't arrive at anything like an answer to why she'd offered her real name, not before she reached the ship, or after she boarded and then undressed in her cabin and went to bed. *He has a lover*, was a last thought before she fell asleep. *Of course he has a lover. Why would he not have a lover?*

Another dream of horses in the night. She didn't understand that, either.

"STRONG-WILLED, THAT ONE," Gaelle said. She remained where she was, so he walked up to her. Her voice was cool. She didn't offer her cheek to kiss.

"You, of all people alive under the moons, are calling a woman strong-willed?"

She laughed. It was good that he could make her laugh.

"This is the partner you've spoken of?"

"Yes."

"How did that happen again?"

He knew he had told her. She knew he knew. He told her again.

"I see. It's dark here. Is she pretty?"

"Gaelle."

"Just a question."

"Not a useful one. Meanwhile, you tell me: when did your brother become like this? Five men to waylay me in the street?"

She shrugged. "He thinks I welcome men into my house."

"I might think that too."

No laughter this time. "Rafel, you are in Marsena a handful of nights a year. You know you have my gratitude forever, but . . ."

"But that isn't enough."

Her remembered smile. "It is enough when you are here. Come, we shouldn't be outside the quarter."

"Why *are* you outside, then?"

"Saving you a beating, or worse?"

"All by yourself?"

"He's afraid of me. Needs my money, among other things. The money you give me."

"And you knew they would be here, how?"

"Servant told a servant. Then I watched his house."

He saw her smile again in the darkness. His eyes had adjusted, and they were standing close now. Her remembered scent, lily of the valley.

"Are they enforcing the nighttime curfew on us again? Really?"

"Not effectively," said Gaelle. "We all came out, as you see. But why stand here and talk? I'd rather have you in my bed. If that's acceptable?" She began to walk, not waiting. Then she did pause, looking back at him.

"It is acceptable," he said, swallowing. "I have a few questions to ask, after."

"After is all right," she said. Then, because she was an impatient woman, used to *knowing* things, "Questions about what?"

"First, the children."

"The boys are well. They will be glad to see their uncle in the morning."

That checked him. "You've told them who I am?"

"They are old enough now. Their father is gone, for years. Dead, or simply having left us. Left them. We have money from no obvious source. I told them this year that their uncle has taken us in his care because he has no wife or children of his own. They like you."

"What they know of me."

"Don't dismiss it, Rafel. The affection of boys that age is hard to come by, trust me. And . . . your other questions?"

"Raina Vidal." He said only the name.

"Ah," Gaelle said. "You are aiming high."

"No. Not in the way you might think."

"And what might I be thinking, Rafel? She is beautiful by report, still young, fabulously wealthy, and . . . she is what she is for our people. And widowed. Unlike me, since I don't know if I am."

All true, he thought. Raina Vidal's husband had also been a business encounter of his. He was proud of that, in fact. Part of why he had thought to find her. One of the reasons why.

"I need to find out where she is," he said. "Do you know?"

They were walking again. She looked over and up at him, a small, fierce (he knew how fierce) woman.

"I do, and it isn't far. We'll discuss her after," she said. And then she finally took his hand, cool fingers laced through his. His brother's widow, or his missing brother's wife.

HE WAS STILL a patient lover, even if some time had passed since he was last in a woman's bed. She was hungry, inventive, generous. Different natures can please each other. They were not in love, but there was a bond. There had to be. They'd been abandoned by the same man, among other things.

Afterwards, as promised, she told him what she knew, which was much more than he did, including where he'd have to sail to find the woman he'd decided to find. He was fortunate: as she'd said, it wasn't far.

She chose not to tease him any more about Raina Vidal. He wasn't going off to woo that woman. Absurd thought. Rafel ben Natan was a modestly successful merchant from Almassar with a single ship, and he sometimes raided under licence from the khalif there (it wasn't a secret, it was why he had fighting men and cannon on the *Silver Wake*). Raina Vidal was the wealthiest, most powerful, most deeply honoured woman in the Kindath world. *Revered* was perhaps the best word. If Rafel even saw her, if he was allowed an audience for whatever he needed, he'd treat her like a queen.

So she told him where he'd find Dona Raina this spring, and charged him with remembering every single thing he saw and heard if he did find a way to see her. How she looked. What she wore. *Everything* she said. Who was with her. Where she lived. How her house was furnished—whatever room it was he saw her in.

She might possibly be good to him here again, Gaelle said, if he did these things for her. "Also," she added, "don't bed that long-legged partner of yours. I've decided I don't like her. And besides, it is never a good idea to have emotional entanglements with someone you do business with."

"Not something that will happen, Gaelle. Though, as to that last, I did business with my brother."

"Not the same," she said. "Different problems."

"Yes," he said.

There was a lot of weight in the one word. She didn't want to address it now. He made her feel indolent and complacent after they made love. And he was good to her and the boys. She didn't like to think about her life, theirs, had he not been so.

They'd see him in the morning, her sons. She'd deal with her fool of a brother after. She knew exactly how. Isacar wouldn't be happy. Which was, of course, the point. It was time to bring him up hard. Like a horse, she thought, though she'd never ridden a horse. You guided your life, Gaelle thought, where you could, as best you could, towards however you defined shelter and happiness in a precarious world. And you prayed to the sister moons and the god for kindness while you lived and after you died.

What else was there for a woman to do, really?

⸎

Choices, as we have agreed, are made right from when and how a tale begins. Truths and lies. People appear, emerging as from shadow or behind doors. Some die. Some have unexpected dreams of horses. A woman walks into it, on a night street in a port city—for a moment, for more than that?

A sailor is angry on board his ship. He is often angry. He drinks for three days and nights in a whorehouse. He is robbed of his clothing and boots and his father's ring when his money runs out. He wakes naked at midday in an alley to find that his ship has gone and he is being mocked by children and men for his nakedness. He manages to stand, takes a flailing swing at one man, then another in the too-bright sunlight, then he is hit, hard, a downward blow with a staff from behind, on the back of his skull. He falls, and he dies. Not the intent behind the blow, but the result. Intent does not always determine.

A sad ending to a life. He'd had parents who loved him when he was a boy. He had fathered two children in two cities, a son and a daughter, though he hadn't known that, and they never knew him.

That ship, the one with which we started, is sailing now from this port of Marsena. Others, south, east, west, also leave ports or continue on the dangerous sea, bearing or seeking goods to trade, hunting or hunted, carrying important people or simply people. There are ships and galleys all over the Middle Sea. Some matter to a given story, others to their own. Some tales are told, most are not. People worship the sun, the moons, the countless stars. There are other stories braided through all of these beliefs, and preceding them. Jaddite sailors often invoke, though always secretly, the son of their god falling from the sky into the sea from a chariot he could not control. His dead, perfect body retrieved by weeping mariners on a passing ship. Mariners. Which is why it is mostly sailors who keep that story alive. It is not entirely gone yet.

And us? We read or hear a new tale and it becomes an interval, an interlude, in our own life, to be forgotten, remembered, perhaps changing us, as we go on . . .

PART TWO

CHAPTER V

A little less than a year before these events, a different ship had sailed for home from Khatib in the east—home also being Almassar in the farthest west. On the way, after taking on wine and information at the great island, Candaria, as was traditional, the ship was waylaid, boarded, and taken by Jaddite pirates from one of the smaller islands north of that one. The sun had only just been rising as their galley appeared out of night at sea, too close by then to avoid.

A common event, piracy, unworthy of note—no ripples from a minor event sent out into the world—had it not been that a man of some significance was on board, and one of the raiders could read Asharic, and did look at the papers found in that traveller's cabin. The man had been trying to throw them out the stern window when they burst in.

THERE HAD BEEN no mystery as to what was happening on deck. Voices were shouting at the crew and captain in Trakesian. He didn't speak that language, but the tone carried its message.

Kurafi ibn Rusad, emissary of the khalif of Almassar, young writer of a great work (he hoped; it was in progress) knew what he had to do if he were to survive this.

First thing, he opened the leather satchel containing his documents. His hands were trembling. Of course they were. He pushed open the tiny round window in his tiny cabin. Then he sat on his lumpy cot and began going swiftly through his notes, spreading them on his knees, crumpling and throwing out the ones that might be incriminating or embarrassing to his khalif back home.

There was an unfortunately large number of those. Almassar's beleaguered ruler, dealing with civil war, had sent ibn Rusad to request urgent aid from Khatib against his brother, while offering, for later, quiet assistance in Khatib's attempt to stay independent of mighty Asharias.

It would *not* be a good thing if the second part of these proposals reached the wider world, specifically mighty Asharias. Gurçu of the Osmanlis, who had conquered Sarantium and now had his ambitious eyes looking for more, in all directions, was not someone to offend.

In fact, if ibn Rusad understood matters (and he was reasonably certain he did), this aid he had proposed and then discussed would never happen. Khatib, for all its history, was not going to hold out against the Osmanlis. And Almassar's worried khalif was almost certainly already writing to Gurçu or his viziers with an offer to share any information he obtained about what Khatib was planning. There would have been an emissary sent there, too. You did that sort of thing to survive. Survival was hard.

The khalif would also be asking Gurçu the Conqueror for assistance.

It was unlikely to be forthcoming.

Gurçu wanted his *own* people ruling the cities of the Majriti, reaping taxes from the west, and tariffs and trading profits. Ruinous civil wars there were useful to him. He could send in his soldiers and fleet, amid devastation. Be seen as a saviour.

The affairs of cities and states were complex. Exhilaratingly so, to the mind of Kurafi ibn Rusad. He was at the very outset of his career. He had great hopes for that career. He was also, just now, on a ship that had been boarded, aware he might *have* no career, no life, even. He raced through papers written in his own hand, discarding out the window any that were obviously dangerous, keeping enough of the others to prove he was a figure of importance. *If* one of these barbarians could read.

Being important mattered! If he was seen as such by these savages, if they could be *caused* to think that, he would be held for ransom. The ship's crew up above, however . . . they were certainly headed for Jaddite galleys, to die rowing. If they hadn't been thrown overboard already. Way of the world. Asharite corsairs all along the Middle Sea did the same thing.

You took your chances when you embarked upon the sea, and not just with storms.

In the event, Kurafi ibn Rusad was ready by the time two of the raiders burst in, smelling of beer and fish and sweat. It emerged there *was* a man who could read Asharic (blessed be the watching stars), and ibn Rusad was not greatly abused. Not sold to a galley or chained to a bench on theirs.

The ship was claimed by the barbarians. Their rank smell was everywhere. Large men, a few with yellow or red beards but mostly dark. Their moods seemed to be anger or wild laughter, nothing between. Ibn Rusad ventured, on the second day, to open his cabin door and make his way cautiously above, to ask what they intended to do with him.

He was clubbed on the back so viciously he fell to the deck. Two men immediately lifted him up and threw him, clattering and tumbling, back down. He bruised himself in several places, banged his head and his right shoulder at the bottom.

He didn't go up on deck again. He didn't know what had happened to his four escorts. He was fairly certain they were dead, or rowing the galley that had captured this ship. Not worth ransoming.

They brought him maggot-infested food and a cup of sour ale twice a day. He forced himself to eat, picking out the maggots. No one spoke to him. He had no idea where they were going. His papers had been taken and he had nothing with which to write. He voided himself into a bucket when he needed to; it was cleared in the mornings, then it sat there, stinking, all day and night. His window was not large enough for him to dispose of his own waste. He'd tried; the wind had blown it back in on him. It would be a lie to say he was happy.

For several days his head hurt from his fall down the stairs. His shoulder and back pained him for longer. He'd probably have a scar on his forehead, he decided, touching it. He didn't feel exhilarated any more. For a time he was angry, then he settled into being afraid. There was a storm one night. He was sick several times into the bucket, and also beside it, unfortunately. He had turbulent thoughts he would have liked to write down.

Unexpectedly, he would end up with the opportunity to do that, the way his life unfolded.

∽∾

In the small coastal city of Sorenica in the southwest of Batiara, where she'd been residing since the previous autumn, Dona Raina Vidal, often called the queen of the Kindath was, of a spring morning in her palazzo, at odds with the world and the discomforts of her body.

It happened too often: headaches, at or near her time of month, shaping an evil, afflicted mood, with an accompanying, ungenerous desire to have people who spoke too loudly around her killed. This impulse to murder would pass, though perhaps not with respect to her sister-in-law. Tamir, still living with her, as she had for years, was obviously a punishment for some sins Dona Raina could not readily identify or recall.

She *thought* she had lived a mostly virtuous life.

It was a pleasant spring afternoon. Not something she could properly enjoy at the moment. Those who attended upon her had learned to recognize (and anticipate) the signs, and the house had been extremely quiet. Tamir, not prone to quiet, and with much (she believed) about which to complain, had gone out in the morning. A blessing, an absolute blessing. And perhaps also evidence of a faint streak of self-preservation in her sister-in-law.

Both their husbands were dead. Raina's, once the most prominent Kindath businessman in Esperaña (and then in the world beyond it, after he was forced to leave), had been burned alive, a decade after the expulsion.

Ellias had kept going back, against her wishes (but what did a young wife's wishes matter?). He would sail in one of their ships—they had six and then eight, and then more—bribing officials beforehand. He wanted to supervise the gradual sale of his family properties in Esperaña, and the transfer of their last assets (as best he could) out of the country.

He had not bribed the right people on that last journey, or one of them had seen more immediate gains and had exposed him. They never knew who that was. A thing that still kept her up some nights. The clerics, notified, had seized Ellias Vidal. And burned him in the main square of Cartada in front of the sanctuary, when he would not convert to the faith of Jad.

She had been twenty-three years old when she was widowed. They had been living in Astarden in the north, where they had been introduced and had married. She'd been born in Esperaña, had no memories of it. A number of Kindath came to that low-lying city on a cold sea. Journeys supported, in many instances, by Ellias's money and then her own management, a task she had taken on. Arranging, from afar, places for people to safely stay on a long, dangerous journey, and often funds to do so.

They'd shared a determination to do all they could to help their people escape to as much of freedom as might be on offer in the world. The Kindath had been welcomed in the north, for the most part. Not every government or monarch or guild of merchants was so wrapped in faith, or controlled by clerics, as to reject the benefits their presence brought. The same was true in Asharias, now that Sarantium had fallen. She had begun thinking about that.

In Astarden, there was an important trade in gems and diamonds, and in gold carried by ships there, out from the Middle Sea and up the coast of Esperaña, after originating south of the Majriti. This trade was very much in Kindath hands. That was largely how Raina's husband and his older brother had continued to expand the family fortune after exile, before branching into other things (many other things).

The taxes paid to be allowed to worship in their faith, build houses of prayer, were considerable. Also the bribes, of course. Bribes were never-ending. It sometimes seemed to Raina that the world ran on bribery. Except when it didn't, and a good man was burned alive.

Tamir's husband, the older brother, had died in Astarden. A natural death, two years after Ellias. He'd had gout by then, and a bad heart, and bone-deep, defining anxieties. He had been the lesser of the brothers, all major decisions made by Ellias. And then by his young widow, who turned out to have a remarkable head for business and who equalled her husband in a determination to bring their people from Esperaña, or wherever else they were now, to better places, since they'd lost their homeland. Their homes.

She was honouring his memory with this, Raina Vidal felt. More than with prayers or candles.

Assuming one could identify those better places, of course. Astarden had eventually become a problem, as Esperaña's king and queen began to threaten the northern cities with war. Esperaña had armies and a large fleet. They could do it, even if King Émery of Ferrieres opposed their expansion desires fiercely and Majriti corsairs tied down some of their ships in the south.

There had been a demand, not made politely, that the wealthy city of canals stop harbouring and sustaining Kindath heretics. It had led to anxious divisions in Astarden, abetted by a feeling among some merchants that there was no particular *reason* the lucrative trade in gems and gold should be so much controlled by the Kindath.

A business opportunity had been discerned. The suffering of some was often a benefit for others. The world worked that way.

Raina had made the decision to leave. Herself, her two young sons, her household, their movable wealth. Tamir had joined her. Of course.

Better to be ahead of trouble, not chased or harried by it. Ultimately, their final destination might well be Asharias, but she hadn't made that decision yet. She sent a cousin there, to open a trading station on the far side of that golden city's strait, where Jaddites and Kindath were allowed to live. To start spreading bribes in the proper places.

There were many things to think about concerning this. She was now in negotiations. Gurçu had a Kindath vizier. He offered freedom of worship in his city to the people known as the Wanderers (with a tax paid for that, of course). Sarantium had emptied out. He wanted it filled again, and brilliant again.

They might indeed be headed that way. Raina wondered, on a spring day (her head was beginning to feel a little easier), if she might somehow be able to leave her sister-in-law behind, or contrive to lose her at sea. Some unfortunate accident.

In the meantime, they were in Sorenica, an autumn, a winter, now spring. It had been a city known for a Kindath presence for centuries. There had been savagery here, too, but mostly the city had let them be. There was even a monument near the market to a woman, a Kindath physician from hundreds of years ago. Her name had worn away and no one remembered it (Raina had asked), but the carved stone image held a urine flask, so they knew she'd been a doctor. Raina liked thinking about that.

It had taken most of a year to prepare the move here and it had been a hard journey south. Guarding a large household and substantial resources over such a long way was not a simple task, and expensive.

They had stopped in Acorsi on their way, with Folco Cino and his extremely elegant wife. Those two had offered to shelter Raina's household. Caterina Ripoli d'Acorsi had shown her the handsome house they'd make available for her. No Kindath quarter, it was a palazzo on the main square, close to the palace.

Folco was an ugly, intelligent, impressive man, and a dangerous mercenary. His wife, Raina had decided, was equally impressive, and probably equally dangerous if crossed. Raina liked her. She was tempted to stay. Acorsi felt as if it would be a *civilized* place to live. Supported by Folco at war, but even so. The city had no harbour, though, and the Vidal ships needed a secure base for loading and unloading and repair.

She'd left them gifts, and gone away with gifts, and come here.

Sorenica had a busy maritime life, an ancient university with a medical school and a law school, and formidable walls, and towers over the harbour, steadily maintained—because being on this coast in this time meant the risk of corsairs was extreme.

The ducal court ruling southern Batiara, inland at Casiano, was currently engaged in an interesting exercise, a striving for religious harmony. Duke Ersani had Asharite guards alongside his Jaddite ones. There were star-worshippers' temples beside the sanctuaries and retreats of the sun god. Asharite farmers had brought the cultivation of indigo from the Majriti, and there was money in that. They bred horses, too.

The duke's efforts, guided by some celebrated thinkers drawn to his court, were not universally applauded, especially after the fall of Sarantium, but he was powerful as well as independent, and a succession of High Patriarchs had tended to leave the southern dukes alone for a long time—in exchange for their making no ambitious movements northwards. Generally, they hadn't. The south of Batiara was its own world, it was said.

Dona Raina (and her sister-in-law, unavoidably) had attended upon the duke shortly after arriving in Sorenica. A carriage ride east through autumn vineyards, grainlands, and those indigo fields. Ersani was a stout, florid, graceful man with a taste for conversation, wine, and music. Wore his hair long and his beard short. He was unmarried at this point; two wives had died. He had only one living heir, said to be frail. They never saw the son, but Tamir had mused upon all of these matters during the ride back to the coast. The son, or perhaps even the father, she said, might be a match for her. She was impossible, really. Pretty? Yes. Appealing to men? You needed to acknowledge that.

"I see. You'd become Jaddite?" Raina had snapped when the musings had gone on entirely long enough.

"Why not? Enough of us have. Ellias *should* have. He'd be alive now. You'll become Asharite when you go east."

"I will not. And I have not made a decision about going east."

"Of course you have!" Tamir laughed. "You're only pretending to be thinking about it. Or afraid to decide. And right now you're just envious that Ersani *clearly* favoured me. Maybe I'll stay when you go, become his duchess, not have to put up with you any more." She was a woman who could flounce while sitting down.

Remembering that exchange half a year later, watching from an upper-level terrace in her home as ships moved in and out of the harbour in the distance below, Raina reminded herself, yet again, that murder was generally forbidden by all faiths, including their own. But, she thought . . . oh, but, but, but . . .

Looking out, without real purpose, though she often had an eye on the harbour to see if any of their ships might be arriving, Raina did notice a trading vessel manoeuvring towards the docks. As she watched, it ran up a flag—the two moons of the Kindath faith.

Not in itself startling—Sorenica had become home to even more of their people since she had arrived—but few ships raised the blue and white moons on a flag. She couldn't remember seeing it, in fact. Ellias might have, she thought, but Ellias had been dead for some time. She was doing what she did by herself, and lay in bed at night by herself. The decision not to remarry had been made years ago. Not one she regretted. She preferred power, she'd discovered, to yielding it to a husband.

She decided to send someone to find out about the ship now coming up to a berth. Knowing more about who had arrived was always a good thing. She also called for food and a glass of wine. She realized she was feeling better.

Maybe Tamir had been eaten by a wolf in town? There were no wolves in the city, but one could dream.

∽⃝∾

They'd parted for the afternoon. Rafel was walking to the Carraza Bank branch here in Sorenica. They had deposited their payment for the assassination back in Marsena. He'd wanted to open three accounts, one in the name of Ghazzali al-Siyab, who had—perhaps in spite of himself—done what they'd needed him to do, and more, but the complication of an account-holder being dead was real. They'd decided to simply take note as to his share. The idea was to send money to al-Siyab's family eventually, though not so soon as to start questions being asked.

Today, Rafel just wanted to confirm the amounts against the documents they'd been given in Marsena's branch, and withdraw a modest sum to establish a process. She said she would do the same the next day. At the moment, as she watched him go off with Elie and two guards (he was willing to accept guards now, at least), she needed to be alone.

Memories and loss were washing over and through her.

Sorenica was not a city she knew, but it was close, it was *very* close, to where she'd grown up. Memories and loss.

She had vowed not to come back, never to reopen those wounds by being here. Twenty years had passed; the farm would have long since gone to someone else. There would have been no one left in their family to keep it going. Her brother had been a child. She had no idea if he and her mother had fled successfully, survived. She briefly had an image of the woman she was now, after so many years, finding her brother, her mother. Seeing their horrified expressions—since they'd know what had happened to her, and so what she'd been.

Too much shame. Too hard a pain in the heart. Embedded, even just thinking of this.

She wasn't going back to the farm. She hadn't planned to ever be this close. It was two or three days' ride (she was not good on horseback). But even here on the coast so many memories seemed to want to come back to claim her. Including her name.

What *was* she to call herself now? Here in Batiara. Was she still Nadia bint Dhiyan?

Or was she Lenia Serrana again? That lost girl.

And when they sailed, as they would, what then? Who would she be? Rafel used three names, one in each faith, depending on where they were. He changed accents, birthplaces. She didn't know if she could do that. Live that way. The Kindath—perhaps they were used to doing so. The need to be fluid, adapt to situations, even with their identity. How they worshipped. In what tongue. She'd not learned how to do that. She'd been an Asharite slave with an Asharite name for so long, and so far from home. From the idea of a home.

She wasn't far now. And still, she was.

They had a purpose in Sorenica. Rafel had explained it. It was the reason (one of the reasons) he'd gone to that woman, Gaelle, in Marsena. For information. For lovemaking, too, she'd thought, but did not say, when he came back to the ship in the morning.

He'd pointed towards a palazzo here before they'd parted just now. Up the steep hill from the harbour. Largest home in town, it looked to be. A queen of sorts lived there, he'd told her.

They'd meet back at the ship before sundown, he'd said, and then left her to herself. A courtesy. It was probably obvious she needed that. She didn't like being obvious. It made you vulnerable. He was the one who'd told her that once, but she'd already known.

She walked alone through the streets of a harbour town in Batiara on a spring afternoon. There was a breeze off the water. Many Kindath, in their blue and white for the moons. Most people just used the colours as an accessory. A scarf, a hat, the trim on a cloak. She knew there had been Kindath in Sorenica for a long time. She had a memory of knowing that from . . . before. Her father had been a man who liked learning things and sharing them. He'd taught her—not just her brother—how to read. Why you'd need to know that on a farm, he never said. He had just decided it was a good thing.

She didn't like thinking about him, or her mother—practical, calm, brisk, but singing to them as children almost every night. Memories could burn you, she thought. Could make you want to weep, or scream into the sky. Or kill people.

So you stayed away in a wide world, and steered your mind (forced your mind) into other channels. That was how she had lived. By not remembering, as best she could.

Harder now, here, in this remembered light, so different from the Majriti where they'd taken her and sold her. Perhaps it would become impossible to stop the memories now. She decided it had been a mistake to come, if that was so. She didn't even know what to *call* herself!

Except, she realized, she did.

For all the rawness of recalling family, farm, childhood, she was not Nadia bint Dhiyan. That had been forced upon her, as he had forced himself on her body, however *kind* he was, normally. She'd carried his name for most of her life (a terrible thought) but . . . she didn't have to, not any more. There were layers of grief in her true name but she could choose to carry those. Her own decision. Just as she'd chosen to kill the man who'd owned her.

She would own herself, Lenia Serrana thought, walking through the market square of Sorenica. Herself and her sorrows. Nor, in truth, was she at all distinctive in having to deal with those. Everyone had different griefs, but everyone had griefs.

She grimaced. Was she going to become a philosopher now? Vie with Rafel in parsing texts and scholars' glosses on them? Unlikely. She stopped at a juice-seller's stand and bought an orange juice. She drank it down, handed back the clay cup. Wine later, after she rejoined Rafel, she thought. Even good wine. They had money now. Possibly much more to come.

And it was in that moment, turning from the juice-seller's stand, that she saw one of the men who had been guarding the ibn Tihon brothers in the tavern when they'd been paid.

He was moving with purpose through the market square, which was being noisily dismantled, past midday now, farmers preparing to head out with their wagons and carts through the city gates to be home before darkness fell.

He was here. In Sorenica. He didn't see her.

She wasn't feeling philosophical now, or wrapped in memories. She followed him. It was not a carefully reasoned decision. It was also life-changing.

෨෧

"I need you," said the woman known as the queen of the Kindath, "to now tell me what happened outside, please. Everything that happened. I prefer my advisers to share information in detail, so I can decide for myself what is significant. I would greatly appreciate if you did the same, signora."

Raina Vidal was a small, handsome, dark-haired woman, about Lenia's own age, beautifully coiffed and dressed, and with a manner that made clear she was accustomed to being in control of a situation, even in the presence of the man standing beside her chair. The enormously formidable man. He hadn't said anything since they'd come inside.

This woman was a queen of sorts, after all, Lenia thought.

She had decided she was *Lenia* again. Nadia bint Dhiyan might be useful at some point as an identity, but it would only be a disguise

now. She'd not introduced herself, or been asked to yet, in this elegant upper-floor reception room. There were tapestries on the walls.
Richly coloured, expensive ones: decoration, warmth, status.

If you were wealthy enough you could do this. Have these. Even
as a Kindath woman.

A second woman, taller even than Lenia, fair-haired, strikingly
beautiful, sat near Dona Raina, leaning forward in a posture of excited
anticipation. Not an appropriate attitude, in the circumstances. Her
eyes were wide-set, large, startlingly blue. She was slender at the waist,
long-legged, difficult not to look at. To stare at. She knew it, too. Used
her smile as a weapon, had done so already, directing it at Lenia.

"My lady, I saw him in the marketplace and knew who he was. I
decided to follow him."

"Very well. Wait, please. Two questions, if I may. How did you
know him? And why would a woman follow such a man alone?"

A quick mind here. She wished Rafel were with them. He'd been
sent for, at Lenia's request. Two guards had gone with a note. She
hoped he was back at the ship by now. She wasn't afraid here, just
aware that this was the woman he was in Sorenica to see, and . . .
this wasn't necessarily the way to have it happen.

And then there was the man. The improbable man standing here,
looking at her silently.

"I saw him when my partner and I encountered his masters in
Marsena a few days ago."

The others knew who that man's masters were by now.

"Marsena. The ibn Tihon brothers? Really? You encountered them
there for what reason?"

Lenia shrugged. "We were receiving payment for a service."

"Which was?"

She shook her head. "Not something I am at liberty to share, with
great respect, my lady."

Dona Raina looked at her. A small smile. Perhaps a recognition of
another woman who would not simply defer. "You are not Asharite,

are you?" The man beside her, Lenia saw, was also smiling now. It changed his features greatly.

But with this question something was here now, upon her. Second time saying it, this time in a public place, not a dark laneway in Marsena. "I am not, my lady. My name is Lenia Serrana. I was born a few days east of here."

"You were *taken* by Asharites? Oh, you poor girl! How long ago? Was it *very* terrible?"

It was the other woman, Tamir Vidal, the fair-haired one. Two widows here, the older with all the power. Rafel had told her a little. This beauty was not the important one, but she might matter, he had said—given what they were here to try to do.

She'd half-understood then. She understood better now, seeing her.

"I was taken, my lady, yes. Many years ago. I was young. Not long ago I achieved my freedom. And joined with Rafel ben Natan as merchants with a ship. He was generous enough to invite me to take a small share."

"Achieved your freedom is delicate phrasing," said the man in the room. First words.

He said it approvingly, still smiling a little. He seemed to . . . well, approve of her. Because of what had happened outside. She was afraid of him, his reputation, his unexplained presence here.

"Why?" It was Raina Vidal again, following her own thread. "Why did ben Natan make you a partner?"

"You know him, my lady?"

"A little. By name. My husband had dealings with him in Esperaña."

Lenia said, "Why he offered me a share is not, again with respect, the matter that brings me here now." Rafel, she thought, would want her to be agreeable, not prickly. So she added, "But . . . I had been taught how to read and do calculations and accounting."

"And you have some skill with weapons, which answers why you felt safe following a corsair?" The man again, quietly.

She looked at him. "Once I saw he was alone."

"You were prepared to fight an Asharite corsair to protect us? How wonderful!" exclaimed Tamir Vidal.

"She did fight one, Tamir." There was no affection evident in the smaller woman's voice.

"Yes!" breathed Tamir. She favoured Lenia with a truly magnificent smile, wide-eyed. "Please go on! This is so exciting!"

Lenia cleared her throat. She wondered when Rafel would get here. She needed him. These were *his* people, this was his devising, they were in Sorenica because *he* wanted to be!

"I saw he was climbing the hill," she said. "And he kept going, all the way up here. Then I saw him sit on the bench opposite this palazzo and pretend to be removing something from his boot. Both of his boots, in fact. To take longer. He was really examining your defences."

"I *told* you that bench was a bad idea, Raina!" exclaimed Tamir Vidal.

"And I told you placing one is seen as a gesture from people with means, offering people somewhere to sit."

"In or near a marketplace, Raina! We are alone at the top of a hill. It serves no such purpose here. It was a mistake!"

Raina Vidal drew a breath. "I have never said I do not make mistakes."

"No, but you never admit when you do!"

Family fight, Lenia thought. Neither she nor the man needed to hear it. Though, Rafel would say, this was information a merchant could use. He was probably right. Also, where in the name of Jad was he?

"Please go on," Raina Vidal said.

Lenia cleared her throat again. This next part was tricky.

"I know his masters, as I said, and I . . . know what sorts of things they do. Especially the younger one. I decided to learn more. I also . . . I didn't *like* what I thought he might be here to do."

"Preparing my abduction! I should say not, Lenia Serrana!" Tamir still sounded more excited than apprehensive. She wasn't a child, Lenia thought, should not be behaving like one.

She said, "I didn't know that then. When he stood from the bench and headed farther up, to look at the side of your house, I drew closer."

"Very quickly," the man in the room said. "I saw you do it. Two knives, and he was flat against the wall. The guards had been watching through arrow slits, from when he first sat on the bench. One of them alerted us he was there. I came down to see. We went out quietly."

"Then you know what happened after," Lenia said.

SHE WAS LIGHT-FOOTED, had been trained to it, and he was over-confident and unsuspecting, moving with the swagger of someone who worked for the most feared men along the reaches of the Middle Sea. She was able to get right up to him from behind. Had a dagger at his throat and another against his back before he even knew he'd been followed.

Careless of him. Unless you were wealthy and powerful and had guards at all times, you were responsible for your own safety in the world. Indeed, guards *were* a taking of responsibility. She really was beginning to see things too much like Rafel, Lenia thought. She pushed the corsair with both blades, so he was right against the rough wall on the side of the street opposite the Vidal palazzo. He turned his face to the left. She moved the other way a little; he couldn't see her.

She pushed harder with the knife at his throat, enough to draw blood. She didn't mind doing that. He drew a breath, afraid for the first time. She said, "Whether you live or die now depends on what you tell me and how quickly. Why are you here?"

She used a slightly deeper voice. He might not know she was a woman. She didn't care greatly, but he'd be more cautious if he thought she was a man. She wasn't unwilling to kill him, but she wanted to know some things first.

"Do you have any idea how bad a death you will suffer if you harm me?" he rasped. Not fearful enough, it seemed, not yet. He spoke Asharic. She wasn't going to pretend not to understand it.

"No one knows I am here. No one will know who killed you. Don't threaten. You are a heartbeat moment from finding out what Ashar thinks of corsairs when he judges them."

It might have been her calmness. Or the fact that this time she pushed with the knife in his lower back, through the tunic he wore, breaking his skin. It would have hurt. "Painful, if you are killed with a knife right there," she said. "You've likely done it, so you know. I don't need to let you live. It is clear what you are doing, and I know who your masters are."

That froze him. "How?" he said.

"You are not the one with questions here. So, listen carefully. I don't care about the Kindath women in that house." A lie, but she needed it. "I have interests of my own. And I don't need you to die, either. Tell me what you are here to do and I might leave you alive. I can do this either way. What do the ibn Tihon brothers want in Sorenica?"

She needed to name them, let this man know he had been identified and was at real risk. He was dangerous, but she had two knives on him.

It seemed as if he realized that. Something in his posture. Or her dismissal of the Kindath women in the house.

He said, reluctantly, "Ziyar wants the younger one. Said to be a beauty."

"For ransom?"

"No." A pause. "For himself."

"In Tarouz?"

"Maybe. Maybe somewhere else. Not my affair."

She knew where else. They had just had the khalif of Abeneven slain. Ziyar would be the one moving west, then. One brother in each of two great cities of the Majriti.

"And how will you capture her?"

"Not in this palazzo. I'm going to tell him that."

"Where is he? Ziyar?"

"City below. Disguised. We can take her when she goes down. She goes to the market. The house is too well fortified."

It was. It would not be an easy place to enter, and there would be guards. She had registered that herself, watching him pretend to clear stones from his boots. She knew nothing about Tamir Vidal going to the market, but it was likely Ziyar did.

"How many of you?"

He was silent. Then, "I didn't like the idea. You need to know that."

"Ah," she said. "You didn't *like* it. But you are here to make it happen?"

"I work for them. You do what they tell you. If you knew any-thing about them, you'd understand that—"

He didn't finish that sentence, although, afterwards, she was quite sure she knew what he would have said had he not died.

He'd twisted to his right, sliding along the wall, more quickly than she'd expected—an error on her part. Errors could kill you. She'd been too caught up in what he was saying. He elbowed her in the shoulder hard, dislodging the knife at his neck. He was reach-ing for his own blade at his belt. She stabbed him in the back as she staggered.

Heard a *thwap* sound and a whine.

Saw a crossbow bolt in him. It passed right by where she'd been standing before he'd made her stumble. It was in the middle of his back, above her knife. It had come extremely close to her.

The corsair splayed flat against the wall, then slid slowly down, his cheek scraped raw as he did. He lay dead in a dusty street, far from wherever it was he'd been born. Lenia decided, standing above him, that she could call this man another Asharite she'd killed. Her knife had gone in first, hadn't it? She turned around.

There were two guards by the door of the palazzo, in blue-and-white livery. They hadn't fired the crossbow. They were holding theirs, bolts still in them. The man who had fired was in front of them and a step to one side. She had a moment to consider how silently the door had been opened. She hadn't heard it, or them. These men were good, she thought.

Then it registered for her—from his appearance, which was distinctive—who the man who'd fired the bolt was. She swallowed hard.

He was of middling years, not tall, powerfully built, broad-shouldered. Not a guard. She knew him: from the long scar on one cheek, and the missing eye above it.

A man conveying formidable assurance, simply standing in a now-quiet street. She drew a steadying breath but she didn't feel steady. She bent down and wiped her knives on the tunic of the dead man, then sheathed them, waist and boot.

She straightened. She said, "That could have killed me. I heard it go by."

"You can't actually hear an arrow or a bolt. It is a common illusion." His voice was grave, thoughtful. "I know it was close, but I had the line from here, as you can see." It was true, for someone extremely confident in his skills.

"That isn't your crossbow."

"Meaning?"

"Meaning you couldn't know how it aims."

He actually smiled. "True enough. A good point. But a very short distance, and I've some experience."

"I see," she said. "I think I had him killed without help."

He nodded. "Likely so. But I couldn't know that. Didn't want him killing you."

She hesitated. "Thank you, then, my lord," she said.

He'd register the honorific. She was saying she knew who he was. He was probably accustomed to being known.

He said, "It will be better you were never here, unless it is important to you to be thought to have done this."

"It isn't. Why is it better?"

"Because the brothers can't come after me very easily. Let it be me, seeing him from the house. Making him say what he said, then killing him."

"You were in this house, my lord?"

He nodded again. "Let's go inside. The lady will want to speak with you. So do I. The guards can deal with the body."

"I know who you are," she said.

"I imagine so," he said. "I am ugly enough to be widely known."

"Why are you here?" she asked. "In Sorenica? This palazzo?"

"Inside," he said, but smiling again. "We will talk. Also: that was extremely well done, with the two knives, right to the end."

"I made a mistake at the end." She wasn't sure why she'd said that.

"Small one. You still drove the knife into his back. I believe you did have him killed with it, regardless of what I did. Who trained you?"

She looked at him. At Folco Cino d'Acorsi. Who was somehow here. Talking to her. Her heart was beating faster than it had with the corsair.

She shrugged. "Inside, as you say, my lord?"

SHE OFFERED HEART-DEEP thanks to Jad when Rafel entered the room.

That was new as well—only a day back in Batiara and she was invoking the sun god reflexively? How the mind worked, where life carried you. Storms at sea. Then you landed somewhere?

That storm had carried her here, it seemed, and to a third man killed. She was quite certain her knife would have ended that man's life, she knew where to drive a blade to do that. She also knew d'Acorsi was correct: it was better in every way if he was the one believed to have killed the corsair. He'd announce it later. There was something to do first, he'd said.

Rafel stopped in the doorway, registering the people in the room. It was darker outside, evening now. Windy, not cold. She was in Batiara. It was . . . it was a great deal.

She saw the moment when Rafel recognized Folco d'Acorsi. He remained expressionless. He was good at not giving things away. She wondered which person he would salute first.

The woman, it turned out. Dona Raina Vidal, whose home this was. He stepped forward, stopped in front of her cushioned chair, bowed low. "My lady," he said. "We have never met. This is an honour for me. I knew your husband."

She was looking at him closely, Lenia saw. Another person who had spent a life assessing people, situations. "I am aware of that, Rafel ben Natan," she said. "You did business the year before he died?"

"Twice, yes. I arranged to get some items of value out of Esperaña for him on my ship. Also, at his request, I took some of our people who had remained and were in danger, as he judged. I was very . . . it was a privilege to assist him, Dona Raina. He was a good man, and is a great loss for all of us."

He bowed again. Lenia was surprised at the tremor she heard in his voice. She didn't think it was feigned. He could do that, but she didn't think this was. So much for not giving things away, she thought.

Rafel bowed to the other woman, the tall, lovely one, then turned to the man.

"I believe I am in the presence of the lord of Acorsi," he said. He bowed, as deeply as before.

There were so many stories told. D'Acorsi was such an unexpected, so unsettling a presence here. Perhaps he meant to be secretly in Sorenica?

Folco Cino d'Acorsi, in this room with them, was only the most feared mercenary commander in Batiara. There had been another one once, a rival, equally celebrated and powerful, from Remigio.

This one's lifelong enemy. The other man was dead. There were different versions of how.

There were no rivals now.

Even in the Majriti, at the far western edge of the world, they knew of this man. His one eye, his scar, his army, his magnificent wife (of the Ripoli family, sister to the duke of Macera). What he was making of Acorsi when he wasn't waging war for whoever hired him in a given spring for a vast sum.

It was springtime now. *What was he doing here?*

"That is indeed my name," Folco said gravely. "I am honoured you know it in Almassar."

"It caused some stir when you bought a large number of carpets last year from our city. I am the more honoured you know where I am from," Rafel said.

D'Acorsi grinned. "Your partner told us while we awaited you. No great trick on my part."

"I understand," Rafel said, not smiling yet, "that someone was killed here. The guards who came said they were instructed to tell me that."

"It is true. Ask your partner," said Raina Vidal.

Everyone looked at Lenia. She kept her account brief. The others had heard it already. Rafel was good at filling in pieces of a tale. At the end she said, "The lord of Acorsi suggested he be the one who killed the Asharite. Safer for everyone."

"I have no doubt of that. I take it he *did* kill him?" Rafel said.

"A matter of debate," said Folco d'Acorsi. "Your partner would like to claim it. She has agreed not to, the wiser path. Tell me," he said to Lenia, "if I may ask a second time . . . how did you learn to handle weapons?"

He seemed to really want to know. "A thing I was taught in Almassar."

"Yes. Taught, because . . . ?"

She tried to avoid showing how she felt about this subject. "Because it was thought I'd make a useful guard for a prominent man there."

"The one who owned you?" asked Tamir Vidal, blue eyes wide again.

"Tamir, let it be," said her sister-in-law. "This is our guest, she did us a service, and she is a Jaddite from Batiara."

"I am only—"

"I think letting it be is wiser, yes," said Folco d'Acorsi. "And more suited to conversing with someone who just helped foil your own abduction?" He turned back to Lenia. "I apologize for asking, signora. I have a reason." His voice was crisp. "Depending on your intentions moving forward, I might offer a proposition to you. I have had a woman in my service before. One who was extremely useful."

"Your niece!" said Tamir, still brightly. Either she really was stupid, Lenia thought, or very sure no one would point it out to her. She didn't know who the other girl had been, but she could see Folco's face.

"Yes," he said after a moment. "My wife's family." A look at Tamir, only that, but unexpectedly she subsided. His gaze came back to Lenia. "Perhaps we can talk after we deal with the matter that has fallen to us."

"And that matter is?" asked Rafel.

He didn't sound happy. Lenia might almost have been amused— was he upset she was being considered for a position away from their business? But she was too shaken for proper amusement. *None* of what was happening was expected.

D'Acorsi said, "Tamir, if she is willing, will go into town in the morning as she customarily does, I understand, with her woman and two guards. Guards from this palazzo will be there before her, and my own men. I have already sent instructions, though they can be withdrawn, of course. She will be carefully protected without appearing to be so. When Ziyar ibn Tihon moves to take her, he and his corsairs will be exposed and captured. Or killed. Likely killed. I am extremely happy to have this opportunity. I can use the goodwill of the High Patriarch just now, as it happens."

"You intend to use my sister-in-law as a trap for him? Is that possibly safe? Can I even permit it?"

"Permit it? I decide," said Tamir, "what I am willing to do, Raina."

"If that is so," said Folco d'Acorsi, "are you willing, Dona Tamir?"

He was moving quickly. Lenia resisted an impulse to look at Rafel.

"I am willing to do whatever the lord of Acorsi should be pleased to ask me to do," said Tamir Vidal sweetly. She had a lovely voice. She clasped her hands demurely in her lap, rings on many fingers. Her sister-in-law made a face, Lenia saw. D'Acorsi was expressionless. He did that even better than Rafel.

"Whatever you ask," Tamir repeated, as she looked up and let her wide-eyed gaze fall, in a practised way, on the lord of Acorsi's ruined, remarkable face.

LENIA AND RAFEL were invited to dine and stay the night, urged fairly emphatically by d'Acorsi to do so. His reasoning was simple: if they had dealt with the ibn Tihon brothers only days ago in Marsena, their ship would be known, and men who lived on the sea would note that ship if it appeared in an unexpected harbour. There was danger in that for them, given what Ziyar was here to do.

They stayed. Rafel would have his own reason, she thought. Her reason, too, really, as his partner.

That emerged after they dined, before they rose from the table. Often, he had told her, it was useful to present people with something you wanted them to do after they'd had wine—especially if you'd been restrained, yourself.

They had been restrained, the two of them. Though Lenia had no intention of speaking a word now.

"I brought them both," he'd said quietly to her as they walked to the dining room.

"*What?*"

"When would it be safer? I had an escort of her household guards! And this is where I intended to come in the first place. It is why we are in Sorenica."

It unnerved her that he'd casually walked through city streets with a diamond like the one they had, just dropped into a leather satchel on his shoulder. The book, too, though she still had difficulty imagining that being worth as much as he thought it might be.

She'd keep quiet, and try not to think about what the lord of Acorsi appeared to be offering her. He'd said they could talk later. After tomorrow. After they did what he'd proposed for the morning, using Tamir Vidal as a trap.

Tamir had been vivid with colour all through the meal, genuinely beautiful. She still was, as they remained at a table ablaze with expensive candles. She was *excited* about the idea that Ziyar ibn Tihon wanted to abduct her. Lenia felt a bit ill, registering that.

It had been an unhurried meal in a palazzo with more wealth on display than she had ever seen. Dhiyan ibn Anash had been an honoured, well-rewarded man in Almassar, but hardly on this scale. This woman, Dona Raina, had been described by Rafel as the wealthiest Kindath in the world, one of the wealthiest people of any faith. She lived, even in a palazzo she'd occupied for less than a year, much like royalty. But she still engaged in the trading ventures her husband had begun. She controlled them. It was interesting . . . a woman accepted as capable of that. There were advantages to being widowed, Lenia thought, aware it was a bitter reflection. She was allowed those, surely?

She and Rafel and Folco d'Acorsi were not dressed at all properly for dinner in such a room. She was in trousers and a belted tunic. The two Vidal women looked elegant: one strikingly lovely, the other thoughtful and alert.

There were only the five of them. After the last plates were cleared by servants Rafel sipped briefly from his glass, and said, "I have a different matter to broach with . . . well, with both of you, but the proposal is for the dona, first, with respect, my lord of Acorsi. She is our hostess and a fellow Kindath, and we are in Sorenica because I learned this is where she is living."

"Learned how?" Raina Vidal asked.

"A Kindath friend in Marsena, my lady. Your movements are, as you might imagine, of interest to all of us."

"And to others," Folco d'Acorsi said.

He was leaning back in his chair, relaxed. He was making some effort to ignore the intense glances Tamir Vidal was directing his way. Lenia wondered, perhaps unkindly, where Tamir's slippered foot was, under the table. She and d'Acorsi had been seated opposite each other.

"So you came to find me, and are happy to see the lord of Acorsi here as well. This promises to be interesting. Go on." Raina Vidal had not drunk a great deal of wine either. Lenia had been watching. She knew Rafel would have been doing the same.

He bent and retrieved his satchel from beside his chair. He was good at this. The candlelight, she thought, would be wonderful for what he was about to show.

He opened the satchel, removed a finely made leather box, and placed it on the table. She didn't know when he'd bought the box. Marsena, probably. Or here today. He opened it, still wordless. He laid it on the table in front of Dona Raina, positioned so they could all see what was inside.

"*Dear Jad!*" said Folco d'Acorsi.

He was actually shocked, Lenia could see and hear it.

Raina Vidal said nothing, only looked.

Tamir Vidal stood up very abruptly, pushing her heavy chair back. She moved to the head of the table, to where her sister-in-law sat with the diamond gleaming before her, green and astonishing in the candlelight. Tamir put a hand to her mouth. She whispered, scarcely breathing, "I know what this is."

"We all do," said Dona Raina calmly. "How did you come by it, Ser Rafel?"

The obvious question.

"I am not, alas, at liberty to say," he answered, sorrowfully.

The obvious answer.

"I see," said Raina Vidal. She didn't push for more.

"May I touch it?" Tamir asked. Without waiting for an answer she picked up the Diamond of the South, on the golden chain Rafel had found for it, and placed it about her neck. It rested at her throat, above the low-cut burgundy gown she wore. She was, Lenia saw, adroit with jewellery clasps. The diamond settled between her breasts. It was a thing of wonder there, bewitching.

"We must have this," she said to her sister-in-law. "Raina, it cannot belong to anyone else."

"We?" said the other woman.

"We can . . . we can both wear it!" Tamir said. One finger was caressing the diamond, tracing its shape. Lenia saw that both men were unable to look away from her.

"At the same time?" Raina said.

Lenia was the only one who laughed. Raina Vidal glanced briefly at her.

Light wavered and danced, orange and gold. Outside, the wind blew; she could hear it in the stillness. Beneath the world now, in the teachings of Jad, the god would be battling demons through the night to protect his mortal children, until he rose again in the east, bringing sunlight back to them, a blessing.

Lenia was remembering killing the young man who had taken this diamond from the palace in Abeneven.

The silence had not yet been broken. Everyone was still looking at Tamir Vidal, at what she wore.

"I must have it," Tamir finally said again. Not *we* this time. "What is your price, Rafel ben Natan? Please name it."

"It doesn't matter," Raina said. Lenia thought she detected regret in her voice, wasn't certain.

"I will always be reasonable with you, my lady," Rafel said to her.

"I have no doubt," said the dark-haired woman. "But it truly doesn't matter. We cannot own this, be seen to own it."

"*Why?*" Tamir cried. You could hear pain in her voice. She had unhooked the clasp now, was holding the diamond between her hands, gazing into its depths like someone adrift on the seas of love, Lenia thought. A line from an old song, that. Her mother had sung it to her and her brother. A sudden memory.

"We are Kindath," Raina said. "This is a famed Asharite treasure. It will become known in very little time that we have it. And our people still live among them, depend upon the Asharites for refuge. Rafel, *you* live among them. No. This cannot be ours, pretty as it is."

"*Pretty?*" Tamir's voice was outraged.

"Well, it is pretty," said Dona Raina. "Thank you for thinking of me, Ser Rafel, but it is not possible. I have too many duties and too many who depend upon me in dangerous times."

She was, thought Lenia, a remarkable woman. She'd been told this, but hearing something and seeing it for yourself were like a foggy day and a sunlit one. Her father used to say that.

She was remembering her parents a great deal suddenly, she thought. Not particularly surprising. Not made easier by that truth. She was alone in the world. Many people were, but she was not . . . other people. You lived your own life, only that one. Hid from or reclaimed your memories.

"If that is so, I believe," said Folco d'Acorsi, "that my wife would kill me herself, in my sleep or with poison, if she knew I had an opportunity to purchase this, and declined."

"Not a knife?" said Dona Raina, a slight smile.

"Not Caterina. Others do that." He returned the smile, included Lenia. There was a conversation she'd been asked to have with this man later.

"Raina!" said Tamir Vidal. "I am begging you."

"You beg for something every second day, Tamir. I have explained this. Think for a moment of people other than yourself and you'll understand. They burn us, Jaddites and Asharites both. This treasure is not for us. I think ben Natan knew it."

"I considered it, my lady," Rafel said. "Although it could be, perhaps, if you stayed here."

"No. It isn't just about me. Not every one of our people can be in Sorenica, Rafel ben Natan." Her voice carried a hint of reproach, Lenia thought.

Rafel bowed his head. "I understand."

"If that is decided, we can discuss your price in private, if you wish," said Folco d'Acorsi. "A purchase made in order to save me from being murdered at home. It would be a kindness on your part."

"Of course," Rafel said.

Tamir Vidal made a strangled sound. She laid the diamond down on the table as if releasing it caused her grief.

"Tell me," said Dona Raina, a voice of idlest curiosity, "where were you going to go next, after I declined? If the lord of Acorsi was not, happily for all of us, at this table?"

"Rhodias," Rafel said simply. "The High Patriarch." Raina Vidal smiled at that, just a little. "I could still do that, of course," Rafel added, casually.

If d'Acorsi didn't offer a fair price was the meaning there. He really was good at this, Lenia thought again. He was also about to make her wealthy. *I owe this man*, she suddenly thought, *so much*.

"No fear of Asharites there, no," said d'Acorsi. "And some desire, one might even say a burning one, to let them know he has a treasure of theirs."

"My thought," Rafel agreed.

"We can talk in my chambers," said d'Acorsi. "I still prefer not to be killed by my wife."

"Is she so dangerous?" Dona Raina asked, smiling still. "The lady Caterina was so gracious when we visited you."

"Dangerous? You cannot begin to imagine," he said. "She's a Ripoli. I live in fear."

There came a small, broken sound across the table from him. Tamir Vidal had returned to her seat. A tear like a diamond slid down one cheek.

"Very well done, Tamir," said her sister-in-law.

CHAPTER VI

Later that night, in Folco d'Acorsi's chamber, two doors down from his own, Rafel ben Natan and the lord of Acorsi settled, easily enough, on the price of a diamond.

It was not enough, and it was wildly too much money, at the same time.

It made Rafel—and Lenia (he was getting used to the name)—wealthier than they could have imagined. It was a sum d'Acorsi might claim as a fee for a season's warring with his army from a city-state that hired him in a given spring.

But . . . there really was nothing in the world like this jewel. It carried an explosive charge in the wars of their time between Jad and Ashar. A minor Kindath merchant might be setting off artillery with this transaction.

Rafel had walked down the corridor, past wall-mounted candles, with the diamond in its box. He'd knocked, quietly. The door opened immediately. He had been awaited. Of course he had. He'd wondered if the other man would come to him, but that would have been wrong. He was a merchant; the other was lord of a city and commander of a military force. Also, d'Acorsi was Jaddite, and Rafel ben Natan was of a beleaguered, marginal faith.

He'd gone down the hall and knocked.

Folco had lamps burning. A flask and two wineglasses on a table. Rafel declined the offer of a drink. His heart was pounding. Of course it was. The other man said, gesturing to a chair, "You have something significant in that box. Dona Raina was correct. She couldn't have been the one to own this."

Rafel took the indicated chair. He set the box down. The room was graciously furnished. Best guest room, surely. A very large bed. Tapestries on two walls.

He said, "I believe she was, yes."

"But you offered it to her nonetheless? Was that showing consideration?" Genuine curiosity.

Rafel said, "It was her decision to make, lord. There might have been aspects I did not know. Perhaps even a gift to Gurçu? If she decides to go there."

Folco poured wine for himself.

"I hadn't considered that," he said. "A very considerable gift, if so."

"Yes."

"Would she have done that?"

"I have no idea, my lord. But she is arranging, and paying, for a great many of our people to settle in Asharias, and their safety will be on her mind."

"A benevolent woman."

"Beyond words. Her husband was, too."

"You knew him, you said?"

"Very slightly, my lord. He moved in circles far beyond mine. I was able to do him a small service, and was honoured to do so."

"Then he died."

"Then he was burned alive, to be precise." He didn't attempt to hide the bitterness.

Folco d'Acorsi nodded. A soldier; deaths did not shake him. Or, not this one, at any rate. Rafel wondered if there had been any that had in this man's life. Surely so?

"We live in a fallen world," the lord of Acorsi said. "We have all lost people we knew—and sometimes loved—to violence. It is why we pray, is it not?"

An answer to his thought. "I don't pray often," Rafel said. He wasn't sure why he'd said that.

D'Acorsi sipped his wine. "I do. All the time. Would you really have gone to the High Patriarch with this, if I had not been here, and Dona Raina declined the diamond? Despite her sister-in-law's delicate tears?"

Rafel did not smile. He thought he was meant to, but he didn't. "Being honest, lord, not with the diamond, no."

Folco was very quick.

"Ah. You have something else to sell?"

"I do, lord. And Rhodias is, I believe, the place for that."

"And if you offered two treasures to the Patriarch that would perhaps push the price down for buying both?"

"You would have made an excellent merchant, my lord." This time Rafel did smile.

So did the other man. "We negotiate all the time in my world. I am a merchant of another sort."

Of war, Rafel thought. They lived in a world shaped by wars.

"Where *would* you have gone, then? With this." He gestured to the box.

"Would you like to see it again?"

"No need. I saw it on the table, and about a woman's throat. I know what you have. However you come to have it." He lifted a quick hand. "I am not asking."

"Thank you, lord. I'd have gone to Seressa, or Macera."

"Oh, Jad!" exclaimed the other man, his voice rising for the first time. "You'd have truly had me killed. If Caterina ever saw Corinna

Ripoli wearing it, and learned I'd had a chance to buy it, and left it for her brother to buy for *his* wife, I'd not have survived that day. Believe me."

Rafel couldn't help but laugh. "Perhaps I should raise the price I have in my mind?"

The other man also looked amused. "Perhaps. And that price is?"

Rafel named it. Not a time for hesitating.

D'Acorsi offered a lesser but fair amount. Rafel proposed a sum exactly midway. D'Acorsi accepted that. It took only moments to conclude a transaction that would entirely change his life, Rafel thought.

"Good. That is settled. Have a glass now, ben Natan. Surely you are permitted?"

"I am," Rafel said. He poured for himself from the flask on the table beside his chair. He lifted the glass. It was fine glassware. "I salute you, my lord. And I thank you."

"And my thanks to you. I am happy I was here. I'll need to arrange financing at my bank, and will do so as soon as we conclude the other matter in the morning."

The other matter involved using Tamir Vidal to trap one of the most feared men in the world. The person sitting with him, Rafel thought, was another of the most feared men in the world.

Not company he was accustomed to.

"Where shall I await you tomorrow?" he asked.

"Here is wisest. Your ship will be watched. And there is no role for you in the morning's dance."

Dance, Rafel thought. "I would never imagine there would be for Lenia or myself, no," he said.

"Ah. That reminds me. I intend to make your partner an offer to join my company. I have . . . I've had clever, skilled women with me before, as I mentioned. There are advantages."

"And risks? For them."

A pair of eyebrows lifted in the scarred face. "Living is a risk, ben Natan. I try to find company members with different strengths—and then protect them as best I can. Both things. My question is, will it grieve you, if she accepts?"

"Yes," said Rafel promptly, surprising himself.

D'Acorsi nodded. His one eye held Rafel's in the candlelight. He was a genuinely ugly man, but he conveyed intelligence and assurance and . . . something harder to define.

"But," Rafel added, "her life is truly her own. I value her as a partner and as a friend, but she will join you or not based on her own needs. Still . . ."

"Still?"

"My lord, I believe that . . . I believe you can understand this. She was taken very young by corsairs. She was a slave for longer than she has been free. Has been in Batiara, not far from her home, for one day. A single day, my lord, returned from exile. It can . . . it can take time to learn again how to be free. To know one's needs and desires. To even imagine they matter."

Silence in the room. He could hear the wind again. Rafel wondered if he'd erred.

"Thank you," said Folco d'Acorsi simply. "You have given me something to think about." No smile this time. "You were . . . you are an exile, too?"

Unexpected, again. "My family was among those expelled, yes. I was young when we left. I have only really known the Majriti. And the sea. But yes, Esperaña was taken from us. A home to which we cannot return."

"But you have done so?"

"Disguised as a Jaddite. It is not safe. As Ellias Vidal learned, my lord."

D'Acorsi was silent again. A soldier who thought about things, Rafel was realizing. There were stories, of both his violence and these other things. He wondered what this man's enemy, Teobaldo Monticola, had been like. The same? Probably not, but he might have been.

"After tonight . . ." d'Acorsi gestured at the box with the diamond in it. "Your own needs and desires might also change."

"I have not even begun to consider that, my lord."

"Another item to sell, first? In Rhodias?"

"Yes, lord. If I can."

A change of tone, briskness returning. "I have taken pleasure in this encounter, expensive as it has been. I will be pleased to receive you any time you wish to visit us." His turn to hesitate. "We have no hatred of your people in Acorsi, ben Natan. The god I believe in is not threatened by the moons or those who invoke them beside him. Caterina and I invited Dona Raina to settle there. She had reasons for not accepting, but the offer was real."

"No port," said Rafel. "She needs a harbour. For her business, and for bringing our people to safety." There was no real safety, but he didn't say that.

"Yes. She's . . . she's better than either of us, isn't she?"

Another unexpected thing.

"I believe she is, my lord. With respect."

D'Acorsi stood, so Rafel did the same.

"I will see you tomorrow, likely in the later part of the day."

He'd be otherwise engaged in the morning, Rafel thought. He looked at the box. "I will leave this with you."

"I have not paid for it."

"It would never cross my mind to doubt your word, my lord."

"And if I am killed by Ziyar ibn Tihon in the morning?"

"I am not concerned."

A quick grin. "For my life or about reclaiming your diamond?"

Rafel did not smile. "Both, lord. Fare safely. It will be a good thing for the world if you do what you intend."

"I know it will," said d'Acorsi. "For our part of it, at least."

It occurred to Rafel that he would not have minded spending time in the service of this man if he'd been a different sort of person himself. An *entirely* from-nowhere thought.

D'Acorsi went past him, opened the door, called softly, "Gian."

Footsteps in the corridor. Rafel had not seen anyone. He imagined if Folco's people wished to be unseen they would not be seen. The man named Gian appeared in the doorway. D'Acorsi glanced towards the box. "Gian, this is to be guarded by two men here tomorrow. Choose two not to come down the hill with us. It belongs to this man, though I have undertaken to purchase it. He is leaving it with me for safety. It is valuable."

"Yes, my lord," said the man in the corridor. "I'll attend." He left, not lingering. A laconic man. Not one to be surprised, or show it if he was, Rafel imagined.

He bowed to the lord of Acorsi and went out himself, back to his own chamber. He had much to think about, more than he'd expected. Lenia was in the room between them. He could knock on her door and tell her what had happened. He decided to wait until morning.

But she wasn't there when he went to do that, though the sun had only just risen.

⚬⚬⚬

She had been awake, not yet in bed. Still in her clothing of the day, but there were two night dresses laid out for her. She'd been given a choice. She had heard some people used such night attire. Wealthy ones. She'd never seen, let alone worn such a thing. There was a white robe beside them, too. And feather pillows on the wide bed.

She heard Rafel's door open and close in the room next to hers. She had heard it when he went out, too. There was a flask of wine here. A brazier for scent. She was standing by the open window (she'd opened it) sipping Candarian wine, breathing the night air. She was being pulled hard by memories and was resisting them. It was difficult. First night back. So many years. The song that had come to her earlier was in her mind again. The one her mother used to sing.

She'd been expecting him to knock and tell her what had happened. So when a soft knock did come she rose, set down the glass, crossed to the door and opened it.

Raina Vidal was there, wearing a night robe of her own, blue as the blue moon, holding a candle.

The other woman smiled. She said, "I have looked carefully, for years, and have found nothing in the teachings of my faith that prohibits women from taking pleasure with each other. Does this go against your own faith and understanding? Or preferences?"

Lenia swallowed hard. After a moment she opened the door wider and let the other woman enter. Then she closed the door, quietly. It occurred to her to hope that Rafel would not now decide to come tell her what had happened with d'Acorsi.

THEY LAY IN bed after, unclothed under the coverlet. Candles burned on both sides of the bed. The tall window was still open. Clouds moving, stars. The moons were on the other side of the house. Raina Vidal, undressed, had turned out to be soft, scented, full-figured, with very smooth skin. Her hair, unpinned, was heavy and beautiful. She said, quietly, "Thank you."

Lenia shook her head. "I think you know I took pleasure, too."

The other woman smiled. "Of course I know. But I could also tell this is not something you've been accustomed to."

Lenia shrugged. It bothered her a little that it was obvious. She pushed her own hair back from her eyes. "While I was a slave, I had no choice in companions." She was determined to get used to saying what she'd been. It was a truth, it was an enormous part of what she was now, right here, tonight. At this possible turning point in her life.

"And since? Since you left?"

She'd left by killing the man who had owned her. She decided she didn't need to say that.

"This kind of encounter, by choice, with a man or a woman, has not been much a part of my life."

"I see. Perhaps it might enter happily at last, then."

"Perhaps," said Lenia. The other woman's fingers were moving lightly along her thigh, upwards, then down, then back up again. It was lovely and unsettling. She couldn't say which feeling was the greater.

"I told only a half-truth at the door," said Raina Vidal. "The teachings make clear that our task, for both men and women, is to have children. So some do conclude . . ."

"That since we can't achieve that, this is wrong?"

"Yes. But I take the view, with some support found in the writings, that it is not necessary to seek company in *only* men or women."

"I see," said Lenia.

The other woman laughed. "You are careful with your thoughts."

"I am," she said. "It has been necessary."

A pause. "I'm sorry. Of course it has. For me it has been challenging in a different way since Ellias died. I am deemed a prize—not for myself but for what I have. I will not wed again. I will not yield our business affairs to any man. Which means . . ."

"That this is easier. And perhaps more pleasing?"

"Certainly as pleasing, yes. I enjoyed the taste and feel of you just now."

"I am . . . I . . . well, that's good," said Lenia. She felt herself flushing.

Another silence. She could tell the other woman was amused now. She *really* had not expected this. If there was a nighttime adventurer in this house, she'd have assumed it to be Tamir. She'd watched the looks the other woman had directed at Folco d'Acorsi.

"I imagine the diamond has been sold by now," Raina said. "I did hear Folco call for one of his men."

"You listen at night?"

"It can be interesting when we have guests. You know that if they have concluded an agreement, you are a very well-off woman now?"

With another valuable thing to sell, Lenia thought. The hand on her thigh was extremely distracting. "I will have to learn to play the part," she said.

"I would guess they settled somewhere between twenty-five and thirty thousand serales." Dona Raina's voice was matter-of-fact, naming numbers that would completely overwhelm Lenia if she thought about them. "The Patriarch might have paid more, I think, or Duke Ricci in Macera, but Folco is an immediate transaction, and he *will* want this for his wife. He isn't really afraid of Caterina, by the way. He just loves her very much."

"That is unusual in a marriage," Lenia said.

"Mine was the same," said Raina Vidal quietly.

She hadn't known that. How could she have known that?

"But," Raina went on (her hand still drifting along Lenia's thigh), "I had a reason for mentioning your being well off."

Lenia turned on her side, took the wandering hand and held it with one of her own above the coverlet, to keep it there, as much as anything. "Tell me," she said.

A brief smile of acknowledgement. "Folco made it clear you impressed him today, with that corsair. And he does have a history of employing women in his company."

"I see," said Lenia.

"No, you don't, yet. My point is, if you are partners with ben Natan, as I gather you are, you will have no need after tonight to serve anyone in the world. Not Folco d'Acorsi, not anyone. Least of all, to become a part of the wars here."

"Batiara, whatever it is, is my home," Lenia said. First time ever saying that, she thought. Voicing the words.

"And war ravages it every spring. Folco is a sophisticated, intelligent man. But he commands a force that attacks cities, and farmlands and villages around them, and brings death."

"I've killed people," she said.

"I didn't imagine the man today was your first."

"Only Asharites," Lenia said, as if it was an excuse, or explanation. Which, in a way, it was.

The other woman looked at her. She disengaged her hand from Lenia's, sat up, then stood in the candlelight, plump and lovely. She retrieved her night robe and put it on again.

"I will leave you," she said. "This was pleasing. For you as well, I will continue to hope. Sometimes I find I need moments like this. It can be intense and unexpected, that need. But listen, I am trying to say something that might matter."

"I'm listening," said Lenia. She sat up, the cover falling back, exposing her upper body. She found she didn't mind.

"I would be happy to welcome you to this household if you are looking for a place to be while you come to terms with new opportunities. If, that is, you decide you don't want to be a merchant or pirate any more."

"Corsair," Lenia said instinctively. "Under licence from the khalif of Almassar. And only Esperañan ships and towns."

Raina Vidal looked impatient. "You know what I mean. You might well decide, the two of you, to buy new ships, expand. But if you want to stay in Batiara for a time, there is a home for you here. As a companion. Though I would value your skills as a guard. Today reminded me again that the Kindath are not safe anywhere."

"Thank you, my lady," Lenia said. "I have no idea what to say." It was the simple truth.

"Nor should you say anything yet," said the other woman. "There are too many new pieces on the gameboard of your life right now."

"I have never considered it a gameboard," she said.

Another impatient look.

It became, suddenly, a little too much of that. "My lady," she said, "we inhabit different worlds. Both exiled, yes, both mourning losses, but I mean what I just said: it is not a playing board for me."

Raina Vidal looked at her from beside the bed. "You are right," she finally said. "It is possible I have become accustomed to thinking of moving people like pieces to make certain things happen, or prevent them."

"You have had pieces to move," Lenia said simply. "I have only myself."

"I am going to think about that," the other woman said. "And perhaps you will do the same . . . about what I said."

"I will think about tonight a great deal," Lenia said. She smiled. Received a quick, pleased smile in return, and realized something: you could wield a certain kind of power through how you appeared in a given moment, how you touched someone, or didn't—even if they were considered a queen in the world.

She had never thought about that. Not as to herself. Not Lenia Serrana, who had been Nadia bint Dhiyan for so long, far from where her mother had sung songs to her when night came.

The other woman took up her candle—it had burned low by now—and left the room, closing the door carefully, without a sound.

LENIA WAS EXPERIENCED at waking when she needed to. She was out of bed and dressed and ready to go before dawn. She hadn't worn the elegant sleepwear offered, wasn't ready for that. The room was chilly, a cold hour. Moonlight and wind came through the window, the white moon setting at night's end over the harbour below. She looked out briefly, then left the room. She didn't have a cloak, wished she did.

She was also good at moving soundlessly. She made her way downstairs in the dark house. There was a guard by the front door, one of those from yesterday. They nodded at each other. He let her out, scanning the street, then nodding again.

She was a guest. Free to go anywhere she liked. For so many years that freedom hadn't been hers. She had been invited last night to stay as long as she wished—or as long as the Vidal women remained in Sorenica. She had also had her first lovemaking encounter in . . . since before she'd killed Dhiyan ibn Anash. She'd conceived twice back in that time. Lost one, had the other stopped by a woman who did such things for those who paid her. Ibn Anash had paid her.

She stepped into the street.

"Good morning," said the lord of Acorsi, leaning against the wall of the house. The guard would have seen him when he'd looked out, and had said nothing. Of course.

He extended a cloak to her. He was wearing one himself. "Cold morning," he said.

She took it, put it on, thinking hard. There was a hood. She put that up, against the wind knifing along the street. She wondered how long he'd been here.

"You knew I'd do this?"

He was looking the other way now, down the hill, scanning for anyone abroad in a still-dark pre-dawn hour. There was a first faint hint of light in the east. More a softening of darkness than anything else. The sky was clear, stars and the low, almost-full white moon west.

"I thought you might," Folco d'Acorsi said, turning back to her.

There were torches on either side of the door but they had burned down by now. A courtesy expected of the wealthy, for people in the streets, their safety at night. The same way the bench across the way was offered for comfort.

Comfort and safety, she thought.

"And you came out to stop me?"

He shook his head, a solidly built figure in darkness. "Not that. I wished to discover your intentions and see if they accorded with my own. For what I intend this morning, random elements are not useful."

"I am to be useful?"

She thought she saw him smile briefly.

"At least not harmful? Or disruptive? Is that acceptable?"

She stared at him. Already, between her eyes adjusting and the slow progression towards grey behind her, she could see him better. He was wearing a sword—mostly hidden by his cloak.

She nodded once. "It is. I'm not entirely sure why I came out. Couldn't sleep."

"Half-truth, Lenia Serrana. You didn't want to sleep. I cannot promise you'll kill Asharites this morning, but I can say you'll be part of what we do, if you want that."

She was still waking up, it felt. She hadn't expected him out here. A bird called from towards the arriving sun. The god returning to the world and his children.

"You want to observe me down there," she said. It was not a question. "How I conduct myself."

He shrugged. "I did say there might be a place for you with us, going forward."

She sighed. "I can simplify that for you. I have matters to attend to with my partner and perhaps . . . other things. I won't make any decisions soon. But . . . I'm honoured and will think about it."

He nodded. "I assumed as much. I did buy the diamond last night, by the way. A very large sum for you. Decisions to follow, I'm sure. I am not in a hurry. Shall I tell you what we plan today, and how I see your role?"

He was treating her like a soldier, she realized. As someone capable of specific tasks in what might be a violent morning.

"I don't have to kill someone every day," she said, as he looked down the street again.

He laughed, turned back to her. There was light enough now to let her see his features. Once you started to grow accustomed to them, Lenia thought, they weren't so ugly any more.

She listened carefully as the lord of Acorsi told her how he saw the morning unfolding. Or, better put, how he expected to *make* it unfold. There was a difference.

There would likely be deaths. He didn't intend those, not necessarily, but he wasn't reluctant to cause them, either. She wondered, briefly, as she listened, about the woman who had been part of his company. How long ago? What had she done for him? Had she killed? Adria Ripoli, daughter of the duke of Macera, Raina Vidal had said.

Lenia carried that thought with her down the hill to the city later. Then it left her, as matters became complex, in the marketplace and within herself.

THE EVENTS OF the morning were straightforward, or one could see them that way, looking back at day's end.

She was to walk with the hood of her cloak up, then simply put it down if she saw Ziyar ibn Tihon—or any of his men. She'd made clear she'd only know two or three of these, from Marsena. And one was dead now.

She was to be a Kindath lady companion accompanying Tamir Vidal to the market. She asked d'Acorsi, standing in front of the palazzo as the dawn wind rose, how many men he was bringing. She raised her eyebrows at his answer.

"I have a military company, this is a military engagement. They are already scattered through that market as the merchants and farmers begin setting up. I expect ibn Tihon and his men to come in through the city gate with the farmers. Do you know how many he has? I don't."

She didn't, of course. Asharites, or some of them, could easily pass for people from southern Batiara. Ziyar himself had blue eyes, born Jaddite. There would be danger here for Tamir, and so for her, walking with the other woman.

She'd gone back in and had a morning meal after all. Raina Vidal at the table was the essence of courtesy and polite concern for a guest, asking how she'd slept.

Tamir was visibly excited by the prospect of being a target for abduction. The idea of it . . . it clearly appealed to her to be a woman so ardently desired. At the morning table, she was still casting reproachful looks at her sister-in-law about the diamond. That wasn't going to be forgotten quickly, Lenia imagined. Another in a long chain of grievances?

Folco d'Acorsi had not come back into the palazzo with her. He'd gone down the hill alone, hooded. There was light by then. She'd watched him go before she went in.

THINKING ABOUT IT later she felt many things, but one of them was astonishment. More than just admiration or respect. She kept seeing again, in her mind, the sequence of what had happened.

Her instructor in weapons, back in Almassar, had told her that at its finest, its most pure, sword and weapons play could resemble a dance. So it had been, in exactly that way, with the movements of Folco d'Acorsi's men—but only after she had urgently, even desperately, pushed back the hood of her blue cloak in front of a leather merchant's booth in the early-morning market of Sorenica.

A dance, but six men died. Not one of them Folco's.

And among the dead was Ziyar ibn Tihon. A thing that might change the world.

His own folly, Lenia thought. He really shouldn't have done this raid, he shouldn't have *kept* to it when a man of his had disappeared the day before while spying on the Vidal palazzo. Sometimes men could think they were invulnerable. Women, she thought, rarely had that feeling.

She'd asked d'Acorsi if Ziyar would stick with his plan or abandon it, when they'd been alone at sunrise outside the house. He had given a precise reply, as to a soldier. "He may leave. Or he may decide the guards here saw his man and captured him, and he'll have had a story prepared. We'll do what we do, and see what he does."

They had. Ziyar was known to be the reckless brother. Perhaps more dangerous for that recklessness, perhaps less so. You could be both, in different circumstances.

He'd been killed by a crossbow bolt while running towards Tamir Vidal with three other men. Running towards Lenia, too, of course. And that—that—was what she kept thinking about at day's end. That was what had her still shaken now, back in the palazzo, listening to Tamir Vidal go on and on about how *frightening* it had all been.

One of the Asharites had moved straight at Lenia, a short, heavy club in his hand.

And she hadn't seen him. She had seen none of them.

And she was the one expected to give warning! The first Asharites hadn't been among those in the tavern last week. And Ziyar had stayed out of sight.

Even though she'd been looking as they strolled, she'd recognized no one. And then . . . and then six men had come out, moving fast, from behind the leather merchant's wooden stall.

They would have been tracking the two women as she and Tamir moved through the market. Had made their move when Tamir stopped and began handling gloves on the wooden counter. Lenia had her back to the stall, scanning for danger, as if idly. And then danger surged out, right at them, from very close.

And someone had warned her. Someone *inside* her head.

Not a moment anything in her life had prepared her for.

Behind you! she heard within her mind—clear as a sanctuary bell in country air. *Lower your hood! Turn!*

And without hesitating, not aware of making any kind of decision at all, Lenia did both things: hood snatched down as the signal, drawing her belt knife with her other hand. No thought. Only movement.

And so it happened that a fourth man was killed by her in that marketplace. Knife between two ribs, in, out, back in again fast and hard, to his heart. The club fell into the dirt beside him, then he fell there, too.

He hadn't expected a blade, resistance. Of course he hadn't. A blue-robed Kindath maidservant? It wasn't a difficult kill, in truth. Once she'd turned. Once she'd been warned.

But if not? If she hadn't been?

And because of her signal, d'Acorsi and his men had also done what they did. Tamir wasn't even touched. She'd screamed because she'd been looking at the booth, at the counter, and had seen large men running at her with purpose. It was not unreasonable to scream.

The man who had gone directly for her was Ziyar. She was to be his prize, a naked assertion that he could appear *anywhere* in Jaddite lands, do anything. Take anyone.

Instead, what he took was a crossbow bolt in the chest. D'Acorsi's men must have hidden the crossbows under their cloaks, Lenia thought. Later. Thought came back later.

D'Acorsi didn't need prisoners, ransom, information. This wasn't about that, he had made clear. He'd have liked Ziyar alive, to parade in Rhodias, offer him to the High Patriarch to execute—Scarsone Sardi seen as a warrior for Jad. But d'Acorsi didn't *need* to do that. He could send—or bring—a feared Asharite corsair to Rhodias as easily. Its own message.

In the end, that is what he did do.

It was uncertain how Ziyar had intended to get away from the market with a captured woman. They did discover that horses had been bought. The guess was that Ziyar had intended to club both women and the leather merchant unconscious, perhaps pretend Tamir had fainted, and escort her (carry her?) to where they'd tethered the horses—be outside the walls and riding for wherever their ship was before anyone knew.

The other woman, the companion, could be killed, or left. She wasn't important. Didn't matter at all.

Such a memorable raid it would have been, another strand in the legend of the ibn Tihon brothers.

Not so, in the event. Or, rather, memorable because fatal for him. He ended there. The story of this morning would indeed run along the Middle Sea, both ways, and reach Asharias. This was an important man.

She remembered d'Acorsi in the market walking over to them. He'd looked calm, alert.

"You left that late," he said.

"I didn't think they'd be behind the stall." It seemed she could speak.

"Clever of them, yes."

"They were djannis," she said. "From the east. Ziyar's men. They carry those clubs. The djannis from Gurçu are their best men."

"I know," he said. "But we dealt with them. And with him. Finally." They both looked to where Ziyar ibn Tihon lay in the dust. A very big man. Dead. It was hard to believe.

"I almost didn't do it in time," Lenia said. It felt as if she had to say it. "I really was late."

He gave her a look, then smiled a little. "That happens. Battles can turn on a moment. You heard them coming? Right at the end?"

It seemed easiest to nod agreement.

"I NOW WONDER," Rafel said to her, after she and Folco d'Acorsi were back in the palazzo, "what will happen in Abeneven. Ziyar was meant to take command there. That was their plan. We were part of it."

She was barely listening to him. Rafel gave her a glance, and she was aware of it, but she really was too shaken to deal with this sort of conversation.

Shaken to her heart's deepest core by that clear, urgent voice *somehow* in her head. Which had almost certainly saved her life. Or . . . she might even have been abducted *back* into slavery.

A shape of horror in that thought. Unspeakable.

So she didn't reply. She had no words.

The man running towards her had had his hand upraised, with the club.

That was why she'd been able to drop down and slide a knife between his ribs and then into his heart. It was possible, it was likely, that they'd not have wanted the bother of carrying a servant out of the marketplace. She would have been struck down hard. Live or die with that blow. Her death, if it happened, of no moment at all in the world, the unfolding of it. Her life to that point? Also of no moment.

But there had been a voice in the early-morning market of Sorenica. In her head. A woman's voice. Only for her. Only her. Only.

Lower your hood. Turn!

∽

There was a chance, Folco d'Acorsi said, that some of ibn Tihon's men had escaped. He didn't think it likely, and he didn't mind much. He had people looking for their ship, and expected to find it. It would be an enormous prize. He couldn't use a ship himself—his city was lamentably without a port and he wasn't a merchant—but he could make a gift of it.

In the same way, the body of the corsair who had intended to be khalif of Abeneven would now be a gift for the High Patriarch in Rhodias. Scarsone Sardi would be pleased in the extreme, and pleasing the High Patriarch was of considerable value to a mercenary leader and lord of a small city.

D'Acorsi was in good humour that evening.

Rafel, as well. Difficult not to be, although he'd been anxious all morning, until the lord of Acorsi had returned to the palazzo with Tamir Vidal, and Lenia.

Lenia had been strange ever since, no avoiding an awareness of that. Something had happened. He hadn't even known she was to be part of the morning. She didn't offer to explain anything. It was likely she'd been tense and afraid, with Tamir offered as bait for corsairs like a small fish on a fisherman's hook. And Lenia had evidently killed someone again, a djanni in the marketplace. Killing one of the legendary djannis was . . . it was an achievement. But it could unsettle you. Perhaps it was only that.

Rafel had never killed anyone in his life, as it happened. Not personally. Had ordered attacks at sea, and there had been deaths, but he had never killed.

D'Acorsi had taken him down the hill, with guards, in the afternoon. Had arranged a banker's note for the stupefying sum the two of them had agreed upon the night before. He, too, used a Seressini bank. The Sardis of Firenta were trying to become as powerful with their own bank, and were making inroads, but most people still used Seressa. Habits, routines. People lived their lives that way, Rafel thought. His own habits and routines might be about to change. And Lenia's.

The bank, he'd noted, was on a street named for a woman. Unusual. He had no idea who Jehane bet Ishak had been. But she'd been Kindath, obviously, from the name. That was pleasing. He'd asked, inside. A physician here, he'd been told, from long ago. The man at the bank didn't know anything more. There was a statue to her somewhere, he said. He wasn't sure where.

Before heading back up to Dona Raina's house, they had stopped at the handsome building on the main square that housed Sorenica's governing council. There was agitation there, not surprisingly. Folco d'Acorsi spoke with the head of the council that year, a fat, grey-bearded, bald-headed man. Rafel noted how diffident he was with d'Acorsi, a man known to be dangerous. And who had killed here this morning.

D'Acorsi had been courteous in the extreme, carefully explaining what had happened, why he had done it with his own men: to avoid panicking the people in the market with the arrival of city guards, and to prevent the corsairs from suspecting a trap. The danger to the citizens, he'd said, was entirely gone now. And an enemy of Batiara and of Jad was dead. It had been, he added, a good day in Sorenica. He hoped the council agreed.

The grey-bearded man, on behalf of the council, had done so.

A good day, Rafel thought, in many ways. In the bank he had simply taken the note d'Acorsi handed him and immediately deposited it into two accounts he opened there, in his name and that of Lenia Serrana. Half in each.

She had only a quarter share of their commerce and raiding profits, was investing her way towards more, but he had made a decision heading to Marsena that whatever sums they received for the diamond and the book would be different. They were not from trading. They were treasures *she* had brought the two of them.

She might argue, being inclined to argue, but he'd win this dispute. Indeed, he already had. Half the diamond money was in her account.

They were extremely well off now. And still had the book.

At some point they would each have to give thought to what was to follow in their lives. He knew the lord of Acorsi had invited her to join his company. She didn't need to do that now, but she might.

He was trying not to think about that. Partnerships formed and dissolved all the time. You changed your life when life forced you to.

Except, in his experience, people driven from home—or stolen from home—didn't like changes. His *experience* included his own, of course. Sometimes he dreamed of Esperaña. Not often, but often enough.

Whichever way the wind blows, it will rain upon the Kindath.

His mother had said that, all her life. Still did. An old phrase. He didn't normally believe in it, but sometimes he did. Made it harder to celebrate tonight as much as was surely proper, even drinking the very good wine Raina Vidal was serving.

He looked across the room at Lenia and saw that she was looking at him. He couldn't read her expression, though he was good at doing that. It occurred to him that habits, patterns, trust could apply to people, too, not just to something like where you banked. More often with people, if you thought about it.

He raised his glass slightly and a well-trained servant brought him more wine.

⧟

Raina Vidal knocked at her door again, late. She knew the knock this time, had almost been expecting it. Lenia opened the door. Same candlestick, different robe, white silk this time, a blue silk belt.

"You might not be in a mood for a visit," the woman in the corridor said. "I could understand that. But . . . you might be, so I thought I'd come and ask." She smiled. It was oddly tentative. Or perhaps not so odd. You could be as powerful and wealthy as this woman was, and still be anxious in matters of desire.

Lenia said, "It was a difficult morning. I am . . . not myself." She managed a smile. "I am still working through what *myself* might mean."

"Because of being back home, you mean?"

"Partly that. Maybe largely that."

"Do you want to talk about it?"

She shook her head. Kept the smile, to make it kind. "I'm not the sort who talks things through."

"And you don't know me at all."

"Perhaps a little," Lenia said. Kindness, and some truth, she thought.

The other woman nodded. Her hair was down for the night. "I was going to offer to escort you to Rhodias, but it seems Folco is doing that."

Lenia nodded as well. "He wants to take the body himself to the High Patriarch. I think he expects to be rewarded. And that is where we need to go, too."

"With the other item you have to sell?"

She nodded again. "Did you *want* to go to Rhodias?"

Raina hesitated. "Not urgently. At some point I should. But perhaps there would be too many Kindath in one party now."

They lived, Lenia thought, by different rules and assessments.

"Are you going to stay here or go to Asharias?" she asked.

The other woman shrugged. Smiled again, a little. "I'm not the sort who talks things through, either, as it happens." She lowered her head, lifted it. "You also have choices to make, it seems, but you *have* choices now. A good thing, even though it might be challenging."

"That sounds like wisdom," Lenia said.

"I try," said Raina Vidal. "You will be welcome, as I said before, if you decide to come back. Thank you for last night. It was a gift."

"Thank you," Lenia said quietly. "More of a gift for me. So is that offer."

The other woman turned and walked along the corridor with her candle. Lenia watched her go until she turned at the end, at a crossing hallway. There was a cast glow of light behind her for a moment, then that, too, was gone.

She closed the door. Wasn't sleepy yet, though she ought to have been. She went to the window, which she had opened again, stood looking out on the night. On the world at night. She suddenly wondered where her brother was, if he was alive somewhere, if her mother was. In the world at night.

Then she found herself thinking again about the voice in the marketplace, the one that had very probably saved her life—and Tamir Vidal's. If Lenia hadn't given the warning, if Ziyar ibn Tihon had seized Tamir, he'd likely have knifed her rather than simply surrender. He'd have known what awaited him, and it wasn't life.

No thoughts came to her about that warning—where it had come from, how, who it was. It was too far beyond her. Beyond anything she'd ever understood about the world. She had been close to talking about it with Rafel tonight, just to . . . do that . . . but there had seemed to be no point. What could he say, even if he believed her?

Still at the window, looking at stars, she wondered why she hadn't let the other woman with her beautiful hair and her generous body and nature and quickness of thought, come into the room. Into her bed. Perhaps when the mind was disturbed and agitated the body's needs could still be assuaged? She didn't know. It was not something with which she had any experience. She had become accustomed to seeking privacy whenever it was allowed. It hadn't normally been allowed.

Eventually she crossed to the bed, blew out the candle beside it, and did sleep.

They left before dawn. Folco d'Acorsi and Rafel both wanted that. They took the *Silver Wake* north, carrying a number of d'Acorsi's mercenaries with them, and a dead man. Rafel meant to catch the tide.

SHE NEVER SAW Raina Vidal again. Not in life, and their faiths guided them to very different beliefs about an afterlife and what might happen to someone there and what encounters they might be allowed.

CHAPTER VII

Entering the second year of his captivity in Rhodias among those he described in his writing as barbarians, Kurafi ibn Rusad was aware that his words on the subject could be regarded as deceptive.

But if he were ever freed, whether finally ransomed or simply released and permitted to sail home to Almassar, it would not do, he had decided, if the words he brought back to share among his people were less than vigorous in their denunciation of those who had captured and confined him.

No, he'd return to the Majriti bearing a tale of savage mistreatment. Of terrible hunger, of sleeping in freezing rooms in wind-ravaged winter, of threadbare woe in a disease-infested city.

He sipped from a glass of wine from some region in the north as he mused upon this. Bare feet! He would say he had no footwear at times . . . on nights when snow fell!

The courtesan he most favoured was just then dressing to depart, slipping her bare feet into sandals. She took her time, knowing he enjoyed watching her gradually become respectable in appearance and manner.

She hadn't been, earlier.

Of course what he would *say* back home (if he were ever back home) was that the women of Rhodias had no least trace of the beauty or wit of those in Asharite lands. None of their allure and sophistication. There were things you thought (there were things you did), and different things you could prudently say and write.

He had abandoned his commentary on ibn Udad. It hadn't, truth told to the self, progressed far. Problem was, he didn't really *understand* the great man's opening pages—which did create something of an impediment to offering a commentary on the book.

Instead, he was now engaged in writing the much more personal, highly dramatic tale of being captured at sea by pirates, abused and beaten by them, borne through stormy days and nights to Rhodias, saved from the roiling waves only by Ashar's grace—then sold as a slave to the High Patriarch of the Jaddite savages! A corrupt, debased man whose hatred of the star-born was well known. Who had vowed to retake Asharias and give it back its old name—burning all the faithful there alive!

Kurafi had allowed himself some choice phrases of intense description as to invented torments he declared he'd been subjected to since he'd arrived in Rhodias. He had been stoically enduring throughout, he wrote, Ashar and the stars always before him, shining lights of inspiration.

The courtesan—her name was Tulia—smiled over her shoulder as she went out. She wasn't talkative. He liked that about her. Ibn Rusad preferred to do the talking. His command of Batiara's tongue was adequate now. A year could do that, for a man of his intelligence!

His main task, though he could never divulge this back home, was an interesting one. He was working in the handsome palazzo of Count Anselmi di Vigano on a translators' dictionary linking Asharic, scholarly Trakesian, and the Kindath tongue. Di Vigano, a man of some learning and culture (also not an observation to be written down), had persuaded the High Patriarch to let him proceed with this three-languages project. Kurafi's arrival a year before had been seen as providential: he was declared a gift from Jad. He'd been purchased from the pirates by the High Patriarch and assigned to di Vigano for this labour.

He was given a tutor in those first months, to teach him Batiaran. Also, because it was evidently necessary, the doctrines and rites of Jad. After half a year, ibn Rusad was formally welcomed among the children of the sun god, converted to that faith in a ceremony in the private sanctuary attached to Anselmi di Vigano's palazzo. Di Vigano sponsored him personally, apparently a significant gesture. Important people had been present. There was a feast.

Kurafi made no objection. There was none, really, to make. Besides which, writings of many scholars and holy men attested that forced conversion from the faith of Ashar did not imperil one's soul. It was a precise argument: since killing oneself was a sin, acting to avoid being killed by the Jaddites was a proper deed.

People converted regularly, for one reason or another. Kindath and Jaddites in the Majriti did it all the time. Converting saved you from paying the head tax on heretics, for one thing.

In private, Kurafi continued to invoke Ashar and the stars, though cautiously. One of the courtesans had almost caught him kneeling not long ago. He didn't kneel to pray after that, and he prayed silently.

He dined, from the beginning, in good company. Di Vigano kept a fine table—not, again, something to be described in his writings. Kurafi sat among scholars, diplomats, high-ranking clerics, and clever women. At least two of the women were poets, not a thing that would happen in the Majriti. He had a bedchamber to himself, with braziers for heat in winter. He had a servant. He was invited to ease his desires with courtesans recommended (and paid for) by di Vigano's steward. He could walk the streets and squares of Rhodias whenever he liked, past and among the ruins and monuments of the Ancients strewn everywhere here. Rhodias had clearly once been a much more populous city than it now was. Almassar had more people now, he told himself. And Tarouz. And Abeneven. All of them! He was pretty certain it was true. He was escorted whenever he walked out by two armed men. For his safety and, well, he *was* a captive here.

Not that he could ever escape, even if such a notion occurred to him.

His writing was a meditation (he liked that word) on just this subject: captivity and exile, the poisonous fruits thereof. How enforced distance from one's homeland over time could set an iron stamp on the soul. He wasn't sure he'd coined that phrase, but he thought it possible he had. He had a skill with words, it had been said of him from very young.

Kurafi adjudged himself well placed to produce a work that would illuminate the subject. Especially if, as any writer must, he permitted himself to amplify or invent a few matters in order to make the insights clearer to the less-educated.

He was, on the whole, not displeased with his circumstances.

Not, again, a feeling to be shared if he ever returned home.

ON THE MORNING he was summoned to the patriarchal palace, Kurafi was working with his fellow translators. One was a mild-mannered Kindath, one a Jaddite scholar. The latter was an old, bitter man who'd fled Sarantium. They were at their great project, di Vigano's dream, the dictionary to link three languages. He had come to enjoy the labour, though the gaunt old man from Sarantium was impossibly arrogant. Kurafi had been told that most of them were, those who'd come west after the golden city's fall. This one, he'd decided, had probably been like this before.

The guards sent to bring him gave ibn Rusad barely enough time to change into proper garb. When the High Patriarch of Jad, the supreme leader of the sun god's faith, wished a man's immediate presence, that man was advised to be prompt.

Kurafi had not been in the palace since his initial arrival—unshaven, in salt-stained clothing, paraded by pirates as a prize. He had no idea why he was being summoned now.

He wasn't afraid, precisely, but there were realities to being exiled among one's enemies, and there had been no warning at all. Events in the wider world could affect a man in Kurafi's position, seldom for the better, and he didn't know about those possible events. The guards who had come for him were extremely tall, entirely expressionless, and armed. They were always armed.

The events of that day, having their origins far away and only now arriving in Rhodias, did affect him greatly, although it was not possible to say at the time whether for good or ill. Kurafi ibn Rusad wept, shortly after arriving in the High Patriarch's reception chamber, startling himself, because the tears had nothing to do with his own circumstances.

∽

They had sailed up the coast to the deep-harbour town of Filonico, which belonged to the Patriarchal domains. It wasn't far, but it was easier to go by sea. They had a body in a casket, and speed mattered with corpses, though d'Acorsi had had Ziyar ibn Tihon's remains treated to delay the corruption attendant upon death.

One didn't want to present to the High Patriarch in Rhodias a decomposing, foul-smelling Asharite. But one did, very much, want to present him.

At Filonico, a self-important port officer attempted to delay them with inspection and paperwork. Lenia had her first glimpse of Folco d'Acorsi allowing anger to show—to extreme effect. The port authority, apprised of the identity of the man currently vexed with him, elected to promptly waive all forms and payments. Bowing repeatedly. Perspiring.

He also provided them with a two-horse cart for the casket, and arranged for the twenty or so horses they needed. A large number, it would not have been easy, but d'Acorsi had taken that many men on board. The seas were never safe from raiders, even along the coast of Batiara, even on a short journey. On the other coast, to the east, the Seressini Sea, pirates from the town of Senjan in Sauradia were constantly inducing rage with raids on merchant shipping. People from other cities were not especially displeased if it happened to be merchants of Seressa who were discomfited.

They lived in an age of piracy. A fact of life, to be dealt with as best one could.

Lenia and Rafel had made a portion of their livelihood that way. The *Silver Wake* had six cannon. A large number for a small ship. The endless calculations of merchants as to whether goods were more safely conveyed by land or by sea were not easily done. Insurance was increasingly expensive, and necessary.

Lenia asked for and was given a gentle horse. She wasn't afraid of them (much), she was just awkward in a saddle, and she knew the ride to Rhodias was going to leave her back and buttocks in distress.

Along the way she realized that Folco d'Acorsi had back pains of his own. He only showed it mounting up and dismounting at midday breaks or day's end. A grimace he tried to suppress. A military life was not, she thought, designed to leave a body without scars or pain, and the lord of Acorsi was not young.

She realized that he was also watching her as they rode. They had to cross a river once, swift, high water in spring, and she wasn't happy doing it. It was tricky enough just riding, let alone through water, the horse swimming. Lenia had a sense that he was assessing her, and it felt unfair. First of all, she had said *nothing* about a commitment to joining his company. Second, she'd made it clear she wasn't used to horses!

He was a surprisingly good companion, though. Several times he let his horse drift back to where she rode, to talk of where they were just then, battles that had taken place there or just ahead, how the terrain had mattered, the importance to Rhodias of the port they'd just left. Other matters, mixing light and substantial. She wondered if he was wooing her this way. She wondered why he wanted her to join him. There were, she thought, roles a woman could play, tasks one could do for a military leader that men couldn't. Maybe assassinate someone? He'd seen her use her knives.

She didn't know how she would feel about being employed to kill Jaddites. Her anger, her very deep anger, lay elsewhere.

Without making much of it, he adjusted her stirrups at one inn yard where they stopped to eat and change some of the horses. Then he showed her, when they were mounted again, how to use her thighs and knees to both control the horse and ease her riding.

It helped a little. The muscles in her legs were going to hurt now, too, however. At least the weather was good, the road well maintained. It was an important route to the coast for Rhodias.

Folco d'Acorsi rarely smiled, but when he did it greatly changed his appearance. She couldn't think of anyone she knew for whom the contrast was so extreme. She wondered how he'd lost the eye, and if the scar came from that same day. You had time for wondering on a springtime ride past wildflowers, trees coming into leaf, men and women working in the fields on both sides of the road.

As best she could, she was avoiding the memory of that voice in her head in the Sorenica marketplace—there was nothing she could *do* with that recollection, though she was not foolish enough to deny it. She'd heard a woman warning her. From somewhere.

She was also trying not to think too much about being in Batiara again, or about her home, inland from Sorenica.

It ought to have been far enough inland to be safe from raiders.

⌗

Antenami Sardi, younger son of the family that ruled the increasingly powerful city of Firenta—in reality, if not in name—had lived a notoriously dissipated existence for most of his years. So had his cousin Scarsone, now, amazingly, the High Patriarch of Jad, the most holy figure of their time. The man whose court he was currently visiting in Rhodias.

Scarsone's elevation to this eminence had been entirely due to Antenami's brilliant father Piero, and substantial sums invested in making it happen. Even Piero Sardi had been unable to quite believe they'd succeeded, Antenami remembered. An investment in a chance, he remembered his father calling it.

Having a family member as High Patriarch was an *extremely* useful thing in the intricate, often violent back and forth of Batiara's city-states. Scarsone's equally extreme unsuitability for the position had, in the event, presented no impediment that could not be addressed by a sufficiency of money carefully distributed among the pious clerics choosing the new High Patriarch.

Real piety had been optional for some years in Rhodias. That's what Piero Sardi had gambled on. And won.

Many things changed when Sarantium fell to the Asharites, however. One of them being the purpose in life of their nephew and cousin, Scarsone. The Patriarch was still young, still enjoying his wine and food and the company of beautiful women, but the fall of the City of Cities had been like a mighty wave crashing over him, as he wrote to his uncle shortly after.

Antenami had read that letter. His cousin, their Patriarch, his former drinking and whoring companion, pre-eminent now of all the sons of Jad on earth, had vowed to send an army to retake the city and spit the head of Gurçu the Osmanli on a pike . . . which is what the infidel had done to the last emperor of Sarantium.

The name Asharias was not to be uttered in the presence of the High Patriarch. The golden city remained Sarantium for him. Lost, but to be regained.

It hadn't happened, and years had passed. Men with any understanding of the world had known it would not happen. Assembling an army among the warring kings and princes of the Jaddite lands, an army and a fleet to sail east to besiege the fabled triple walls . . . no. No, alas. Not a thing that could be done in the world they knew, however much the High Patriarch thundered and threatened.

They hadn't sent men to *defend* the city, had they? They wouldn't send them to the far harder task of reclaiming it. Indeed, it was more likely that the Jaddite world would lose more land, more cities and fortresses, to the ferociously aggressive Gurçu.

The world had altered when Sarantium was taken. They were living through that.

Antenami Sardi himself had been changed greatly in these last years. Not by the city's fall—*he* was not going to bear the burden before Jad and history of having been High Patriarch when that happened—but by events in his own life and within his family.

He was trusted by his father now. In its own way, an astonishment. It had only ever been his older brother who'd had Piero's confidence. But Antenami was in Rhodias now as the family's emissary, relied upon to use his best judgment—and that would not have happened only a few years ago. He had never been thought to *have* a best judgment.

His assessment, unfortunately, was that the time was not propitious to push their cousin to amend his edict concerning Firenta's long desire to conquer a nearby city and the lands and towns around it, the ones paying taxes to that other, vexing city.

There were wars everywhere. Mercenary armies roamed up and down Batiara every spring and summer. But the High Patriarch had made a firm (and deeply unfair, in Piero Sardi's view) decision that his cousins would not be permitted to take Bischio. Not and remain within the light and shelter of the god. It would upset the *balance* of things. Any mercenary, the Patriarch had proclaimed, who took Firenta's gold to lay siege to Bischio would be exiled from the protection of Jad and the rites of his clerics, along with all that mercenary leader's soldiers, and the citizens of any cities or towns he might control.

This included Folco Cino d'Acorsi, of course, who had been hired by the Sardis some years back to take Bischio for them. A momentous spring, that had been. Folco had withdrawn his forces from the field when Sarantium fell. And he had stayed withdrawn from that fight afterwards. Every commander had, because of the Patriarch's decree. The hope of light with the god after dying was a bone-deep part of the Jaddite world.

Antenami had some affection for Bischio, vivid memories of its famed horse race, but those didn't interfere with his awareness of how much claiming it would enhance Firenta's resources. He wouldn't have understood this four years ago. He did now.

So he had come to discuss it again with his cousin, and gently remind Scarsone just how he had come to this extravagantly beautiful palace and life. Induce, if he could, a renewed awareness of gratitude, loyalty. Without family, what were you in this hard world? He'd say that.

But the circumstances of the day had now altered. Circumstances had a way of doing that, in his experience.

Who could have expected that Folco d'Acorsi would arrive—the day after Antenami came to Rhodias—and be granted an audience immediately? Well, no, the *immediately* part was understandable, given that this was Folco, a man he knew and admired (and feared, as most people did). Folco was a part of Antenami's memories of Bischio. They had ridden to the city together once, also in spring. If Firenta could change the Patriarch's mind on this, his father would want to *hire* d'Acorsi again!

But what was the man doing here now? It was clear he hadn't been summoned. Unease and surprise rippled through the reception room. Folco had entered with two merchants, one a woman, the other . . . a Kindath! It was highly unusual.

Their names were called out with an absence of enthusiasm by the steward of the Patriarchal court. Antenami was prepared to nod gravely to Folco, but the other man hadn't noticed him yet in the crowd near the dais.

Perhaps because he'd been thinking about Bischio, because he was *here* to talk about Bischio, the name of one of Folco's companions caught Antenami's attention. He had become better in the last few years at making connections, registering things he might once have permitted to float serenely past him. He looked more closely at the new arrivals. Nothing occurred to him, however, and it wasn't an uncommon name.

Folco had a long, narrow wooden box carried in. That was more noteworthy. It appeared to be a coffin.

It was.

༄

The High Patriarch of Jad would not have said he was *angry* with his cousin but he wasn't entirely pleased with him, either. He liked Antenami quite a bit—they'd shared memorable nights when they were younger than they were now—but he knew exactly why Uncle Piero had sent his younger son to Rhodias, and he was not of a mind to accede to requests in the matter.

He could have invited Antenami Sardi to stay in the palace. He probably should have, but he didn't. The Sardi residence in Rhodias was a handsome one, and it wouldn't hurt for his cousin to take a point about not being especially welcome if he was here to ask, yet again, for permission to send an army to Bischio.

There were reasons for refusing. Macera and Seressa were urgently opposed, and their views mattered. So did those of an increasingly confident Duke Ersani, south in Casiano. A man to watch—and not idly offend. Supporting their position in this matter of Bischio and Firenta's ambitions had been useful to the High Patriarch in several ways, chiefly financial.

Besides which, though this really mattered only to him, Firenta's armies had actually been on the way to Bischio when they'd all learned of Sarantium's fall. Scarsone Sardi was a man prone to believing in omens and auspices, and that moment was . . . well, it was at the centre of his life now. He still had nightmares about it. And he somehow felt (though never said) that if he were to let Bischio fall he would never achieve his goal of retaking the golden city in the east. The two things had become linked for him.

Not that he was ever likely to retake Sarantium, but the world needed to know that if this didn't happen it was not because the High Patriarch had been lax in his efforts!

It was years ago now, but he *still* woke from those terrible dreams of what it must have been like within the city's walls on the day Gurçu's army broke through. His companions in bed on such nights would have to go to great lengths to soothe him. Some were better than others at that. None could take the dreams away.

He hated Gurçu the Destroyer with an intensity that shocked him sometimes.

He had never been a hating sort of man. But he grieved bitterly that Sarantium had fallen, and that he'd be the one blamed—so unfairly!—for it. It blighted his life and endangered his soul. And so he'd lie locked and lost in darkness when he died if he willingly let his Uncle Piero renew that attack on Bischio!

And today, as another omen, there now came to him the commander who had called off his army from the Bischio attack he'd been leading! After Sarantium's fall, Scarsone had sent a message to every figure of significance in the Jaddite world that no wars would be allowed that season. All were to wear mourning and add prayers of repentance to their rites for the rest of the year.

But Folco d'Acorsi had withdrawn before that command. Even though Teobaldo Monticola, who had been hired by Bischio against him, lay dead, leaving the city undefended.

And then . . . he'd guaranteed the safety of Monticola's own city of Remigio, and of his family.

No one could have predicted it. It was still in place, that guarantee, and it was still unsettling. Any force (even the Patriarch's!) moving on Remigio, where Monticola's widow and brother ruled as regents in the name of his young son . . . *anyone* approaching those walls would find Folco d'Acorsi making war on them.

Not a threat to ignore. But you could modify a threat into something you honoured and supported, and let the world know you did so. Turn a necessity into something that spoke to your own benevolence. He was learning how to do that, more and more. He'd had some years here now, hadn't he?

He ordered d'Acorsi and his companions—merchants, he was told, not names anyone knew—admitted on the very day they arrived. Of course he did. This was a man he might need. A man he probably did need.

On impulse (and impulse shapes much in the world) he had his cousin summoned to be present. He had a vague memory that Antenami knew Folco d'Acorsi. Something from that campaign against Bischio.

Antenami arrived early, showing a little too much alacrity. The High Patriarch greeted him warmly enough, allowed him to kiss his ring instead of his foot. He *was* a cousin, his father *had* made Scarsone High Patriarch.

Antenami withdrew to one side, properly situated among the higher clerics and courtiers, towards the front, near the dais, which was proper for a Sardi.

Shortly after that, Folco and his companions were announced.

They brought a dead man.

Wonderfully, *wonderfully* dead, eternal praise be to holy Jad of Light—given who it turned out to be.

~

Folco d'Acorsi did everything Rafel could have hoped for.

He seemed to feel he owed them a debt for guiding him to Ziyar ibn Tihon, allowing him to present a feared and hated—and newly dead—Asharite to the High Patriarch, to claim what rewards might be linked to doing so.

D'Acorsi remained grave and serious as the Patriarch and his court grasped who this was, how he had come to be here, and then began celebrating the death of a man who had terrorized the Middle Sea for years. The paeans to Jad of the Sun and the praise for the lord of Acorsi were loudly triumphant. Prayers were spoken and shouted. The sun disk gesture was made, over and again. It wasn't decorous.

Scarsone Sardi (a younger man than Rafel had expected) didn't even bother trying to appear calm or judicious. He was exultant. He stepped down from his dais to stare at the dead man in the now-open casket. Then he spat on him.

Instructions were given to sever the corsair's head and display it. The Patriarch ordered the head impaled on a spike on the outer ramparts of the palace for carrion birds to attack the eyes. This man had done worse things in his day—to living captives, it was said. A proclamation was to be written and read out all over the city, and sent by messengers through the Jaddite world.

The headless body would be dragged behind horses through the streets of Rhodias in the morning then left in the dirt for the dogs.

This was not Gurçu the Destroyer, but this man had been one of his most feared commanders in the west, and the High Patriarch was going to make as much of this as he could. It was why d'Acorsi had come here with the body.

And with them, Rafel thought.

The corpse of Ziyar ibn Tihon, once ruler of Tarouz with his brother, once a scourge of the sea, was covered up again in his coffin. Few in their world had escaped seeing dead men, or were unaware of how their corpses or heads might be used if they'd been a certain kind of person. There were no surprises in any of this. Observing the extravagant celebration, Rafel did suppose he'd expected more dignity. How much, he wondered, did dignity matter in their time?

Only after ibn Tihon's corpse had been carried out and a measure of calm was restored did d'Acorsi step forward again to explain who his companions were, and why they were present. They had something of importance to offer, he said. Something else that might very greatly please the High Patriarch. He had urged them to come with him.

This last wasn't true—d'Acorsi didn't even know what their second item was—but it was generous of him. There was no doubt it helped them that the first words were spoken by the lord of Acorsi in a moment of triumph to a supremely pleased High Patriarch, and not by a Kindath merchant wearing the mandatory blue and white.

They had always been unlikely to succeed here, he knew. But they did have alternatives, which was useful when you were trying to sell something.

He received the gaze of the High Patriarch, bowed three times, did not approach any nearer. Even kissing Scarsone's foot was an honour beyond him. Beside him, Lenia also bowed properly. They wore acceptable clothing, nothing stylish. They were here to sell something, not to fit in with an opulent court.

Scarsone Sardi nodded graciously. A plump, fair-featured man, thinning hair, no beard.

"You have something for me?" he asked.

An invitation. In that moment, a sense of the comedy of a man's life assailed Rafel ben Natan, born in Aljais in what had once been Al-Rassan, exiled from there, now a merchant of Almassar.

Who was he to be standing here? In this company? To be about to speak to the most powerful man in the Jaddite world? Perhaps, he thought, he should use this opportunity to ask the High Patriarch to order the king and queen of Esperaña to allow the Kindath to return from exile. That would go well, surely.

"I have a book," is what he said.

༺༻

Later, back in the modest but handsomely furnished house d'Acorsi kept in Rhodias (the lord of a city, even a small one, needed to have such a residence here, it seemed), Lenia was in a wonderfully hot bath, trying to soak away the aches of their ride, and to grasp what had happened in the palace.

Grasping was proving difficult. She had thought Rafel's sale of the diamond to Folco had been an astonishment, the sum they received. The book had sold today for more. A *book*.

It seemed that Ghazzali al-Siyab—whom she had killed—had been correct in his assessment of how valuable it was to the right person.

There had been confirmation. From an Asharite captive summoned to the palace, a scholar of some sort. That moment, too, had been remarkable.

The bath was deep, the water scented. She had a woman attending her in a room dedicated to this purpose. This was all entirely new for her. D'Acorsi had said, before heading back to dine with the Patriarch, that his wife had insisted on this when they had bought and redesigned the house. Lenia felt gratitude in this moment to many people. Caterina Ripoli d'Acorsi was one of them.

So was—a wry thought for her—that Asharite who had arrived, sent for in haste, when a high cleric had suggested it to the Patriarch as a way of testing the extravagant assertions of the Kindath merchant about this book.

They had waited for him. Wine was served by tall servants. The death of Ziyar ibn Tihon was celebrated anew. The High Patriarch led them in prayer. She watched Rafel perform the Jaddite rites flawlessly. She'd seen him do that before. A man who could assume many guises. She thought about that, kneeling herself and rising, chanting words she remembered.

She'd risen, they all had, as the prayers ended.

It was likely, she thought in her bath, that she had changed Rafel's life, by killing al-Siyab, taking the diamond and book, then following and killing a spy outside Raina Vidal's house. But with what he'd done in that house, and now today, here, he'd changed hers forever, as well. Again.

In the palace, the Asharite scholar had been announced. He'd entered and bowed, head to marble floor. The captive—ibn Rusad was his name—rose cautiously, remaining a proper distance from the Patriarch. He was instructed to examine a book being handed to him by the steward and tell them what he knew about it.

He accepted it, opened it. Stared.

His hands began to shake, Lenia saw. He opened and closed his mouth. He swayed where he stood. It seemed clear that he wished to fall to his knees again, and was afraid to do so.

It was powerfully persuasive. Decisive, really.

He declared, barely able to speak, that this was indeed the original copy of the *Prologue to Knowledge* by ibn Udad, infamously stolen some years ago from Khatib in the east. Probably the most treasured book, outside the earliest copies of sacred texts, in the Asharite world.

It was, he said—before someone took the book from his hands, for fear he would drop it—the most valuable book he had ever touched.

The High Patriarch of Jad instructed his treasurer to convey a properly generous gift to the two visitors to his court in exchange for their bringing him this highly valued and unexpected prize.

That was how such things were done, it seemed.

That proper gift was discussed by Rafel and the treasurer before they left the palace. Folco d'Acorsi had elected to be present for that conversation. Rafel reported to her that d'Acorsi had said nothing, merely looked on, listening attentively. His presence, Rafel thought, had mattered. The treasurer was not about to negotiate aggressively. Not with the lord of Acorsi there.

Perhaps because she was excited, a little overwhelmed, lying naked in a luxuriously hot, pleasingly scented bath, with a good meal to come when she rose and dressed and went downstairs, Lenia imagined, briefly, what it might be like making love to Folco d'Acorsi.

Not as a reward for him—she didn't imagine herself so rewarding—or even one for herself. It wasn't like that.

It was just a fancy, a flicker of physical need.

She hadn't allowed herself such things for most of her life.

⌘

The Sardi palazzo in Rhodias was very near to Folco's smaller one. On his way to dine in the palace, Antenami Sardi stopped—on what could only be called an impulse, with something nagging at his mind. He had one of his attendants knock on the door of d'Acorsi's house. He was running late, as often, assumed that Folco had already gone. He climbed out of his litter and waited for the door to open.

He was correct about d'Acorsi. The steward confirmed it. It wasn't Folco he wanted to see, however.

He asked if the female merchant, the one named Lenia Serrana, would be good enough to receive him, briefly.

She came down the stairs a few moments later. Her short dark hair was appealingly damp and disordered from a bath. The steward ushered them into the reception room at the front of the house and asked if they would take wine. Antenami said yes; the woman declined. She ought to have accepted, since her guest had, but he didn't imagine her to be familiar with these courtesies.

They stood in an awkward silence until the steward returned with a tray and Antenami's wine. The man served it and left, closing the door. Antenami noted it was glassware in the newer style. Caterina, d'Acorsi's wife, was celebrated for her taste.

He sipped his wine and saluted the woman. She was tall, slim-hipped, wide-set brown eyes, wide mouth. A direct gaze. Her clothing acceptable. He guessed it had been provided by Folco. She wasn't the sort of woman Antenami preferred, but she was pleasing to him. That wasn't why he was here, of course.

"Have you asked for me, my lord?" she said.

Direct, in that way, too. The Sardis of Firenta weren't lords but people tended to address them that way, he'd gotten used to it. Enough, even, to detect a slight when it was withheld.

LENIA HAD NO idea why this man was here for her. It made her anxious. *Being* in Rhodias made her anxious. There was too much power in this city. She'd been looking forward to a quiet dinner with Rafel.

With d'Acorsi at the palace it would be a chance to talk about what had happened today.

Instead . . . a Sardi was here for her. More power.

He smiled. Antenami Sardi seemed a mild, genial man. But no one trusted that family, she knew, just as no one trusted the Council of Twelve in Seressa. Or the high clerics here, for that matter. There wasn't a great deal of trust in the world, she thought.

He said, "It is but an idle query, something tugging at my mind. Because of horses, which, well . . . because of horses. Yours isn't an unusual name, but I do business with someone called Serrana, and I . . . well, I wondered."

"Business?" she heard herself saying, but her heart had already sped up. The world could attack you, ambush you. On your farm. In a morning market. In a palazzo in Rhodias. Anywhere, really.

"He is a horse breeder. I have a magnificent stallion, my joy, Fillaro, and we have bred him to some of Signore Serrana's mares, with happy results."

"I know nothing of horses," she said.

Antenami Sardi smiled cheerfully. "A shame, but that isn't it. I just . . . I wondered if you were related."

"I can hardly imagine so, my lord."

"He comes from the south, and there is even some resemblance of features, now I see you more closely, though he is a smallish, solidly built man, and you are handsomely tall for a woman, signora, if I may say so." He smiled again.

Lenia found herself staring at him. It seemed to her as if he might be able to *hear* her heart. She felt suddenly light-headed. And terrified.

She said, clearing her throat, "Where is it you do business with this man?"

"In Bischio. His ranch and stables are outside the walls. His name," Sardi said, "is Carlo. Carlo Serrana, of course. Before he stopped racing a few years ago, he was the most celebrated rider in Bischio's race. Won it many times! I was there for his last race and it was such a remarkable . . . Signora! Are you all right? Please! Allow me to . . . !"

She let him help her to a cushioned bench. She needed that help. She was finding it difficult to breathe. Sardi shouted for the steward, who came promptly. She declined wine, water, food. She said she was all right. She wasn't.

ANTENAMI APOLOGIZED PROFUSELY, took his leave. The woman clearly didn't want him hovering and he was late for a banquet. He was carried through the windy streets of Rhodias to the palace. There was no opportunity to talk privately to his cousin. The food and wine and entertainment were excellent.

Such a strange encounter with the merchant woman, he thought later, back in their own palazzo. He felt badly about it. He had shaken her with his query, though that hadn't been his intent at all. He was only curious. Thought it might be a pleasing discovery, a coincidence.

In Antenami's considered view, there were pitfalls in almost everything you could say to people. It was a wonder, really, that friendship ever happened, that business dealings sometimes concluded successfully! Or love. The woman he loved was living in another country.

In the morning he was finally able to speak with his cousin. As expected, it was not a fruitful conversation. Despite the High Patriarch's fervent expressions of love and gratitude to his family, he made it clear he had no intention of lifting his ban on Firenta taking Bischio. There were, he said, many reasons.

Pressed for these, he demurred. As expected. They exchanged gifts and embraces, and Antenami left the palace. He could have tried being more severe, he thought, but he was sure it would have achieved nothing, and possibly had a negative effect. His father, listening carefully when Antenami reached home, agreed.

It wasn't in Antenami's nature, in any case, to be severe with people. Possibly a weakness.

LENIA HAD NO doubt, not for a moment, not a single one, that this was her brother.

There was no reason to be so certain, but she was. Carlito was alive. It terrified her. Joy, yes, yes, of course—and wonder. But mostly . . . terror.

She had been a slave for most of her life, compelled to the bed of an Asharite whenever he wanted her. Available for his friends, had he wished. Many owners of slaves treated them that way, men and women. A valued guest in your home? You offered him a slave for the night. The fact that her owner had not done so was merely chance. And had not stopped her from killing him.

She told the steward she'd take a glass of wine, after Sardi left. It didn't help.

Rafel came into the room. She saw concern on his face as soon as he looked at her. Was it so obvious? She wanted to stand up and say something, words that sounded customary, to show she was all right. Instead, she began to cry.

He came over quickly, knelt on the carpet beside her. That would likely have hurt, she thought, he had a bad knee. He took both her hands. She let him do that. He didn't speak. She kept weeping, soundlessly, exposed, tears impossible to stop. A feeling so difficult.

"I have to leave Batiara," she finally managed. "I must never come back."

Rafel ben Natan, her partner, her friend, her only friend, looked at her, kneeling by her seat. He was expensively dressed, she realized. He said, softly, "Of course we can leave. We can do anything, *you* can do anything you want now, Lenia. Everything has changed. But . . . will you tell me why?"

Sometimes you needed to, it seemed. She told him why.

He didn't release her hands. She didn't make him do that. It was all right, his holding them.

NO ONE, RAFEL ben Natan thought, could grasp another's sorrows. Not the deeper, enduring ones. He kept up a stream of talk as they dined that night in Folco d'Acorsi's home. There were four attendants for the two of them. He had caused some discomfiture by rejecting the seating that had them at opposite ends of the table. The steward had come in, apologized, and smoothly supervised a rearrangement of plates and glassware. Rafel had Lenia at the head of the table; he sat beside her.

The wine was remarkable. He made sure she had some more. And that she ate at least a little.

For himself, had he learned that a brother believed dead might be alive after all, it would have been a source of complex feelings, as well. Because he did have a lost—or dead—brother. With two children Rafel was supporting. He had none of his own. A different sort of sorrow. Some of the exiled Kindath had produced half a dozen offspring, quickly, after they'd been driven from Esperaña. The need to say *we are still here, in the world.*

Grief and loss acted differently on different people. Just as fear or desire or greed did. Or love. Just as everything did, really.

He was thinking this while telling her how he thought they should initially invest some of their considerable sums now, subject to changes later. She was, of course, entirely free to make her own decisions, he said. These were just his own thoughts, he said. He kept talking. He told her he had already made plans to transfer a portion to Ghazzali al-Siyab's name, to be sent to his family. He knew how to do this. He had been a merchant for a long time. Sailors died, and you arranged for their last wages to go to their families, if you were decent and honourable.

He tried to be that. Decent and honourable. Partly his nature, partly a sense that your reputation mattered. There was a saying, that the Kindath needed to be twice as virtuous to be thought half as much so. Truth to it: there weren't enough of them.

Lenia, who was not Nadia any more, could be said to be home now in Batiara. Perhaps not on the family farm, but among those with a shared faith, in a place where she and her ancestors had probably lived for a long time.

But she had just said she *needed* to leave. And he couldn't ever remember seeing her weep. It had to do with the possibility of her brother being alive. He struggled to understand. Still, he hadn't been abducted by corsairs and sold into slavery, forced to convert to Ashar's faith, owned by a man who could do whatever he wished to do with her.

Her brother, she'd said in the reception room, could *only* want her dead. For the shame she'd brought upon their name. Rafel had begun arguing right away, debating this. He really didn't agree, he'd said. Her eyes had made him stop.

He wasn't a woman, he thought. He didn't live in the world women inhabited. He didn't know her brother.

Neither did she. He'd said that, trying one more time. "You said he was a child! Younger than you. Who knows what sort of man he's become? If this is him. Don't be so certain he won't feel joy if he sees you! Lenia," he added, "I would feel joy."

She'd shaken her head. "He will have wished I had died. He will have prayed all these years that I'd been killed, or killed myself, and wished for my soul to find light with Jad."

"He wasn't even ten years old," Rafel had said again, feeling helpless before sorrow.

THEY WERE IN the reception room again, in chairs by the fire. There was a portrait above it, a young woman with red hair, standing at a window, hills behind her, vineyards, a distant town. It was well done, as best he could judge. He wasn't expert. The woman had strong, intelligent, confident features. There was a knife in her belt, which was unusual, he thought. He didn't know who she was, or who had painted this.

It occurred to him again that he had more than enough money now to retire from the sea, become a backer of other merchants' journeys on the Middle Sea or overland, if he wanted. Or become an insurer. He could do that. There was a great deal of money to be made in insuring ships and land parties if you had good information and skill with numbers. He could *buy* paintings like this one, learn to judge them, see them properly, meet the artists. He could own glassware like the kind he was holding. Drink wine like the wine in his glass.

He could bring the children and their mother to him. Or move to Marsena where they were. It was a perfectly good place to live, if you chose a Jaddite city.

He could marry again.

But . . . the idea of place, a home, settling in? Building the rest of a life? Where should *home* be, in the world of Ashar, or of Jad? Where was safety? Was it anywhere at all? He wondered what Raina Vidal would say.

He heard the front door of the palazzo being opened by an attendant, and a moment later Folco d'Acorsi came in to them.

With a proposal. Brisk. Little preamble beyond a greeting.

Lenia accepted it as soon as she grasped what was being said. Rafel did so, as well, after asking a number of questions and receiving answers to all of them.

He was never certain, after, why he'd agreed. It was not an obvious thing to do just then.

Lives change, turn, pivot on small things, accidents of timing. We are proceeding in a given direction and then . . . we are not. Sometimes for reasons we don't grasp, even if we have a nature that causes us to look back.

But he did say yes to Folco d'Acorsi that night, sitting before the fire, holding a glass of wine, under a painting of a woman with red hair.

༄

They did not find the galley Ziyar ibn Tihon had used for the raid on Sorenica. The raid that killed him.

Ayaash ibn Farai, son of a great father who had long been with the brothers, third in rank to the two of them in Tarouz, had been posted outside Sorenica's walls with the horses on the morning of the planned abduction.

He was alone with them in a copse northeast of the city. He hadn't picked the place. This was his first raid; he was too young to have any judgment or authority. He was here only because of his father, and he knew it. A gesture from Ziyar. He was a burden. He felt it. He was terrified of blundering.

He was to stand guard here, in a place chosen by wiser men to be invisible from the road leading to and from the city. He was to have the horses ready to race away when Ziyar and the others came out with the woman they were there to seize, in an exploit that would become famous, he'd been told. The whole world would know of it!

He was worried. Of course he was. But it was peaceful among the trees and it wasn't a difficult task. His only challenge was keeping the horses quiet. He had oats for that purpose. He was to feed the ones that seemed restive. He'd been doing that.

Time passed. The sun rose, began to set. It should not have taken this long. He'd been told to expect them by mid-morning. Anxiety settled into him, took root.

Ayaash moved nearer the road, on his belly amid the undergrowth. His hearing was good—he would listen to what people were saying, perhaps get a sign as to when the raiders would be coming.

What he heard, what men and women were saying, was terrible! It was calamitous!

Ziyar ibn Tihon was dead, people on the road were crying as they left the city. They were shouting it to those heading in. There had been an attempt at the capture of a woman! But the great Lord Folco Cino d'Acorsi had been in Sorenica and had foiled it! He had killed the evil corsair himself. It was a miracle of the god! People were laughing and crying for joy.

Ayaash felt his belly clench in spasms of terror. He suddenly needed to void his bowels. He crawled backwards and did so amid the trees. He was sweating; he felt ill. What was he to do? He had no idea! What if these people were wrong? What if it was all . . . a plot to make him leave?

No, that couldn't be so. They didn't know he was here!

He needed to *think*!

What would his father do? He would ride for the galley, Ayaash thought. The galley and the men on it needed to be saved, and carry word back to Tarouz! It occurred to him: the Jaddites knew there was a galley! How else would Ziyar have come here? They'd be looking for it! Perhaps already!

He examined his own thinking, the way his father had taught him. He decided it was correct. He'd leave all but one horse here, in case this *was* some sinister plot by the people he was overhearing, or a mistake, Ashar and the stars willing. He'd leave them so Ziyar would have horses to escape with if he was alive. Ayaash would ride for the ship as fast as if evil djinn were pursuing him. Which they might be doing!

It was while he was untangling the one horse from the others—some of them neighing and nickering at his presence among them—that Ayaash ibn Farai heard a rustling in the copse. He wheeled. His heart stopped, or it felt that way.

"Who are you?" a man said. He seemed to be a farmer, or the son of a farmer. He was Ayaash's age, younger. He seemed curious, not alarmed.

Ayaash understood Batiaran a little. He spoke it terribly. His father was from the eastern islands: born a Jaddite, going to sea as almost everyone did there, ending up among the Asharites as a corsair, as many did.

Ayaash, by appearance, could pass for Batiaran—until he had to talk.

He grunted at the other man, continued to untie the horse he needed. His hands were not steady.

"A lot of horses," the other boy said.

"Horses," Ayaash muttered. "Yes."

"Why so many?"

He didn't answer. He almost had the horse freed. Several others were stamping now, even more restless because of a new person here. It wasn't peaceful in the wood any more.

"Your dagger!" the other boy exclaimed suddenly. "You're with the raiders!"

Ayaash swore. His dagger was curved. Of course it was. He was from Tarouz! His father was a commander for the ibn Tihon brothers! He was on his first raid!

The other boy turned to run, to give a warning.

Ayaash was fast on his feet. He sprinted, he drew his curved blade, he plunged it into the boy's back, pulled it out and drove it in again where his father had told him you needed to, to best kill a man from behind.

He killed that man from behind. Before he could shout his warning.

Ayaash stood over him, breathing hard. He looked down at this Jaddite. At this boy. No. This *man*. It was a man, he told himself, not a boy. "Why did you come here?" he cried softly, in Asharic. "*Why did you make me do this?*"

He stumbled away and threw up against the base of an ash tree. His first killing. This boy. This *man*, he told himself again. Killed only to save his own life, perhaps the lives of many others. To get word back to Tarouz!

He left the body where it was. He didn't want to touch it, but he did. He found an old knife at the other's belt. He threw away his own revealing blade, deep into the trees. It felt as if he were throwing away his life up to that moment.

He finished freeing the horse and mounted it. He wasn't a good rider—there had been little reason for horseback riding in his life— but he'd been on enough camels and mules, and he could manage. He didn't go south to the crowded road. There was a way through these trees north. That had been the plan.

It came out at a trail, the one they'd taken coming here from the galley. He rode quickly then. The trail widened into a path. He saw two people walking towards him. They stepped aside, as one did for a mounted man. There were labourers in the fields on either side. It was planting season.

He rode, he concentrated on that. He went as fast as he dared. He still felt sick. He thought he might throw up again. The killing. What seemed to have happened in the city. The disaster there.

Ziyar dead? Impossible. Ashar would not permit it to be true. What would become of those who had come here with him? What would become of Ayaash ibn Farai?

What would his father say?

He did come safely to the strand among pines where they'd beached the three small craft that had brought them ashore. And were to take them back, with the woman. The galley had been anchored a distance out, for safety, if it needed to move quickly away.

There were no Jaddites, the place had not been found, the small boats were here.

The galley was not.

Ayaash scanned the sea. Emptiness. The ship was supposed to be back by now from the run it had made north for water and food after sending their party ashore yesterday.

(There had been contrary winds at night and again at sunrise. The galley could not make any speed back south, under sail or rowing, and there had been danger from the rocks. It was delayed.)

Ayaash remained on the strand. He sat down, knees up, hands clasped around them. He was hungry now. He made himself not cry. At one point he heard noises behind him, inland, and grew even more frightened than he already was. It was woodcutters at work among the pines, but he didn't know that. He feared that whoever this was would come down to the beach. See the boats. See him.

What would his father do? He didn't *know*!

He left the horse tied to a tree and pushed one of the boats off the strand, began rowing, awkwardly, because it was too big for one man. But he did get it out into the bay. He took it to where he remembered the galley being anchored. Or thought he remembered. He wasn't sure. He waited there on the water, alone. Rowing to stay in place, keep from drifting shoreward again. He was hungry and thirsty. He felt ill. And terrified.

He kept looking north, staring a hole in the wind, as the saying went. The galley did not appear. It ought to have *been* here. It was not. The sun set and the sky darkened and Ashar's first stars appeared, and a wind. Ayaash spoke the evening prayers, fervently. He realized that when night fell he'd be unable to see any ship approaching. The galley would not be showing any lights. It wouldn't see him.

He didn't know what to do.

⚬

Arsenius Kallinikos doesn't understand why he seems to be floating in the air above his body, looking down at himself and his lacerated wrists, where he lies in a palazzo in Rhodias, far from his home.

He knows he is dead, that he's killed himself, which is a sin in most faiths, including his own. Though there have been texts written—and he has been a scholar of such texts—that suggest it is acceptable in certain circumstances, including to save others. Or, for some people long ago, when honour has been too deeply compromised. There have indeed been times when honour was more highly valued than in the present days. He has written on this subject. He could quote himself. His memory was always good. Many ancient writings memorized.

Still a scholar, even dead, he thinks. How useful.

Can you be ironic when you've died?

Kallinikos, philosopher and linguist, once teacher to the emperor's children in Sarantium, a part of the empress mother's circle of thinkers and artists, a man of renown in the east, looks down at the blood pooling where he lies on the floor of his room, and decides that since he is in fact being ironic, then you can indeed be so after you have died. At least briefly. While hovering like this. The hovering, the seeing himself, are unexpected.

Insights he might have wished to share in writing, if . . . well, if he were not here. Wherever here *is. And, teasing the thought further, were he not here, he wouldn't have the insights, therefore . . . ?*

Questions rather more suited to a living man.

In life, he had ended up in Batiara, wreckage washed ashore among ignorant westerners led by an uneducated High Patriarch not worthy of the title—or respect. Nothing like their own Eastern Patriarch before the City's fall. A man Kallinikos had been proud to know and dearly love.

The fall. It had changed so much, destroyed so much.

Including, though it hardly mattered by any real measure, Arsenius Kallinikos's life.

He had accepted the command of his emperor and fled with the empress mother on one of the last ships to leave Sarantium. Came here, to Rhodias. Where there were, at least, libraries, and some scholars. Including others like him: exiled, lost, destroyed—just as their world had been destroyed.

More than four years now. The bitterness of life in an exile you knew in your heart would never end. Bitterness of bread made in a different way, of different ways of praying, of picturing the god on walls and canvas and domes, on medallions. Living among people who had such an inferior, vacuous grasp of the proper worship of holy Jad. They had understood such matters *back home. They had debated doctrine with learning and passion.*

Here they largely debated which wines were best and who were the strongest mercenary captains or the most in-demand painters of portraits. And courtesans. They talked a great deal about courtesans and prostitutes.

He realizes, lingering in this strange space, these moments after dying, that a part of him had died with exile, when Sarantium fell.

He'd tried to make a life here. Accepted the patronage of Anselmi di Vigano, a decently intelligent man—for an aristocrat and a westerner.

He had laboured at his own writings, despite the absence of his library, and also at di Vigano's project, the dictionary of Asharic, Trakesian, and Kindath, meant to assist future scholars and readers with sacred and philosophical and medical texts, or the great Trakesian tragedies of two thousand years ago. Works dear to his heart. To what had once been his heart. Before he was exiled. Before he died.

"For the betterment of those who follow us," di Vigano had said, grandly.

It had not been a dismal labour. His had been the Trakesian part, of course, though he spoke Asharic and had some of the Kindath tongue, and of several other languages—as any proper scholar did. At least in the east. Not so much in Rhodias.

And then, some time ago, di Vigano had brought into his palazzo a new man: a young, fatuous, arrogant (why did those so often go together?) Asharite, seized in a raid by pirates, brought here because they thought he might be worth something.

They ought to have drowned the vain fool, had been the considered opinion of Arsenius Kallinikos.

Ibn Rusad was a drunkard, a whoremaster, and had a comically inflated view of his own sagacity. A superficial cleverness did not excuse any of these things! He was impossible to work with, but di Vigano regarded him as a prize. He'd wanted an Asharite scholar for his project from the start.

Little use explaining that this man was no scholar. Kallinikos had tried to do that, twice. Each time he'd been rebuffed, the second time harshly: accused of envy, ill will, hatred based on faith.

The idea! That he was envious of . . . of that man! And as if a Jaddite should not hate the people who had destroyed the City of Cities.

Of course he hated the man. Their Kindath colleague expressed no views, ever. He did his work, was quiet and acceptably capable. Cautious—as a linguist, as a man. As the Kindath had to be, for the most part. But Kurafi ibn Rusad, the Asharite, had driven Kallinikos mad.

Evidently.

Because earlier today, when the young man was abruptly summoned from work to the palace (Why him? Why not Kallinikos?) and their work for the day was suspended, Arsenius Kallinikos had followed an impulse, a madness of the god, and entered the other man's chambers, adjacent to his own. (He had been forced to listen, over and over, to ibn Rusad loudly fornicating with Jaddite women.)

He'd had no purpose, only a restlessness akin to a burning within— and his grief, which never went away. He went to the other man's desk. There was a manuscript there.

Kallinikos looks down at his own dead body. It seems to be farther away now, as if he is rising, floating. Or perhaps his vision is blurring. He is dead, after all.

But before dying, he had read some of the pompous, insufferable Reflections *of that false scholar, that preening, ignorant, dishonest fool: his musings on the agony and pain of exile among barbarians, savagely treated, suffering so very much.*

Suffering! It had scarcely been a year for him, he was living in an opulent palazzo, and his *people had destroyed the walls of Sarantium and killed the emperor and Eastern Patriarch and spitted their heads on spears to parade through burning, ravaged streets of the dying, and then spiked them both on the walls. And they had forced the exile of tens of thousands of men and women. More! More people than that!*

Yet this mewling man-child was writing fabrications about his current life, and offering—only a few pages were required to see it—thoughts about the pain of those exiled. And perhaps the worst thing, the very worst, was that the thoughts were dishonest but the phrasing, the writing, the words, showed . . . skill. He could tell, even in Asharic. You could be clever and a fool. Kallinikos had always said that!

It had become, suddenly, too much. This was the man summoned to court by the High Patriarch? Valued by Count Anselmi? Enjoying the wine and food and whores of Rhodias while posing as a victim of terrible hardship?

Arsenius Kallinikos, in what he could only call a moment of madness, like some flawed hero of a Trakesian play assailed by a god, stood staring blindly at the wall. Then he took the manuscript from the other man's desk, carried it to his own room, and burned it on the fire there.

After which he took the knife lying on his own desk, spoke the prayers of the eastern rites, invoking his beloved, sustaining, dark-haired, dark-eyed, suffering Jad who battled evil for his children every night—and ended his own too-bitter life.

Hence and therefore, obviously, arriving here. Wherever here was.

Drifting now. Higher. Away.

He ought not to have burned another man's writings, he thinks. It was an ungenerous thing to do. Ibn Rusad was very young, he might grow. People did do that sometimes.

He ought not to have been forced to flee Sarantium. To end up so far away from all he'd loved. To imagine the burning there when the City was taken. To live with that imagining. All the dying. People he'd known.

He thinks, on the whole, that he'd lived a virtuous life.

He hopes he might find mercy now. Light. All any man could do was hope.

An almost-clear thought comes. A memory and a vision: Valerius's great sanctuary in Sarantium, the lanterns suspended on their chains, swaying high above, the many-coloured marble pillars rising into shadow. There had been mosaics on the walls and dome when the Sanctuary was built a thousand years ago. Wars of doctrine and belief within the Jaddite faith had taken those down.

He had always wished, even if it was heresy, that he'd seen them. The descriptions were wondrous.

You never did do all you wished to do in life. Some lives were more blessed than others. Some tasted more of sorrow. But . . . he had known the City. Sarantium. It had been his city for a time. There was that. There was that.

Last thought, then gone.

༉

For some, the reality of exile, each and every sunrise, twilight, nightfall revealing a self understood as displaced forever—rootless, unhoused, alien where they live, depending upon the charity of others—that can become unendurable.

Carrying on might be a matter of never reaching, or being forced towards, the moment, the awareness of that *unendurable*.

The effect of being violently driven from home, and that home being despoiled . . . it can go on and on like sea-surf against rocks. On and on within a man or a woman, or within a child as it grows up somewhere else, never at home, only *away*.

If that is our fate, we may be able to endure it, until something significant occurs, or nothing very dramatic happens but it is still suddenly too much, and then . . . then some cannot do it any longer. The going on, the enduring, in what has become their life. They shatter. Sea-surf on rocks.

The rain misses the cloud as it falls into the sea.

PART THREE

CHAPTER VIII

Lucino Conti, duke of Seressa, head of the Council of Twelve, a man widely respected and widely feared, had endured a terrible stroke some years ago. It had left him, sadly, incapable of fulfilling the demanding duties of his office in turbulent times.

The presently acting duke had expressed the view, in private and in meetings of the council, that disruptive events could be good for trade if assessed shrewdly as to options and responses. Seressa, as he was prone to observe, had the best network of spies in the world—and needed it. It was also the city where the phrase *For the god and trade* had been coined.

That was the story about the phrase, at any rate, that it had originated here. Stories were not always true, Duke Ricci thought, but were often useful. Or they could be dangerous. He put on his spectacles and scribbled a note as to that. Writing things down was a habit.

He was mildly anxious this morning, which was not like him, but the letter on his desk—he had read it three times already—and the man presently to be ushered into his larger, more formal reception room were both cause for uneasiness.

"You know him well, don't you?" he asked the younger man standing beside his desk. The only other person in the room.

"I wouldn't say that. We did have dealings some years ago. As you know."

"As I know, yes, or I wouldn't have raised the matter."

It was unlike him to be peevish, as well.

Guidanio Cerra, his adviser, smiled briefly. He wasn't a smiling man, and his recent loss had left him even more thoughtful and quiet than usual. Ricci liked him a great deal; trusted him, too (not the same thing). He was sorry for the younger man, but he didn't have time just now to address that. He needed Cerra to be sharp and observant. Seressa did. Still, the wry smile, the knowingness of it, amused him. And reassured.

Danio—most people used the short form of his name, it suited him—was tall, dark-haired, with a large nose and large ears and appealing eyes. He was lightly bearded of late, in the fashion for younger Seressinis. He said only, "I would never presume to offer predictions about Folco d'Acorsi, lord. He is what he is in part because he is difficult to anticipate."

Ricci shook his head. "Not the problem this morning. We *know* why he is here. We need to decide how to deal with it."

"That means deciding how to deal with the High Patriarch, no? D'Acorsi is his agent here."

Which was true. A formidable agent, however. Thank the god there had been a letter first. If Folco d'Acorsi had entered now to inform him, without warning, of the Patriarch's expectations, and his threat, Duke Ricci's celebrated poise would have been sorely tested.

More likely, in truth, it would have cracked like a new-laid egg thrown at a wall. Another phrase he liked. He wrote it down.

As it was, the letter had preceded Folco by barely an hour. A time frame carefully calculated? Or simply a delay because a messenger had stopped for a drink or a morning whore? How would he know?

Well, he doubted that last possibility. D'Acorsi wouldn't have allowed it.

The acting duke of Seressa felt himself growing, in short, *extremely* uneasy as he waited for a knock on his door and their visitor to be announced.

"We just have to listen this morning," Danio Cerra said.

Duke Ricci wondered if he should be bothered that his disquiet was so obvious to his adviser, even after several years. He decided he had other things to be concerned about just then.

He said, "Your daughter? How is she?"

"Thank you for inquiring, my lord. She is with my mother and father during the days. She is loved and cared for. What more can we ask?"

"What more, indeed?"

The young girl's mother, Cerra's wife, had died two weeks ago in childbirth. So had the child she'd been carrying. A boy, evidently. It happened. It was a terrible thing. Sometimes even more so than usual. His sense was that it had been a good, affectionate marriage, though he knew things about Guidanio Cerra, his history and his heart, that had made that doubtful at the beginning.

A man of strength and wisdom accepted his past, carried it within himself, moved forward with it. He was about to write that down, too, when the knock came and his door opened.

Three people entered. He hadn't expected that. He really didn't like it when unexpected things happened.

⌇

Rafel had some guesses as to why d'Acorsi wanted them with him when he spoke with the duke of Seressa (the *acting* duke, as everyone kept reminding him), but they were only guesses. He was, he'd admit it freely, unsettled by the company they were now keeping, he and Lenia. And he still wasn't sure why he'd accepted the invitation to come north. An aspect of being unsure of his own future? Wanting an interval? Lenia had shown no hesitation at all.

They could now be considered wealthy, both of them. The invitation to accompany d'Acorsi might not be unconnected to that. Seressa valued money, perhaps more than anywhere else in the world did.

But . . . he was still just a Kindath merchant (with less-palatable aspects to his history at sea) and she was a woman taken into slavery in the Majriti as a girl, with everything that implied. It seemed reasonable to find all of this unsettling. His life, from the time of their first encounter with the ibn Tihon brothers, and a proposal to kill the khalif of Abeneven for a fee, seemed to have been moving much too fast.

That khalif was dead. So was the man who'd done it with them. So was one of the brothers now. A trail of the dead. And here they were, clothed extremely well, after travelling with Folco d'Acorsi by sea up the eastern coast to Seressa, and about to be introduced to Duke Ricci of Seressa, said to be brilliantly shrewd.

Life, Rafel ben Natan reminded himself, *could* move swiftly at times. You did what you could to keep up. Or afloat. Or whatever word you wanted.

He bowed, for a start. Saw Lenia do the same. She preferred bowing to essaying a woman's sink-to-the-ground salute. Also: she was here as a merchant, part-owner of a trading ship, and this was not a social or courtly visit.

It was, in fact, a first overture to war.

And not one this duke or his city would be enthused about, for many reasons. Ricci had only one attendant with him, a tall man with watchful eyes and a grave expression. Pale—perhaps recovering from an illness? He hadn't been introduced.

But d'Acorsi was nodding to this one. And his first words were spoken to him, not the duke, which had to be a breach of protocol? Not that Rafel knew much about protocol at this level.

"I was sorry to learn of your loss, Signore Cerra. I was told when we arrived. I have vivid memories of you. We shared some moments a few years ago."

"It is extremely good of you to say so, my lord. Both of those things." The man—he was still young, but didn't have a young man's manner—spoke calmly. "I hope *vivid* is not a bad thing in your customary use of the word."

D'Acorsi smiled. The other man—Cerra, it seemed—smiled back briefly.

"Not customarily, no," said Folco d'Acorsi. "Not in this case, either."

"I am greatly relieved," said Duke Ricci's adviser. He took a half-step backwards from beside the duke's chair, as if to now withdraw himself and his own affairs from this morning's engagement.

Ricci looked over at him with, also, a small smile.

This is just like selling or buying something, Rafel told himself. *More powerful people, more at stake, but the same.* The thought didn't reassure as much as it should have, perhaps. He reminded himself it was likely he wouldn't have to commit to anything, perhaps not even say anything.

"May I ask your companions why they are here, d'Acorsi?" Duke Ricci said.

So much for not saying anything. Inwardly, Rafel ben Natan sighed. He also laughed at himself, though didn't let that amusement be seen. This man would be good at seeing hidden things, though, or he'd not have the office he held.

He was about to speak, but Lenia answered first. A woman, yes, but a Jaddite, and he was here as himself, a Kindath, a blue-and-white hat to mark it.

She said, quietly, "We are merchants, my lord duke. As you will have been told. We hope to conduct some dealings here. But my lord of Acorsi has been good enough to regard us as having aided him with something in Sorenica, and that bears on . . . why we are with him." *Something.* The killing of Ziyar ibn Tihon and bringing his corpse to the High Patriarch.

"It is as my partner says, my lord," Rafel added when she stopped and looked at him. "We will be pleased to provide what assistance we may."

"Thank you, of course," said the acting duke of Seressa. He seemed puzzled. "But what assistance might you imagine we could require of you?" Ricci's manner was not hostile, it was careful. He was, Rafel decided, busily learning things even as he sat before them holding his reading glasses, a notebook open in front of him. That sort of man.

Now he stood up from his desk, his place of authority, and moved around it, neat-footed in his movements. It was a large room. There were low-backed chairs towards a window over the canal on that side. The shutters had been folded back. There was a breeze, the smell of salt. The room was bright. Morning light. The duke gestured his guests that way. They moved there and sat down, d'Acorsi first. The young adviser stayed by the desk, watching and listening. It really was a dance.

And it was his turn to dance, Rafel thought. To choose the opening music.

"Before I answer," he said, "may I say, Duke Ricci, that I had very happy dealings with your father, and I grieved when I learned of his untimely death."

Choosing the music, indeed. He saw that had startled Ricci. As he'd expected. Even men skilled in hiding their reactions could be caught unawares. It was useful in an encounter like this to do that.

"You knew my father how?" the duke asked, brow furrowed.

"I assisted him on more than one occasion in getting quantities of alum out of Esperaña, when Seressini merchants were not welcome there."

"And Kindath ones were?"

Rafel shook his head. "Not in my lifetime, my lord. I traded under a different name. As a Jaddite. A number of Kindath and Asharites converted under duress, as you'll know."

"And some did so falsely."

"Indeed. Duress is an excuse accepted by clerics in your faith as well, for converting yet retaining one's own beliefs."

Ricci said, "You are right, of course. You traded with my father? He paid you for shipping alum?"

Rafel nodded. "As I said, my lord. He also permitted me to secretly bring a number of men and women of my faith out of Esperaña on those ships, as part of our contract. He was a good man, in my humble estimation. His murder distressed me."

"You brought these people, your friends, here?"

"Not friends. But people of my faith, yes. I did, lord. Many have remained here, in your Kindath quarter. Some will have moved on by now. People were being burned in Esperaña, my lord duke."

"What was your name there? In those dealings?"

"Not an important matter, my lord."

Folco d'Acorsi remained quiet, waiting.

"May I ask, however? My father might have told it to me."

It was in the nature of a plea, not any kind of demand. Fathers and sons. Dead fathers and living sons. Duke Ricci's father had been killed on a bridge by rivals here.

Rafel nodded. "I have been known as Ramon Comares at times," he said.

Duke Ricci of Seressa leaned back and smiled.

"Then I do know of you, and it is as you have said it was. My father commended you to me, under that name, as someone who could be trusted."

Rafel blinked. His turn to be surprised. "I am touched, my lord. And honoured. Kindath are not often so described, particularly Kindath merchants with ships, who have also been corsairs."

He was aware of Lenia looking at him. He hadn't needed to say that last thing, but it felt right. It wouldn't remain a secret. The Seressinis were going to begin investigating them the moment this meeting ended, and the information-gatherers here were what they were.

He looked back at her. He wondered what else she was thinking these days. He couldn't ask yet. Some things he might never be able to ask.

॰॰

She had been thinking, since they'd arrived the previous day and docked by the Arsenale, alongside the impressively cobblestoned walkway there, of how, as a girl, she'd always wanted to see Seressa.

Neither of her parents had ever been here, of course. Neither had travelled at all from their farm in the south. Farmers didn't go much beyond the nearest market town. Perhaps a son might go out into the world if he joined a mercenary company or became a cleric, if there were too many sons to share the farm. But there were always stories told of the great city-states, of powerful men and women, beautiful, richly dressed, bejewelled. She'd had images in her mind from very young: a city built on water! People travelling from house to house by boat! Bridges over canals, one after another after another. It had seemed magical, wondrous.

Childhood had been a sheltered place for her, she thought. It wasn't so for everyone, but for Lenia and her brother it mostly had been. Some real hardship at times, ongoing uncertainties and fears— too much rain before the harvest, plague reported too close, wolves in a harsh winter, disbanded soldiers roaming nearby, shortages of food or firewood, raiders on the coast (mostly just there, until the last ones). But she'd had parents who were decent, caring.

A gift, the adult Lenia Serrana had come to understand. Until it died.

Well, no: gifts were stolen or broken. People died. Dreams died.

Yet here she was now in Seressa, walking across those bridges, seeing the slender boats being poled along the canals. This had been her dream, hadn't it? And now, now that she was here? What was she to *do* with all that was happening to her?

They'd crossed Batiara eastward from Rhodias to the coast with Folco d'Acorsi and twenty men. They'd booked passage at Orchioli on that coastline, boarding a good-sized ship going north. Faster and safer, usually, than riding overland. There were pirates from Senjan on the other coast, but they had fighting men on board. D'Acorsi was unconcerned.

Lenia had been grateful to be back on a ship. Hadn't wanted to be on horseback going so far north. She really wasn't happy riding.

Her brother, if it was her brother, bred horses, Antenami Sardi had said.

That *couldn't* be her brother—she'd been thinking it since that night in Rhodias. A well-known breeder of horses? This man had raced them, too, Sardi had said, been celebrated for it! It was not a thing that made any sense to her. But . . . *His name is Carlo. Carlo Serrana, of course.*

Sardi had said that so lightly. Just words spoken, like any other words one might say. A casual query of her on his way to a banquet, curiosity, no more. Like commenting on the prospect of rain that day.

On the way to Seressa they'd docked at the coastal city of Remigio. There seemed to be a history there for d'Acorsi. An enemy. A dead one, now. He had been present when Teobaldo Monticola died, apparently. They'd been about to be on opposite sides of a war: Firenta besieging Bischio.

She and Rafel had not gone to the palace with d'Acorsi. They'd explored the market. Didn't buy anything to trade. It wasn't a time for that. It wasn't their ship. D'Acorsi had come back quiet and thoughtful.

She didn't care.

He could be as private as he liked. It didn't mean anything to her, this story of two mercenaries. She was leaving Batiara. She'd vowed it to herself, and told Rafel. She couldn't go back to the Majriti, of course. Ferrieres was possible. She did know Marsena a little by now. Esperaña? Possible. She didn't think so, however. She could go north. Astarden was a growing commercial centre: diamonds, furs, amber, other things. She had the money to set up as a merchant there, buy a warehouse and a home, find a partner—because it was challenging to do it alone, as a woman. She could go to Candaria. There was something appealing about living on an island, Lenia thought. Could she buy a vineyard there? An olive grove? Embrace that sort of life?

So many things to choose among. The choices that decide your life.

But first came the matter for which they were travelling to Seressa. The one that might allow her to kill Asharites again. She realized that she still wanted to do that. She wondered if she always would, and what that said about her. It wasn't really a virtuous thing, though some clerics would approve, she knew. She wondered if the god did.

The High Patriarch in Rhodias, Jad's principal agent on earth, had exulted to see the body of Ziyar ibn Tihon. He had almost *danced* in his joy. He'd sent word around the known world that the corsair had been killed.

He'd approve of killing Asharites. He already had. It was his message they were carrying.

It wasn't retaking Asharias. But it was a plan, an attack Folco d'Acorsi had proposed to him. It was something. Same for her, Lenia thought: it was *something*. To fill the emptiness, assuage a seemingly endless anger.

She tried to not dwell on that, to steer her thoughts to other channels. She seemed to be considering now, for example, if men or women were attractive. A new thing, entirely. She could blame Raina Vidal. She decided she would.

The acting duke of Seressa, for example, was a handsome man with eyes that had assessed her when she entered, and appeared to approve. His young adviser had a composed look. Proper for his role.

A pleasant face. She thought she saw sadness in his eyes. D'Acorsi had mentioned a recent loss. He hadn't named it.

In the meanwhile, in a handsome room over a canal, Folco d'Acorsi and the duke were discussing war. A conversation that mattered. For their world, and for her. Rafel had already said he would not participate except by way of paying for a ship for the campaign. Lenia had told d'Acorsi she would go with him, on that ship, if this attack happened.

This attack was on Tarouz. Where Zariq ibn Tihon ruled. And might not even know his brother was dead. He would, soon enough.

In Rhodias, in the Patriarchal Palace over dinner, d'Acorsi had apparently proposed taking and sacking it. Killing or capturing the surviving brother, ruler of that city in Gurçu's name.

She and Rafel had made it as clear as they could that Zariq would be planning a campaign of raids as soon as he did learn. Revenge for his brother was coming, and it would be fierce.

They couldn't stop his raiding. Zariq could have ships on the water by summer, or sooner. But if Rhodias made it evident that a great fleet was being prepared, was coming for him, he'd have to assign resources to Tarouz—walls and armaments, finding more fighting men—and be cautious. He might not, for example, be able to leave his city to command a ship.

In Seressa now, Folco d'Acorsi was speaking, in a chair opposite Duke Ricci. "In addition to the fleet the High Patriarch wants assembled for next spring, we intend to recruit land forces from the Majriti."

Duke Ricci raised an eyebrow. "You think Asharites will fight *for* us?"

"No. But they may fight for independence in the Majriti, against Zariq ibn Tihon, who serves Gurçu. Especially those from Abeneven. It is known, or soon will be, that the brothers killed the khalif there, seeking to take control. You have had word of this, I imagine? Keram al-Faradi is dead. Poisoned."

Seressa had not had word.

They'd travelled quickly. Outpaced the tidings. The duke was unhappy to have important information reach him this way. She watched him make a note. He asked questions. D'Acorsi answered, then Rafel did. Ricci wrote the answers down. She was proud of Rafel. He was speaking with precision. He tended to do that, but this was on a larger scale than any he'd have known.

"You really intend to invite Asharites to prepare an army for next spring?" It was the duke's adviser this time. His first words spoken to the matter at hand.

"The invitation has already been sent to Abeneven, Signore Cerra," d'Acorsi replied. "As a first inquiry."

He and this man knew each other. More history. She didn't care, Lenia reminded herself. She was *leaving*. But she wanted this attack to happen first, this siege, this war—and to be a part of it. If they bought and equipped a ship, she and Rafel, they couldn't really stop her.

"You have assumed this will happen, then?" The duke this time. "This fleet?"

"The High Patriarch's letter is before you, Ricci."

Just the name this time, no title. Subtle shifts in balance, in power in the room. D'Acorsi was the agent of Jad here, of his High Patriarch. Seressa, notoriously, preferred to stay out of conflicts with the Asharites, depending so much on trade with the east. They were going to have trouble avoiding this one.

Indeed, they might not want to. There were ripples here. The ibn Tihon brothers had indeed been the agents of Gurçu the Conqueror, his most powerful figures in the west, his naval commanders. When, that is, they weren't acting for themselves. Which was much of the time. And acting for themselves, they had punished Seressini merchants over and again.

Insurance rates had almost doubled in their day. Merchants were even choosing to travel overland again, the dangers there, which were real, being judged to be less in some seasons, along some routes, than trying to go east or west along the Middle Sea.

Seressa paid close attention to insurance. To all issues of commerce. Especially, Folco d'Acorsi had said in a conversation on the way here, since the Sardis in Firenta had begun taking the lead in offering maritime insurance, a lucrative thing, if the costs were carefully calculated.

The Sardis calculated carefully, it seemed.

D'Acorsi was headed for Firenta and Macera from here. This was his campaign. He'd been named commander, hired and paid by the Patriarch. His reward. It was to be a holy war. The Batiaran city-states, and Ferrieres, and Esperaña would be expected to build and send ships and men and contribute funds. Large sums. Money would be demanded from the northern countries, as well. Some might even be sent.

She wondered, idly, if Folco's fee would cover the purchase of the Diamond of the South. Likely so, and more. She realized it was the first time she'd thought of him by his name. That was unsettling, too.

This was not the great war to retake Sarantium, but it was a response by Jad to what had happened on the triple walls. It *would* be a blow to Gurçu if Tarouz fell. And, of course, there was the matter of sacking a wealthy city of unbelievers. Having a share in that pillaging. You couldn't raise an army without such a promise.

As if cued by her thought. The duke turned to Rafel. He said, "You were about to answer my earlier question, about how you might assist us. We moved to other matters, including your knowing my father, signore. If it is not impertinent of me, would you be good enough to finish that answer?"

If it is not impertinent. Sometimes a certain phrase, used a certain way, could reveal the gulf between people. Be the opposite of what it appeared to be.

Rafel smiled affably. "We did move elsewhere in conversation, yes. It is good of you to bring us back, my lord. My partner and I are here because we intend to arrange for the building of a ship to join this campaign."

"Really? You have assembled enough partners? Among . . . the Kindath? How interesting. Already? But this matter has just—"

"No partners," Rafel said, with the slightest emphasis. And interrupting. "We'll build it ourselves, and arrange for men to sail it, and will carry as many fighters as we can to Tarouz."

Of all men on earth, a duke of Seressa, acting or actual, would know what a ship built in their Arsenale cost. Rafel was making it as clear as could possibly be that he and she were well off. Extremely so.

"You would have a war galley built?" It was the younger man.

Rafel laughed aloud. "Hardly, Signore Cerra! We will earnestly hope our ship survives a successful attack on Tarouz, and is allotted its share of what emerges from taking the city. Then we will deploy it in our own trading ventures after, if fortune allows. This is an investment in future dealings, as well. You'll need carracks with cannon mounted. To carry large numbers of men, and then to carry back—with the blessing of the god and moons—the fruits of your efforts there."

Carracks were the largest, three-masted, merchant ships. He was reinforcing his point about money, Lenia knew. She was, in spite of her own state of mind, enjoying this almost as much as he would be. The Seressinis would not, of course, have any idea how they'd come into such funds.

A murder, a diamond, a book.

Duke Ricci cleared his throat. "I apologize, of course," he said. "I had not been properly informed as to the scale of your resources, Signore ben Natan. The commander of the Arsenale will be only too happy to discuss the building of such a ship. I will arrange to have your needs addressed by him personally, and immediately. Often there is a delay in such matters. We are always busy with shipbuilding here."

"Of course," Rafel said gravely. "I feared we might need to cross to Dubrava to ask there about building a ship. Knowing how many are the demands on Seressa's Arsenale, I feared it might be a difficulty. With those demands possibly to increase now."

The duke did not reply hastily; that would have been too revealing. He said, "Well, the demands, as you say, are many, but that will not matter once I send word to the commander."

"You will do that for us?"

Ricci shrugged dismissively.

"But does this mean you commit Seressa to the campaign, my lord?" Folco d'Acorsi asked, almost sweetly. Also beautifully done. Delicate words from a ravaged face. And a *my lord*, again, she noted.

More than one clever man in this room, Lenia thought. She believed she detected the hint of a smile, quickly suppressed, on the face of Guidanio Cerra, still standing by the desk.

Duke Ricci laughed aloud. Either real laughter, or he was good at simulating that. He shook his head. "Ah, my lord, you know our ways better than that! The Council of Twelve will take up the Patriarch's request expeditiously. But we can certainly go ahead with the commissioning of a merchant vessel. Dare I assume your two friends will want that regardless of what else happens?"

"Possibly we will," said Lenia. It felt like time to speak. She wanted to speak. It was not like her, but what she was *like* now was being sorted out, wasn't it? "It would be better to know that our proposed investment here was also serving the holy cause of Jad against the infidel, before it is turned to our own needs. That is our wish, is it not, Rafel?"

"Exactly so," her partner said.

"And so it should be," said Folco d'Acorsi briskly. "Incidentally, my lord duke, friend Cerra, you may possibly not know another thing. It was Lenia Serrana who discovered the plot to abduct a woman in Sorenica, enabling us to trap and kill Ziyar ibn Tihon. She is, if I may say so, of significance in many respects."

They couldn't have known that, she thought. Folco, for reasons she didn't grasp, still wanted her in his company.

Duke Ricci cleared his throat a second time. He made another note. He might be hating this, or he might be happy to be learning things that could matter. Or both.

He said, "Yes. Clearly so." He nodded to her again. "I trust we will be granted the company of all three of you at dinner this evening? To discuss this, and whatever other matters arise?"

Lenia didn't smile. It was an important invitation. They had, just this moment, been elevated in stature. In Rhodias, Folco had gone to dine at the palace, leaving them at his home. Here in Seressa . . .

But here in Seressa money spoke of power. And was allowed to dine with power, it seemed.

"We would be greatly honoured," she said, and held Duke Ricci's eyes for a moment. Not a thing she was used to doing, with anyone, let alone someone so far above her. You could learn this skill, too, she thought. It suddenly struck her that he was a man who appreciated women. Something to bear in mind. Another new thought in a changing life.

⤖

I don't remember a great deal from the period after my wife and new-born son died. My memory, I have often thought, is strange, uneven. Intense and painfully vivid for some times and people, mist-shrouded for many other intervals of my life. I don't know why that is. When I've tried, once or twice, to ask others about this, as to themselves, I've encountered odd glances and incomprehension.

I was grieving at that particular time, twenty years ago. The duke had offered to let me stay home, or to travel. He suggested I visit my old teacher in Avegna, whom I loved. A kindness on his part.

I'd chosen to stay, return to work. I'm not certain I know why. As I say, there isn't much that is clear about the days immediately after Julia and the baby died. I'd loved my wife, unexpectedly. She'd loved me, perhaps even more unexpectedly. It happens with arranged marriages. Not often, but it does.

Folco d'Acorsi and Caterina Ripoli were ultimately a love match, weren't they? And that marriage had been entirely about worldliness when it happened, joining military strength to power and wealth. My own first marriage, to Julia? Just Guidanio Cerra, a young aide to the acting duke of Seressa, marrying the daughter of friends of his parents. Duke Ricci hadn't arranged that marriage for me (he did make my second one, much later, a very different matter).

My mother appeared to grieve for the two deaths as much as I did. She threw herself entirely into caring for my daughter, who was only two years old then and didn't understand anything of what was happening, except that she couldn't see her mother. We hadn't brought her to the burials. It isn't customary.

So I really don't know why I recall the morning we met the Kindath merchant and the woman who was his business partner. I even remember much of what followed. I know we were startled— the duke and myself—to learn they had the resources to build a trading ship. That was not a common thing at all, and these two were, well, they were a Kindath and a woman.

I'd taken note of their names. Of course I had, it was my job, or part of it, to retain such details, then investigate, or assign men to do so. I was already at the stage of having others report to me that year.

But I did not, in any way at all, link her name to Bischio that first day.

If I'm honest, I tried to avoid thinking about Bischio for a long time. Some things had happened to me there, and on the way there, not so many years before. Seeing Folco that morning had brought that time back. How not? I could see in his eye, his one eye, that meeting me with Duke Ricci had done the same for him. To him. Maybe that's why I recall that morning.

We were bound, he and I, by moments and people from that earlier time.

That connection to Folco never amounted to a great deal through my life, but it was there whenever we did meet. A woman, a man, a horserace. And after.

Duke Ricci remained in the reception room after walking his guests to the door. Arrangements for the evening banquet were made. I escorted them to the top of the Stairway of Heroes, with the dreadful sculpted figures at the bottom.

We bowed and the two men started down. The woman, Lenia Serrana, hesitated, then turned to me.

"Forgive me, but I don't think I'll attend this banquet, signore. I am honoured to be invited, but would not be good company tonight. I can only hope the duke will not be offended."

"Offended? Of course not," I said. "Though his chef is wonderful."

She smiled briefly. I studied her face. I had gotten better at that, through my years with the duke, and travelling for Seressa. She said, "Wasted on me, if so. Will you convey my regrets?"

"I will," I said.

She turned to go. Turned back a second time. We were at the top of the stairs. Her partner and the lord of Acorsi were now waiting for her at the bottom.

"Why," she asked me, "is there so much sadness in you, Signore Cerra? If I may?"

LENIA HAD NO idea why she'd asked that.

She didn't know the man, might very well never see him again. But he was courteous, had a gentle face. And that sadness. *None of your business*, she told herself. But she'd asked.

He was startled, she saw it. Well, of course he was. She'd startled herself. If she was changing into someone new, was this sort of thing to be a part of it? What *was* this sort of thing?

He said, "I'm sorry. I . . . my wife died recently in childbirth. And the child."

Lenia blinked. She felt intrusive in the worst way. She said, "How terrible. But why are you here then, signore? You should be . . . I don't know. Not working, though!"

He smiled. A tall man, slender. A diplomat, not a fighting man, by his build and manner. "The duke said the same thing. I find my work helps. I remember others saying it was so for them in times of loss, and now I discover it to be true."

Lenia nodded. "I hope they find light with the god."

Most people said *I will pray*. She wasn't able to say that yet. It wouldn't be true. She didn't pray often. For a long time now. Her own soul, she thought, must be so much at risk.

He said, before she turned again, to go down the steps, "And you? Why the sadness in you?"

Lenia felt abruptly exposed. That was the problem with asking a question! It led others to think—and to be correct—that they could or even should ask questions of you.

She said, "It is so obvious?"

"Something is," said Guidanio Cerra. "I don't know what."

"I shouldn't be," Lenia said. "I should not be that way at all. Extremely good things have happened to us. To me."

She left it at that. This was a Seressini, after all. You were careful with them.

"I am happy to hear it," he said. "But even so . . ."

"EVEN SO," I SAID. And expected that would end it, that she'd go down the stairway, joining the two men waiting for her.

She didn't. She said, "I was abducted from my home by corsairs as a child. I was a slave in the Majriti for many years. I escaped, and joined Signore ben Natan. This is . . . I have not been back in Batiara since I was captured. It . . . what happens to us young can shape a life, signore."

It was surely because of Julia's death, the baby's death . . . I was feeling an ache, and it reached to this intense, dark-eyed woman just then.

I said, "Where was home?"

"Not far from Casiano. We had a farm."

"Have you gone back?"

She shook her head decisively. "I have had no time, but I won't. I . . . I was a slave, Signore Cerra. Do you know what that means? For a woman?"

I was silent, thinking. Trying to think. Eventually, I said, "I don't think anyone can truly know if they haven't experienced it. You have decided your family will reject you? Be ashamed of you? Instead of being proud of your strength and courage? Your escape. And your . . . and the good things you just said have happened."

"Proud," she said bitterly. She looked away and then back. "There's no one left on the farm, I'm sure. My father was killed. My mother and brother . . . I . . . well, this is not your sorrow. Yours is new, mine is very old. I do wish you well, signore."

And *that* is the moment I made a connection.

A brother, she'd said.

"I know of a man named Serrana," I said to her. "In Bischio. A man from the south who rode in their race for years and now breeds horses. Carlo Serrana is his name."

She looked at me with what seemed to be terror, her face suddenly white. Not a thing that really happens very often, just a phrase people use. But I saw it that day. I grew frightened for a moment, because of where she was standing, right at the top of the long staircase.

"Goodbye, signore," she said. "Please give my regrets to the duke for tonight."

She went much too quickly down the stairs. Almost fleeing, it felt. I think it was.

⟡

What happened that night in Seressa changed her life.

It felt so to Lenia at the time, even though many different moments change our lives, sometimes when nothing significant happens. Our lives are endlessly changing, it might be said. Indeed, the *absence* of the significant can matter. The person we don't meet, missing them by moments. The chapel we decide not to enter, when doing so and looking up, perhaps at a mosaic on the dome, might have shattered and then remade us. A truthful answer given, or withheld, which causes—or averts—catastrophe. A moment lingering in a corridor— or not doing so, going down stairs and away. The act of courage no one sees or knows but which takes root in the soul, a thing we know, ever after, we *can* do. The door at which one knocks after climbing stairs away from the wildness of a carnival at night, or doesn't . . . doesn't climb, doesn't knock.

We are not at the mercy of randomness, or fate, but both are present for us.

She told Rafel and d'Acorsi she didn't feel inclined to go to a formal dinner that night. Yes, it would be interesting. Yes, a new experience. But no, it was not one she wanted just then. She couldn't say exactly why, even to herself, only that she felt like someone clinging to wreckage in rough seas, hoping to sight land. Two people had now told her they knew a man named Carlo Serrana in Bischio. A man who had raced and now raised horses.

If three people told you something, the folk belief was, you needed to follow where it led, or you would anger the powers of the half-world, or the demons the god battled.

It was, she thought, the half-world that had reached out to her in Sorenica with a warning. What she had told that man today, Cerra, was true: she didn't have any illusions at all about being welcomed here. Not when her story became known, as it would. A woman who'd been a slave to an infidel. By day. By night. How did she dare show her face in Batiara after such shame? How could she even live on? People would think that. Some would say it.

A man escaping and returning was a hero, a valiant warrior of Jad. A woman was . . . something else.

She didn't bother to lie about being unwell or anything like that. She was a person, she told herself, who could now be *disinclined* to do something. She had that freedom. Money, if it did nothing else, could give a woman that. It might be a wrong decision but it was hers to make. She had already decided she was not staying in Batiara. Her choice there, too.

She'd help do what needed to be done as to building a ship, and would wait for it somewhere else until spring. Then come back and board it for the attack on Tarouz. If that happened. If not, she would make other decisions, but it wouldn't involve a life lived here.

She could, she really could think that way now. She could live anywhere she wanted. Once she knew what she wanted. Other than killing Asharites.

She wondered if she secretly hoped one of them might kill her, end this sorrow. She didn't find or feel death inside of her, though. She found anger.

Neither of the two men tried to change her mind about the dinner. Rafel could represent the two of them in whatever might happen back at the ducal palace.

He told her he was sending a message to Almassar on a ship headed for Esperaña. He'd gone back to the harbour, earlier, to arrange for that.

It would take time, there'd have to be another ship encountered at some point—one crossing to the Majriti. Not an easy or sure encounter. His message might never arrive. He was going to send another as soon as he could find a ship going to Marsena, where there was trade with the Asharites. That might be a likelier link to get word to Almassar.

He wanted his mother and father away from there. There was at least a chance Zariq ibn Tihon would learn that Rafel had played a role in Ziyar's death. And many people knew where Rafel ben Natan was from, and his parents could be found.

"It wasn't you," she'd said, in a sitting room in Seressa. "It was me following his man. You went to do our banking!"

"Ah. And I can trust to Zariq thinking that way?"

She'd shaken her head. He was right. They couldn't trust to that at all. Ziyar ibn Tihon's was a death that would lead to other deaths.

"What do we do with our ship?" she'd asked.

Rafel had changed for dinner. He looked courtly in black. It occurred to her, since his revelations about working with Duke Ricci's father years before *and* his links to Ellias Vidal, Raina's husband, that there were many things she didn't know about her partner.

People, she thought, were allowed their pasts, their mysteries. It was provoking though. Unreasonable of her, perhaps, but you weren't always reasonable in how you felt about things. Rafel would argue that you should try to be. He could be exasperating that way, she decided. She also decided it was all right.

He said, "I think it is best on the west coast for now, we'll have Elie harbour it at Padrino. We can bring it around and up here, but I'm not sure it is a good time to do that. For one thing, Ziyar's war galley is out there somewhere."

It was. It had not been found, though ships had gone looking for it from Sorenica and all along the western coast. It would be faster than any that were searching, better manned, very good cannon on board. And possibly bending like a bow towards the first stages of revenge.

Which was, of course, why Rafel was trying to get his family away from their home.

Folco came downstairs, also in black, gold accents on his sleeves.

He said, "We should go, ben Natan." He was wearing a sword. Rafel was not, of course. Kindath were not allowed swords. Properly, they were supposed to live only in a Kindath quarter, be inside it by nightfall, and wear blue and white. *For their own protection* was the way it was explained. Rafel was staying with the lord of Acorsi here, however. Exceptions were made and licence taken in Seressa all the time. It was a city of licence taken.

As if cued to her thought, Rafel said, "You'll stay inside tonight, Lenia? Please?"

"Where would I go?" she asked.

"He's right, though," said d'Acorsi. "Seressa has about ten thousand whores in years without plague, and men at night make that assumption of a woman abroad."

"I know," she said, though she hadn't known the number. It was, she thought, a large number.

The two men left, to dine with the duke of Seressa.

She waited a decent interval to be sure they were gone, then she put on her cloak and went out, nodding briskly at the steward by the door, not giving him a chance to say anything. Outside, she put up the hood and looked in both directions up and down the street. No one to be seen. Didn't mean no one was there.

She smelled salt—and tar. D'Acorsi's palazzo was towards the Arsenale, but not too near for the smells of shipbuilding to be present.

She was not in what anyone might call a normal state of mind, and she was disinclined by nature to accept instructions. Or live fearfully. She had done that for too long.

She didn't have a destination. Only a memory of how as a girl she'd heard tales of Seressa and wanted to see it. At night was one way to see a city. Not the wisest, but—Rafel's opinion notwithstanding—you couldn't always do what seemed wise.

Or, she couldn't. A small canal lay behind the house. She picked her way carefully along the laneway beside the palazzo, heard rats skittering, and sounds from the Arsenale, where they worked all night. She came out to d'Acorsi's small, private dock. A single lantern was at the end of it.

It wasn't especially late, but both moons had risen and the stars were out, Jad's sun under the world. Under land and water and the world he'd made, where mortal men and women lived out their days, short or long, free or unfree. Sheltered, or not so.

She walked to the end of the dock, stood by the lantern, in its glow, and hailed one of the long, narrow boats approaching. The boatman pushed over towards her with his pole.

"I'd like to just ride through the city for a time. Will you show me some of Seressa? Can we do that safely?"

"Signora, it is safe as long as you are in my boat. Less so if you leave."

"I understand. Do you love your city?"

"Every Seressini loves his city, and also knows why others might not, signora."

A philosophical man in a boat, she thought, and entered the craft.

"Would you like me to sing for you?"

"Thank you, no," she said, perhaps a little too quickly. "Just show me your city."

It wasn't really quiet on the water, too many boats, too many people, and some of the boatmen were indeed singing. But it was quiet enough, and mostly dark.

She felt she needed to think, make decisions, choices, but she didn't feel *ready* to do that. If the plans of Folco d'Acorsi and the Patriarch came to fruition, in about a year from now a fleet would make its way to war and she'd be with it, going to fight Asharites.

A year could pass swiftly or very slowly. You could die in that time. She might, she thought, stay with Folco. D'Acorsi. She seemed to be using both his names in her mind now. He was clearly prepared to make her an offer to join him. He'd impressed her a great deal. He had things to teach, Lenia thought. She wondered what his wife was like. He'd bought a wildly expensive diamond for her. But that could be an assertion of his power and wealth as much as anything else. The ability to possess such a treasure.

They were on a larger canal now, approaching the ducal palace, with the enormous square in front of it, but the man poling the boat turned before that, up another small canal to meet a different large one. They went along that towards a high-arched bridge. There were shops along it, lit with lamps, people doing business at night. Buying and selling. A crowd. *Seressa*, she thought, without really knowing what she meant.

They passed under the bridge, and he turned again, away from the lagoon and its pathway to the sea and the world.

Folco d'Acorsi was one path. So was going to Astarden, or Ferrieres. Or Esperaña, she thought. Rafel couldn't go there, not as Rafel ben Natan, and it was ferociously dangerous to try to be there as Ramon Comares, his Jaddite name. Too easy to be found out. Raina's husband had been burned alive.

He had no reason to take that risk.

Were they to remain partners? Did she want to still be a merchant at sea? Did she have *any* idea what she wanted?

Not really. She realized she was hungry, though. There was that.

She could go back to the palazzo and be given food and wine.

She didn't do that.

The man poling the watercraft didn't like the question she asked. He repeated that the city was not safe for a woman alone at night. She acknowledged this, and repeated the question.

He poled them east along the canal they were on, then north on another. It was an astonishing city, she thought. The child she'd been would have been wide-eyed, mouth agape with delight and awe. That child was so far away. Not just in years but in the marred life that lay between now and then. You didn't really control it, Lenia thought. You were smashed on rocks, splintered to fragments, or you might find a harbour out of the wind. And it wasn't just about how skilled you were at sea, or at living. Or how much you prayed. Life wasn't like that. Not as she understood it.

The man pulled his craft to a mooring post and she handed him coins, more money than necessary. He looked at what she'd given him and said he'd wait if she wanted. She thought about it and accepted. He seemed a kind man. She had no idea if he really was. How could you know?

The man who had bought her as a girl in the slave market of Almassar had been a kind man by almost any measure.

She followed the boatman's directions to the fifth doorway on the left. There was a lantern outside it. A mist had descended now, or risen, diffusing the light. On the way, an instinct, Lenia looked over her shoulder and saw another boat pull up to the next mooring pole. A man got out quickly as she watched, leaping to the pier before the boat stopped entirely. She couldn't see him clearly. The *quickly* was her alert.

She didn't look back again. She entered the tavern, the glow of it. It was warm, with two fireplaces and many people. Smell of food and smoke and sweat. Not a large room. Crowded but not oppressively so. Loud talk. Laughter. She found a small table towards the back, on the side away from the bar, sat where she could see the door. Watched for a few moments, but no one entered. If she had been followed and they'd seen her come here, they didn't need to also come in. Could wait for her to leave. It was cold and damp on the street. She wasn't about to feel sorry for them, but . . . why would someone be following her in Seressa with ill intent?

A tall man with disordered hair came and quickly told her the food on offer. She asked for a lamb pie and a glass of wine. There were only two other women in the room. Both clearly with clients of their services. *Ten thousand whores.* Hard to credit, but she wasn't going to dispute it. You disputed when you knew what you were talking about, or thought the other person didn't.

The wine came, and then the meat pie, which was hot, and tasted better than she'd expected. She supposed the men who poled the boats here would know where good food could be found. Her boatman was waiting for her, which was either kind, or showing a shrewd awareness she was likely to pay well again. Or both. People could do things for more than one reason.

She finished her wine too quickly, decided against another glass. There might be a man following her. She could drink back at d'Acorsi's palazzo.

Someone came over to her table, blocking the light.

"You shouldn't have to sit alone," he said. He was well-dressed, carried a sword with a jewelled hilt. Young. Not sober. The sons of the wealthy, she thought, could be a problem. Everywhere.

"My preference," she said, politely enough.

"Really? You'd have more company if you smiled more," he said. "You'd be pretty if you did."

"Thank you, but as I said, I am happy alone tonight."

"I can make you happier," the man said. "And you could make me happy. Isn't that a good thing?"

He moved to sit on the stool next to her.

"If you sit down," Lenia said, "I will slide a knife into your ribs."

He stopped, straightened, stared down at her. Not a big man, even younger than she'd first judged. Had a large ruby ring on his left hand. "What? Are you crazed, woman?"

"No, just alerting you. I value my privacy."

"And if I want company?"

A fool, or drunk, or both. People could be more than one thing.

"Then go and find it, signore. Paid or otherwise."

"You are reckless for a woman alone," he said. Which wasn't untrue.

"I am skilled with blades. Also, I am a guest in the palazzo of Folco Cino d'Acorsi, and attended a meeting in the palace with Duke Ricci this morning. Perhaps the recklessness might be yours if you continue to offend me?"

"Hah!" he barked. "If all that's halfway true why are you by yourself at night?"

Fair question. But he'd exhausted her patience. "Because I have things to think about. And I cannot do so with you standing there. Go."

She pushed her belt knife, drawn swiftly, about an inch into the front of his thigh. Close enough to his groin to make him aware of the fact.

He yelped.

"Bitch!" he swore.

"I am," Lenia said. "I am also exactly what I just said to you. Go now!"

The knife was still in his leg. As he shifted away, her hand moved with him, keeping it there. "I've killed people, signore," she said. She felt almost happy now. "And the duke will protect me if you die here. Believe it."

She thought it might even be true.

So, evidently, did he. He swore again and backed away. She let him, withdrew her blade. He strode across the room, still swearing.

Lenia returned her knife to its sheath and continued eating. She was calm. She could deal with this. He was at the bar, talking animatedly to another man, nodding back towards her. If the two of them went outside now they would be doing so to wait for her.

So many strangers wanting to greet her in the night. She met his glance. She smiled. He had said she should smile more, hadn't he?

He turned quickly away. His companion, also looking at her, did the same. The companion said something to the tall man behind the wooden counter. Another flask of wine was brought for them. They weren't leaving yet. They might follow her out, though.

She felt a thrumming in her blood. Not fear, anticipation. She had no actual desire to fight anyone here; the urge to kill was, for her, directed at those who had stolen her childhood and broken her life. But at the same time, she wasn't, it seemed, unwilling to deal with men who threatened her.

Could get you killed at night, though.

Especially, she realized, when she paid her reckoning and stepped outside, if the mist had turned to fog. She moved back the way she'd come along the street to find her boat, if—she suddenly thought—it was still there. The boatman hadn't owed her anything on a cold, damp night.

She listened as she went but sounds were muffled in the fog. No stars or moons now. A mixture of smells, not pleasant ones. A feel of mystery and danger in the dark. The first mystery being, still: *Why would anyone want to attack her here?*

And then: *Who was the man who got off the boat that had pulled up after hers, too quickly?*

Footsteps behind her. Two sets. She hadn't looked back to see if the man she'd stabbed had followed her out. A mistake? But the tavern doorway would have been swallowed in fog unless she'd waited right there.

Then: more footsteps, farther behind, moving fast. Running, in fact. Were there two pairs there, too? Hard to tell, but she thought so.

She quickened her pace. She refused to run, but she did pull out both knives. She was afraid now. If you didn't feel fear in circumstances that demanded it, you were a fool.

"Stop, you two!" she heard. One of the farther voices.

"You fucking plan to make us?" That was the man from her table. He *had* come out. As soon as she'd left.

"I do," said the other voice.

"And I." A new voice.

"What? Who in Jad's name are *you*?"

And that, unexpectedly, was not the man from inside, it was the one who'd just ordered those chasing her to stop. He didn't know the newest man?

"Doesn't matter," that new voice said. "These two do."

"I'll decide what matters. Who are you?"

"Fuck you both!" said the man she'd stabbed in the tavern.

She was at the pier now. The boat was there.

"*Get in!*" the boatman said urgently. He had stayed.

"Not yet," she replied. She turned, knives ready.

"Amaldi," came a new voice. "I'm not fighting in fog. Not for this. Gentlemen, we are leaving. Make way and we'll go back the way we came."

The friend from the bar counter, had to be.

"Go on then. I'm making way. Can't speak for this bastard who won't name himself."

"This bastard has also made room for you. Watch how you go. Drink some more, buy a woman. I have my sword out and I see quite well, even in fog. Leave the woman to me."

To me?

A silence. Then, "Amaldi, come on! We're going. I mean it. Or fight and die here alone."

"Fuck you, Bustino!" the one called Amaldi said. "Fuck you with a sword!"

But a moment later she heard their footsteps going back, receding. She couldn't see any of them, though, in the fog.

"Now!" said the boatman. "Signora, quickly, we must leave! We don't know who these other two are!"

"We don't," she agreed. "But I intend to." She raised her voice. "I will fight either of you if you come much closer. Drunken fools in a tavern didn't disturb me. Two armed men who followed might do that. I have knives, I can see you both, and I know how to throw them. I will do so, right now."

She was lying about seeing them.

They are not enemies. They are guarding you!

Her heart thudded, thumped, then felt as if it would overwhelm her with its racing.

It was the voice from Sorenica, from the market. In her head again.

"Did you hear that?" she demanded of the man in the boat.

"Hear what?" he said. As she'd known he would.

Who are you? she demanded within, to this voice of the half-world. *Why are you here?*

I do not know! came the reply, a woman's voice. *But they are not there to harm you!*

How do you know? Are you alive?

No answer.

And where . . . where are you?

One beat. Another. Again, no answer.

But on a pier in Seressa in night fog, Lenia heard, "My lady, I don't know the one near me, but I am the lord of Acorsi's man, Gian. You know me from the ship."

She did. Hard, taciturn, trusted. "*He* sent you after me?"

"Yes, my lady."

"He knew I'd go out?" It was suddenly unsettling.

"He thought you might."

"Then who is beside you? Say your name!"

"Yes," Gian snapped. "My sword is still drawn!"

"So is mine," said the other man, calmly, "and I was a captain of the civic guard here for years, so I know how to use it."

"And now you are . . . ?" Gian said.

"Now I serve Signore Guidanio Cerra, and he sent me to watch the lord of Acorsi's house and defend Signora Serrana should she venture out of doors tonight. My name is Brunetto Duso, and I mean her no harm. Or you."

"You couldn't harm me," said Gian.

"I believe I could," Brunetto Duso said quietly.

"Indeed? Then shall we—"

"In Jad's name, stop it!" Lenia exclaimed.

At which point, though it was not in her nature now, had not been since childhood—although she did remember being different as a girl in this, her mother had called her silly and mischievous—she began to laugh, helplessly.

She listened for laughter from the half-world, from this other woman, living or dead, but there was none. No sound within. That voice was gone for tonight. She knew it. Somehow she knew. Her laughter, she thought, had an element of desperation in it.

How not? Really, how not?

CHAPTER IX

Lenia was angry, Rafel saw. It was rarely difficult for him to know when this was so, but it was . . . well, it was obvious tonight. Her face was rigid with barely controlled fury.

She had waited in the sitting room for him and d'Acorsi. She had a glass of wine, was in a chair (sitting extremely straight, one might even say rigidly) by the fire, which had been built up for her.

It was a damp, fog-shrouded night. He walked over to warm himself.

"Don't come near me," she said. "I might hurt you."

A clever man could extract a clue from that. He was, however, angry himself.

"You did go out! You said you would not."

"And I owe you—or *you*, Folco d'Acorsi—an accounting of what I do?"

"You might owe friends a disinclination to lie to them."

Folco said it mildly, but bluntly. Rafel approved. He liked this man.

"There were weapons drawn in fog," d'Acorsi added. "Never a good thing."

He was a lord of a city, Rafel reminded himself; they were . . . what they were. He hoped Lenia remembered that.

She glared at them both. There was something else in her face. Rafel was tempted to say fear. According to Gian, he and someone else, another man sent to guard her (that needed sorting out), had chased two attackers away. Not serious men, he'd said. Drunken youngsters, sons of powerful fathers.

Drunken men could assault and kill you, though. Perhaps frighten even a woman such as Lenia?

He didn't think that was it. But something had disturbed her. He knew her well by now. As to some things, at any rate. He still didn't have a sense of why she felt so urgent a need to leave Batiara. He thought he *could* understand it if she talked to him. She had shown no inclination to do so.

And was not likely to do so tonight, he judged. About anything except *their* transgressions, his and d'Acorsi's. He wondered if Folco d'Acorsi was accustomed to a woman being so forceful with him, then remembered how many stories there were about his wife. Caterina Ripoli was not said to be placid, or passive.

There came a knocking at the door of the palazzo. He and d'Acorsi looked at each other. It was late. Not a time for visitors. No one, not even a mercenary commander, liked unexpected arrivals at night. They waited. The steward came to the double doors of the room.

"Signore Cerra, my lord. Requests a word."

"And I want a word with him!" Lenia snapped before Folco could reply. "Let him in. Please." The last word an afterthought. She really was furious, Rafel saw. Spots of colour in her cheeks now.

"I would never turn the duke's adviser away," d'Acorsi said. He seemed slightly amused. Not wise, necessarily. He didn't know Lenia very well.

The steward went back to the door, returned to announce and admit Guidanio Cerra, still in his dinner clothing.

"Thank you, my lord," Cerra said. "I will not trouble any of you for long. I need to get home to my daughter."

"You stopped here before doing that?" d'Acorsi asked. Not amused now. Paying attention.

"I did, yes. To explain and apologize."

"To me?" D'Acorsi raised his eyebrows.

"No, my lord. To Signora Serrana. I greatly presumed when she said she would not dine with us. I . . . it seemed she was . . . I thought she might decide to go out at night and we know that can be unwise."

"Unwise!" Lenia said coldly, and it was unclear whether she was echoing his last word or commenting on what he'd said.

Guidanio Cerra bowed to her. "I am here to apologize. It was an instinct. But meant kindly. After our conversation."

What conversation? Rafel had seen them talking at the top of the staircase. Had thought it innocuous.

"You decided I needed to be protected?" Lenia was now glaring at the duke's adviser.

Cerra hesitated. Looked at the other two men, then said, "Many of us do need that, at some moments. I know I have."

There was a silence.

Folco d'Acorsi cleared his throat. "If it matters, signora, I have great respect for Signore Cerra, from dealings some years ago when he was still quite young."

Lenia opened her mouth; Rafel could almost *hear* the acid words she was readying. She drew a breath. And when she spoke it was only to say, "I am, perhaps, being unkind to people who were concerned for my well-being. It is not a thing I am accustomed to."

Rafel took a chance.

"That," he said, "wounds me deeply."

She looked at him, and he watched her face change, finally, as she yielded to amusement. He gave silent thanks to the two moons. He realized that not only did he not want her angry with him, he did not want her sorrowing.

"It was still a presumption on my part," said Cerra. "But I am pleased to be forgiven. If I am. My reasons were honourable, yes. Also . . ." He hesitated.

Rafel looked at him, suddenly apprehensive.

"Also?" said Lenia quietly.

Guidanio Cerra looked down, then back at her. "I took another liberty."

"Are you the sort of man who does that?" she asked, voice cold again.

"No," he said. "Normally not."

"But you did so with me?"

"*For* you, was my thought, signora."

"For me. With what possible licence, signore?"

Rafel discovered he was breathing shallowly again.

"I cannot truly say," Cerra replied. "I am not entirely myself just now, perhaps. My own life."

"Which ought to have left you entirely indifferent to someone you'd spoken to for a few moments this morning."

He smiled briefly. "It ought to have."

"Tell us, then, and go home to your daughter, man," said Folco.

Cerra was looking at Lenia, as if waiting for permission. After a moment she nodded her head.

Rafel still found breathing to be curiously difficult. He couldn't say why. The night, the fog. So many changes at such speed. But he was a man of reason and calculation, he reminded himself, not given to premonitions.

Guidanio Cerra said, "I asked people who might know, this afternoon. About . . . about the person with your name in Bischio."

Oh fuck, thought Rafel ben Natan.

SHE WASN'T CERTAIN why she'd nodded at Cerra to go ahead and speak. Maybe weariness? But she wasn't, curiously, unhappy about the fact that d'Acorsi was in the room to hear what was said. He wasn't the concern for her.

She still didn't think, however, that any of the men here—any men, perhaps—would entirely understand. Or even mostly understand.

Guidanio Cerra added, "His story is mysterious, but three people who go to their race every year told me he was the best rider for years, from when he was very young. Won many times. Became celebrated. And . . . and he's from down south, signora. That much is widely known."

"What is widely known can be wrong," she said.

Cerra nodded his head. "I know this, signora."

Folco d'Acorsi was listening intently. He said to Cerra, "Wait. This is the Serrana we both saw . . . the man we watched some years ago?"

Cerra nodded. "He stopped racing after that, it seems," he said. "Still a young man. He breeds and trains horses now."

Antenami Sardi had told her that, in Rhodias.

"I didn't know he'd stopped riding," said d'Acorsi. "I haven't been back."

"Nor I."

Lenia wondered why the man had stopped riding, but that wasn't the question, was it? It wasn't even close to the question, was it?

Her weariness became suddenly very real. It was late, and had been a difficult day in too many different ways.

She said, "Thank you, Signore Cerra. I do believe you mean me only well. I am grateful. Go to your daughter. It was good of you to stop by."

"I am forgiven?"

She managed a smile. "Yes."

"For both things?"

"It matters so much to you?"

"It does," he said.

"Then yes, both things."

He bowed and went out. A man who'd suffered terrible losses two weeks ago. Who had come here nonetheless to tell her something he thought she might want to know. A kindness. There could be kindness in the world, she reminded herself.

The steward took him to the door; they heard it open and close again.

"I am going to sleep," she said. "The dinner went well?"

"Well enough," Rafel said. "Nothing is easy in our world. I'll tell you in the morning."

Was anything easy in any world? Was there a better world? She had a faint memory of her mother telling stories of one.

She went upstairs. Hers was a large room with a brazier and another soft bed. She could grow accustomed to these beds and pillows, Lenia thought. Not necessarily a good thing.

She had too many thoughts chasing each other in an overtired mind. He was from the south. A young man, still. Carlo Serrana. Not a very common name, but not *so* uncommon, was it? Was it?

Just before exhaustion claimed her, and sleep, a thought arrived, and a question.

You are in Bischio, aren't you? she asked of the voice she'd been hearing in her mind. Expected no reply, of course. And so, of course . . .

I am. Come and see me?

Third time. There it was. Third pull that way. To Bischio. Three of those meant fate taking a hand, spinning fortune's wheel, leaning on the scales, choosing a path, guiding you—for good or ill. Three times meant power. The old belief.

She didn't want to go. She didn't want to go. She didn't want to go.

At some point she fell asleep. No dreams, a blessing.

∽

As night deepened over the sea and along the coast just north of Sorenica, bringing wind and the threat of rain, Ayaash ibn Farai brought his small boat back to the strand.

There was no point trying to remain out on the water in the hope of a series of miracles: that the galley, moving without lights, would return in the dark, that he would somehow see it, that they'd be close enough for him to hail.

It had grown increasingly choppy in the bay. Harder to stay out there against wind and waves. His arms ached with the effort. He'd have achieved nothing in life if he died here, he thought. He couldn't swim. Few mariners could. It was seen as bad luck to be able to, among the Asharites. If you could survive in the sea, you became a candidate for fate sending you there.

There were rocks towards the shore, but he didn't strike any on the way back in, by the grace of Ashar and the stars. Those stars were hidden now above clouds that probably meant rain. Ayaash dragged the boat up on the stones as best he could. Not easy: one hungry, thirsty, frightened, weary youngster, and a boat meant to carry eight or ten.

It made a loud scraping noise, but there was no one around now. No one would be here at night. Animals might be. He could be killed by wolves as easily as by waves or rocks. His life would come to a solitary, unknown end. No burial, no rites. No one to weep for him, or even know.

It did begin to rain. Ayaash cried a little for himself, huddled under a tree at the edge of the woods. The spring leaves dropped water on him. He didn't dare go farther in. Wolves, and whatever else there might be in a forest here. Bears. Wild boars. It was cold, and too wet to make a fire. He couldn't even see to look for firewood, anyhow.

He cursed the Jaddites who had done this to him by killing Ziyar and the others in Sorenica. How had that even happened? Ziyar was a terror of the world. A great man. He was invincible, they all knew that! So how did it come to be that Ayaash ibn Farai found himself alone on a rainy night by a strand in Batiara with no galley out there to carry him home to his father?

He didn't curse his father. His mind did not allow for that possibility.

The rain stopped. It hadn't rained long. The clouds moved east and stars came out from behind them. The white moon was up. Some light. A little light. He prayed. He waited for dawn. He even slept a little, against the trunk of his tree. There might be snakes, but he couldn't worry about *everything*, could he?

Morning finally came, a cold greyness.

Ayaash stood and stretched. He was wet and chilled, thirsty and very hungry. He went in search of water under the dripping leaves. The first good thing was that he found a pond, not so far into the woods. He watched it for a while before approaching, which he knew was the correct thing to do, then he went forward and dropped on his belly and drank. He filled his leather flask, then urinated into the bushes. He said the morning prayers, honouring the stars that were always in the sky, even when daylight hid them.

He still didn't know what to do.

He walked back to the edge of the sea, looking, always looking, for the galley's return. By the grace of Ashar he found some small tidal pools and there were shellfish in them, crabs, and small, quick fish. Enough to eat. He broke open the crabs and sucked the meat. He swallowed the tiny fish whole. He drank from his flask. He sat down and watched, though listening for sounds behind him. It was still possible the Jaddites might come here, looking for Ziyar's galley. He watched the sea, he listened.

He remembered, suddenly, that he had a horse!

He was a fool. The son of a great father, but a fool.

He went to find it. The horse was hungry too, and wet. Ayaash didn't know what to do about those things. He untethered it from the tree where he'd left it, and led it to the pond, and it lowered its head to drink.

He stayed in that place all day. Looking out to sea. He had never thought before how empty the sea could seem, hour after hour, the sun slowly climbing, slowly starting to go down. He didn't take the boat out again. If the galley came, surely it would anchor here. He'd have time to see it and be seen coming out. He would wave at them.

He heard sounds behind him again. Woodcutters, he decided. Distant, far side of the woods, it seemed. He felt curiously passive. If someone came through or around the trees for some reason, and saw him . . . well, then they did that. He'd be captured, he would die. But by mid-afternoon the cove and grove were silent again save for seabirds and the sea.

The passage of time can impose a decision upon us, even when we are afraid to make one, or agonizingly undecided. Ayaash came to realize he couldn't spend another night in the wood by this stony strand. If the galley wasn't here by now, he thought, it had gone. Somehow, for some reason, even if he would never know why.

He never did know why. But he did leave that place late in the afternoon after eating more of the shellfish and small fish and filling his flask again. He let the horse drink and he rode east. He came after a short while to a grassy meadow with small yellow-headed weeds growing in it, and he dismounted and let the horse graze there. He wondered if he should name it, but he didn't do that.

He offered the sundown prayers a little early, then mounted up again.

He knew it was dangerous to go anywhere near Sorenica, where an Asharite raid had happened, where by now a dead boy (man!) would surely have been found in a copse nearby, and the horses meant for the raiding party.

He did have a thought, a direction, and it didn't feel like a terrible idea, though probably it was, since he knew almost nothing about Batiara. He had no business being here, and he was young and alone.

THE GALLEY OF Ziyar ibn Tihon, recently deceased in Sorenica, came back into the bay towards sundown that day.

Had Ayaash waited just a little longer he'd have seen it coming, backlit by the sun. He could have waved from the strand, rowed out to tell them what had happened, been taken aboard and away.

He wasn't there. They saw no one, looking towards the land. They knew they were terribly late, two full days. Wind and weather, then Jaddite galleys patrolling after the squall passed. Normally they'd not fear them—they were a large war galley with significant firepower and superbly trained fighters still on board. But the idea was to get to the bay near Sorenica unseen, to pick up three small boats carrying their best men, and Ziyar. And the woman he'd come here to take.

If they brought Batiaran galleys to the bay, chasing them, there would be real difficulties in getting their fighters back on board, rowing small craft through waves into cannon fire. And Ziyar would be in one of those boats. Not good.

They'd stayed hidden in a cove, moved out only at night, but not far and not easily, a west wind pushing them towards rocks along a coastline they didn't know well.

No one was happy on the galley that rainy night. Part of what caused this was terror as to what Ziyar would say—and do—when they did pick him up. He had made it clear he might be pursued or tracked, that they'd need to get away swiftly. They hadn't been where they were supposed to be, and Ziyar was not a predictable man, except as to rage.

They came into the bay, finally, alone. They anchored offshore at day's end. No one to be seen, though the three boats could be spotted if you knew they were there. Six men rowed ashore. Came back. No one there, they said, but one of the boats had been taken back out recently. It was only partly pulled up on the stones. They had no idea why that was so. It was unsettling. One more thing that was.

The galley stayed through the night. The mariners nervous, the fighting men even more so. Ziyar was not a *reliable* leader. Not a safe man. Wildly successful, but that was partly because he was terrifying. It was a bad night. In the morning, still nothing on shore.

Then they spotted Jaddite ships again, north of them. Three of those, one a war galley this time. They could not stay in the bay. They'd be trapped downwind and would die. Heads on pikes in a Jaddite land.

They left. Didn't even claim their boats from the strand. Raised anchors and rowed, double time, to get out to where they could catch the breeze. They fled south. They weren't caught. They passed Sorenica on the way, keeping well offshore. It was a bright, clear day. They could see activity in the harbour, no signs of distress. A merchant ship was coming in, the sort they'd devour in a different time and place.

They carried on down that coast, without their commander and his best men. Not good. Not a good thing in any possible way.

There were discussions towards evening. They had no idea what had happened to the shore party. They had been late to the bay, Ziyar hadn't been there, with no sign he ever had been, other than the one wet-keeled boat. No explanations were available to them. Not at sea.

They decided it would be unsafe to return to Tarouz.

If Ziyar had somehow been captured he was certainly dead. If he wasn't, *they* were, every one of them, when they got home. Because they'd have left him behind. You didn't survive that.

That galley, *Night's Fire*, continued south but then went east around the bottom of Batiara and kept going that way. Not home. They made quick landings and raids for food and water. Galleys always needed to do that. They couldn't go more than two or three days without. They continued east, afraid.

They didn't go as far as Asharias. Ziyar and his brother were Gurçu the Conqueror's khalifs in Tarouz. Asharias held terrible risks for them because of that.

The Middle Sea—the whole world, really—held terrible risks for them.

They ended up making a base, one corsair galley among others, in the sea around Candaria, using the smaller islands. They painted over the galley's name before they got there—normally bad luck, but they had no choice. They changed the sails to the darker ones they carried, threw the distinctive figurehead at the prow overboard. They got rid of the ibn Tihons' flag. Threw that in the water, too. They didn't fly a flag for a time.

They survived for several years as pirates. Some left, most stayed. The men at the oars died, as galley slaves did. They were replaced. A reason you raided. Eventually, the galley that had once been called *Night's Fire* was rammed and sunk in a battle with Jaddite ships. They'd been drunken and careless, gotten themselves trapped on the shoreward side of a fight, with the wind wrong.

There were many ways for men at sea to die.

IT WAS EXTREMELY likely that if Ayaash ibn Farai had been in the bay when they'd finally come in, back in that terrible time near Sorenica, and had rowed out to tell them that Ziyar had been taken and killed, they'd have done the same thing—fled east.

Zariq, the older brother, was not as dangerously mad as Ziyar, but he was unlikely to forgive a crew and fighters who came safely home while his brother was spitted on a rampart in Rhodias. (They learned about that, eventually, everyone did.)

The boy, likeable though he was, was too much tied to his father, who was the ibn Tihons' most trusted man, and terrifying in himself. The crew and soldiers would almost certainly have thrown young Ayaash overboard when they made the decision to head east. Not happily, but you did what you had to do, as best you could judge, in a world largely without gentleness.

~

Ashar and his stars could be kind to the virtuous. Nisim ibn Zukar, once vizier, now acting as khalif in Abeneven, found himself thinking this as the winds of spring shifted towards summer's heat and storms and the caravans continued to come up from the south to find the city and the sea. And he continued to remain alive, and in power.

The murder of one khalif, the emergence of another in the city, even if he hadn't yet claimed the status . . . why would that matter to merchants bringing goods from beyond the mountains, or those faring on ships from the harbour here, carrying those same goods across the water, bringing other goods back to trade?

If he could hold the army to him and keep the walls defended, the merchants who used Abeneven for their own purposes would have no trouble with his succession.

If, of course, he didn't do anything foolish with tariffs and duties.

Ibn Zukar did not intend to do anything foolish. For one thing, he'd been overseeing the taxation of both merchants and citizens for some time; he knew this process better than anyone.

He really *was*, he told himself, the best man to succeed an unfortunately slain young khalif.

Having his likeliest rivals dispatched on the day Keram al-Faradi was murdered had been a brilliant stroke, done at speed in a challenging time. *Someone* had to sit on a throne when it was vacated, to keep order in an important city. Too many people depended on it.

Why should it not be the lamented khalif's calm, trusted vizier?

He hadn't been especially calm that first week. Who would have been? For one thing, he had been the one who'd invited the killer into the palace. Innocently, but innocence hardly signified. Not in the matter of an assassination. He'd done (he thought) a good job of hiding his bone-deep fear of dying.

The more he'd thought about it, the more it seemed likely that the ibn Tihon brothers had plotted the khalif's death. Hired the man who'd killed him. Which meant that Zariq and Ziyar planned to move on Abeneven.

He'd have done that himself. And they had the real khalif—Gurçu in Asharias—supporting them.

Perhaps. Perhaps not?

Might the great man, the Conqueror, possibly be persuaded the brothers were too ambitious, too much about themselves to be his best servants here in the west? Ruling two cities? Was that wise? Wouldn't an ongoing balance of power, a *distribution* of it here in the Majriti, serve the grand khalif's purposes better?

Ibn Zukar had set about selecting gifts. He chose an emissary and he wrote a letter.

As to one of the gifts, he was in difficulty. There were two great beauties in the palace harem of Abeneven. Keram al-Faradi had not had much to do with any of the women, of course. Nisim was of a different nature. The vizier had been permitted at times to see the khalif's women making music or dancing after a dinner. One of them, in particular, he had instantly desired. She had visited his dreams, uninhibited, unclothed. A flame in his nights.

He acted upon this desire, those dreams, in the days following al-Faradi's death. Despite his great fears in that time, his pleasure taken with her had also been great. Hers, as well, or else she was skilled at simulating this. She was from Esperaña, taken in a raid, offered by the corsairs as a gift to Abeneven's khalif.

He was therefore inclined to send the other beauty to Gurçu. His thoughts as always—he was that sort of man—turned to danger, however, possibilities of it. Imagine if someone were to say to the great lord of Asharias that the new man in Abeneven, ibn Zukar, had sent to the exalted one only the *second* most comely woman of the harem. The insult in that!

Someone might say this! It was very possible. It was . . . it was almost certain!

But . . . surely this was not so. Surely this was nothing but fear speaking in his restless mind. And if ill-wishers wanted to malign him to Gurçu they would find ways to do so, whatever he did in the matter of gifts.

He made himself be bold. He sent the other woman, and a pretty boy who had a pleasing voice. He sent gold and diamonds, and a desert lion from the palace menagerie. A lion was a good gift if it survived the journey. He kept the black-haired woman from Esperaña for himself. What, truly, was the point of aspiring to power, achieving it, if you denied yourself the delights that came therewith? She really did seem to derive much pleasure from their nights together.

As it happened, he'd made a mistake. We do that.

Sometimes our errors can be seen as such to someone with a clear eye at the time. In other cases, decisions turn out to be flawed, with nothing to warn us. Looking back, we can see the moment when a path led towards ruin, but we could not have done so when we took that road.

This mistake was of the second sort.

In the meantime, later in the summer, well before the future came upon Nisim ibn Zukar in his bedroom at night, with a man's curved knife and a woman's cold laughter, there arrived a letter on a merchant ship from Ferrieres, delivered up the hill to the palace by the ship's captain himself.

It had been entrusted to his hand, he said, to be presented only to the vizier of Abeneven. Ibn Zukar was still not calling himself khalif. He didn't know if the lion had reached Asharias. Or the woman and the boy and the gold and the diamonds.

They did know by then that Ziyar ibn Tihon was dead and that his war galley had vanished. An absurd death, a foolish, reckless one—in Sorenica, on the coast of Batiara. Pursuing a Kindath woman! Ibn Zukar told the story to his favoured concubine, the black-haired one from Esperaña. She spoke softly—he loved her voice, the sibilance in her Asharic—and agreed. No woman was worth that, she said. And smiled at him. He loved her smile.

The letter, however. The letter. It was from Folco Cino d'Acorsi, the mercenary, writing as commander of the High Patriarch's forces, inviting him to join them in something. Something that might end any threat Zariq ibn Tihon posed to Abeneven, he wrote. The letter mentioned that d'Acorsi knew for a certainty that ibn Tihon had had the late khalif assassinated, and it presented details. He suggested that these details might not please Khalif Gurçu, if he were to be informed of them.

Zariq was not, Folco d'Acorsi wrote, likely to hesitate in following up on his ambitions in Abeneven, despite—or even because of—what had since happened to his brother. If Vizier Nisim had thoughts on any of these matters at all, the ship's captain who had brought this letter was prepared to carry a reply back north.

There were a number of specific proposals included. Interesting ones. Dangerous, but also perhaps promising an end, as suggested, to other dangers. It needed thought. Balancing. Nisim prided himself on being good at that.

You navigated your life, he thought, like a ship between rocks, in night and a storm.

It was a hot, dry day. The wind was from the south, carrying sand. A bitter wind. Summer in Abeneven. Being by the sea helped, but there could be a white, blinding heat in the middle of the days, and a gritty taste in the mouth.

The bells for midday prayer began to sound from everywhere, including the palace tower. That tower overlooked the courtyard of the harem from high above. By tradition, the man who had the honour of ringing the palace bells was blinded, that a commoner might not look down upon the women of the khalif.

Once, long ago, this blinding had not been done and . . . well, there was a story.

There were, ibn Zukar thought, always stories.

∽

There was a man—a Trakesian metalsmith recently recruited to Seressa for a considerable sum, a small palazzo, and servants—who had devised a new way of casting bronze cannon for ships that made them lighter and less prone to explosions. Exploding cannon were, Rafel was informed by his companion, in a dry tone, regarded as bad, generally.

That companion, late afternoon, sun going down, was a high-ranking official here at the shipyard. A letter hand-delivered from Duke Ricci that morning had ensured it.

This summoned official understood, as of yet, only that this Kindath merchant, Rafel ben Natan, intended to have a large merchant vessel built for himself and a partner (not with them on this visit). That got you attention in Seressa. Today, it had gotten a tour from the deputy commander of the Arsenale.

The man might be Kindath, the official thought, but he evidently had the duke's support, and was preparing to pay for a significant ship with his own resources. Which were therefore considerable. And might possibly extend to a second vessel, in time, if he were pleased. Clients of any shipyard who could do that were coveted. There was a rival shipyard in Dubrava. A good one. No real way of denying that. People could easily build their vessels there instead. The Kindath merchant had even asked, casually, if Dubrava had the ability to supply these newer cannon yet. The deputy commander hastened to say it was not so, but he wasn't certain. Such things were hard to keep secret for long. Men went back and forth in the world, they carried information, filled their purses sharing it.

Dubrava was becoming more of a nuisance all the time.

In the event, Rafel ben Natan proved a very good negotiator as to price and the Arsenale's commitment to a delivery date. And he blandly mentioned, before leaving to let them draw up proposals for the ship, that, of course, all stages in the construction would be monitored from the ducal palace, because this carrack would be employed initially in an activity on behalf of Seressa and the High Patriarch.

A copy of the proposed plans should be sent, he said, directly to Duke Ricci's attention.

The merchant only smiled when queried about what this *activity* might be.

But the message was extremely clear: no skimping or stinting as to materials or details. Whatever else was going on, this Kindath was obviously protected: he had the highest-ranking patron one could have in Seressa.

After escorting his visitor to the tall iron gates of the Arsenale, bidding him a courteous farewell, even bowing to a Kindath, the deputy commander of the Arsenale was left with many questions. He intended to get answers. Information was what Seressa traded in, as much as anything else. Worth gold. Worth more than gold, on occasion. Worth access to power, worth power. Worth someone's life, at times. That had happened, in the deputy commander's experience.

IT WAS A MATTER of low street comedy, Rafel ben Natan thought bitterly, a work performed among acrobats and fire-eaters. Travelling players in patched costumes acting on boards laid down over mud and dung in a village, or claiming a corner of a town square on an afternoon when it did not rain. But really, *really*? A man coming at him with a sword, steps outside the Arsenale? Who in Seressa could possibly want him dead?

He even had escorts. One of Folco d'Acorsi's men and one of Guidanio Cerra's had taken him here and remained waiting by the gates to take him back. They were walking alongside the lagoon, a very wide path. The noises and smells of a ferociously thriving city, crowds at day's end. Folco's man close, Cerra's farther back.

Crowds made for problems, sometimes.

The assassin was in front of Rafel, sword out, before his nearer guard could react. None of them had expected there to be anything to react to. The men with him were meant largely to confer dignity and stature.

He saw the blade. He didn't recognize the man wielding it. It was such an absurd way to die. Stupidly, *randomly*, in a time when life had changed in ways that were almost entirely good, creating choices, offering promise. Presenting hope.

He heard d'Acorsi's man shout. He twisted away from the levelled sword. Bumped into someone who stumbled away. He saw light glint from the blade. So *stupid*, he thought again. Life, the world, dying like this.

But . . .

"We are not here to hurt you," the man with the sword said. "Not at all. I'd be grateful if you came quietly with us."

"Why the weapon, then?" Rafel snapped.

"Well—"

"*No!*" said d'Acorsi's man, stepping forward, his own blade out. "That is not happening! This man is protected by—"

Rafel turned in time to see his escort clubbed down. Hilt of a dagger to the back of his head. The man with the sword had not come alone. The second assailant caught d'Acorsi's man, breaking his fall, lowering him to the street. Less conspicuous in a crowd, but people were still watching this. They were not interfering. Shouldn't someone be calling for the civic guards? Rafel opened his mouth to do that.

"Really," the man with the sword said calmly, holding the blade point downwards now, "I wouldn't. They'd never get here in any usefully short time. It would be better if you just came. I mean it: you will not be harmed." His voice was assured.

"And the man escorting me? Who has already been harmed?"

"These things happen," said the one confronting him.

At which point a knife was pressed to Rafel's back, low down, unobtrusively. Not a pleasant sensation. It pricked through both his doublet and tunic, breaking the skin. The man in front sheathed his blade. People were moving all around them, both directions, chattering. Rafel heard laughter. D'Acorsi's man lay on the ground. Men and women stepped around him. Did this happen all the time in Seressa?

"Basso, be careful. No need for injury," the leader said. "Shall we walk, Signore ben Natan? It is not far, where we are going. Just across two bridges."

※

Come see me. A voice from the half-world, Lenia thought.

Half-world, and Bischio. Where her brother might be. Racing horses once, now breeding them. Of all impossible things in the god's world, that he might be doing that. But why so, really? Why more impossible than anything else? More than Lenia being a trader on a ship, a corsair?

She didn't want to go to Bischio.

Shame and grief can embed themselves in a person, she thought. That had happened to her. Had been done to her.

Rafel would say there was no shame to be felt, and that everyone lived with griefs. He wasn't wrong, but he wasn't a woman. Could she say that to him, as an answer? Would he understand? Perhaps he would.

The Council of Twelve had been convened. The duke would report to Folco what they decided as to joining the force the High Patriarch wished sent to the capture of Tarouz. A wish supported by the threat of sanctions as extreme as Scarsone Sardi could wield throughout the Jaddite world. With looting of the city offered, of course, if they succeeded. A prize, to balance the threats of the god he would levy.

A wealthy port city, Tarouz. Full of Jad-denying infidels. Men to be killed or sent to the galleys, women for whatever one wanted them for. Gold from beyond the desert. Gold, and more. It was not Asharias, not reclaiming Sarantium, but . . . it *would* be a response. A blow struck. A fleet sailing to exact vengeance. And not even very far!

The council was to meet tonight. They did that sometimes, she'd been told by Guidanio Cerra, who continued to keep them informed. Folco was engaged in discussions he didn't share. They had no reason to be told what he was doing. But d'Acorsi was to command this force if it happened. He would speak to the council tonight. It was said to be a majestic room, where they met in the palace. Portraits of past dukes lining the walls, up very high, all around. Seressa had been a power for a long time. Queen of the Sea.

There were also, on an infinitely smaller scale, plans to be made for the building of their new trading ship. The carrack the two of them were to offer for the assault, then use for their own purposes. If it survived. If their partnership continued.

She had told Rafel she'd leave arrangements to him. He knew ships by now, liked planning things. And she trusted him entirely. A deep truth for her, she thought. The trusting. If their partnership were to end in days to come it would be a sorrow. She could admit that to herself. She was trying to be better about acknowledging such things.

In the meantime she had walked the city alone yesterday. Or, almost alone. Duso, Guidanio Cerra's man, had come with her, staying a few steps behind. After the encounter in the fog, she didn't feel she could protest. It chafed, but also . . . if she was going to at least try to be honest with herself, and she *was* trying, it also reassured. He was a reassuring sort of man, Brunetto Duso. Had been a captain of the guard here. How he'd come to be with Cerra she didn't know. He might answer if she asked, but she didn't.

She had never been someone who asked a lot of questions. Watched, and thought about things.

They'd covered a great deal of ground, mostly on foot, a few times on one of the narrow boats. She'd been remembering all through the day how, as a child, she'd wanted to taste the world. The wonders it might hold.

A windy day, chilly in the shade and on the water, but she had worn a cloak. She bought a hat at a shop on a high-arched bridge lined with merchants. Duso had warned her to watch her purse. Later, she stopped and listened to a blind beggar sitting astride a barrel by another bridge. He told stories of the sea, announced he could tell someone's fortune from their palm. Somehow he knew she was there, and a woman; offered to tell hers for a copper coin. She didn't let him do that but she gave him the coin.

On the far side of that bridge the smell proclaimed they were nearing the tannery district, and after looking into a small sanctuary with mosaics and leaving more coins in the box for those, she turned back. She prayed before leaving, though. Hadn't done that in a long time. At the doorway she turned back to the altar and made the sign of the sun disk before she left.

She asked Duso for a suggestion and ate a meal where he pointed as they walked back the way they'd come. He declined to join her, stayed outside the door. He was a guard. She was someone who had a guard now.

She'd had an unexpected thought while eating. It shook her, then settled in to be considered.

It concerned Jad, faith, a life she could possibly live. An absurd idea, seen one way, less so if looked at differently. Many things were like that, weren't they?

At the end of their walk, back at the palazzo, she had asked Duso to request Guidanio Cerra to be good enough to call on her when his work day was done.

Cerra did so, late in the afternoon. Neither Rafel nor d'Acorsi were back yet. The steward let him in and brought wine to the sitting room.

A quiet man, this Cerra. A sense of humour, though, and still young. Perhaps not *always* quiet, she thought. She'd asked him some questions. He'd answered.

It was impulsive and she knew it, was almost certainly folly, but she had another day, at least, without obligations here. She'd accepted his offer to make arrangements for her to pay a visit outside the city the next day.

She was really not accustomed to people looking after her. Even paying attention to her. She had tried to live so as *not* to attract attention. Escorts, guards? And a man dealing with grief who seemed to want to be a friend? Who might be recognizing her own grief?

When she stepped out of the palazzo the next morning, Guidanio Cerra was waiting. She'd thought he'd send Duso or some other man. Rafel was going to the Arsenale for meetings concerning their ship. She didn't know where d'Acorsi was. He'd be in the palace tonight with the Council of Twelve. In that great room. She wondered if she'd ever see it. She'd heard there was a door at the back that led down to dungeons and torture rooms. Seressa was not a soft place, its citizens were not to be crossed. Or trusted, usually.

"You have no tasks for your duke today, signore?" She was wearing her new brown leather hat from the day before. The morning sun was bright, reflecting off the water, doubling the palazzos across the way in their reflections.

"Always those," he said, with that brief, small smile.

"Yet you are here?"

"I keep a horse at a stable on the mainland, signora, and I ride when I can. This journey becomes, if you will allow it, an excuse for me to do that. The way to where you are going is not obvious. Deliberately so, of course." He hesitated. "Riding is a joy for me. Or a relief. Both."

"I'm not good with horses," she said.

THERE WERE IRON GATES, quite high, darkened by weather and time, shadow and light on the almost-black bars as the breeze moved the leaves of the very tall trees on either side. She could see a well-groomed garden beyond. Fruit trees, a pond. Pale stone walls surrounded the large property. The sunlit, coppery dome of a sanctuary was visible through the gates. She had thought about turning back several times on the way here.

The Daughters of Jad retreat was indeed remote, as Cerra had said it would be, down a long track off the last road they'd taken, winding through trees, in leaf now. It had been chilly in the shade as they approached.

Guidanio Cerra had given her only two suggestions as to riding, one being an exact echo of what Folco had said. His horse—he called it Gil—was handsome, and his love for it was evident. They'd given Lenia a small, extremely gentle mare at the stables.

Now, in front of these tall gates, Cerra turned to her and cleared his throat. He looked awkward. "I should tell you . . . this is not the . . . not the holiest of the retreats for women in Batiara. It is, well, it isn't necessarily a *good* place, signora."

"What does that mean?" she asked. But she was listening. She felt an unease, had no idea why. These were just women in a retreat.

"They are very wealthy here, many donations and endowments. And they . . . the current First Daughter acts so as to ensure that this continues, and it . . . it affects how they live. Also, they . . . they receive daughters of noble families who have, well, who are . . ."

"Who are with child, embarrassingly for their families? And a sum changes hands?"

He nodded.

"Is that a bad thing?"

"Not always. It can be," Cerra said soberly. "Sometimes . . . well, these women sometimes leave, to serve Seressa in various ways."

"Various ways?" she said. *Spying* was one of the things he probably meant.

He flushed. "Shall we ring the bell?" he said.

She nodded, but as he pulled the long rope and the bell rang in the stillness, a lonely sound, she added, "Thank you for that."

∽

"You understand, Rafel ben Natan, we only wish information about tonight. After which, you will be escorted wherever you like. I can even offer you a purse."

He decided not to take offence at that last. There was already too much to be enraged by. Rafel drew a breath. Calmly, he said,

"Abducting a man, assaulting his companion? That is the way you solicit information?"

"It is often effective," said the seated man facing him. Rafel had been offered a chair. He'd declined.

They were in a reception room just to the left of the front door in a handsome palazzo. The furnishings were expensive, impeccable. The man facing him was extremely well-dressed, as if prepared to go out for the evening. He was, Rafel now knew. He was going to the palace.

This was, he'd been informed, Signore Branco Ciotto of the Council of Twelve. Recently named to that, Rafel guessed; he was very young for such a rank, almost certainly arrived at via family influence. He was handsome, with unfortunately receding hair.

"I am a merchant visiting your city and I am commissioning a vessel at the Arsenale. By what right do you accost me? And risk that commission for Seressa? And why do you think it will be permitted?"

The other man smiled and sipped from a glass of wine. Rafel had been offered wine. He'd refused this, too.

"As I said, no harm will come to you, Kindath. But don't try my patience. I don't care about whatever boat you want built. Just tell me what Folco d'Acorsi wishes of Seressa and you are on your way."

"And you don't think you'll learn that from Duke Ricci tonight?"

"Acting duke. And I prefer to know it *before* Ricci shares what he chooses to share. Information, you know what they say about it." He smiled again.

It was not a pleasant smile, Rafel decided. It was smug, complacent. This man, he thought, was stupid.

He didn't lose his temper often but it had been known to happen. Now it did.

He said, "Despite the notorious Kindath love of offered money, I'm afraid I will try your patience. You are rude and vulgar. And you oughtn't to have struck down the man escorting me."

Behind Ciotto, the other man, the one who'd escorted him here, made an urgent calming gesture with one hand. Rafel thought he was being decent. That he was trying to keep this encounter under control.

He didn't care.

"In my experience," Ciotto said airily, "servants tend to recover quickly. Something about their hard lives. Vulgar lives? Who was he? One of Cerra's? He's been seen with you."

A weakness revealed. You exploited those if you saw yourself in a battle. And were angry.

"Alas for you, signore, it is not so. I fear that man was a high-ranking member of the military company of Folco d'Acorsi. The man you are going to hear tonight in the palace."

It *was* a weapon, that name.

Ciotto swore. His handsome face grew somewhat less handsome.

"Lord Folco has also been seen with me, of course. And will be again."

"Tazio, this is true?" Ciotto snapped, without looking back.

"It is. It was unfortunately necessary, or there might have been greater violence by the Arsenale, in furthering your desires in this matter."

"Fucking Kindath!" Branco Ciotto said. "I hate them!" He swore again. It was almost amusing, but it wasn't.

Tazio, Rafel decided, was not a servant. He didn't speak like one. Probably a relative, a trusted man. Seemed a good one, despite having shown a sword to Rafel. And forcing him to come here.

He was still angry. "Oh really?" he said. "Fucking Seressini is what I prefer to say. Some of them, at any rate. One in this room."

Ciotto stared at him, reddening. "Be more careful. You think you are safe here?"

"I know I am," Rafel said. Although, in truth, he didn't.

"No one knows where you are!"

"I suspect they do, cousin," said the man named Tazio. "There was another escort with Signore ben Natan. Cerra's man. I knew him, he'll have known me."

There was a silence. A pleasing one.

Into it, as if on cue in the staged drama he'd imagined before, came a heavy knocking on the double doors of the palazzo, just behind Rafel.

∾

"I confess, I am intrigued to know what you believe we can do for you here," said Bentina di Gemisto, First Daughter of the retreat nearest to Seressa.

She offered a severely limited smile. She was tall, handsome, thin, with long fingers and high cheekbones, not as old as Lenia had expected. But First Daughters assumed that position by way of family rank and power as often as through seniority. She wore the prescribed colour of the god's servants, but in an iridescent silken fabric, more gold than yellow.

Lenia was aware that her own appearance and clothing had been swiftly and dismissively judged as she entered. She was trying not to feel hostile, and was failing. Not good. She'd come for a discussion about staying in this place, hadn't she? Changing her life. She already felt as though she'd acted on a foolish impulse, but she was here, might as well follow through with a conversation.

She took the stool the other woman pointed to. She removed the gloves she'd worn for the ride and set them down. The First Daughter was in a comfortable seat by a built-up fire. Rank and power on display. She had risen briefly as Lenia entered, then seated herself again.

Guidanio Cerra had absented himself to attend to the two horses before the return ride. It occurred to her that he might have wanted to be here to form some thoughts about this woman, for the duke. More details for Ricci's notebooks. But he'd left her alone, in privacy.

He might not have long to wait, Lenia thought. The other woman had elicited an immediate, visceral dislike. It wasn't common for her.

Lenia Serrana hadn't lived a life where she'd been allowed to feel such things. Fear, yes. Not this.

She wasn't afraid, or intimidated. She had left many fears behind, it seemed. Not all, but many. She had killed people.

She looked around, taking her time. A sumptuous room. Images of the god in tall paintings on two walls, Jad fair-haired and triumphant. Lenia knew nothing about artists, but was quite certain these would have been done by celebrated figures. A large sun disk rested in its stand on the mantelpiece above the fire, the shape of the god's sun engraved upon gold, gleaming in the light from the window. There were several tapestries hanging and a thick carpet on the floor. Two, in fact: another by the window, where there was more seating. Where someone—Bentina di Gemisto, one assumed—might look out on the beautiful garden and the wide grounds of the retreat.

She looked back at the other woman. "I'd had a possibly idle thought I might take vows to the god and join you here," she said.

A hand lifted to a mouth, to hide a smile. "As easily as that?"

"It is never really easy, is it?" Lenia said, her own hands quiet in her lap. "Withdrawing from the trappings of the world . . . as you evidently have."

She didn't get a reaction. "Truly not easy," the First Daughter said. "And especially not . . . well, not as to this retreat."

"It seems a *very* elegant one," Lenia said, as if overawed.

"We have some extremely well-born women who have sought the peace of Jad within these walls, yes. They arrive, and remain, with considerable support from their families. We are expected to invoke in our prayers the god's light and blessing for the dead of many of the great families of Seressa—and beyond. Some of them are buried in our graveyard."

"I see," Lenia murmured. "Candles and prayers cost a great deal here? The remoteness?"

The other woman's eyes narrowed slightly this time, as if hearing a distant trumpet. "Not especially. It is not inappropriate, surely, for women of birth to have some of the comforts they once knew, when they come to Jad?"

"Some say it is, do they not? Some teach that it is the very reason to come to a retreat. To cast off those earthly comforts for the purity of faith."

Bentina di Gemisto was not to be easily outfaced. And by now she'd know she was being challenged. Lenia hadn't come here to do so, but that is what this had become, it seemed. You couldn't plan for everything. "Is that what you hope to find in a life of piety, Signora, er, Settana, is it?"

"Serrana. I am uncertain as yet about what I hope to find in life."

The other woman smiled, as if kindly. "The family endowments we are accustomed to receiving when women join us are, it would be wrong not to say at the outset, considerable."

"Obviously so," Lenia said. "I am admiring your tapestries as we speak."

"They are worth admiring," the First Daughter said, with poise. "Ah. Well. I have much to do before prayers. I'm sorry if you had a long journey to no useful—"

"I can arrange for ten thousand serales to be deposited wherever you hold your money," Lenia said. "Or, of course, deposited for the credit of whichever retreat I eventually do choose, if this is the path I elect to follow in life. I do my banking with Seressa, as it happens."

There was a pause. Lenia realized she was enjoying herself.

The other woman shifted in her seat. She had been on the edge of rising. A sequence of expressions flitted across fine-boned features. She really was a good-looking woman, Lenia thought.

"Your family is in a position to—"

"My family owned a small farm in the south. Any sums I convey will be my own."

The First Daughter's brow knitted. She said, "Forgive me. Are you by any chance in an embarrassing circumstance?"

Lenia laughed. "Expecting a child? No. Were you, when you sought the god?"

Bentina di Gemisto flushed. "Why would you ask such a thing?"

"Why would you?"

"Signora, *you* are the one seeking admission to our retreat. I have a duty to—"

"No. I am the one possibly offering ten thousand serales to a retreat I choose. I am accustomed to making inquiries as to where my money goes. It is only prudent. I'm sure your father was the same. Was he a merchant? A banker? Or is he alive yet?"

"By the grace of Jad he is indeed alive, and sits on the Council of Twelve."

"How fortunate for him, and you. Does he send to you for some of the young women who *have* borne a child? To come serve Seressa?"

Her anger, Lenia realized, was considerable now. Perhaps recklessly so. It had to do with an image of those girls. She had a thought: they were probably treated viciously here, to make them more receptive should the Council of Twelve request their services. Were they turned into well-bred prostitutes? Likely, for some. And spies.

Bentina di Gemisto leaned back in her deep chair. This time she was the one taking her time. She said, "You seem troubled in your soul, Signora Settana. Perhaps it is indeed a wise thought to seek to spend your life in pious works, making recompense for deeds done? I wouldn't know, of course. But this might not, despite your alleged resources, be the best place for you. I imagine"—another thin smile—"you are feeling this, as well."

"I might come here," said Lenia, "to be named First Daughter, to bring a more substantial piety to this place."

Yet another smile. "Ten thousand might get a woman admitted, but not to any power. And I enjoy my role as spiritual guide to all those here."

"I wonder what twenty thousand would do, and a specific proposal to Duke Ricci, next time I see him."

An arrow. She saw it strike.

"Next time you—"

She was interrupting the other woman a great deal, Lenia thought. She didn't mind. She said, "I am staying with Folco Cino d'Acorsi while we conduct business here, which includes having a carrack built in the Arsenale. Folco will be with the duke and council this evening. I shall certainly ask him to greet your father for me. And I might also ask him to speak with the duke on my behalf. I would make my own appointment with Duke Ricci, of course. I saw him two days ago. It is always useful to have powerful men advocating for you, don't you find?"

Twenty thousand was an absurd amount of money to bring to a retreat. She would never do it. And she would *not* spend her life here. Or anywhere withdrawn from the world, she was realizing, even as she sat here. Clarity arriving. But this woman didn't know that, or need to know it.

Grief might make you do some things, and fear, but this sort of existence was not for her. Not her life to come, whatever that might turn out to be. It had been worth riding here to affirm it.

Lenia stood. She collected her gloves. Another assertion of power, to be the one bringing the encounter to a close. She had seen Rafel do it in negotiations.

The other woman also rose. Two tall women, of similar age. One born to wealth. The other . . . what she was, but also what she would *make* herself now: not defined by what had happened to her. A new thought.

It felt a very good thought.

"I appreciate your granting me this time," she said. She even meant it. "I will go find Signore Cerra, who has been kind enough, even in his sorrow, to escort me here himself."

She hadn't been certain Bentina di Gemisto would know Cerra's name and his association with the duke. She did, however. It showed in her face. Many arrows, Lenia thought, successfully launched. You could battle someone this way, with your words, your eyes. She didn't know what she'd won here, but she knew she had.

But then, outside again, walking through the herb garden, headed towards the stables with a young woman in pale yellow guiding her, there came that voice again. In her head. The one that did terrify her.

Hurry, she heard. *He is in danger. Your friend.*

What? Cerra?

No! The Kindath. Your true friend.

How do you know?

A pause. Then, almost plaintively, *I don't know! I don't know how I know. But hurry!*

Lenia began to run.

Your true friend, she thought.

༄

Branco Ciotto stood up quickly as the knocking at the door continued. "Don't answer!" he shouted to the servant in the antechamber.

But Rafel was still angry, and feeling reckless, and he said, "Don't answer? Unworthy of your distinguished family! Allow me, signore— a Kindath can surely serve as doorman for a member of the Council of Twelve!"

He spun, heard a cry of anger, ignored it. He crossed the floor to the antechamber and opened the front door before the footman could intervene. It might be no one useful. It might be . . .

"Ben Natan. You have obtained new employment, friend?" said Folco d'Acorsi.

The lord of Acorsi smiled, but thinly. He stepped inside, broad-shouldered, daunting. Three armed men followed him. The footman stepped back to the wall, hastily.

"Testing the role," Rafel said. "How is your man?"

"He'll be all right. Some others might not be." D'Acorsi's glance went past Rafel.

"Ciotto, is it? The son? You have made a grave mistake. You will present a sum I name to Signore ben Natan, as apology and compensation for insult and injury, and on our walk to the palace now I will tell you *all* the ways in which you have erred."

"Why would I do that?" Ciotto said. "Give a sum." He was pale, however, Rafel saw. From flushed to pale very quickly. Trying to keep his composure.

"Because this is a friend of mine, a guest in my home, and you had him abducted. And your people assaulted and injured one of my own company today. These things are not permitted, Ciotto. I need no further reasons to denounce you to the council this evening, before the session begins."

"What? You would not—"

"Denounce you? Of course I would! What do I care about shielding a junior member of Seressa's council, in a seat bought by his father's bribes? I care about my own people, and the plans I am here to address. And I would write the High Patriarch, declaring these things."

"The High . . . for a Kindath? In Jad's name, you would do this for one of those contempt—"

It was the loudest slap, Rafel ben Natan would later tell some people, that he'd ever heard.

Perhaps it was because of the way sound carried in that high-vaulted antechamber, but Folco d'Acorsi's hand striking Branco Ciotto's cheek sounded like a gunshot.

"Yes, I would," d'Acorsi said quietly, in the silence that followed. "I would do it for a Kindath. For any friend wronged as you have just wronged Signore ben Natan. Ciotto, hear me: the man who struck down mine will be turned in to the authorities. This evening. Not tomorrow. Attend to this. And the payment to Signore ben Natan? Two thousand serales of your father's money will do it. Also tonight, not later. He was threatened and seized in the street. He is my guest. I am therefore an offended party. Do these things, or I *will* speak to the council about your conduct, and write to Rhodias. You are," he added after a pause, "remarkably stupid for a Seressini. It doesn't bode well for the future of the republic."

For the first time, watching, listening, Rafel understood in his blood and heart, not just as a reflection upon power, why people were devoted to Folco Cino d'Acorsi, as well as afraid of him. *He* felt a little afraid of the other man now, this scarred, one-eyed mercenary commander, lord of a city, who had come for him here, who had named him a friend.

You didn't want him as an enemy.

THEY WALKED OUT together, d'Acorsi, himself, the three men Folco had brought. D'Acorsi had said he'd wait outside for Ciotto, they would walk to the palace together. He probably had something he wanted from him now. Turn this to advantage.

Rafel had no doubt at all that he'd receive two thousand serales from Ciotto tonight or tomorrow. The sound of that slap lingered.

"I don't need his money," he said to d'Acorsi.

"I know. But he needs to pay it. A different thing. Do whatever you want with it. There is a hospital for orphans here. And I am sure the Kindath have their charities."

"Yes," said Rafel. Then, "Thank you."

"I don't think he's reckless enough to have really hurt you. And his cousin—Tazio—I'm told he's a good man. I think he'd have stopped it."

"He wanted advance word about tonight's meeting. Whatever I knew."

"Seressinis love advance word. They lust for it. The prostitutes here ask questions about ships and goods expected in, and invest accordingly."

Rafel smiled. "Again, thank you. He might have held back, but I was . . . I was not being courteous. Or cautious."

"Angry?"

"Yes. Not safe for a Kindath."

Folco d'Acorsi looked at him a moment. "Not safe for most people. But yes, more so for you. Acorsi really is a safe haven, by the way, if you decide you can live inland. I offered it to Raina Vidal, as you know."

Dona Raina would, Rafel thought, have brought a considerable—and useful—fortune to Acorsi. He didn't say that.

"I'm not looking for havens, my lord. I . . . we are building a ship."

"You may need a home in the world."

Rafel said nothing. *A home in the world.*

D'Acorsi smiled again. "How was it at the Arsenale? I think—"

Footsteps heard, running.

D'Acorsi turned. Rafel saw his hand go to his sword. His three men did the same.

Lenia, Guidanio Cerra beside her, ran into the street. They came to a skidding stop, breathing hard.

"Good," said Folco mildly. "Useful that you have arrived. Catch your breath, then you can escort ben Natan home. I'm going to the palace from here."

He smiled at Cerra. There was a history there, Rafel remembered. Not one he was ever likely to learn. It occurred to him: you met people, spent time with them, a conversation, or several, journeys, meals . . . and would usually never know what days and nights had brought them to the moment of encountering you. What had made them the person you met.

Lenia said to him, "You are all right?"

He nodded. "How did you know where I was?"

She said nothing. Looked away, in fact.

Cerra answered. "My man had come to the city's edge, was waiting when we took the ferry from the landward side. He told us." He looked at Lenia, but said nothing more.

There *was* more. Clearly so. This sounded like a story, not a truth. He might not ever know what this was about, either. Life overflowed with things unknown. You tried, despite that, to gain at least *some* control over what might happen to you.

He really did understand, Rafel thought, the Seressinis' hunger for information.

BUT BACK IN d'Acorsi's palazzo, just the two of them, he did learn more, in fact. Because she said, quietly, "Let's sit down. There are things I need to tell you."

And she did. Tell him. A story about the half-world he found almost impossibly hard to address. He didn't *have* to address it, however. He was only hearing it. It was hers. Her life. *She* had to deal with this. And she was going to Bischio, after all.

CHAPTER X

Saranios della Baiana, a high cleric of the god, stood in his beautiful Sanctuary of Jad's Mercy, in Firenta, and smiled. The Feast of the Springtime Sun was upon them and it was one of his most-loved days of the year. It had once been a pagan festival (he knew that, most people didn't—and they didn't need to) but now it was a joyous day in the Jaddite calendar; it belonged to the god and to those who worshipped him.

Strictly speaking, Saranios knew he should repent for thinking of the sanctuary as *his*, but it was a habit now, and . . . well, really, other than holy Jad himself, who could claim it as theirs if not the high cleric appointed to lead the rites here?

Him. Saranios. He could claim it! For ten years, come midsummer. Surely the god in his mercy (and this was a sanctuary named for the mercy of Jad!) would allow that much? It was prideful, yes, but he felt he had devoted himself for so long and so attentively to this place, he might be permitted that, especially as he looked around now: early morning, light streaming beautifully through the high, narrow eastern windows. And the quiet. It was blessedly quiet now, before the doors would open (at his command) and the crowds begin streaming in on a holy day.

This was not the largest sanctuary in Firenta. That was the Great Sanctuary, with its enormous dome, over by the palazzo that housed the city administration. This was only the most beautiful, and it was becoming more so all the time, because it was Piero Sardi's favoured sanctuary and he spent generous sums to enhance it, year after year. There was a chapel marked off for, eventually (years hence, Saranios prayed), Piero's tomb. His wife was there now, waiting for him.

She had waited for him a great deal, was the story. Not that Piero was known to have strayed with women (though he probably had), but the man who had ruled Firenta in all but name and title for a long time seldom left his offices before darkness fell, even during the long days of summer, and he was back there by sunrise. Every day.

You could never accuse him of not working hard for his bank, his family, his city.

Saranios della Baiana, named for the great emperor who had founded a golden city in the east, now tragically fallen, regarded Piero Sardi as a man halfway, at least, to being among the god's blessed. He had only to look around him for evidence: paintings on walls and dome, sculptures in alcoves and chapels, marble and alabaster everywhere, brought from the celebrated quarries of Barignan. The elegant curve of the stairs ascending to the pulpit where Saranios spoke on days such as this. Or the library above, through the door behind the altar or a separate entrance from the street, with its own handsome stairway.

Saranios had a room back there, for himself. There was a small painting of the god, shown in his chariot, done by Viero Villani of Seressa. Not a famous artist, but a respected one. He had bought that himself, years ago. But in the sanctuary itself? The most famed artists and artisans in Batiara and beyond came when Piero Sardi summoned them, and they made things of beauty and piety, and then left, well paid for their work.

Timely payment by a patron was not always the case in these times, and Piero had earned their trust. Often they returned to Firenta because of that, bringing even greater glory to the city with new work. Even the master of them all came, Matteo Mercati: a beautiful man, almost too beautiful. And so gifted. Almost too gifted. Both things made him arrogant. You accepted that, Saranios thought, when someone was genuinely magnificent. Just as people accepted it—or should!—with the Sardi patriarch.

But of course not everyone loved Piero as much as Saranios and the family followers and a dozen artists did. Envy was part of the human condition, after all. Piero had for years been wielding power in a city that called itself a republic. There were elections, yes, but they were controlled by the Sardis. Everyone knew it. It was for the greater good, though, surely: just look at how Firenta was flourishing!

Still, a flourishing city would be filled with ambitious, worldly men, and some of these might think they could do even better at governing, that *their* families might as well reap the benefits therefrom.

Saranios della Baiana, short, plump, balding, clever, legitimately pious, thought they were wrong. He believed that Jad in his wisdom had elevated Piero Sardi here.

He himself had chosen the god's service when he left childhood behind, younger son of a good family in Baiana, and he had chosen his mortal lord not long after arriving in Firenta to take up this position—after serving in other towns, then other cities, and for a time in Rhodias. He was a high cleric now and had earned that, he felt. Not the most powerful religious figure in this city, but powerful enough, since it was widely known that Piero favoured him and his sanctuary. Saranios's goodwill, his intercession, both religious and in mortal affairs, was solicited.

He was, accordingly, well pleased that morning with his sanctuary, his city, his life, with where the god had brought him, and especially happy because of the day it was.

He checked the angle of the sun through the eastern windows. Saranios knew the light in his sanctuary as it changed through the day, the seasons, sunshine or clouds or rain. He nodded at Musseo, his most trusted cleric. Musseo signalled to those standing at the doors and they were opened, allowing the throng in the square to begin coming in.

Men and women in Firenta did not enter a sanctuary, or anywhere, in what could be called an orderly fashion. It was not in the nature of the city.

People burst through the tall bronze double doors, talking and laughing, filled with the joy of the season and the day. Saranios didn't even think of quelling them. He felt the same way. He knew most of these people, of course. Each sanctuary had its regular attendees. Here it was largely families associated with the Sardis, or those who wished to be, or desired to at least not be regarded by them in a hostile way. Where you worshipped had a significance that went beyond the god.

It was a wealthy, well-dressed crowd for the most part. People knew where they should sit, how near or far from the pulpit where he was now, with the altar just beyond it where the magnificent sun disk rested. Where he'd lead the service after he welcomed them all and spoke his words of piety. He tended to be brief. Piero Sardi didn't like long sermons. It had been conveyed.

Saranios looked over his shoulder on that thought. He knew the rhythms here. Behind the altar, the door had just opened and he saw the three Sardis, father and two sons, along with cousins and the family's women, begin to enter. The three men were dressed in black, even for a celebration. Expensively made clothing, expensively trimmed, but in no way ostentatious or attention-getting—unless you knew the price of fabric and good tailoring. And in Firenta, a cloth-making city, most people did.

You wanted people to see how rich you were, without them being able to murmur about how you were *trying* to make them see it. Piero knew all about this, and he'd taught his sons.

The women moved to take their seats, greeting other women as they went, formal embraces, kisses on both cheeks. Real or feigned affection. It was loud in the sanctuary now, and happy. This was a happy festival, Saranios thought. Piero and his sons aside, people had bright colours on display. It made Saranios feel even more festive. His prepared remarks were about rebirth in this season, but also on every morning, as the god returned from under the world.

He was aware—how could anyone not be?—that spring always brought wars to Batiara, but he wasn't going to talk about that.

Piero and Versano and Antenami Sardi walked forward together, moving around the altar to mingle among friends before they'd take their seats just in front of him. There was, always, a social component to days like this. You were here to be seen. And to be petitioned, if you were a Sardi. Piero took his time, letting people come to him. The sons moved on, Versano grave, emulating his father, always, Antenami smiling happily at people he knew. He was a man who often smiled.

Piero glanced up at Saranios in his pulpit. The high cleric adjusted his yellow robe and nodded. He would summon the sanctuary to order, or to the first movements towards order, when he received a second look from the elder Sardi. They had their procedure down by now. He felt honoured to be here, to be trusted. To be this man's spiritual adviser.

The sons continued forward and people gathered around them, too. Saranios liked the younger son, it was difficult not to, and he was happy to see how Antenami had changed in the last few years, earning his father's confidence more and more, after a long time devoted to horses and women.

It had been surprising, this change. Nothing had prepared any of them for it, and no one really knew the reasons. There was talk of a woman, one not even in Firenta now, but Saranios personally wondered if it had to do with the fall of the City of Cities. If holy Jad had touched the younger Sardi, made him see the tasks and duties a man

254 Guy Gavriel Kay

of his stature now needed to assume. He wasn't married yet. It was probably time.

Saranios was looking benevolently down at Antenami, who was standing close to but not actually beside his older brother (they didn't like each other, not uncommon), and so he saw what happened.

Everyone in Firenta wore a sword wherever they went, even in a sanctuary.

You didn't draw a blade, however. Not in here. Ever. Except, now someone did.

Later, the events of that morning and its bloody aftermath would become known as the Briachi Conspiracy, with the Soncino family also implicated. That was later. On the day, in his sanctuary at the outset of the celebration and rites of the Springtime Sun, Saranios della Baiana saw Odo Briachi, heir to that family's fortune, young but not *so* young, pull his sword from its scabbard as he approached the Sardi brothers, and . . .

And Saranios screamed a warning from the pulpit, so loudly it was heard above the babble of sound. *"A sword!"* he cried. *"Sardis, be warned! Assassins!"*

It was almost enough.

He spun quickly to look for Piero, saw men approaching him, too! With weapons coming out.

He screamed again, wordlessly this time. And then he saw what he saw, and would never forget. The foul, murderous desecration of a holy place. *His* holy place.

૭૭૭

Antenami knew he ought to have died that morning. He was aware of this for the rest of his life. It was the second occasion, in fact, when he might have been killed in an attack, and he was *not* a man of violence. Theirs was a violent world, however.

One cannot live—or most people cannot—entirely in the shadow of such moments, memories, but it is fair to say they infused his days, and his dreams on many nights.

The idea that every breath drawn, glass of wine sipped or swiftly downed, every woman encountered, sunrise seen, horse ridden, travels undertaken (love revisited, just the once, after a journey) . . . all such things existed for him, going forward from that day and hour, only because della Baiana had screamed from the pulpit and Antenami had moved backwards instinctively, and . . . people had intervened, who ought not to have even been there that morning.

It didn't save his brother.

Versano Sardi died that day, assassinated in the Sanctuary of Jad's Mercy, with consequences for Firenta and Batiara and, arguably, the world, since Batiara mattered greatly.

Piero, their father, was the best-guarded of them, and his guards did step forward, and they intercepted three men coming at the Sardi patriarch and . . . one of the guards died, and all three of the would-be assassins. Two of the Briachi, and a Soncino, the latter only fifteen years old. Good with a blade, but not good enough. The Sardi guards were skilled, but the speed and surprise of the attack—in a sanctuary, on a holy day!—had been great. The remaining guardsmen hustled Piero out of the chaos back the way they'd entered, through the door behind the altar. They defended him in that chamber; they guarded the door to it.

As for Antenami, he'd had only one man with him, just as Versano had, not far away. Perhaps a mistake. This was changed, afterwards. Many things changed afterwards.

A Soncino killed Versano Sardi, sword into chest, screaming, *"Death to tyranny! Freedom for Firenta!"* There were three others of that party there: one plunged an unnecessary, vicious blade into Versano where he lay on the marble floor, already dead. Antenami saw it happen.

Two others came for Antenami, weapons out, also screaming about tyranny.

They never reached him.

One was intercepted and killed outright by a person extremely lethal with a sword. The other died of a dagger thrown, striking him through the eye. But not before that assassin had stabbed someone else, an unarmed man who'd moved quickly forward (foolishly, bravely, recklessly) to block his path, slow him down.

It was established later that the Briachi had expected support, a rallying to their name and cause, once the three Sardis had been killed and word went forth from the sanctuary. Piero Sardi was not loved overmuch, only greatly feared.

Only one of the three was slain, however, and it was not Piero, and so there was no rallying at all, whatever level of unspoken support there might have been. Instead, people displayed their loyalty (such as it was) by hunting down Briachi and Soncino family members, dragging them out of their palazzos, both the men and the women. Some were killed, inside or on the streets in front of their homes. It was a savage time in Firenta.

So the city never found out the true depth of feeling as to *tyranny* in the republic. Within days the Briachi and the Soncino, who were numerous, were destroyed. Almost all the adult males were killed, and *adult* was loosely defined in those days.

The women and the very young were exiled for life, to whatever life they could make or find. That degree of mercy was seen as a mistake by some. It was remembered how Duke Arimanno Ripoli of Macera had slain *all* members of the families that had risen against him in his city a few years ago—and left their bodies to rot for days in the city's central square. Even the women. And the children.

Piero Sardi chose a slightly different course. Although those exiled were not allowed to return in his lifetime or that of his surviving son, who would eventually succeed him, they were not killed. And some did make a life for themselves elsewhere.

There was a difference, a subtle man wrote, years after, looking back at those days, between a duke and a banker, ruling his city-state in reality but without a title of any kind.

~

Rafel knew he'd been a fool and that he was dying because of it. An enormous consequence, but folly at some levels carried that possibility, didn't it?

How did a man regarded as prudent and shrewd do a thing like this? Really, how? Rushing forward unarmed—he was *always* unarmed!—to block an assassin wielding a sword against someone he scarcely knew?

It wasn't entirely folly, he protested to himself, breathing shallowly, a hand to the wound in his chest. He hadn't considered (insofar as he'd thought and not just *acted*) that he could do more than jostle and slow the man rushing for Antenami Sardi. He had hoped to impede him, bump him from the side, perhaps, allow d'Acorsi or Lenia time to intervene, for the Sardi son to back away, for his guards to step in, or . . .

Well, Lenia seemed to have killed the man, and young Sardi was alive, so he'd done what he'd intended. There was that.

Why he'd intended it was a bitter question for these last agonizing moments of a life, he thought. Antenami Sardi meant nothing to him! Who ruled Firenta meant nothing!

Had he been, somehow, Rafel ben Natan thought, an *ethical* person all this time? Virtuous?

Really? A merchant? A corsair? He'd have laughed if it were not impossible to do that just now. He was in a shocking amount of pain. There was a great deal of blood. Of course there was.

He became aware of Lenia kneeling beside him. He turned his head to look at her. He said, with difficulty, "You know where my money is to go. Marsena. You have . . . authority. Documents at the bank. I arranged that . . . when I created the account."

"Be quiet, Rafel!" she said. She tried to make it sound stern, but she was crying. He didn't want her to be doing that. And yet, even if it was wrong, he didn't entirely *mind* the idea that he'd be mourned. What had your life been if no one grieved for you?

There were more things he needed to say, however. And it was already difficult. "Also . . . the carrack, go ahead with it? I pay my share. Insure it properly when it is done. If we end up making profits, or if you sell it, send my share . . . to the same place. You know I trust you. More than trust, Lenia. More."

She was holding one of his hands between both of hers. Gripping quite hard.

"Be quiet," she said again. "They've sent for a physician."

"They just kill you faster," he managed. Old joke.

It really was remarkable, the pain he was feeling. He hadn't known something could hurt this much. The sword had gone in high. In and out, the assassin wanting to get by him fast. He hadn't. Not fast enough. That man was lying not far away. There was a knife in his eye.

"Lenia, let me in! I need to see the wound." It was Folco d'Acorsi. That made sense, Rafel thought, trying to remain capable of thought for a little longer at least. Clear thinking had always mattered to him. A military man, d'Acorsi. Would have seen many sword wounds. Had probably killed men he'd led who'd been mortally wounded, to put them out of pain, make their dying easier. Send them to their god.

Rafel had seen that once, on the *Silver Wake*. Elie had done it. A mariner on the deck with two bullets in him; a raid on a merchant ship that had succeeded, but with three casualties. More resistance than Rafel had expected.

If they were your men, your orders, had you killed them when that happened? Or . . . were they not free to choose their own life paths?

Questions he had liked to wrestle with, by himself or debating others. That sort of mind. Not a fighter, never liked it, even when he'd ordered an attack. So this, where he was now, this was unexpected.

You could say inappropriate. Except . . . except if you were genuinely a thoughtful person you knew that sudden death lay as a possibility on the path of life for everyone. Sea or land, market square
or palace, stony beach. Quiet farm, if raiders came.

Lenia wasn't getting up, or letting go of his hand. D'Acorsi walked
around to Rafel's other side, also knelt. He said, "That was brave,
ben Natan."

"I didn't do much."

"Only saved his life."

"And placed people who depend on me at risk. Not wise."

D'Acorsi said nothing to that. Gently moved Rafel's hand from
the wound. Looked closely. Closed his one eye. Briefly, but it was
enough. He said, to no one in particular, "Clean linens, boiled water.
Wine for the wound."

"Quickly!" Another voice, Antenami Sardi's. "Saranios, have this
done!"

"I will." The high cleric had come down from his pulpit, was standing beside them.

"I don't care where I'm buried," Rafel said to d'Acorsi. "I do care
that my parents be brought out of Almassar. Will you help? Get
them to Marsena."

"I will do that!" Antenami Sardi again. "I'll make it happen, and
bless your name."

Rafel turned his head. Sardi was weeping, too, it seemed, standing
above them.

"My lord." An urgent voice beyond him. "Your father insists you
come to the back."

"Tell my father I am guarded, and staying with the man who
saved my life."

"He's right. You should go, Sardi," d'Acorsi said. "We don't know
how many there were here. Are you certain of your guards?"

"Of course, I—"

"*WATCH HIM!*" THAT voice in Lenia's head. Again!

She rose quickly on the words, already drawing her short sword as she did.

Folco was faster. Even without a warning from the half-world.

Of course he was. A lifetime of this. One guardsman had not been standing with his back to them, watching for another attack. Had instead been looking at Rafel and her and—rather more so—at Antenami Sardi.

He was killed with efficiency, almost casually, by Folco d'Acorsi as he was drawing his blade. There was something chilling and reassuring in it, both. How a danger was addressed, how easily a man died. The guard's sword clattered on marble.

D'Acorsi looked down at him with an expression of distaste. "Rival families with a plot is one thing. A traitor offends me."

"He's no longer alive to offend," Antenami Sardi said. "Thank you, my lord."

He sounded astonishingly calm, Lenia thought. That was unexpected. He looked such a mild, ineffectual man. No beard, ought to have had one, perhaps, to make him seem older. He looked like a man who'd prefer a drink and a song to policy meetings or war. That was his reputation. And horses. He loved horses.

He was also, given that his older brother lay dead nearby, the heir now to the Sardi bank and fortune, and perhaps to governing Firenta.

"It really would be best if you went to the back room," d'Acorsi said again.

"No," Antenami Sardi said again, in turn.

"Join your father. You can't *do* anything here, Sardi!" Folco sounded angry now.

Lenia knelt again by Rafel, heedless of blood on marble, of tears still on her face.

"I can try," she heard Antenami Sardi say. "I can try to do something."

ALL THE SEAS OF THE WORLD   261

"And I will pray." The high cleric had come closer, he was just behind her. He hadn't retreated from the sanctuary either. "I saw what happened. This man was unspeakably brave."

"Unspeakably foolish," Rafel muttered. "A Kindath dying in Jad's sanctuary?" He was still breathing. But Lenia had seen Folco d'Acorsi's face when he exposed the wound.

"I have always believed we should pray for every soul," said Saranios della Baiana.

She didn't know his name then, only learned it later. The cleric knelt beside her, also ignoring blood on his beautiful golden robe, and he began to pray to the sun god for Rafel's life. There ought to be a Kindath prayer spoken, Lenia thought, but there wasn't going to be. There was no one here who knew such a thing. Those words. She looked up and saw that Antenami Sardi had closed his eyes. His hands were clenched at his sides, as if he was straining to do something.

THOSE WHO PLAYED a part in what happened next never spoke of it. And the people around them, the guards, clerics, citizens who had not yet fled the sanctuary, never understood what took place, or how.

Not that any of us entirely understands how things happen in our lives. We do not, we truly do not, fully grasp the world we have. The one we move through all our days and nights. We fear what cannot be explained. We seek shelter with a god, with his sisters, with a visionary, the stars. Other beliefs at other times. It is a longing shaped by need. A yearning for shelter while alive, and perhaps after. That is a prayer, or a wish, for most of us. Or else we can feel naked in a storm. Along with those we love.

ANTENAMI SARDI WASN'T even sure what he'd meant, saying he would try to do something. Was he just . . . speaking words in confusion, in the chaos? But he did feel a need to help, seeing this man bleeding on the sanctuary marble. He had accepted the Kindath merchant's calm assessment that he was dying, then something, *something* urged him, demanded he push back against that. He had closed his eyes.

What did pushing back even mean? Prayer? Saranios was doing that.

His brother was dead. He would see Versano if he opened his eyes. Assassins had come for them. In Jad's sanctuary. The high cleric was offering the Importuning of Mercy now.

Antenami didn't join in. He didn't kneel. He just kept his eyes closed, standing where he was, and he thought, intently, of a person in his past. An image of her. He named her in his mind. And then did so again. Nothing happened. Of course nothing happened.

Not for him. But . . .

THE SARDIS' PRINCIPAL physician came up, hustled between two guards. He had, it turned out, been in the sanctuary but had fled, prudently, with the crowd as violence burst forth. The guards had caught up with him halfway to his home. He had, at first, thought they were there to kill him. They might have, had he not come to understand who they were and returned with them, however reluctantly.

The doctor was breathless, pale, and afraid, Lenia saw, looking up. She was still clutching Rafel's hand. The man didn't kneel, didn't touch Rafel. Just looked at him, not as carefully as Folco had. He winced at the amount of blood.

"I cannot do anything," he said flatly. "Not with so much bleeding in the chest. I'm afraid—"

He's wrong! And there was the voice again. *I . . . I don't know how, but I am being told he is wrong! Say that bleeding isn't always fatal. It can be stopped, stitched. If the sword didn't sever a major vessel, she says he will bleed but might live if they stop it now! Say this! I am told to tell you!*

She? She says?

Say it!

Lenia understood nothing. She was terrified for so *many* reasons right now, but she looked up and said it. Exactly the words she'd been given.

And Folco, listening, suddenly added, "I have seen this, yes. I might have been wrong about the bleeding. We must clean it and close the wound. We have to try!"

How do you know this? Lenia asked of the woman's voice in her mind.

I don't! I don't know anything! There is . . . there is someone else with us! Because of the man . . . the one without a beard. He called her!

Her?

Yes!

Lenia looked at Antenami Sardi. His eyes were still tightly closed; he was swaying where he stood. He looked as if he might fall.

She said, "Signore Sardi. My lord, what are you doing?"

He opened his eyes, stared at her. "I can't explain it to you. But I'm . . . I am trying to help."

"You might be doing so," she said.

She turned to d'Acorsi and the physician. "How do we stanch bleeding? How do we do that?"

"It doesn't matter," the doctor said. "If he is wounded where we see—"

"Stop the bleeding, Pelachi, you fucking leech, or you're dead the moment he dies!"

It was mild, genial Antenami Sardi. He looked at Lenia, a frightened hope in his eyes, then back at his family's doctor. "Your task is to do what you are told, Signore Pelachi. Exactly that. At risk of your own life if you fail."

Folco d'Acorsi looked at Lenia, then at the physician. "Signore," he said, "if he should die after you try what is suggested, it is not your fault. If you fail to contend with this, it is. I *have* seen chest wounds survived. It depends, as Signora Serrana has said, on whether a vessel that carries life has been cut. Bleeding doesn't mean it has been."

He looked at the guards. "Where are the linens, wine, the water?"

"They are coming, my lord," said a cleric. "See, we have linens, and the wine. The water is boiling in our kitchen."

The physician said, even more ashen-faced, "We'll need to move him to—"

No! came the voice in Lenia's head. *He'll die if he's moved, she says. Ligatures, she says. I don't know what those are. Wine in the wound now. Then pack it with clean linen until the ligatures are here, then it is to be closed up. The physician can do that!*

It was past impossible, every single part of this, but it might save a life that mattered more to her than any other. Lenia repeated, again, exactly what the woman talking to her said.

The doctor opened his mouth as if to object again. Antenami Sardi said, "His lordship of Acorsi may be more generous-minded than I right now, Pelachi. Identify what you need. My guards will go for it. We make him comfortable, we bring light for you, you treat him here." He sounded commanding. Cold, even.

The high cleric summoned a man, gave crisp orders himself about making Rafel comfortable. Lenia had her cloak under his head. He was still bleeding. So much.

She looked up. The cleric who'd been given the orders wasn't moving to obey. "My lord high cleric," he said, fierce with self-importance, "this is a Kindath! Look at his clothing! The blue and white! Are we to profane this holy—"

"You are dismissed," said the high cleric. Another voice gone cold as winter rain. "Remove your robe and leave. Mazzari, escort him out. Fillipo, get what I sent him for. Do it swiftly. There is a man who may die here."

People in yellow robes began moving, quite quickly. The one dismissed was protesting. He looked as if he'd been poleaxed, Lenia thought.

"I seem to be causing trouble," Rafel said.

"Shut up!" she said. "Stop joking." She squeezed his hand. Hard. "They are going to try. Pray to your moons. Stay alive for those who love you."

"Am I finally handsome?" he asked.

"Rafel, if I kill you, it won't help anything," she said.

Antenami Sardi, standing above her, said, "Will you step aside with me, signora? Please? Just for a moment?"

She pushed herself up, stiff after kneeling, her robe bloodied, heavy with it. She wiped at her eyes with the backs of her hands. They walked a short distance away. Two guards followed, frightened and watchful.

Sardi said, quietly, "Who is telling you to do these things, please?" His voice was anxious, not commanding now.

"I . . . I cannot properly explain, my lord. It is very . . ."

"Is it a healer? One not here?"

Tell him it is! It isn't me. She is speaking through me.

Lenia bit her lip. "I do not hear her at all. I . . . hear someone else. In my head. Someone devout in the faith of Jad, who . . . who says a healer is speaking to *her*. And then she is telling me what we are to do."

What she saw then on Antenami Sardi's face was joy. He said, after a moment, quietly, "Jad bless you and give you light, signora. This stays between us, for both of us. I know who this is. She might save your friend. If anyone can, she can."

"Who is she?"

He shook his head. "The name doesn't matter."

Her name is Jelena, came the voice in her head. *She said I could tell you. And to greet Signore Sardi.*

"I am told by her to greet you," Lenia said. Was she going to refuse? Really?

Sardi reached out a hand to steady himself, gripping her by the shoulder.

"Oh, Jad. I understand none of this," he whispered. "But I am so happy! Please let him live."

"You think *I* understand?" Lenia said. *Please let him live,* she thought.

I don't either! came the inner voice. *But I don't think we are meant to. This may not be a woman who believes in the god, but she is serving Jad now. I believe that.*

It is a Kindath we are trying to save, Lenia said.

She knows. I know. I am . . . I'm the one who needs this to be coming from Jad.

I don't care who it is from.

I know that. Do you love him?

A pause.

Yes, Lenia said then. *Yes, I do.*

THE PHYSICIAN TURNED out to be capable with his hands. Piero Sardi was too meticulous, too aware of so many aspects of life and his current roles, to have had one who wasn't, Folco d'Acorsi thought.

Rafel ben Natan's wound was cleansed with wine, which caused him to scream in an almost empty sanctuary, the cry echoing from dome and walls, through spaces holding and dispersing light from high windows, with motes of dust in that sunlight.

He then fainted. An entirely good thing, d'Acorsi thought, as long as the man kept breathing.

Folco did not know how the woman, Lenia Serrana, knew what she seemed to know about treatments for a sword wound, but this wasn't the time to ask. And she wasn't the talkative sort. Reliable though, he had judged. Also angry, in ways that might be useful. She was too well off now to *need* to serve him in any role, but people sometimes took on tasks for their own reasons and desires. It had happened before in his company.

He didn't try to sort out *why* he hoped a woman would join him, but he more or less knew.

The wound was packed with clean linens to slow the blood loss, and wrapped. He had seen blood vessels tied off. Challenging. The doctor who knew how to do that wasn't here. He didn't even know if it would have been suitable.

The linens needed changing twice before guards came running back with the implements the physician had requested. Hardly medical implements, really, Folco thought, but he knew what they were for. With sheep's gut thread and a tailor's needle, the physician began stitching shut ben Natan's wound.

There was no way to know how this would play out. If a significant vessel in or near the heart had been cut, the man was dead. Surprising he was still alive this long, if that was so. If it hadn't been severed there remained the danger of pus. The green hue of it meant death was imminent. Ben Natan could also die from simple loss of blood. Or from uncontrolled coughing if one of his lungs had been cut. Or if his heart gave out.

You could die so easily, Folco d'Acorsi thought.

He found himself thinking about how long it had been since he'd been home, where there were people he loved. He knew Caterina would be pleased with the diamond; it would earn him some relief from her anger at his absence, even if he was almost always away in spring. In a way, he thought, it might be a good thing that she was still angry with him when he was away for too long, even after all these years. Meant his absence was a sorrow, still?

He missed Acorsi very much, he realized. He had a stop after this one, in Macera, then another, longer journey. And then he could go home to tell his wife he'd be going to war against the Asharites next spring.

Perhaps. It still needed assembling, this campaign. It was now going to be difficult to speak to Piero Sardi about funding a war across the water. There would be chaos and violence in Firenta. Necessary deaths. Likely some unnecessary ones, as well, but who was he to judge? Piero's older son, his heir, had just died. Traitors in the city (and in the Sardis' own ranks) had revealed themselves. It might be wiser to move straight on to Macera, come back here later, summer's end, perhaps.

He decided to do that. Leave tomorrow or the next day. He was, by now, swift to make decisions. Had seen his share of necessary and unnecessary dying. Had caused both.

He did hope the Kindath merchant survived. The man had done a brave thing, on behalf of someone he scarcely knew.

The doctor finished with the suturing. The sword had gone in and straight back out, the cut, as best Folco could judge, not as deep as it might have been. A cleric had been sent to the kitchens for honey. Folco knew about that, too. He remembered someone, a woman healer, using it on a wound some years ago. For the last woman, in fact, to be in his own company. Odd coincidence, in fact. It wasn't widely used.

Indeed the doctor balked at doing so, until given orders again by Antenami Sardi, whose forcefulness here was another surprise. Perhaps it ought not to have been. The dead older brother was . . . dead. There were going to be changes in Firenta. Deaths first. Then other things.

Yes, wiser to go to Macera. Come back here later.

Rafel ben Natan was still unconscious. Breathing shallowly, but breathing. His wound had been stitched and the honey applied. It was impossible to know what was happening inside his chest, of course. Just as it was impossible to know sometimes what people were thinking or feeling. What lay within . . .

He sent two of his men to obtain a stretcher to lift the wounded man. He couldn't stay in the sanctuary, on the floor in blood. The men of Folco's army were familiar with how to make them if they couldn't find one. You learned many things through years at war. Almost every springtime. This year an exception. He didn't mind that, though it affected his finances. He'd used the quiet season to go south, visit Duke Ersani in Casiano. He'd never been employed by

Ersani. He hoped that might change after hunting together, dining, drinking. Ersani liked wine.

He'd stopped at Sorenica to see Raina Vidal, whom he admired, before heading north to home and . . . and unexpected things had happened. The ensuing contract offered by the High Patriarch to lead a holy army south was generous. Folco's finances were stable again, and more. Which meant his city would be for another year or two. For himself, he thought, the idea of revenge taken for Sarantium was not displeasing.

He could still hear the bells that had tolled when holy men had come walking through a field to bring them the news of that fall.

⚮

Rafel woke in a soft bed in a dark room.

He had no idea where he was. Or the time of day. It was dark, but not entirely black. He was in considerable pain. You could call it extreme. He decided he would. But . . . he had awakened. Was among the living.

"Welcome back, ben Natan. The next stages will depend on whether there is pus, what kind, how much."

He turned his head cautiously. The room spun, settled. He saw Folco d'Acorsi.

"Have you been here . . . ?"

"No. Just stopped by now. I told Signora Serrana to get some rest. I said I'd wait with you a bit. She's the one who has been here since they brought you."

Rafel asked a question with his eyes.

"Yesterday morning. Your wound was cleaned and stitched and you have wound dressing on it under bandages. There is some debate about the best response to the pus if it comes, but I won't tax you with it. I'll just say that, for reasons I don't understand, Antenami Sardi has instructed his family physician with exactitude. You are being treated in a fashion that tries to reduce that pus, not encourage it."

"I see," said Rafel, though he didn't. It was something to say. He was alive, hearing words.

"Honey," said d'Acorsi. He smiled. "Not a term of endearment, though I am very pleased to see you awaken. They are using honey, oil, lint I think, some other things I forget, to try to reduce what might be engendered in the wound. The stitching," he added help-fully, "is from the intestines of a sheep. Some use silk, I believe, but you have sheep's gut."

"I see," said Rafel again, for want of a better response.

"I have seen it used," Folco added cheerfully.

"Does it all . . . does all of this succeed?"

"Sometimes. People do survive. We'll know in two or three days, I think. Crackling sounds in the wound will be bad."

"I . . . would imagine so."

"But you'd be feeling extreme pain before then, of course, and would probably look . . . grey."

"I see," Rafel said a third time. "Grey." He really didn't have a more cogent response. "Where am I?"

"The high cleric's chamber, in back of the sanctuary. He offered. Meant moving you less. It is likely you saved his life, you know. Young Sardi's."

"Lenia's dagger."

"Which needed to be drawn and thrown. You allowed time for that."

"No idea why. Mistake."

"Perhaps. Also brave. They can go together."

Rafel closed his eyes.

"Sleep," said Folco d'Acorsi. "I'll tell Signora Serrana and the doctor that you are with us again. And young Sardi. He's been here several times. I am going north tomorrow, but will stop in again before I go."

Rafel opened his eyes. "Macera? Because of chaos here? And because they are needed too?"

D'Acorsi smiled briefly. "I do like a clever man, ben Natan."

"So do I, my lord," Rafel said. And fell back asleep hearing the other man's laughter.

LENIA HAD THOUGHT it would be difficult to explain why they were telling a physician how he should treat his patient, but Antenami Sardi had solved that. He'd been wounded himself some years ago, he said, arrows, an incident near Bischio. Perhaps Signore Pelachi remembered it, he said.

Signore Pelachi did. Sardi added that the healer who had saved him there had been good enough to explain her regimen as to dressing and coating wounds, and what she had her patient drink, for easing pain and increasing strength, and to encourage sleep. Sardi had recovered wonderfully well, except for an ache in his shoulder when it rained. He was simply intervening to have this man treated as he had been.

Pelachi, he said, would not be punished in any way if it failed to succeed, so long as he followed the instructions.

They'd placed a cot on the floor for her. Lenia was in the room much of the time, so she could see that Pelachi was doing this. Indeed, the physician had scribbled notes for himself. Not a foolish man, it appeared. Set in his ways, but most people were.

She didn't hear the voice of the woman from Bischio now. And she'd never heard the other one's voice. The healer. It might be cowardice, but she tried not to think too much about what had happened in the sanctuary while Rafel lay in blood, expected to die.

In the streets and squares of Firenta people *were* dying. Piero Sardi had not waited to begin his response to what was already being called the Briachi Conspiracy. A family called Soncino were a part of it. Lenia didn't know why their name wasn't also attached. She didn't much care.

She smelled smoke, even in here. Houses were being burned. Carefully, that the fire might not spread, but they were coming down in flames. She wondered if people were being trapped inside. It might be so.

The Sardis, father and son (remaining son), were very grateful to her and to Rafel. They really had saved Antenami's life. Folco d'Acorsi found her in the Sardi palazzo and said her partner had awakened. She'd accepted an escort back to the sanctuary. The city was dangerous.

Rafel had been asleep again by the time she got there but she sat by the bed and waited and saw him wake, and was able to say, astringently, "You are an impossible man."

No smile, a ghost-thin voice, "You expect me to defend myself against that?"

Which made her, unfairly, begin to cry again.

"How is it," Rafel whispered, head turned her way, eyes on hers, "that I have a partner so woman-weak and frail?"

She didn't answer. Couldn't even glare at him properly. Tears made that difficult.

⧉

Sometimes people could surprise you.

Folco had thought he might be asked to attend on Piero Sardi before leaving, but he wasn't prepared for what the older man said.

"You came to Firenta for a reason of course, my lord of Acorsi. A lucky spin of fortune's wheel for my family, that you arrived for the feast day and were in our sanctuary."

"Not lucky for your older son. I am sorry about that, Sardi. I have children of my own. I can imagine."

Sardi nodded. "Thank you. You still did us a great service. Will you share what it was that brought you?"

He was a man who prided himself on his self-control, d'Acorsi thought. They had had dealings before. Folco had been hired by Firenta to take Bischio some years ago, a much-coveted jewel. It hadn't happened. Sarantium had fallen, and all wars in the Jaddite world had stopped. For a time. Folco had offered to return the money he'd received. Sardi had told him to keep it, against a future contract. Generous. Shrewd. Both things.

Piero Sardi was a small, trim man with a large head, thick grey eyebrows, and almost no hair any more. There was a case to be made, amid many candidates, that he was the cleverest man in Batiara. Folco might have made that case himself.

Sardi used reading spectacles now, like the duke of Seressa. He held them as they talked. Folco had thought about getting such devices for himself. It was probably time. There was a great deal of reading involved in what he did, and there wasn't always enough light to make it easy. You didn't wear them to destroy a city's walls or kill a man with a sword; you did to write the letter reporting you had done so. His wife would laugh at him, but gently enough. And he could survive Caterina's laughter if he needed spectacles to read. They still crossed often through the unlocked door between their rooms at night when he was home, often enough to reassure that need remained, as well as love.

He *really* wanted to get home, he realized again.

He told Piero Sardi, a man with much on his mind, of the plan to take war to the city of Tarouz and Zariq ibn Tihon next spring, killing or capturing him, or driving him to flight, sacking and looting his city. For Sarantium. For Jad.

It was the High Patriarch's campaign, he said. And every ruler of every country, and the Holy Jaddite Emperor in his cold northern city, and the leaders of all the city-states in Batiara were to contribute, on pain of—

"On pain of banishment from the rites. The usual," said Piero Sardi.

But he made the sign of the sun disk, as if in contrition for being wry. When men grew older, Folco thought, they often seemed to become aware of their approaching end, and of what might come after. The holy rites, access to them, mattered even more? Hadn't happened to him yet, but he could sense that state of mind, as a distant cloud on a clear afternoon turning towards twilight.

Sardi asked him what sum they had in mind for a contribution from Firenta, and what their allocated return would be if Tarouz were taken. Of course they'd have no ships in the fleet, being a land-locked city. "Like your own," Piero Sardi added. "Despite your efforts through the years, my lord."

"We don't always achieve our desires," Folco said. He didn't mention the conquests Sardi had been trying to make and had not yet achieved. Not the time for that.

He answered as to the sums and percentages. He asked for what they'd agreed upon in Rhodias, and offered what he had been authorized to offer as a return, but added a little, because this was Piero Sardi and because his son had just been killed, and Folco had spent much of last night thinking about how he'd feel if it had been a child of his own. He mentioned, because it seemed useful, that he'd ask the same of Macera.

Sardi agreed outright.

Didn't bargain as to Firenta's investment or return. He might even have guessed that Folco had just raised the sum he'd intended to offer. The man was like that, even now, a son murdered, violence in his city, the sound of screaming coming into the palazzo, smell of smoke.

Folco looked in on ben Natan again towards evening, because he'd said he would. They spoke briefly. He agreed to something. Then he did indeed leave Firenta, his men riding in close formation through streets of smoke and flame and crowds and ash, dead bodies and the dying everywhere. They went out the northern gate, and away.

CHAPTER XI

Bischio, seen at a distance from a rising of the road as she and her escorts approached from the north, was clearly smaller than Firenta, and quite a bit smaller than Seressa, but it was not an inconsequential city, and the walls, even from far off, reflected that.

They would reach the city gates this morning. In peacetime they'd be open on a market day. Lenia was anxious, frightened, really. She kept pushing back against an inner query: *why are you here?* There were answers, but they didn't bring comfort.

There was some comfort in being escorted.

She was aware, because one of the guards had told her, earlier, that two other men were riding behind them along the road south, keeping a steady distance. They were not, the Sardi guard leader said, trying very hard to be unnoticed. What did the lady want him to do?

The lady decided to ride back to them herself.

She allowed the guard leader to come with her, bringing three others. It was his job; he'd suffer if she were hurt. She needed to think that way now.

Riding was a little easier, however. Antenami Sardi had chosen her horse himself, a life's passion deployed in her service. And had assigned his own men, eight of them, to go with her. She had killed a man trying to assassinate him. She had accepted the gift of a horse, and the escort.

Rafel was recovering in the Sardi palazzo now. He had asked her to wait, said he'd go with her if she gave him time. She didn't want him with her. Not for this. Not a man who knew her, cared for her. This was too complex, too entangled in what she was. What she'd been made to become.

She was so afraid.

But he *was* recovering, and the physician, Pelachi, had turned out to be a decent man, proud of his success, prepared to learn from it. Of course neither Lenia nor the man who was now heir to the Sardi fortune was about to explain what had happened. Antenami Sardi had spoken of being healed himself some years ago, at an inn near Bischio, in fact. They'd probably passed that inn, Lenia thought. There had been several along the road. He'd been there for the race, he'd said. The celebrated race had already taken place this year. Bischio ought to be quiet now, he'd told her before she set out.

She came back to where the two men following them had now paused on the road. As expected, she knew them both. Men, she thought, could be predictable. Not in a bad way, sometimes. She was close to smiling, but didn't.

"You don't trust me to eight guards of the Sardi family?" she asked.

"Of course we do!" said Brunetto Duso, companion to Guidanio Cerra of Seressa.

The other man, d'Acorsi's, the taciturn one named Gian, just nodded.

"Yet you are here."

Both of them nodded this time. Amusingly synchronized.

"Do you like each other now, at least? Has it been a pleasant ride?" They'd tracked her separately through a fog in Seressa. Had almost fought each other that night.

"He snores," said Duso. "Otherwise he's all right."

"Same," said Gian. He looked as if he wanted to smile, and that it would destroy him to do so.

She shook her head. "And so here you are, far from those you serve, because . . . ?"

"Because Signore Cerra felt that when you entered the city you would refuse an escort from Firenta, and he thought you should still be guarded."

"Same," said Gian. Predictably. Men were. And yet also irritatingly clever sometimes, because she *had* decided she wouldn't enter Bischio with men in Sardi livery. They were an enemy in that city.

Folco had gone north to Macera two weeks ago. She wondered how Gian felt, left behind to guard a woman. She looked at the other man, Duso.

"You are saying you followed us all the way from Seressa, because Guidanio Cerra *thought* I might go to Bischio?"

"He's . . . a thinking sort of man, signora."

"And then you two rode from Firenta together?"

"Not together," Duso said. "We saw each other on the road."

"How nice for you," she said.

But it was oddly difficult to be angry. She didn't seem to have access to as much anger just now. Different emotions, different channels of thought and memory, and the fear.

SHE DID INSTRUCT the Sardi guards to stay outside the city. She made it clear this was not something to be discussed. She reassured them that the other two men would follow her into Bischio and she trusted them, knew who they were.

It was decided that Antenami's men would wait for her in a town they'd passed, off the main road. Dondi, it was called. She and the two men who'd go with her into Bischio would find them there. Or she'd send a message. She did urge the eight of them to go back to Firenta. They respectfully declined to do so. The leader eyed Brunetto Duso and Folco's man dubiously. They eyed him in much the same way.

LENIA AND HER two escorts left their horses at a stable outside the northern walls. A good location for a stable, she thought, inconsequentially. They probably had a successful business. She walked through the open gates of Bischio. The men stayed a distance behind, had agreed to do that. The city's race had been weeks ago—or it would allegedly have been impossible to navigate the streets. Now there was a feeling of aftermath, though a market day. She didn't know anything about the race, who had won; she didn't care, though she did know her brother used to ride in it, and win. If this was her brother.

Shops and stalls and streets that twisted the way they did in all cities. It occurred to her, as she walked, that she had been in so many cities this spring. Almassar to Abeneven, then to Marsena. Sorenica, Rhodias, Seressa, Firenta. And now . . .

People wrote books about their travels, the wonders they saw, dangers encountered. She felt exhausted just thinking about it. *Good* things had happened, mostly, but good things could also change your life, or force you to think about what you wanted from it.

She still had no idea. She didn't even know where she was going in Bischio right now! Chances were good she could ask anyone where Carlo Serrana's ranch was. But she had something she felt she needed to do, first. Or try.

And she was so afraid. Painfully unsure. You could travel to a place, to something that might be there, and still turn back, Lenia thought. People did that all the time. Often it was the wise thing to do.

She had even gone to a Daughters of Jad retreat. Considered withdrawing from the world at one of those. Find peace, and piety. She'd turned away from that.

She didn't think she was suited to peace and piety, quite apart from how she'd reacted to Bentina di Gemisto. But that woman had clarified a larger truth for Lenia. About herself. And so she *was* in Bischio now. Not withdrawing. Not hiding.

She walked the streets of a busy city, midday, and heard the bells beginning to ring. Some people began going to sanctuaries to pray; others remained abroad, buying and selling food and merchandise at stands and stalls. Faith took different forms, she thought. A man led a donkey laden with firewood past her. Another stood juggling and singing a ribald song in a small square, even as the bells continued. Lenia walked. She didn't know where she was going, had no idea how to find the person she needed to find.

This encounter she was setting out to have first . . . this one frightened her, too.

It was interesting, if you could manage to think that way: she had been a woman in Almassar, but she didn't remember living day by day in fear, not after the first months. There were things that had frightened her, but they'd deserved to. She'd registered such moments, such people, and it was . . . proper.

This was different. She was trying, with no idea how to do it, to find someone who had spoken to her inside her mind. Who had said she was in Bischio.

And so, eventually, pausing at another square, in sunlight, Lenia asked the question.

Where are you?

She expected no reply, and so, of course . . .

I'm here, said the now-familiar voice.

I don't know where here is.

Yes you do.

So Lenia Serrana, sighing, did another thing she had never done. She started walking again, just following where her footsteps led, trusting in whatever this was.

Trust was not natural for her. It was difficult.

She approached the central square of Bischio, walked around its edge and away, moving on. She paused a moment, though, and looked back. It was more an oval than a square. Handsome. They ran the race here, apparently. That had to be dangerous, she thought, imagining a huge crowd, the thunder of horses. She tried to picture her brother here, but couldn't. He'd been a child when she was taken.

She walked on. Passed a small and then a larger sanctuary, people entering both. She turned down a wide street, then a narrower one, sunlight hidden by houses close together, overhanging the street.

Another sanctuary, another street intersecting the one she was on. She stopped. Turned to her left. The heart was on the left side. Rafel was alive because the sword that stabbed him had missed his heart and hadn't reached his lungs. She had felt such fear seeing him on the marble floor. Such an awareness of loss. The two men watching her were somewhere behind. She didn't look back now.

An even smaller street, sunlight again at a crossing, small shops, most of them closed at midday. It was cool, pleasant. Springtime. Boys playing ahead of her. A dog barking beside them. She saw a shoemaker's sign swinging, a shop with the residence above, as usual. The shop was still open. Beside the door, a low window on the street. A small child sat on the window ledge doing needlework. Children started working young. You needed to earn your food.

Then she realized that the child wasn't doing needlework. Her head was bent but she had a book in her lap, was reading in the better light falling on the window ledge.

There you are, she heard.

Lenia stopped.

She made a sound in a strained register.

The child looked up from her book.

"Hello, signora," she said aloud. And smiled.

She was, seen closely, no more than four or five years old. A child's voice. Of course a child's voice. But reading a book almost too big for her to hold.

She must be just looking at pictures, Lenia thought. *But . . .*

"Hello," she managed. "I have no idea how any of this has happened. How I'm here."

"I don't either," the child said gravely. "But it must be from Jad?"

She framed it as a question. She looked a little frightened herself. Lenia saw that there were no pictures on the open pages of the book on her lap. She was perched on the window ledge, her short legs dangling over.

"What are you reading?" Lenia asked.

The child held up the book. *The Book of the Sons of Jad.* Not a picture book. Not for children.

"You are . . . who taught you to read?"

"My aunt," the child said. "My father's aunt. She learned numbers and letters when she entered our family business."

"Your family are shoemakers?"

"Yes," the child said, happily. "All the way back to my grandfather's father!" She beamed. "I'm Leora," she said. "I'm going to a Daughters of Jad retreat in the fall."

"You're young for that," Lenia said.

"Everyone says that. But I was promised to Jad when I was just born. They thought I would die," she said. "But I didn't. There was a miracle."

"I see."

"Everything changed because of it."

"Miracles can do that."

The child nodded. "Exactly!"

"I still don't understand anything of how you . . . how we . . ."

"I don't either. I *told* you that. Maybe it's part of the miracle? From the day of the race, when I was supposed to be dying."

"What would I have to do with that?"

"I don't know. Do you want to pray together?"

Lenia shook her head. "I don't really do that very often." She cleared her throat. "If your aunt taught you to read, you must both be very clever."

"We are!" Another smile. Then, "That sounds prideful. I'm sorry. I will ask for forgiveness."

"I forgive you," Lenia said.

A face. "Not *you*! Jad who watches over us all! Why don't you pray?"

Lenia hesitated.

Really, why not?

It was deeply unsettling: the inner voice was not a child's but the spoken one was entirely so.

"You sound so much older in my head." Avoiding the question.

"I know. I think . . . I think that will become my voice? Maybe?"

Lenia drew a breath. This was almost impossibly hard. She said, "You saved my life. And other lives."

The child looked uncertain. "I am . . . I'm happy, but I'm not sure how. I can't do anything to make this happen. And with you is the first time it ever has."

That didn't reassure, Lenia thought.

The girl said, "Your friend. The one who was hurt. He is all right?"

"I think he is. Thank you."

A quick shake of the head. Curly hair, dark, to her shoulders. Bright, blue-grey eyes. A simple tunic, green, good fabric.

"I didn't do that. The . . . other woman did."

"You drew her in, though?"

"I don't think so. I didn't . . . I didn't try. Someone with you did that. And . . . I don't think she believes in the god." A worried expression.

"We all believe in something," Lenia said, though she wasn't certain it was true.

"We must believe in Jad." A firm nod.

Lenia looked at her. She said, "Does your family know you can do this?"

The child named Leora shook her head. "Only my aunt. I told her. I think it would scare my mother and father because of my going to a house of the god. Everyone used to say my aunt was a witch, but they don't any more. She can't walk, and people are cruel about that. But she's not a witch. She teaches me things."

"Good," said Lenia.

"My aunt rode in the race," the child said. "She was hurt. That's why she can't walk."

"But she can read and do numbers? Those are good things. And she's teaching you?"

A vigorous nod. "She says it will be useful for me. It already is!" She lifted the book.

"I'm sure that is true, Leora." She was talking to a child. It was too strange. There was a short silence.

"I'm very young, you know."

"I know. I can see that."

"I lied before. I shouldn't do that. I think . . . it may be I am a little afraid of going to the retreat. It is very far."

"Where is it, Leora?"

"They say near to Rhodias? I think that's far."

A little afraid.

She smiled at the girl. "I am very sure they will welcome you."

Her own fear was receding with every word they spoke, on a street with people walking past, talking, laughing, the noises of everyday existence. This child was about to be taken away from her life, too. Lenia felt an unexpected tenderness. It was rare for her, there had been so few occasions for it. And this had not been a moment when she'd thought it could arise.

She added, "I think you will make everyone proud."

The child lifted her head. "Really?"

"Yes, really."

"Do you think . . . if *this* stays with us, you might talk to me sometimes?"

"I will always do that. If this stays with us."

Thank you.

You are truly welcome, child. You did save my life, and that of some-one I care for.

And then the switching back to words . . .

"You want to know where the man who may be your brother is, don't you?"

A cart rumbled behind her, she waited for it to pass. "Do you know if he is? My brother?"

Leora shook her head. "I don't know anything about him."

"But you know why I'm here?"

A small nod of a small head. "Jad lets me see some things about you."

Lenia managed another smile. This was a child, whatever else she was, and she needed that smile.

As to what she herself had expected, or had been preparing herself to find . . . it was not a small girl reading a holy text, and *seeing* her. Being seen was unsettling for someone who'd lived most of her life trying not to be.

"My father will know where he lives," said Leora.

It turned out that her father was named Carderio Sacchetti, a clearly successful maker of shoes, a man with an easy, generous manner to him. He came to the window when his daughter called him, and he did, indeed, know where the horse ranch of Carlo Serrana was, outside the walls. He didn't ask questions, for which Lenia was immensely grateful. He did say, "Our family's fortunes, a great change in them, are tied to the last race in which Serrana rode. I am not ashamed to say that."

"The last race? Was he . . . was he hurt?"

"Not very much. Not like my aunt was. He had a fall, the usual injuries. He was fine after, but he never rode again. By choice. He has a very successful trade in horses, though, breeding and training and selling them. And much respect in Bischio. He won the race so many times!"

"Thank you," she said. And then, "Goodbye, Leora. Thank you."

"Goodbye."

Not really, though? she heard within.

No, she replied the same way. *Not really.*

And meant it.

There can be miracles, or things impossible to explain or understand in the stories of our lives.

"I am extremely grateful," said Piero Sardi. "I would like to know why you did what you did, at risk of your own life. I confess I am curious. And I dislike owing a debt to people, I find."

Rafel looked at him. A slight man with a light voice, though Rafel had a sense it contained different registers. He was feared and respected and immensely powerful. He was standing in the bedchamber where Rafel was recovering, having appeared with no warning. He was dressed in black, as he apparently always was. He wasn't smiling, but his expression was . . . well, you could call it benign. Or simply curious. He had just said he was curious.

Sardi had spent the last little while killing and exiling people and having their homes burned. There was, Rafel had been told by his doctor, a grim quiet in the city. He could still smell smoke when his window was open.

It was morning. He was propped on pillows in a bed in the Sardi palazzo. The window was indeed open, light streaming through. Some doctors would not allow an open window in a sickroom, but Rafel had told the physician that he wasn't sick, he was recovering from a wound, that he'd been inside for too long and he needed air, even if there was smoke.

He'd dreamed the last few nights of being at sea on the *Silver Wake*. Salt, wind, sun, and clouds. He'd also had a dream of being in Bischio, protecting Lenia—though she'd be far more likely to protect him if danger came. He had no idea what was happening to her. If she'd arrived, if she was still there. He didn't like not knowing.

He said, "I didn't save your son, my lord, but I thank you for the thought. My partner did."

"Your partner was unlikely to have done so without your stepping forward to face a man with a blade. I have been told as much. Modesty befits a man, but so does acknowledging truth."

Rafel said, "I am happy to have done so, then." He was a Kindath, a minor merchant; this was the man who governed Firenta.

"And so my question remains," said Sardi.

Rafel drew a breath. "If we could know why we do all the things we do . . ."

"Not all the things, ben Natan. This one thing." Hint of a smile. "I am aware of the Kindath propensity for debate and deflection."

"Are you, my lord?" Rafel also smiled. He added, as the other man waited, "There was violence in that sanctuary, some of it was suddenly directed towards your son, where I was. It . . . offended me. And we had met him, in Rhodias. I didn't intend to be stabbed, if you're thinking that."

"No, I imagine you didn't. So, not enough time for careful thought? An impulse?"

"I think that is correct. I am not debating or deflecting, my lord. It really can be difficult to say why we do some things in life. Do you not find that?"

"On occasion," said Piero Sardi. Then, "But rarely."

Rafel smiled again. "If anything," he said, "I thought the lord of Acorsi might intervene, given a moment to do so, before the man reached me."

"He was killing someone else, I understand."

"He was, my lord."

A pause. "I usually know why I am doing the things I do. I try to avoid impulse."

"I see."

"Your partner, the woman, Lenia Serrana, she has been trained with weapons?"

"Yes, my lord."

"While a slave in Almassar?"

He hesitated. But there was nothing to conceal. Piero Sardi had some of the best information-gatherers in the world.

"I met her when that time had ended for her."

"Obviously so," Sardi said. "It is unusual, that's all. For a woman, a slave."

"I suppose it is, my lord."

"And she has gone now to find her brother in Bischio?"

Another hesitation.

Sardi registered it. "Antenami told me what he said to her in Rhodias."

"It might be her brother," Rafel said. "It is a common name."

"Somewhat so. I imagine she's fearful of this."

That surprised Rafel. Because it was true. She'd told him so.

He said, "I believe so. I found it difficult to understand."

Sardi shook his head. "I don't. A woman escaped from slavery is not the same as a man who does so. It is unfair, but much of life is."

Lenia had tried to explain this to him. He'd grasped what she meant, but had still said if he knew a brother lost in childhood might be alive, he'd want to know. Need to know. The fact that his own brother had been missing for so long—dead, or escaping his family and his life—that might play a role in his own thinking, but he hadn't told Lenia that. He felt badly now that he hadn't. He ought to have done so. He *was* too secretive. Or careful. Both?

He said, "I would never debate that last point, my lord. About unfairness."

Sardi had grey eyes. Northern blood in the family from some-where? He said, "A Kindath will understand unfairness. You are from Esperaña?"

The question was a politeness. Sardi would know the answer. Not a man who entered many conversations without being prepared, Rafel thought.

"I am. We were expelled when I was a child."

"And went to?

"Almassar."

Sardi nodded. "You should know that I have no issues with your people or your faith. The Kindath are useful in a growing city. The clerics here know my views. My gratitude to you is real. I could have lost both of my sons that day. You will have an honoured place here should you choose to stay, Rafel ben Natan. And we will reward you and Signora Serrana for what you both did, of course."

"No reward is needed, my lord. I mean that. And I suspect she will say the same." He spoke firmly.

"She already did, in fact. You feel you can speak for her?"

"Never," said Rafel. "One would be a great fool to do so with Lenia."

Sardi smiled again, moved a hand to his mouth, as if to hide it.

"Everyone can use a reward for a virtuous deed," Piero Sardi said.

"Do your clerics not teach that virtue is a reward? That Jad knows of it?"

"They do. They still like their comforts and rewards, most of them. Not all, to be fair."

"We are, and I say this with humility, fortunate in our finances, my lord. Your goodwill and your son's survival are reward enough. And I remain deeply sorry about your older son."

"Children can become a way for the world to wound you," said Piero Sardi.

Unexpected. Rafel said nothing. He nodded his head. There was a silence. Not a bad or worrisome one.

Sardi was leaning against the wall by the bed now. There was a chair, he hadn't taken it. He said, a change of tone, "I do understand you have resources. I am told you are building another small merchant ship?"

It was a weakness, even a displaying of pride, but . . . "A carrack, my lord. In Seressa, yes. It will be part of the expedition to take Tarouz. Then we will use it ourselves as we need, if the sisters and the god are kind."

He could see he'd surprised the other man, despite Sardi's attempt to hide it. A carrack was a very expensive ship, and Seressa's Arsenale built the most expensive ones.

"You have assembled enough partners to do that? Good for you." Everyone assumed this.

More pride, or honesty? He said, "Just the two of us, my lord. As I mentioned . . ." He left the sentence unfinished. He'd already said they didn't need a reward.

Piero Sardi looked at him. "I would, of course, like to know more about this."

Rafel smiled. "I would like to know the secret to a swifter recovery from a sword wound in the chest."

Laughter, sudden, almost explosive, from the famously grave man who ruled this city.

"I deserved that," Sardi said, still laughing. His expression changed. "Have you considered the cloth trade? Here? You need not consider it a reward if I invite a man of means to stay with us, invest and participate in Firenta's principal activity. Especially if you have a ship, or two, and places to dock and load them?"

"I have considered nothing yet beyond getting upright again, and the building of our ship. As part of the invasion the lord of Acorsi will lead for the High Patriarch."

"And for Jad," Sardi said. "We have committed to funding ships and men. Did d'Acorsi tell you?"

"He did, my lord. He visited me before he left for Macera." No point denying it, no reason to.

"It will be a year from now. You really have no purposes in life before that?"

"I am very willing to discuss an engagement with trade here." He hadn't given it a thought before this moment. You needed to adapt to what came to you.

"I'm pleased. I will send one of your fellow believers in the moon sisters to you. A merchant named Cardeño. Cardeño ben Zaid. He came here a few years ago. Antenami befriended him. They had another friend in common, a woman, no longer with us here."

"I see," said Rafel, though he didn't, of course.

"There is a good-sized Kindath temple here, as I am sure you know. About fifty families and one of your Elder Teachers."

"I do know that, my lord. I had intended to visit it, pray there."

"I hope you will be moving about soon, and can do that. I have visited it myself."

Another surprise.

His visitor, he saw, had intended that. "I enjoy debate and good conversation," Piero Sardi said. "I have had enjoyable encounters there. I am happy to see you recovering. I am a friend now, Rafel ben Natan, if you want one. Also a friend to Signora Serrana, if she comes back here. Or even if she doesn't."

"Who would not want a friend such as you, my lord?"

A shrug. "There are families who have . . . who had a differing view."

Rafel said nothing. Saying nothing, if you could manage it, was often the best course.

Sardi left. Rafel fell back asleep not long after. He was recovering, but his chest still hurt, and he wasn't strong. The sheep's gut stitches were to come out soon. The wound had a quill inserted, for drainage of pus, but there hadn't been much of that at all, and the doctor now believed there wouldn't be anything substantial. The doctor was very pleased with himself.

Rafel dreamed again, in morning light, of salt and sea. Wind blowing.

⚭

Carlo Serrana had not ridden in the Bischio race for some years now. He had announced it formally: that he was withdrawing to dedicate himself to breeding horses. Still a young man, too. There had been attempts, at intervals, to cause him to change his mind. Large sums of money offered. He was, by a good deal, the most successful rider of the day. He was also quite successful with his ranch, however, and famously incorruptible.

A grim-looking man for the most part—though less so, it was noted by those who had dealings with him, since he'd stopped racing. He attended the race every year, of course, given an honoured place by the start-and-finish line, among the most prominent figures attending. People fought to be seated beside Serrana, share their recollections of his triumphs. He never said what district, horse, rider he favoured in a given year, and was never seen to wager, though *everyone* wagered on the Bischio race. People from all over Batiara and beyond came to watch, and join in the raucous festival that led up to and followed it.

This year the Giraffe District had won. A surprise, as they rarely did. Serrana had been there to offer a handshake and clap on the shoulder to the mud-spattered, grinning rider who had won for them. His first victory. A young man of promise, it was agreed.

That had been weeks ago. Life had returned to normal in the city; it had remained largely unaffected on the Serrana ranch out-side the walls. It was breeding season, and some mares would be dropping their foals soon and needed watching. He had his own four stallions here, plus three sent from aristocrats and merchants in other cities to be bred to his mares. And a truly splendid mare had been brought to the ranch a few days ago for Tarsenio, his most coveted breeding stallion. Normally stallions travelled to the mares, but Serrana did many things differently, and people were willing to pay a great deal, and change their routines, to allow him to do so. No one ever questioned his integrity, his expertise, or the care he offered their horses.

A reserved man, not prone to smiling, but when he did—after a mare's successful dropping of a foal, say, or when his young son suc-cessfully rode a difficult horse—it was a warming expression. His daughter made him laugh, often. Sun after rain—his wife always said that about his laughter. She knew him very well; it didn't unset-tle him any more.

When he'd been a rider, it had been useful to be intimidating, feared on the track, but there was no call for that now. He had even become known, on days in the city for business, stopping at a tavern, as a good storyteller about horses, racing. Always about those things. He never let anyone buy him a drink. He was admired more than he was liked, but some did say they liked him, latterly. He was from the south. Had that colouring. Had learned to ride down there, evidently.

One of the mares would have her foal soon, a matter of days. He was walking back from looking in on her when he saw someone riding alone up to the gate, along their trail off the Bischio road. The rider stopped some distance from the ranch. Unusual.

It was a woman, he saw, belatedly. Also unusual, that she'd be alone. It wasn't especially dangerous here, in daylight, afternoon, but it wasn't *wise* for a woman to do this. For anyone, really. She wasn't a very good rider; he registered that without any actual thought. A lifetime with horses.

She stayed where she was, too far away for him to make her out clearly. She was looking at his ranch. It was a handsome property, pastures, barns, training rings, the wide, low house he'd built in the southern style, then expanded. There were many horses to be seen. Of course there were.

For some reason he stopped walking, too. He stood where he was, looking at her. The sun was on his left, beginning to set, a windy afternoon, white clouds scudding. The blue moon was rising in the east, faint in the daylight, but present, like a memory.

Motionless between the main barn and the front gate, looking north up a road that led only here, Serrana felt his heart thump once, very hard. And then it seemed to him as if it actually stopped for a moment, before starting to beat again. His hands began to tremble. When he resumed walking towards the gate, he realized that his legs were trembling, too.

The woman began moving her horse forward. Very slowly.

Carlo Serrana began to cry.

THEY MET BY the wide, slatted, chest-high wooden gate. He got there first, was waiting.

Riding up, Lenia saw that he was weeping. It broke her like a hammer.

It was him. She'd known it from far off, after two decades and more, after what time and life had done to both of them. Seeing him walking on his own property, then stopping abruptly when he saw her, as she had also stopped in the road. A boy, not yet ten years old, when last . . .

When last seen, known, loved. With a full heart, unbroken.

SHE WAS TALL. Had been tall as a girl, as he remembered her, but that might have been because he was younger and she was his sister and protector. You could have distorted memories for reasons such as that. He remembered his father as tall, and he hadn't been.

It was also difficult just now because they were both crying. Neither had said a word yet. Neither had been able to. He wasn't a man of words, and this felt . . . too much beyond speech.

She dismounted. Not too awkwardly, he thought, watching her every move, hungrily, urgently.

She came towards the gate where he was but stopped (again, stopped) a little distance away.

She left the horse untethered, which you shouldn't do, but . . .

She was so beautiful to him, and such a grief and a reminder of grief.

"I never cry," Lenia said. First words.

Which only made him weep harder. It was difficult to breathe. Raggedly, feeling it as pain, he fought for control.

He said, finally, to his sister, to Lenia, after so long, "I killed people at home. Asharites. Even those who taught me to ride. I said . . . I said your name and father's whenever I did. I was certain you had died. Then mother died, not long after. I buried her where people had helped us bury father, by the olive trees."

A speech. It was close to a speech.

She shook her head. Kept shaking it. Wiped her eyes on her sleeve. Her dark remembered eyes.

"Oh, Carlito," his sister said.

He had not been called by that name since she'd been taken. He placed his hands on the top of the gate for support. He really felt he might fall. But then he extended them over the slats of the gate and his lost sister came forward into his life again, from loss and memory, taking the few remaining steps on Jad's earth that lay between them near the end of what had been an ordinary spring afternoon, and she took his hands in hers and the child in him let out a heart's cry. There was joy in it and pain and so much awareness of time lost and gone by.

SHE HAD TO say it, gripping his hands.

"Carlito, Carlo, I was a slave among them."

"I thought that," he said, He was gripping her hands as if he would never let them go. "If you were even alive. It is . . . it is why I killed, Lenia, as many as I could, before I came north."

"When did mother die?"

"Four years after. She was never the same, Lenia."

Used to sing to them, tell stories. *Who could be the same after what happened to us?* she thought.

"I did, too," she said. "I also killed Asharites." It was astonishingly difficult to form words. "The man who owned me, first. Then others."

"Good," was all he said.

"I . . ." This was so hard. "I thought you might not accept my coming back."

"*What?*"

His tone, the dismay, the disbelief in his voice at the very idea—
an idea that had ruled her life from the moment she was free again.
Balm to a wound festering from that day.

"Carlito, a woman taken away is—"

"They *took* you, you didn't choose *anything!*" He was almost hurt-
ing her now, squeezing her hands so hard. "Lenia, you are here! You
escaped. You are *alive!* Oh, Jad, this is the best day I can remember
in my life."

She lowered her head and kissed his hands.

"Really?' she said. "But . . . I heard you won some race here a few
times."

It took a moment, then he understood that she was teasing him.
Carlo smiled. In turn he lifted her hands and kissed them both.

"You have a wife? Children?"

He nodded. "The boy is Strani, the girl is Aura."

Their father's name, their mother's.

Her heart was full, it was overflowing, like a pitcher filled too high.

"Will you come in and meet them?" he said. "And Anni? And see
my horses? There is . . . there is a home here for you, for as long as
you want it. For always."

"You have to open the gate first, Carlito."

He smiled again at that. A well-built man, not tall, but clearly very
strong, easy in his body. He looked like their father, she thought. As
a boy he'd smiled all the time.

"I can do that," her brother said.

His voice healed the world a little more with every word he spoke.
It frightened her, how much so. *Were you allowed to be happy?* she
thought.

He opened the gate. She walked through. He gestured to someone as he followed her, and one of his men ran over and out on the
path, to bring her horse.

CARLO SERRANA WOULD remember all his life the time when his sister came back to him—from the dead, from exile, from the hollow shaped inside him by her absence—unlooked for, loved.

Two weeks. They told each other stories: shared memories, and those that only one of them had, since they'd been ripped apart so young. He taught her how to ride properly, or better at least. He was a patient teacher. Horses the love of his life, along with his wife and children. And Lenia now. Lenia again.

Anni, his wife, a gift of Jad he felt he had never deserved, took to her as she took to everyone who was good, and even more because this was his sister and she made him smile. The children discovered they had an aunt, an unknown sister of their father, who had come to stay for a time.

Only for a time. Only that for now, she said. She would not say what might come after. She had things she needed to do, she said.

She was, it emerged, a woman with assets. In a Seressini bank.

He had done well over the years, because of the racing, from the time he'd arrived, very young but already strong—extremely good, ferocious even, on the track. He'd won the would-be riders' competition to be entered in the draw to ride the race his first year here, and his name had been picked. Randomly then, just fortune's wheel turning. He'd known no one, had no district desiring him as their rider, offering bribes to the officials. He was unknown. Last time that was so.

He won that first race. Broke another rider's arm with the club they all carried. It was permitted, expected—you'd hit the others, they'd swing at you. Never at the horses. You could be beaten or killed after the race if you did that, even by chance.

Being extremely good in the Bischio race was a path to fortune here.

And Lenia? She had become a merchant with a partner and a ship, and then . . . just this spring, just *now* . . . she was suddenly wealthy, and she and that partner were building a ship for a fleet that might be going south next year.

To take the city of Tarouz from Zariq ibn Tihon. A name every-one knew. A man who sent raiding ships, like the one that had destroyed their lives.

Lenia had come here looking for him after Antenami Sardi had told her there was a man named Carlo Serrana in Bischio, raising horses. Sardi! Of all people! Could the world, or your own insignifi-cant part of it, change because of such a casual thing? Something so random, so . . . capricious?

It seemed it could. It had. She was alive and had found him.

That his sister had the resources to build a ship, and planned to go to war with it, that she was—apparently—skilled with knives and a small sword and intended to kill men herself when they got to Tarouz, these were things he needed to make room for in his understanding.

"BUT IT IS the same for me, Carlito, understanding you as the best rider of horses here and a breeder with a ranch like this," she said when he told her this one evening, as they walked under emerging stars on the land he owned. "How could we have guessed?"

"Guess the future? How can anyone alive?" he said.

"Oh, dear," Lenia said, laughing. Her laughter was rain in a dry month for him. "A philosopher, too? *That* I am not ready for."

He had to laugh with her. But added, "Too much time has gone by, Lenia."

"Perhaps not," she said. "We're here."

But that was also when she told him she'd be leaving soon. She'd try to return. Return often, she said, though she didn't know when yet. Too much had changed for her, was still changing.

Try to return collided in his heart with *going to war*.

"I don't think I could bear to lose you again," he said.

"You never will now," his older sister said, stopping and turning to him. More stars were coming out. A soft evening, little wind, no clouds, horses quiet in the pasture beyond the fence. "We have seen each other, and we know what we know, and it is good. Your family are wonderful, Carlito. It eases my heart to see you with them."

"But you have none."

She shrugged. "I've had a different life."

And so, amid joy, there remained the awareness of pain, sorrow like a stone. How could there not be? The world was what it was, and their parents were buried under the olive tree at the edge of the farmyard that had been home.

Two days after that a man came riding up the path, also alone, though Carlo saw that others had stopped on the road a distance behind him, so he could approach by himself.

There were clouds that day, and a promise of rain, though it was not here yet. The man was a better rider than Lenia had been, Carlo saw, because he couldn't *not* see how people rode, but he was sitting carefully on his horse (a good horse), as if uncomfortable.

Lenia had been with him at a pasture rail, watching Strani work with a horse. The boy was very young, but had the hands and instincts already, the reassuring voice. She followed Carlo's glance, saw what he saw in the road.

He watched her walk towards the gate to meet this man, realized that she was unsurprised to see who had come, decided to go and be there, too. Was aware, in the moment, that she would be leaving now. The world calling her away. Not lost as before, but away, still.

They spent the night at the ranch, she and her Kindath partner. He liked the man immediately, ben Natan. There had been Kindath down south. Sorenica on the coast held a great many of them, had for a long time, and Duke Ersani welcomed them at his court, along with Asharites. This man was courteous and amusing (he did tricks with coins for the children), and he was Lenia's business partner, had helped her escape, then make her fortune. He'd have to like this man, wouldn't he?

And Rafel ben Natan wasn't the reason Lenia was leaving. *She* was the reason she was leaving. In control of her own life now. At least to the degree any person could be, he thought.

RAFEL WENT OUTSIDE with Lenia after they ate. Her brother and his wife left them their privacy. He walked slowly, but it was more stiffness after riding than pain from his wound now. He was healed, they'd told him in Firenta. His stitches were gone. He had a scar. Someone looking at him without a shirt might think he was a military man. Amusing. There was still something strange about how he'd been saved that day. Antenami Sardi, visiting, had started to talk about it once, almost proudly. Then stopped himself, started again, stopped again. Rafel hadn't pushed him.

There had been good things emerging in Firenta. It hadn't been *anything* like a planned action, what he'd done in the sanctuary, but it had consequences. He'd asked the younger Sardi, the heir and successor now, to help him with something. A search. The Sardis were well-connected everywhere. Antenami had been genuinely happy to try.

He saw Lenia eyeing him closely as they walked. He told her again that he was all right. He'd been telling her since he'd arrived. Didn't think she entirely believed him. They came to a fence surrounding a pasture. He could see horses, shapes in the gathering night. They stood beside each other, arms on the top rail under stars and both moons, east. It was chilly.

"What happened in Firenta? After I left." She was almost always direct, he thought.

"Deaths, many more exiled in the two families, some of their supporters. The burning of houses stopped."

"It doesn't make sense to burn houses if you've exiled the people who live there."

"No, it doesn't. Piero Sardi mostly does sensible things, I believe."

"You spoke with him?"

And here it was. Quickly.

"He came to see me a few times. I was moved to their palazzo from the room in the sanctuary."

"I see. And that was . . . good?"

"I think so, Lenia. He offered me one of the now-empty houses, and one for you. Gifts, for however we want to use them. He's suggested we live there, invest in their cloth trade, use my connections in Ferrieres and Esperaña, maybe even Almassar, to help expand the markets they want to control."

"I see," she said again.

"He isn't a man who thinks about just entering a market."

"Controlling it?"

"Yes."

"Does this . . . is this a thing you can see doing?"

"It is one thing. Sardi had a Kindath, a man named ben Zaid, come see me. To tell me how we are treated there."

"I see. And how are you treated?"

He smiled. He was a little tired, but the air was bracing. "Much as everywhere, I'd say. Tolerated when useful and if times are not troubled."

"But more so if you've saved the life of an important man?"

"That, too. I think they feel to be in our debt."

"They are, Rafel. But . . . Antenami Sardi is also how I found Carlo. I owe him for this."

An owl called in the darkness to their left.

"He seems to have done extremely well, your brother."

"Yes. He has. He's . . . he's wonderful, Rafel. They all are. I still cannot believe it."

He looked at her, smiling. "You cannot believe a good thing can happen? Has happened?"

She shook her head. "Don't mock me. It is difficult, yes. I . . . assume bad consequences. I was sure you'd die in the sanctuary. I was so angry with you!"

He looked at her. He shook his head. "Such an affectionate response."

She met his gaze, though it was hard to see her eyes now. "It was, Rafel. I was not ready to lose you. Whatever we end up doing."

Whatever we end up doing.

SHE FELT SUCH confusion within. Happiness, apprehension, turmoil, flux . . . so many *words*. Too many, Lenia thought. Sometimes it wasn't about the words.

He had been asleep. She saw that when he opened his door to her quiet knock. It was late, she didn't want to wake anyone else, but she also knew it would be all right if she did. This was as safe a place as there was in the world for her. Such a thought.

But she couldn't stay. Not yet. Maybe not ever. There was no *role* for her here, no proper task. It was Carlo's life, not hers. There was, Rafel had said, a house waiting for her in Firenta, if she wanted it. There was also the offer from Folco d'Acorsi. There was a ship they were building. For Jad. Maybe even for Strani and Aura Serrana, lying in graves on what had been their farm. And for vengeance also, perhaps, for their daughter—in her own name, with her chosen weapons, at Tarouz.

But now? Tonight, on a ranch near Bischio? Amid all the words, thoughts, choices, memories, decisions to be made . . . ?

"Are you feeling well enough," she asked her partner, her friend, the man it seemed she did know best in the world, "to make love to me? Or let me make love to you?"

His room was dark, she held a candle in the hallway. She saw his eyes widen. "Are you certain, Lenia?"

"I am certain of nothing," she said. "I have decided uncertainty is all right. But I know that this feels needful to me."

"Needful," he repeated.

"I can go," she said.

"No. Please. Please, do not," Rafel said, and what she heard in a handful of words aroused her even more than she already was. He reached out a hand and she took it with the one that was not holding a candle and he drew her into his room and then, when the candle was set down, she drew him into her arms for the first kiss they had ever shared.

Needful. She whispered it to him again. There was agency in desire, she thought, and there was urgency, as well.

"Will this change everything?" he asked, later, as they lay together on his bed.

"Change? Everything always changes," Lenia said. "Also, you look very handsome just now."

"That," Rafel said, "is because there's only one candle in this room."

She laughed aloud. It was good to feel laughter, to release it. To believe it was permitted. That many things might now, finally, be allowed.

We are vulnerable when we feel that way. But not, in truth, any more than when we live curtailed, held back, enraged, afraid. Everything is, indeed, always changing. And not usually to be controlled by us, the children of earth and sky, with fortune's wheel always turning and a future we cannot know.

BROTHER AND SISTER both wept in the morning, parting at the gate. Carlo Serrana thought his heart would break, watching her ride away. But that had occurred long ago, he thought, the breaking of his heart.

It seemed it was a thing that could happen again and again until you died and the god judged your soul and took you for his own or left you to the dark.

She had said she'd come back. He clung to that the way he clung to his family, and hope.

༄

Ayaash ibn Farai made his way south and east carefully from the coast above Sorenica. A boy on a good horse alone was at risk. Also, he was an Asharite. Any spoken words would betray him.

He rode at twilight and at night, dangerous for different reasons, but he judged it less so than daylight when he could be seen, noted, questioned. He had no experience, no real judgment, but no choice, either, but to try.

He stayed off the roads mostly, moving through fields or picking his way along the edge of woods until full dark when it became too hard to see where he was going even under moonlight, and then he moved back to a road.

The roadway he finally took grew wide, better maintained, and he suspected he was getting close to where he was going. The only destination he'd been able to think of, alone in a foreign land where they hated his faith and his people. They'd also hate him for himself, if they knew he had been part of a raid by Ziyar ibn Tihon.

It was important to get away from where that had happened.

He was working his way into the lands ruled by Duke Ersani of Casiano, at the bottom of Batiara. The only idea he'd had. The duke, like his father before him, was known to employ Asharites: at court, in the indigo fields now, as horse-trainers, palace guards. Those men were despised by the ibn Tihon brothers and by Ayaash's father as traitors to their faith and tribes, but they did exist.

He needed to see some of them, to be sure he'd come far enough into the duke's lands. He might be able to approach someone who worshipped Ashar's stars and would help him—out of fellow feeling, kindness. Maybe pity for someone lost and alone?

Towards sunrise one morning, seeing the hint of grey and then a flush of pink in the east, Ayaash moved again off the road, into fields of indigo and then grain. He'd need a place to stop and hide until darkness fell again, but there were no woods here. Maybe farther ahead. He saw too many farmhouses, smoke rising from chimneys already, people preparing for the day. He was hungry, had eaten nothing since the morning before, but didn't dare try to steal anything with the sun rising. Ought to have done so before, but he'd heard wolves in the night.

He kept a distance from the houses, hoped no one would care about a rider going past, though they'd wonder that he wasn't on the main road, probably. After a little time, no obvious shelter to be seen, he found himself nearing a farmhouse that looked rundown, no chimney smoke. There was a barn at a little distance and the fence was broken in places.

He'd head for the barn, he decided, shelter there until day's end. He'd done that before, coming this way. It was too bright now to be abroad and he was tired as well as hungry.

He rode carefully past the house and barn to the far edge of the property, and then turned. There were trees now, finally, a small grove of olive trees. He dismounted among them and tied the horse out of sight. The trees weren't that tall, but they were all he had. He'd check the barn first. If it was as empty as it looked he'd bring his horse in there, try to find food and water for both of them. Wait out the day again.

He walked out of the trees. There were two graves here, he saw. Wrong season for olives or he could eat those, he thought. He looked at the graves with little interest. Inscriptions on the headstones in Batiaran, which he could not read. The graves were untended. It gave him more hope this might indeed be an abandoned farm.

Hope can be misleading.

"A good horse," said a voice behind him. "How do you come by it?"

Ayaash spun around, terrified, then gasped in relief. The speaker was Asharite, even to a necklace of stars on silver!

"Thanks be to the holy stars," he said in his own language. "I am so happy to see you."

"Really?" said the other man, not switching from Batiaran. "Why? And why are you here?"

"Many questions!" Ayaash said, trying to smile.

"Awaiting answers," the man said. He was of middle years, not a big man but extremely calm, which unsettled Ayaash. "You are from where?"

A bad question, that one. He temporized. "I am looking for shelter and work. I am a hard worker. Is this your farm?"

"It will be," the other said. "We are repairing the fences and the barn, then the house."

"I can help!" Ayaash said.

"I don't think so," said the man. "I think you are from the Majriti, by your accent. I think you were part of a raid. I think I even know which one it was. News," he added, "travels fast sometimes."

"No!" Ayaash exclaimed. "No, I—"

"As I said, a good horse for a boy alone, and hiding it, too. Or trying. Were you on the ibn Tihon raid? And ran away?"

"No," said Ayaash, less emphatically. He was so tired, so afraid.

"I think you were," said the other man, still so calmly. "Thing is, it would be very bad for my brother and myself if we were discovered to be employing someone from that ship, just when we've finally been allowed land of our own."

His voice had changed.

"I understand," Ayaash said. "I'll just carry on, then. I did not . . . I wasn't part of any raid, though. I just want work. And shelter?"

"All of us want shelter," the other man said, in Asharic this time. Almost as a kindness, Ayaash thought. "I'm sorry, boy. But you're in the wrong place."

He drew the sword at his belt.

Ayaash gaped. But he wasn't a coward, just weary and alone, and he quickly drew his own sword, which he did know how to use, being his father's son, taught from childhood (not so long ago) and he could—

He could die there, Ashar's stars hidden by the risen sun on a springtime morning. He was not killed by the blade of the man in front of him, who was not, in truth, a fighter, and Ayaash might have dealt with him. He was clubbed down from behind, his head cracked open by a blow from a heavy staff.

Wielded by a second man, the brother (though Ayaash never knew that) emerging from the olive trees behind the two graves. On which the inscriptions read, carved deeply into dark-grey, moss-covered stones: *Strani Serrana,* and *Aura Serrana,* and *Rest forever loved in Jad's Light.*

IT WAS WASTE, *it was too little time, he had done nothing, achieved nothing, experienced so little, and now it was done. What was the point of life granted to you, birth, infancy, childhood, entry into manhood, if this was all it was? All it would ever be?*

He was looking down at his own crumpled body, blood flowing from his smashed-open head. He could cry. Could you be dead and cry?

No one would ever know where he'd died. His father would never know. His father . . . his father had made *him join this raid. He wanted to hate him, blame him, he'd never felt able to do that. Never been strong enough. His father had said it would be good training, a step in his career, if Ayaash wanted a life at sea. Ayaash hadn't ever really known what he wanted, what kind of life. What choices he might have, if any choice at all, son of the father he had. Never would know now. Or choose. Make any choices at all. It felt . . . unfair. So much he'd never done and never would now do. Was it for* this *that children rose up and walked, then ran from their mothers' and nurses' sides and entered the wider world, travelling through their lives?*

What wider world? Ayaash ibn Farai thought. What life travelled through? He'd not even have a grave, no rituals, no prayers spoken above him, to help his passage through the afterlife. Dead in Jaddite lands, at Asharite hands.

He didn't really know enough to think in terms of irony, as he looked down at the star-worshippers who had killed him, but he had a glimmering, a glimpse of it. I might have done things, *was his last thought, suspended here. He looked up, away from that broken body on the ground, his body. He looked for stars, above and beyond the morning sun. Didn't know if they'd be there. Didn't know if anything was there. Here. Wherever he was.*

Felt such a weight of sorrow on what had been a springtime morning in the world.

HE WAS BURIED properly, as it happened. Right there, near the other two graves, though not with a headstone, just a low mound, since the brothers who now owned that several-times abandoned farm had decided it really was best to say nothing of this encounter, or leave any sign of it. But after they dug and covered over his grave they did offer the prayers of their people for his soul, that it be conducted to Ashar among the shining, eternal stars. They were not cruel or violent people at all, they reassured each other, just living in the world as it had been given to them.

Part Four

CHAPTER XII

As spring turned towards summer—dry and too hot in most of Batiara and southern Ferrieres, windswept in the north, and with unusually frequent thunderstorms towards Esperaña and the western Majriti—there was real fear in Jaddite coastal lands that Zariq ibn Tihon would begin to execute a savage vengeance for his brother's death, which had become known because the High Patriarch wanted it known.

There was no secret as to how the brother had died. Ziyar had been killed in Sorenica by Folco d'Acorsi, an equally formidable man. It was unclear why Folco had been there, but he had been, and the head of Ziyar ibn Tihon was displayed soon after on the ramparts of the Patriarchal Palace in Rhodias. It was still there, rotting. His headless body had been dragged through the city streets, then left for hungry dogs. That had been seen and reported, also as intended.

Vengeance was demanded, for many reasons.

Zariq ibn Tihon, however, had difficulties to address in the city he ruled. Substantial ones, and they'd be more so when word of certain things emerged. That hadn't happened yet. It would. People told tales. Men and women loved telling tales, hearing them. The coinage of the world. And there were those who had an interest in his troubles occurring.

The brothers' scheme to take over Abeneven with the blessing of Gurçu the Conqueror in Asharias . . . that plan had required both brothers: one to remain in Tarouz, one to go west to seize power in Abeneven.

It had also depended on chaos in the other city after the khalif's murder, and—obviously—that blessing of Gurçu. Of course, as his agents in the Majriti, they ought to have informed him of their plan in advance, not gone ahead with an assassination. Zariq had written a letter, explaining, or trying to. Had dispatched it, and had prayed that evening, with intensity.

Someone else had written to Asharias already. He was sure of it. He felt threatened and alone. Ziyar was dead and sheltered among Ashar's stars. Or so his brother hoped. He might not be. Who could know? And there had been no burial, no rites.

But it was a certainty that a message to Asharias had been sent from Abeneven right after the death by poison of Keram al-Faradi. If so, this would have been done by the vizier there, ibn Zukar—who had acted (it had to be admitted) with decisiveness, and appeared securely situated now, unexpectedly.

If Gurçu had learned of events in that way, it was not a good thing.

The assassination itself had happened much as planned. The assassin was dead (usefully), the Kindath merchant and his woman partner paid. (They would be too fearful to ever say a word.) But the *consequences* had not been at all as expected.

All of this meant that Zariq ibn Tihon found himself in his city of Tarouz feeling—for the first time he could remember—fearful, as summer's heat came with the southern winds. There were stories that the vizier in Abeneven, acting as khalif and probably claiming the title soon, was preparing to come after *him*, with support from the western tribes. If Gurçu were to withdraw support from Zariq—turn his countenance away, as the phrase went—the older ibn Tihon brother, the only ibn Tihon brother now, was . . .

Well, he was not in the best position, it could be said.

If Zariq's soldiers from Asharias received word from Gurçu that the ibn Tihons had overreached, that agents of the grand khalif who failed to remember they *were* merely agents became expendable . . .

Not good thoughts amid heat and thunderstorms. Zariq ibn Tihon knew he was a powerful, feared person in the world, still in the prime of life—but he felt old that season, and he missed his brother. Nothing assuaged him. He smoked a great deal of hashish; he summoned women every night from his harem. Once or twice these women, even his most favoured ones, were unable even to arouse him.

That had never happened before.

As a consequence of all these things, no plan emerged for a fleet of vengeance driving across the Middle Sea to savage coastal Jaddite cities for slaves, and create a carnival of death. That should have happened. It did not.

One ship only was sent, under his best commander. Farai Alfasi's young son had been with Ziyar on his raid. He was among those dead. Or missing with the galley. It was not known which.

Zariq's hesitance as to a campaign of retribution was not known in Jaddite lands. Hence the widespread terror there, urgent watchfulness along many coasts. You could not kill a man like Ziyar ibn Tihon and disgrace his corpse without expecting a response.

Some wondered if Folco d'Acorsi might even be afraid. Others knew he was not.

A few clever leaders in Batiara did speculate that the older brother might be in a difficult circumstance—since they had information from a Kindath merchant and the Jaddite woman who was his partner. But that was all it was, information, speculation. Certainty was not usually given to mortals, though you could weigh chances, take actions. Make mistakes, too.

It was a summer driven by fear, in many places.

⚭

Folco d'Acorsi had proceeded from Firenta to Macera on his campaign of recruitment for the campaign against Tarouz.

There he met with his wife's brother, the tall, cold, cautious duke of that extremely powerful city. Caution notwithstanding, Arimanno Ripoli was not in a position to refuse his brother-in-law, not when Folco had been given formal command by the Patriarch and a holy war was to be declared. Not when he also presented documents of Seressa's commitment of ships and sailors. And perhaps especially, the report that Piero Sardi of Firenta had ordered monies transferred to the Patriarchal account.

Not just promised, already transferred.

The landlocked cities led by Ripoli and Sardi were rivals. And of course the High Patriarch was a Sardi, and from his palace in Rhodias he could press a holy thumb heavily on the scales of power if he wished. Macera needed to match Firenta. There was always the grim possibility that the Patriarch would permit Firenta to capture Bischio, which would be extremely bad for the other powers.

Arimanno Ripoli knew all of this.

He exceeded Firenta's contribution by a carefully judged amount.

Folco hadn't needed to say much. Duke Arimanno was another of the leaders of that time who could lay claim to extreme shrewdness. Power, endlessly fickle, demanded as much, or it moved on, seductive and alluring, to dwell with someone else.

FOLCO STAYED A time in Macera with his wife's family. They hunted every day, enjoyed entertainments at banquets. There were musicians and wrestlers. He declined an invitation to wrestle one of the courtiers. The offer was made in jest, mostly. It was known that the lord of Acorsi had killed a man wrestling when young. An accident, but memorable. As always, there were stories.

He was accompanied by a number of his men, and one woman who joined him, coming north with a Sardi escort, later. The escort didn't linger, turned right around and went home. The woman was newly with Folco's company, it seemed. Only for the coming year, he explained to the Ripolis, who expressed interest in a handsome woman being with him. They inquired, for many reasons, though not, as it happened, the one that might have seemed most obvious, or salacious.

There were things women could do for a military commander that men could not, although he was the only one of the mercenary leaders who had ever employed a woman in this way. They knew this, in Macera.

Also, the Ripolis' spies informed them, this woman was well off, to the point of building a ship for the invasion fleet, and after, a group organized by a partner who was said to be of the Kindath faith. All very interesting.

It was curious that she'd agreed to serve with Folco. Corinna, duchess of Macera, sent a letter to the lady Caterina in Acorsi, her husband's sister. She wrote, as always, of silk, deaths, the weather, painters, events in the world. But she did mention, as if indifferently, that Folco had a woman with him again. Did Caterina know much about her? She seemed, the duchess added, pleasant enough, attractive, if quiet.

The lady Caterina smiled reading this. She was entirely undisturbed, though later at night, alone in bed, she grew troubled and sad, tangled in memories and absence.

Folco also wrote to his wife, reporting that he had one more journey to make before coming home. There was no significant danger, he added, but because it might involve some time, and he didn't want to carry a certain item so far, he was taking the liberty of sending her a gift, with four of his men. He hoped it would serve as an emblem of his devotion, he wrote, and of his urgent impatience to see her again. And hold her, he added. Perhaps, his letter ended, she might wear it to receive him when he came home? If, of course, she was pleased: by the gift, and by the prospect of his return.

The lady Caterina Ripoli d'Acorsi was a great beauty and a subtle woman, in a marriage unexpectedly loving from the start, and still so. She took pride in her composure. She gasped aloud, however, when she lifted the clasp of the sandalwood box presented to her and saw what lay within, green and glorious, unmatched in the world.

ॐ

Lenia could not have named with clarity the reasons why she had chosen to spend the year with Folco d'Acorsi while their ship was being built.

Part of it was the simple fact of the invitation from this man, given what he was. Another was that this became a way to delay, create time to think before making larger decisions. Sometimes you needed that. Perhaps the god would send her inspiration. Or . . . something would?

How *did* people make choices in life? she wondered. If they lived a life that allowed choices. Did they really make them? Or mostly drift into things then look back, years after, and wonder? Or were choices made *for* them. Or . . . ?

She'd told d'Acorsi she'd come with him to Ferrieres and stay with his company after, until they sailed for Tarouz, if they did.

She wasn't sure what she could do to help make that fleet happen, but she very much wanted it to sail, and there was no doubt being with the man chosen to command it would . . . well, it would give her *some* chance to play a role. Her thought was that it would be the last time she went to Asharite lands. She had been forced to go once, now she would *choose* to do so. Choices again. That word.

That little girl in Bischio, Leora Sacchetti . . . perhaps she had a clear course before her. She'd be entering a retreat soon, embracing that life. Or having it given to her. But even there unexpected things might happen. And that child was many things, but not ordinary.

Rafel had remained in Firenta. He'd accepted the Sardi invitation to invest in the cloth trade there, though he'd also go back and forth to Seressa to oversee the building of their ship.

She had stopped in Firenta on her way north, long enough to accept a small palazzo from among those seized from the rebel families. Antenami Sardi had promised to staff it for her. She liked him. A hard man not to like. And the great man, his father, seemed to have taken to Rafel. Her partner had told her that late at night on Carlo's ranch, after they'd made love.

After they'd made love.

She was still coming to terms with being a woman who could do, who *had* done, what she'd done that night. Was she really allowed to make such decisions in what seemed to have become her life? Extend affection, accept desire? Her own, someone else's? To be a woman who seduced a man? And not just *a man* but one who cared for her.

These were, Lenia Serrana thought, the dilemmas of a free woman with some standing in the world. It *would* take getting accustomed to. A year with d'Acorsi might help with that.

She hoped she would adjust. It was hard to accept the idea that happiness, different forms of it, might be allowed.

The surprise that night on her brother's ranch had been that Rafel was a skilful lover. Should she have guessed he would be? How? She had so little experience of lovemaking as pleasure, guided by need. But her body had given her some answers twice now, with Raina Vidal in Sorenica and in Carlo's house, before she'd ridden away.

ON WHAT TURNED out to be the end of their time in Macera, Lenia reluctantly joined the court in a morning hunt.

She had no objection to hunting, she just disliked riding, still, even if she was better than she had been. You rode a horse when you needed to get somewhere, in her view. Not to leap fallen trees in a wood to kill something for entertainment.

That it became her last day, and Folco's, and the rest of his company's, was partly her fault. Or entirely so, someone might say.

She had been riding with Corinna, duchess of Macera, who was predictably skilled on a horse. That came with rank; perhaps you also needed a passion for it. Folco was up ahead with his wife's brother, the duke. They weren't riding fast, nothing had yet been scented by the hounds. It was a beautiful morning to be outdoors, Lenia had to concede. It would probably be hot later, but it wasn't so yet, and the effects of light and shade as trees screened and allowed the sunlight were lovely. You could understand why people did this, she thought, if leisure was their gift from life.

The duchess had drifted back a little when the path widened, so they rode side by side now. A tall woman, more handsome than beautiful, younger-looking than her husband. Likely she was, but they'd had several children. Some had died, of the usual causes, and in a rebellion here years ago. Lenia didn't know much about it. Similar to Firenta's, she'd gathered. Rivals for power in the city.

"You don't like horses?" Corinna Ripoli asked, smiling.

It was, it seemed, evident.

"I have had little chance to ride. My brother raises and breeds them near Bischio, my lady. He has said he'll teach me properly in time."

"He hasn't had the time yet?" Still smiling.

They would know her history, Lenia thought, or some of it.

She smiled back, catching the first faint hint of an unexpected challenge. She said, "As you might know, I was enslaved in the Majriti for much of my life. Not many slaves ride horses, especially women."

A trace of disappointment in the other's fine-boned features? A desire balked, a wish to unsettle her? Lenia veered around a fallen branch in the path; Corinna Ripoli just had her horse go over it. Together again, the duchess said, "I envy you, going to see the king of Ferrieres. They say Émery is a beautiful man."

"I have heard as much."

"Folco is also a powerful, handsome man to be travelling with, isn't he?"

Careful! Lenia suddenly heard within, clearly as ever. The adult voice of a child in Bischio.

There you are, she said, the same way. It was still unsettling, but was also something else by now. A part of her life. This child. This voice.

Why doesn't she like you?

No idea, Leora.

"Handsome? Folco?" she said aloud to the woman riding beside her. "You think?"

"You don't?"

Lenia let herself laugh a little. She *was* amused, though aware of the need for caution. "Not why one would follow him, I suspect."

"Why *would* a woman follow him?" the duchess asked. No laughter now.

"He has other qualities, my lady, as the world knows. But if I were to be attracted in that way to someone, it would more likely be you than him, to be honest."

Lenia! Is that honest?

Probably not.

Probably?

Hush, Leora!

The duchess of Macera had flushed. Had turned her gaze to the path ahead. Lenia added, feeling reckless, and also a little angry, "Your colouring just now is exceptionally appealing, my lady. If I might be permitted to say."

Corinna Ripoli had done too many verbal dances to remain disconcerted for long. She said, "The morning air is always good for us. But why are you joining a company of soldiers, then, to travel so far, and the only woman?"

"I have only ever been to Marsena in Ferrieres." She decided something else was probably not known by the other woman, and could be another blow. She said, "There are things I want to learn and see. I have a year before our ship is built in Seressa and I join the Patriarch's fleet. I assume the duke has told you why Folco is here, and going on to King Émery? Does he not confide these things in you, my lady?"

"What? Well, of course he does!"

Lenia knew she shouldn't do it, but sometimes . . .

"Ah! He didn't tell you yet? I'm sure it is just an oversight."

The other woman flushed again. "He said something. I wasn't paying attention. There is always something. A ship, you said? *You* are building some sort of craft, signora?"

"A carrack, yes. You know what that is, my lady?"

Hesitation. "A larger sort of ship, yes. We are landlocked, of course, sea trade has never been our access to fortune."

"Indeed. Everyone knows that."

"So, a ship. How very exciting. You're somehow part of a group that—"

"No. My Kindath partner and myself. We're having it built ourselves."

It was extremely likely that the duchess of Macera, however landlocked they were, knew how expensive it was to build a large ship. She remained poised, though. It was impressive. She said, "But you are leaving it behind, staying with Folco this year . . . while he's away from home and family?"

Again, Lenia knew she shouldn't, but it felt as if her life might have reached a point where she was allowed to show anger, not hide it.

"My lady, do you think the men in his company want to bed him? Or just any woman who joins them?"

A longer silence. Sun and shade as they rode. A light breeze stirring leaves. The other woman, for some reason, looked as if she'd been slapped.

Why would people want to sleep together like that?

Oh, child, I don't have time to—

"You are rude, signora," Corinna Ripoli said finally.

"No," Lenia said. "You are born to power and feel entitled to be, but the rudeness was yours, your grace. You've insulted me *and* your brother-in-law. Meanwhile, I am investing in the High Patriarch's army and going with the fleet to war. Where in this lovely countryside will your morning rides be taking you next spring, my lady, while I do that?"

I don't like her! Ask her about . . . Diedo Galleoto?

What? How . . .

I don't know. From . . . her? I can hear the name. And . . . she hugs him.

So, so reckless, but there was an undeniable pleasure. A wind blowing through the aridity of what life had allowed her to do.

"Also, do tell me," she asked, without taking time to think it through, "how is Signore Galleoto these days? Diedo. As charming as ever? He's said to be!"

The other woman reined her horse hard. Lenia did the same, a little ahead, turning it sideways, looking back. There was a space behind them before the next riders. Those back there also stopped, seeing them. They were still alone, more or less.

Corinna Ripoli was very pale. "How dare you!" she said. "I could have you whipped."

"For asking after a member of your court, my lady?"

"How do you even know to ask of him?"

Lenia could feel anger rising again. Blocked and balked for so long.

"You might consider how discreet you've been if someone newly arrived knows to ask, my lady."

She heard a sound, turned her head. Saw Folco riding back, smiling. He came up to the two of them.

"I wanted to see if you'd fallen off your mount yet."

"Not yet," Lenia said. "The duchess has been keeping an eye on me."

"Good."

"She's upset because I enquired about Signore Galleoto. Seems to want to whip me for it."

Oh my, said Leora, within. *Was that wise?*

No, Lenia said. *Don't care. Actually, it might have been. Harder for her to attack me now. He'll know why, if she does.*

That's clever! And I still want to know about the hugging. And why people sleep—

Not now, Leora!

"Diedo?" Folco said. "He's still in Macera? Do they not miss him in Avegna? A polished courtier. They love him there. The brothers pride themselves on that at their court. But . . . whipping one of my company, Corinna?"

He was keeping his voice mild, Lenia saw. But it was a dangerous moment. She'd made it so.

A silence on a forest path. Then Corinna Ripoli said, "This latest woman to join your company seemed to be suggesting something untoward. That was disrespectful."

Folco looked at Lenia, waiting.

Lenia knew what she had to do. The world was what it was. She said, to the duchess, "I offer my most abject apologies if I seemed so. You are right, my lady, it was not my place to speak in such a way. I took offence at something, and it was wrong of me. Impertinent."

Another pause, her words being weighed.

The lady of Macera inserted her voice, as if reluctantly, into the silence. "No, I was ungracious. You are our guest here. Folco, I didn't know enough about Signora Serranio, her resources, her devotion to the High Patriarch, and I admit I was jealous that she is now to travel with you to Ferrieres. It is I who was unkind."

"Serrana," said Folco.

"Serrana," said Corinna Ripoli.

She turned to Lenia. "I mean it. I was unkind. Folco has had women in his company before, serving with honour. I am well aware of it. Will you accept my apology and forgive me?"

She means it?

I think she does.

Lenia said, "With an open heart, my lady." She bowed in the saddle. Then turned to Folco, grinning. "We were discussing, among other things, whether you are a handsome man." Same jest she had with Rafel.

"Of course I am!" he said, laughing. "What man needs more than one eye? And I'm so tall, and slim!"

"With *such* an alluring scar!" Corinna Ripoli said. "I have asked Arimanno to consider achieving one but he always declines."

"Not a man to chase fashion," Folco said ruefully. "Never has been."

"Not a chasing man, no. Except on a horse in the woods. Shall we carry on?"

"We should. I need a word with Signora Serrana first."

"Of course. Do take care she doesn't fall."

"I'll do what I can," Folco said.

They watched the duchess ride on, waited until those following approached and passed. Then they were alone.

Is he angry?

Most likely. I was foolish.

"I should be angry, of course," Folco said quietly.

"I'm not sure you have rights in that regard, my lord. I am travelling with you, and will assist as I can, but you do not command me."

"Oh? Even to give you a task?"

"That, yes. But not in what I say when someone attacks or belittles me."

"She did that?"

"She did."

He hesitated. "It is . . . there is some complexity to this."

"Ah. Complexity! Far beyond my poor capacity to—"

"Lenia. Don't bristle so quickly. There is a history, as to women in my company, and it isn't entirely mine to share."

She was silent.

I think I like him.

I do, too.

"I'm sorry, then," she said. "I appear to be a bristling sort of person."

"I should have asked ben Natan about that. Would he have warned me?"

"Undoubtedly."

They rode on together.

THE FOG CAME soon after, out of nothing, in the woods north of Macera where the court liked to hunt.

It was not a season for fog. And there had been blue skies, high white clouds. The birds fell silent first. Lenia didn't realize it, then she did. Then the wind changed, then it died. The mist descended heavily on the forest, cloaking trees, muffling sound. They rode as through a shroud.

She and Folco had caught up to some of the party. An uneasy silence fell. They came to a place where the path opened into a clearing, trees just visible on the far side. The duke had halted with his entourage; his wife was beside him now.

It had become difficult to see anything. There was a dampness to the air. Lenia caught a whiff of something. Not pleasant.

"I don't like this," said Duke Arimanno. His words sounded faint, hollow, fell as if to earth. "I don't ever remember—"

"Look!" said Folco d'Acorsi.

Lenia looked, caught her breath. It was difficult to discern anything across the clearing, but at the edge of the trees, in the open, there now stood a stag, head high, looking right at them. It was white, amazingly. It might have been just an illusion of whiteness in the mist that had come to blanket the forest, but Lenia was sure—for the rest of her life—that it hadn't been. There was a white stag here, creature of legend and dream, within a fog meant for such things.

Arimanno of Macera raised his bow. "Jad's love and mercy, it is magnificent!" he whispered.

"Arimanno," Folco said. "No. Listen!"

Lenia didn't understand him at first. *Listen?* But then she heard it too: a deep, resonant, animal sound she never forgot. Fog swirled, dispersed and gathered, lifted and deepened—the stag present, then only almost-seen, apprehended.

Like a thing from the half-world. She startled herself with the thought.

I'm scared! said Leora, within.

So am I, child.

"Folco's right!" said the duke, a man said to be cautious in all things. "Turn! Go! We don't know what that sound is! What any of this is!"

The company turned. He was their duke, and he had released them to their fear. They fled the way they had come, twenty riders from a great court, urging their horses to a dangerous speed in the now dense obscurity of familiar woods.

Lenia never knew why she stayed.

Why Folco did. Only the two of them. Maybe he remained to defend her? She never asked; he never said. Your life, she thought, could bring you a moment when you *could* not explain what was happening, or explain yourself.

From across the clearing the sound grew louder, and nearer, something between a roar and a vast snarling. An announcement. A *presence*.

Staring, sweat on her skin, heart pounding, trying to penetrate shifting grey and mist with her eyes, Lenia saw, thought she saw, something colossal emerge from behind the stag. She never could decide for certain, after, what it was. A forest bison? A bull? It seemed larger than both. A bear?

And it stank. That was inescapable. She gagged from the smell. Thought she would throw up in the saddle. It was rank, rotten, meaty, and . . . so heavy. Even from across the clearing.

"Dear Jad," whispered Folco d'Acorsi. "Defend your mortal children."

Lenia? said Leora.

Only her name. Whispered within. Child's plea in a woman's voice.

A different sound, higher in pitch, from the stag this time, which she could barely even see now. And this sound was not fear, which was what it *should* have been.

It was—the word leaped to her mind—it was submission. Acceptance.

Stags run from such a danger, she thought, feeling terror within herself. Stags fled from the least hint of something like this.

This one did not run. Or move. It was unnatural. She saw it clearly for a heartbeat: white, graceful body, glorious branching horns. She lost it, saw it, the dark shape behind, a vast, appalling bulk. There came that deeper sound again, almost below what she could hear, as if the earth itself was making it. And then something, *something*, struck the stag and it went down, and the fog became entirely too thick for them to see anything at all.

The sounds from across the clearing ceased.

Nothing to see, nothing to be heard.

Only that smell lingering, penetrating, as if it was nearing *them* now in that heavy sightlessness, and Folco said, "Lenia, we must go! We are not meant to be here for this!"

They fled. As the stag had not. They fled through the mist as if there were no god at all behind the sun, no light, no shelter to be found—in this forest, in life, in the world. Nothing that a mortal man or woman, cast into time for an uncertain number of days and nights, could ever understand.

Except, perhaps, that they had been *permitted* to go.

It was not a choice they made. It was a thing allowed.

FOLCO WANTED TO pray before returning to the palace. So, Lenia discovered, did she. Leora, she thought, would approve, but the child did not answer now when called from within. She had been very frightened when the fog came in. How, Lenia thought, could someone not be, especially a child?

She thought—she *thought*—she had seen, however briefly, a monstrous head, with horns, loom behind the stag, above it. An animal that much larger than a fully grown stag?

"Did you . . . see it clearly?" she asked Folco d'Acorsi. Needed to ask.

"No," he said, too quickly.

They walked into the enormous, sumptuously decorated sanctuary of the god in the centre of Macera. She saw Jad painted on the dome, golden and benign, behind four horses in his chariot. Blue sky, soft white clouds. The reassuring serenity of it.

Outside, the fog had gone. As soon as they left the woods. There had been sunlight again as they rode back, as if it had never gone away. It came in here now through windows in the dome and stained-glass ones along the walls. There were statues all around. The floor was rich marble in three colours, at least, and so were the pillars. She saw family chapels on both sides, gold on many of the railings that marked them off. Gold everywhere. Macera was a wealthy city. You needed to show the world your wealth because that signified power, and power could protect you.

It could. Didn't always. There were sometimes more powerful people, places. There were those who might seek to claim what you held. They'd just seen that tried in Firenta.

She owned a palazzo in Firenta now because of that day.

The world was inexplicable, Lenia thought again. Her mind seemed to keep going that way. Perhaps the folly was in even trying to understand it. Or was *this* thought the real folly? Didn't you need to at least try to find a purpose to your days?

But what could you decide about, what could you *do* with what they had seen (half seen, almost seen) this morning? Conclude that men and women lived in the world like children, however powerful they might think themselves? That mercy needed to be endlessly sought, whether or not it might come?

There was no service taking place now. The huge sanctuary was not empty—it would never be empty here—but it was quiet. Distant voices talking, praying, footsteps, but quiet, soft echoes. She knelt beside Folco d'Acorsi and followed his deep voice into one of the oldest, simplest prayers: exactly the one she'd been thinking of, her-self . . . beseeching Jad's mercy for his children in the world he had made. She had known this prayer from childhood, had said it with her mother when she went to sleep at night.

There hadn't been much mercy in her life. Or the lives of her mother and father.

Or was that too grudging a thought? Look where she was. Look where her brother was. Perhaps Jad just needed *time*, or chose to take his time?

Beside her, Folco's hands clasped a sun disk he'd taken out. Lenia didn't carry one. She decided that she'd buy one today, or in Ferrieres perhaps, keep it on her again, as she'd done as a girl.

They had encountered something primitive and immense today, not a thing she'd ever deny, whatever the monstrous creature was that had taken down a white stag in mist.

We are not meant to be here for this, the lord of Acorsi had said.

She didn't know if he was right. She didn't expect to ever know.

They prayed together, remained kneeling in silence after.

In that quiet, it suddenly seemed to Lenia Serrana that she heard singing. That was often the case in a sanctuary, whether there were services or not, but this was different. She couldn't place the voice, it was as if it was above her, suspended, and—

Don't listen!

Leora, what? Why?

I don't know. It scares me again!

Oh, child. Why?

I don't know!

It was impossible to not listen. Or try. Just as it had been impossible to not see in the forest. Or try. Folco showed no sign of hearing what she heard. His eyes remained closed in silent prayer. A cultivated, pious, violent man, she thought. The warring contradictions of their time. But there was, there *was* someone singing, a woman's voice, in the air above her, somehow, and Lenia couldn't—she *couldn't*—make out the words. She thought she heard *children* and maybe *sky*, but even that much was uncertain, elusive.

It was, she thought, exactly as it had been in the fog. Something almost seen. Something almost heard.

I can't make it out, Leora said.

Nor I.

I'm still afraid.

This is so difficult, I know. I wish I could be with you, Leora.

I do too. I need to think about so much now.

And she was gone again. Child. More than child.

She would, young Leora Sacchetti, grow into a woman greatly honoured—well before a long life ended—by many of the pious and mighty in the world, for her wisdom and compassion, and her devotion to the god.

In the great sanctuary of Macera, Lenia Serrana thought about the gifts that had come to her that spring, including an impossible half-world link to a child in Bischio. And she had just been allowed to glimpse something else from the half-world. And almost hear something now. Almost. Was that to be her life? Her destiny? Or . . .

"We don't always need to understand." She said it aloud.

Folco turned his head and looked at her with his one eye. Muted light, a quiet sanctuary. Footsteps at a distance again. Someone praying, off to their left.

"Not an easy thought for me," he said finally. "My nature is to need to understand. But I imagine you are right." He stood up. "I have one thing I do when I am here, then we can leave. And we should go tomorrow."

She also rose. "Away from Macera's palace, or away from that wood?"

He offered a wry smile, a little more himself now, she thought. She was too, she realized.

"Both have their dangers."

She said, "Did you . . . did you hear someone singing? Just now?"

"I did not. You did?"

She nodded. She would not deny this, either. But he didn't ask anything else.

The one thing more for him was lighting a candle before the sun disk in the largest of the side chapels. Lenia didn't go through the gate in the railing with him. There were stone coffins there, names carved that she couldn't see. Two statues of tall men in armour. A very large painting on one side wall. She caught a glimpse of it from where she stood. A woman on a horse. She had unbound red hair, was holding a sword. Probably done by a celebrated painter, Lenia thought, given where they were, but she hadn't lived a life that allowed her to have any awareness or understanding of art or artists. One of many such limitations.

Like horses. Or maybe happiness.

THEIR LAST NIGHT in the palace was uneventful, though she overheard Folco arranging with Gian to post a guard outside her door. There was music after the banquet. Some members of the court danced for the duke and duchess of Macera. People did not speak of the morning's fog, or not openly. She and Folco had been the only ones who'd stayed behind.

They left in the morning for Ferrieres, for the court and king at Orane.

There were events there, too. Someone died.

☙

It turned out, unexpectedly, that Rafel had an eye and touch for fabrics and a quick gift for the cloth trade as it ran (lucratively, for some) across the world.

The Kindath merchant in Firenta, Cardeño ben Zaid, helped him learn. A generous man, his family also from Esperaña. And Antenami Sardi, whose family had begun in the cloth business before becoming bankers, was attentive, visibly pleased that Rafel was staying in Firenta. He was a good-natured, genial, readily amused man. He would be burdened now, Rafel thought, by a new role, with his brother slain. It would change him—whether a great deal or only a little, and how, would have to be seen.

He discussed one particular matter with Antenami, and elected not to move in to the palazzo they'd offered him. He was a Kindath, it was still his defining identity in the world. They were tolerated in Firenta under the Sardis, but were still expected to live in their quarter, across the river, amongst each other, and tolerance could fray. It would draw too much attention, Rafel felt, to accept that palazzo.

He wasn't even supposed to ride a horse, but he'd done that with Folco d'Acorsi, and again when escorted to Bischio. He'd ridden in the Majriti as well. Being an emissary, however minor, for the khalif of Almassar had carried some privileges. Those days were over. He supposed the same thing might apply here, with his link to the Sardis, but he felt better being careful. You needed, Rafel ben Natan thought, powerful friends if you were to survive and rise while retaining your faith, and you needed to be cautious.

Some did abandon that faith. You might feel you owed it to your family, shaping opportunities for your children. Or simply a thing done to stay alive in a dangerous time. What was the price of religious devotion?

He wasn't a particularly devout man, but he wasn't prepared to do that. Change his faith. Because of his father, perhaps. Or maybe because he was fairly certain his brother had done so when he'd left his family. If he hadn't died. Families shaped you, in different ways.

Dissembling, taking a Jaddite or Asharite name and identity for a time, that he could do. That was simply a business practice. He'd been Ibadi al-Murad at times. Couldn't remember how he'd chosen the name. And he'd been Ramon Comares when he'd gone, briefly, back to Esperaña.

There were lines here too, he thought. Shadings. He wore a silver and lapis lazuli bracelet on his left wrist. The Kindath were to mark themselves with those colours. He did it this way. Had for years. Sometimes did more, depending on where he was. He didn't think he'd die for his beliefs, but he didn't think he *wouldn't*, either.

Exile, the endless inward reliving of what had been done to you: that was also a thing that defined some people. In a sense, Rafel had often thought, he'd always remained the child on a crowded sea strand with his father and mother, driven from their home among weeping people. Would that ever change? Salt sea, salt tears?

He was concerned for his parents.

He had done what he could to get his mother and father out of Almassar. He wouldn't know for some time if he'd succeeded. He'd sent very specific instructions, and arranged money for their passage to Marsena.

It pained him, that the two of them might feel themselves exiled again, forced to move once more, this time as age descended upon them. But it was important. There really was a risk. Marsena was where their grandchildren were, with Gaelle, who had been married—might still be married, if he was alive—to Rafel's brother.

His request of the Sardis had been about that: could Piero offer his intelligence network, as a courtesy, to the small task of discovering if a certain Sayash ben Natan was alive, and where, if so?

"He is likely using a different name. Jaddite. Asharite. Depending on where he is. That makes it—"

"More difficult, yes," Piero had said. "Nonetheless, I have good people and we will do what we can. I even have a Kindath among them. I will send a man to you, you will tell him what you know."

That had happened, a conversation with an attentive person. Rafel didn't know much, of course. If he'd known much, he wouldn't have needed Piero Sardi.

He'd also sent money to the family of Ghazzali al-Siyab. It was a bitter sort of amusing, that he and Lenia had both accepted that al-Siyab had had to die because of what he'd done—but were not happy depriving his family of his share of their fee.

He had ongoing conversations with Piero Sardi. The man seemed to have taken a liking to him. Gratitude, or something more? Curiosity? Sardi lived for his work, sitting all day behind a large desk in a large room, papers in front of him to be read, other papers to be signed after he wrote or dictated them. His son (his only son now) sat nearby much of the time, doing the same. There were clerks, advisers, runners, often hangers-on lingering in the room, seeking to be noticed by the powerful, to have their lives changed that way.

Rafel would be summoned at times, would arrive, and Sardi would rise from his desk with his thin smile, and they'd walk the perimeter of the room, talking quietly, or go out on the balcony overlooking the city and the river.

"Do you name the moons?" Sardi asked him once.

Rafel blinked. "Our liturgy says we are not to speak or write the names of the goddesses. We say only the white and blue moons. There was a sect, since gone, that named them Birth and Death, which all men and women know."

"Indeed. We do. Though we prefer not to think about the second of those."

"Yes."

"As I get older, I find myself doing so."

Unexpected. They'd been on the balcony, a warm day, noises in the square below. Sounds of construction. Shouts, hammering, the creak and rumble of carts. Piero was expanding his palazzo and reshaping Firenta's main square.

Rafel said, "You just lost a child, my lord. It steers our thoughts."

"Yes. Have you children?"

He shook his head. "Not of my own. A sorrow. I am responsible for my brother's, however."

"The brother I'm to try to find?"

"Yes, lord."

Sardi nodded. "I've sent three men. They'll start in Marsena."

He'd sent men. Already? Rafel wasn't sure what he'd expected, if he'd even believed it would happen.

The names of the two moons. He thought about the question, after. He wondered why Sardi would want to know.

He had a fighting man's scar now. His chest still hurt if he exerted himself, but it was easing. He'd been able to ride to Bischio, then around it to a ranch they'd been directed to. He'd been able to make love to Lenia, when she came to his door.

He thought about that night too often for peace of mind.

Peace of mind was a good thing, but there were, Rafel believed, other good things in life. You needed to be grateful. Not have too many expectations. Do what you could to avoid the worst happening. Know that there were times when there would be nothing you could do.

At one point, her body had curved backwards above him like a bow. Then she had drifted slowly forward and down, and let him hold her in the dark.

A FEW DAYS after this, he received a letter from Guidanio Cerra, about the ship they were building. There were decisions that needed to be made, mainly as to cannon. Antenami Sardi insisted on giving him another escort, and Rafel went back to Seressa.

There were events there, too. Someone died.

∽

The spies of the Sardis, a network of them, were indeed among the best in the Jaddite world, only outdone, perhaps, by the agents of Seressa.

Three men were sent to Marsena to inquire as to the fate of a certain Sayash ben Natan. One was, indeed, a Kindath. They didn't ask why they were doing this: a good spy, receiving orders, never did that. It was understood that the Sardis wished to know more about this person. They were well paid to do their work—what more did they need to know?

The Kindath of Marsena appeared to be much as they were in Firenta: inclined to close ranks against outsiders, but also, as people everywhere were, amenable to inducements.

The Sardis' Kindath agent did not talk to the missing man's wife, though he observed her at a distance with the two children. He addressed himself to members of the community, and his companions did so also, when the Kindath came out in the morning from behind their gates to do business at the harbour and elsewhere.

The Sardi spies spoke with trained courtesy. It was not a threatening subject. There were, they explained, business reasons why Piero Sardi wished to know what had happened to Sayash ben Natan, the merchant. No more than that.

Of course *business reasons* had killed people, and those they spoke to would be aware of that. If ben Natan had fled from a debt, for example . . .

No one admitted knowing his whereabouts. Or any reason he might have left. Yes, he had lived in Marsena for a time with his family. His wife and children were still here, awaiting his return. Yes, he'd been gone for three, maybe four (it was difficult to remember) years. No, they truly had no idea where he might be. Or why he'd gone. Debts? No one knew. He'd been in the gem trade, yes. Perhaps Astarden? Had they considered Astarden? There were many of their people there. It was the diamond and gem centre of the world now, as was widely known.

Astarden was possible. It was even likely, the three agents agreed at night over dinner in a place between the harbour and their inn. If the man was alive. There were reasons he might not be. There were, of course, always reasons for that. It would be easier if he was dead, but their task was to ascertain if he was. They had been down to the docks, had conversations there, offered sums, carefully judged. Piero Sardi demanded precise accountings of expenses. A generous enough man for a banker but . . . precise. No one on the harbour had seen Sayash ben Natan, the gem merchant, leave Marsena. And certainly no one had seen him return at any time.

Or, no one admitted doing so.

They had finished dining on the fish soup Marsena was famed for, were preparing to head back to their shared room, quite sober— Sardi had been known to have men observe his agents, reporting on how they conducted themselves. As they were settling their bill, someone approached their table. A conversation ensued.

The person asked for a sum of money. A portion of it was placed on the tabletop, the rest to come if the information was important.

It was. It wasn't about the man they were seeking. It was about themselves, and danger.

You can die so easily, Hilario Ascani was thinking. Not a useful thought. Not a time for such reflections. The three of them were walking briskly back to their inn. Their swords were drawn. They had an escort of four men. He'd have preferred more, and evidence these guards knew what they were doing.

Hilario's real name was Hilal ben Rashir. He'd been born in the Kindath quarter of Firenta almost twenty-three years ago. He used that name at home. He wasn't home much. He worked for Piero Sardi. He was a spy.

So were the two men he was with in Marsena. The practice was to use three for an assignment such as this: they'd chase information in different ways, compare notes. Ascani had been picked because it was a Kindath merchant who was missing.

Now, in the darkness of winding lanes, the day's heat cooling, smells of cooking, refuse, and the sea, few lights to be seen, things had changed. Someone might be looking for them, instead. Hunted, not hunting.

A ship had come into the harbour late in the day. That was what they'd just been told at the table where they'd had their meal. And not just any ship. Marsena was a port, traders came and went, from everywhere.

Including, it seemed, Tarouz in the Majriti. And questions had been asked by those on that ship when they came ashore as to whether there were any people from Batiara in the city.

Asharites were allowed to dock here. The king of Ferrieres had a quiet agreement with them. In return, the merchants and goods of Ferrieres were safe from their predation. King Émery even exchanged gifts with Gurçu in Asharias. In a normal time, a galley from Tarouz, even a large one with many cannon, would occasion no more than conversation.

This was not a normal time. Ziyar ibn Tihon had been killed this spring. His severed head was displayed in Rhodias. There would be deadly displeasure in Tarouz regarding all Batiarans at the moment. And the ship that had arrived this afternoon from that city was a notable one.

Someone, seeing it come in, overhearing questions being asked, had thought the three spies from Firenta would pay a decent sum for this information— as it might touch upon their lives.

Someone had been right.

PIEDONA VALLI, LEADER of that group of three, had also wished for more than four guards. But he judged it more dangerous to stay where they were, waiting to see if others would arrive, than to get back to their inn and barricade themselves there. He had paid someone to alert the city authorities. Ferrieres might permit Asharite ships, but it could not safely countenance attacks on Jaddites. That could blow up the cynicism of their practice with the Majriti ships. There *were* limits to such things.

Or so he hoped.

The guards who arrived were from the Kindath quarter. Not the best-trained, he suspected, but they were good-sized, armed with cudgels (no swords, of course), and they'd come quickly, at a request from his companion. Hilario had sent to his own people. Piedo had sent a runner to the harbour for the night patrol, and someone else to try to find a civic guard or two. No one had come from the port, no civic guards had arrived.

You worked with what you had.

It wasn't far to the inn. He thought they'd be safe there. If there was even any actual danger. He reminded himself that this was all just caution, no threat had been made or overheard. Just a dangerous man arriving at a time of, well, danger for Batiarans.

They were, he reminded himself, hardly the only people from Batiara here. And Firenta was in no way linked to what had happened to Ziyar ibn Tihon. That would be Sorenica and Rhodias— and Acorsi, since it was no secret who had killed Ziyar.

Still, he was uneasy as they walked and they moved quickly. Vengeance was not necessarily calculated with precision as to targets, and Zariq ibn Tihon *would* want revenge. Was there anyone who doubted that?

Piedona Valli certainly didn't. And rather less so when their party of seven was stopped on the night street at a place where no lights reached from any doorway. Stopped by a group that looked to be about twice as many.

It was difficult to tell in the dark. They carried two torches, the seven of them, but those didn't penetrate far, or illuminate much.

"In a great hurry?" a large man with a deep voice asked. He spoke Batiaran. Accented but intelligible. The choice of language revealed that he knew exactly who they were.

"It is late, we are headed back to our beds." Valli kept his voice calm. "Why would you be accosting us?"

"Accosting is a harsh word," the other man said. "I'd merely like a conversation."

"In the dark?"

"Our lives move from darkness to darkness," the other man said. Probably quoting something. Bastard. "I am Farai Alfasi, by the way."

Not a *by the way*. This was exactly who they'd feared. The ibn Tihons' captain. If Zariq was intent on vengeance, short of a fleet, this man would be the one he'd send.

Piedona Valli realized that he might die here.

"What would you like to converse about?" he said. His voice was still easy enough. It occurred to him that the four Kindath men who had joined him might decide to run. They hadn't, yet. Alfasi had half his men behind them. Valli and the other two spies knew how to fight, but they were intelligence-gatherers, not street brawlers. This was, in all respects, bad.

He prayed then, silently.

"I know what happened to my khalif, Ziyar. I want to know where his ship is."

"We are from Firenta, you know that, don't you? We are an inland city far north of whatever happened. I have no idea, none, about any ship."

"My son," said Farai Alfasi, "was on that ship."

"Then I will pray for his safe return home," Valli said. "But I know nothing about the ship."

"Why are you here?"

"For matters to do with Firenta's interests in trade. This is what we do. I believe you know it."

"Why would I know that?"

"Because you are a powerful man serving another."

Alfasi laughed. Not a pleasant sound in a summer night.

"Why," asked Hilario, from beside Valli, "are you doing this? How do we have anything to do with Ziyar ibn Tihon? Will you really risk losing access for Asharites to all the ports of Ferrieres just to attack three men going about their business? Will you then seek and try to kill every Batiaran in Marsena?"

Valli didn't much like Hilal ben Rashir, who used a different name some of the time. He didn't actually like any Kindath, but the questions were good. They induced a pause.

"I am accountable to you, now?" Farai Alfasi said. He was a genuinely large man, you could see that even in the night. He had a drawn sword, too.

"Surely not. Only to your khalif, and perhaps the grand khalif in Asharias, for the safety of all the ships of Ashar. The right to dock in Ferrieres matters, and the king of Ferrieres will be tasked with responsibility if Jaddites are assaulted by you here. You know this. So I ask again, how is this proper revenge? *We* are your vengeance?"

Hilal, or Hilario, was being very brave, Valli thought. It needed to be acknowledged. Pino, on his other side, was keeping quiet. He usually did. Was the best of them with a blade, though.

"Our vengeance, *my* vengeance, will take many forms and involve many deaths," said Farai Alfasi.

"And when the fleet of the High Patriarch arrives before Tarouz, to take *his* vengeance for the fall of Sarantium, what then? What happens then?"

Piedona Valli caught his breath. He was not married, had no children, but there was a man he loved back home, who loved him, and he didn't, in that moment, expect to see him again.

"That is a desperate lie."

"No lie," Hilal said. "Giving you information. We trade in that. The lord of Acorsi is to command a fleet being assembled. He is going to all the leaders of Batiara, is at the court in Ferrieres now, or will be soon. The Esperañans, who you hate, will also send ships and men, no one doubts it. They hate you, too, after all."

A long silence. Stars, one moon riding through swift clouds, two torches.

"And this stops me from killing you, why?" But Farai Alfasi's voice had changed a little. Valli was trained to detect such things.

"Because if you do, the King of Ferrieres will send money—and ships—and will close his ports to you. To all of you. *And* he will write to Asharias to say why that is so. Who caused it to be so. You are standing in a very dangerous moment tonight, even if you can easily kill us. We are," Hilal ben Rashir, the Kindath, added, "not your proper enemies. But we can become the cause of enemies gathering if you make a mistake."

"You might simply have been beset by thieves," Alfasi said, but again that new thing in his voice.

Piedona Valli said, "Seven of us? Armed? So many thieves!"

He left it there.

And then, by the grace of Jad, Alfasi snapped something in Asharic, which Valli spoke, blessedly. What he said was, "*Leave them!*" and those in front and behind melted away, as snow melts on slopes when spring comes.

On the walk, when they resumed it, for the short distance remaining to their inn, an arrow took Hilal ben Rashir from behind and killed him in the street under a waning blue moon. His people would attach some meaning to that, Valli thought, kneeling beside the fallen man, in grief and fury. Above, standing guard, Pino was cursing savagely, through tears.

An event in Marsena, as well, then. Someone died.

PEOPLE DIE IN STORIES, *as in life. It is embedded in the world we have and in many of the tales we tell, if they are to register for us as containing, sharing, certain kinds of truth. Sometimes these are figures at the heart of what we are reading or hearing. Sometimes they are not. But even so, even if they have only just walked into it on a night in a city far from their own, we must imagine them as having people who loved them, for whom their absence will loom large, even if it does not in the story we are being told.*

If we take a moment for them it is also a moment taken for ourselves. For those who love us, those we love.

CHAPTER XIII

Tarouz lay very close to the ruins of an even greater city, built in the time of the Ancients, long since destroyed, the ruins said to be haunted, and undeniably mysterious.

It had allegedly been founded before the days and nights of Jad or Ashar, if such a thing could even be imagined. The Kindath had been present in those days, it was said. It seemed to Zariq ibn Tihon that they had always been present.

He didn't like them, even if he'd used one, a merchant, for a mission that had seemed extremely clever—at the time. It didn't seem as much so to him now. Well, clever, still. But you learned, over time, that ambitious plans carried, implicitly, the possibility of failure.

It had begun to look as if the murder of the khalif of Abeneven might not have been his own best devising.

For one thing, his brother was dead. Unconnected, but also not. Ziyar had always done reckless things, when enraged, or when elated. All the time, really. For another, he had just learned from Farai Alfasi, his most trusted man, his *only* trusted man, in truth, that the accursed followers of the burning sun god might be planning an attack.

On him. On Tarouz. When *he* was the one who was meant to be planning raids now, taking a terrible vengeance for his slain brother.

Farai had indeed gone across the Middle Sea to kill Jaddites for Ziyar. Vengeance was important, instilling fear even more so. You survived when enough people feared you enough. He had gone to Marsena first, to gather information, and to seek out men from Batiara. He had killed one man there. Only one. Which was nothing! Then he'd returned home swiftly, with grave, unsettling news.

It might not be true, but . . . it might. It very well might. Zariq had wanted to kill the High Patriarch of Jad, hearing it. Flay him alive, stuff his skin with straw.

He currently wanted to kill a number of people. His brother was dead. An impossible thought. Ziyar had been disturbing and disturbed, but their trust had never been shaken, nor had their love for each other wavered from boyhood. Zariq felt alone. He *was* alone.

No reply to his letters had come from Asharias.

Gurçu tended to send his letters on two ships, for better assurance they'd get through. A careful man. Nothing had come through. No response to Zariq's careful explanation of the assassination he'd caused to happen in Abeneven, how it had been done, as everything always was, in devoted service to the grand khalif.

Silence, he thought, could sometimes be loud.

When the wind was south in summer the heat was like a punishment for all the worst things you had done. The sand got into everything, your food, your bed, your skin and eyes. A torpid lassitude fell upon the Majriti. It occurred to Zariq that he might be in real danger. He had an enemy now in Abeneven's vizier—an unexpectedly confident one, by report.

He began eyeing his guards with some anxiety. He would not be the first khalif in the Majriti to be murdered. Indeed, he'd just murdered one. He was not a man accustomed to being fearful, or alone. His brother had been beside him all his life.

In the white heat of midday, when even the birds were still, he had his women wipe his naked body down with cloths soaked in cool water. He drank the fermented mare's milk he loved. When the bells summoned, he prayed to Ashar's holy stars with fervour. He had three thieves decapitated one evening in the square before the palace and watched from his balcony. You did what you could to take your mind off your troubles.

Autumn came, finally, a shifting of winds. No letter from Asharias. Tidings arriving with merchants suggested the Arsenale in Seressa was loud, night and day, with the construction of new ships. Someone said the same was true in Dubrava's shipyard across the narrow sea.

He thought at night, lying awake, of boarding his own beloved galley, manning half a dozen others with trusted mariners, and going away. But where? Where in the world as they knew it could he go?

All men made mistakes. Some mistakes were worse than others. He had come a long way, Zariq ibn Tihon thought, from their fleck of an island in the sea between Trakesia and Candaria. He could go home. Didn't all men want to go home, in some way? If they could. If it was still what it had been.

If they were still, somehow, what they had been.

His memories of Tihon, their island, were not vivid. They should have been, he'd been sixteen when they were captured. He had images of his mother wearing black, endlessly praying, especially after his father died. He remembered a sanctuary of Jad in the hills inland from their home, a fresco behind the sun disk that showed— he had been told—a forbidden subject: Jad's son, a boy on the edge of being a man (maybe that was why he remembered it?), driving his father's chariot. A banned image, heresy. You were not to speak of that son, let alone pray to him.

His memories began to be clearer from the time of their capture by Asharite raiders, he and Ziyar and two friends. Eight men at twilight, boarding their fishing boat from a small ship, looking for Jaddites to sell to the galleys. They weren't hardened raiders, the Asharites who took them. It was just easier and better money than fishing.

You died rowing the galleys, usually. Jaddite or Asharite.

They hadn't died. They hadn't gone to a galley. They'd overpowered the man guarding them at night on that ship. Ziyar, extremely strong even at fourteen, had worked free of his binding and strangled the fisherman silently with the rope in darkness at sea. They'd taken the man's knife and old sword and killed the others, half of them asleep under stars. They'd thrown the bodies overboard and claimed the small ship.

They could have gone home. To this day, in his city of Tarouz, Zariq doesn't know why they didn't. They weren't exiles. They really could have gone back to Tihon. Perhaps a life fishing off a small island had already begun to feel limiting? Perhaps killing eight men had opened up a sense of what the world might offer someone bold enough?

The sun god's only son had seized his father's chariot and horses, hadn't he? His name was Heladikos. You weren't supposed to even say it.

They took ships and seized goods, both Jaddite and Asharite. They didn't care. They raided fishing villages and farms, flying no flag. They offered mercy to young men who joined them, and they grew in number. Claimed a second, larger boat, then a third, a real ship, two masts, cannon.

It had begun that way. Eventually they'd adopted the faith of Ashar and the stars, and later accepted an offer from Gurçu to serve him. Gurçu didn't have Sarantium yet, but he intended to take it, and Zariq thought it would happen. He made a choice. Certain things flowed from that.

Your faith, Zariq ibn Tihon believed, was a decision, a calculation. A way of surviving.

It had taken him here.

He ordered the city walls repaired, and had all captains ensure their ships were cleaned and caulked and ready. He didn't know what he was readying for, but there might be a fleet of invasion, come spring. He would beat it back, he told himself. He knew these waters, his walls were strong, he had many ships. He began gathering food in the granaries, water in the cisterns.

The winds changed again, were stronger, bringing rain. He sent again to Asharias, in rough seas. He wrote of evil Jaddites preparing an invasion against the loyal servants of Ashar and the grand khalif. He didn't beg. He said he was asking for guidance and for aid.

Asking for guidance was a good phrasing, he thought.

It was reported that the vizier of Abeneven, Nisim ibn Zukar, had been crowned as khalif there on an autumn morning, then blessed in the temple across from the palace when the sun set and the holy stars came out.

Someone said he wore a diamond about his neck. Someone said it had been sent from Asharias.

⁖

The course of a life, Raina Vidal thought, as the weather turned towards the season of the wine harvest, could create challenges for a person or, unexpectedly, solve problems.

In Sorenica the sea breeze eased the heat now, especially towards twilight. Visitors would come later in the autumn. People knew better than to come south in summer.

Autumn was predicted, by those skilled in such assessments, to be wet throughout Batiara, breaking the heat, yes, but worrying farmers. Harvest was always an anxious time. Deaths followed upon bad harvests; it was simply true. You prayed, lit candles, watched the skies morning and night. Some invoked night spirits to defend the fields. Others sought forbidden auguries: flights of birds, entrails of birds, bones of animals, readings of the heavens, wisewomen, alchemists . . .

Raina didn't believe in such things. It was not in her nature.

She was alone in the palazzo now, save for servants and advisers. Her sister-in-law had remained in Casiano after their second visit to Duke Ersani there. Tamir had remained, more particularly, *with* Duke Ersani. It was not a thing that could have been anticipated.

It amused her, mostly, but it did resolve a dilemma, both domestic and for the Vidal family business. Their husbands had been brothers and partners in a hugely successful enterprise of many facets. Facets like diamonds, she thought—which were an important part of what they traded.

Raina had taken over management of this. All of it. Tamir had been a fountain of envy and ill will living with her, wherever they were. You could say, if you were disposed to be kind, that she might fairly resent being pushed aside, except that she hadn't been pushed at all. She had never shown the least inclination for business of any kind. She enjoyed *having* money, and was adept at disposing of it, most often in ways that accentuated her comfort and her beauty. The beauty being indisputable, even famed.

So much so that Ziyar ibn Tihon had died trying to abduct her as a prize. His death, pursuing Tamir Vidal, might change the balancing of the world, amazingly enough. It remained to be seen, but it was possible.

A tale like that could make a woman even more celebrated, Raina thought. A proposal from an increasingly powerful duke to become his newest mistress might emerge—and be accepted. Tamir might not have skills in commerce, but she certainly did with men, and proposals of this sort could be guided and induced if one wanted them. Tamir had been interested in Duke Ersani from the first time they'd met him, just after they'd arrived in the south. An impressive man of considerable power . . . ? How would she not be interested?

A Kindath could never marry a Jaddite duke, obviously. But someone could, evidently, welcome becoming an adornment at an important court, with the stature—and power—that carried.

Mistresses *could* have power, very much so, if they were a certain sort of person. Raina didn't think her sister-in-law was one of those, but more surprising things had happened, and she was fairly certain

Tamir was skilled in intimate activities. That could be a path to influence. Especially, if one was inclined to be cynical, with an older man of diminished capacities and desire. She had no idea if this was true of Duke Ersani, but it was certainly possible.

Raina's own belief, another cynical one, was that he'd grow bored with Tamir, but be courteous enough to keep her at court, with attendants and the status of a prized mistress, even if she was a worshipper of the Kindath moons. She would, after all, always be the woman an Asharite khalif had died trying to claim. An adornment in that way.

It did not occur to her that Tamir would convert to the faith of Jad.

Her sister-in-law did do that, in a ceremony at the harvest festival in Casiano. What would come of it, Raina had no idea. It might be a mistake, cause Tamir to appear dangerous to those at court with an interest in matters remaining as they were. The duke was, after all, unmarried currently.

Raina was not in a position to advise her. And wouldn't have been listened to.

It was, Raina Vidal decided, a *good* thing if your life could throw surprises at you even as you grew older. Not, by preference and hope, dangerous or violent ones, but unexpected things that amused, or even solved problems . . . those were excellent!

She'd made a proposal, a generous one, to Tamir and whoever would be advising her, as to a settlement of her sister-in-law's interest in the Vidal businesses.

It was accepted.

There would be some challenges in realizing the sum involved, but not insurmountable ones. By spring she expected to be entirely free of Tamir. She would become, at that point, the sole possessor of one of the larger private fortunes in the world. And still controlling it.

Women never did that.

She remained more than a little solitary. There were people in her life, of course, correspondents, visitors. If you were wealthy, you accrued both. Sometimes they just wanted to make use of you, but a few were interesting and rewarding. It became an additional task to distinguish between the two. She wasn't afraid of tasks.

She had no real time to think about intimacy, nor did she have any immediate willingness to explore an answer. No, the decision she *needed* to make, the thing to think about (not love, not companionship) was whether to leave here, sail east, take up residence in Asharias, that had been Sarantium not long ago.

She had left homes, cities, countries before; she was not afraid of doing so again.

She had been corresponding directly with Gurçu, named the Destroyer here, for almost a year. He was an impressive man, she'd decided. She sent him gifts; he sent back gifts of greater value. He was, after all, the grand khalif of the Asharite world: he needed to be more generous than anyone.

And he wanted her in his city. Which mostly meant that he wanted her fortune, her trade, taxes and tariffs paid. Perhaps the sophistication she might bring by being there. Artists and writers, musicians, they might come to her. They had tended to, wherever she was. Asharias was not even five years old under his rule. Immensely powerful, but with a long way yet to go to match Jaddite Sarantium and its thousand years of history.

No surprise in any of this. She'd have wanted Raina Vidal there, had she been him. An amusing way to think of it.

She had two dozen men already in Asharias; they had residences, warehouses, and an office, trading for the great enterprise her husband had created and she now controlled. Their reports were almost invariably positive. An enlightened, ambitious leader, undeniably the most important in the world, given the wracking divisions in Jaddite lands.

It almost certainly made sense for her to go east. She knew it.

And Asharias was, for whatever that might be worth, about as far as one could really go in the world from Esperaña, where her husband had been burned on a pyre.

♒

In the time and place the figures in our story travel through (and through which we travel for moments in our own lives), there was a world of difference between living along a coast or inland.

It was not just about corsairs. The citizens of Khatib, far to the east, a port famous for grain shipments and much else, did not go about their days offering prayers to Ashar's stars in fear of some Jaddite fleet arriving out of the dawn mist. They were too far away, and too important to the western lands. Famine could follow if their harvest was poor, or if, say, they decided to withhold a portion of it—for whatever reason. That was unlikely, since they needed the revenues from Jaddite cities, but it was within their power nonetheless. And sometimes the harvest did fail. Deaths in many places when that happened.

The fear in Khatib was of Asharias now.

Gurçu was a man who seemed intent on dominating the world. Sarantium was not enough. Some said distance and insurrections would limit what his armies could do. That he would try, and fail.

These voices, in the end, proved correct. But when time needs to pass, when truths become clear only in the end, that doesn't help those living through the time of uncertainty, the threat of war, waiting to see.

Uncertainty conjures many things. Sleepless nights. Piety. The repair and expansion of city walls, hiring and training armies, building fleets. For some, there comes a recklessness in wine-drinking, or in love. For others, a drive for wealth, in the belief that it can protect. (Sometimes it can.) For a few, there might be withdrawal from the world to retreats of one kind or another. These retreats can also be targets, of course, depending on where they are.

There are, a philosopher of the Ancients had written, no perfect answers to the unknown.

Trakesia of the Ancients, long fallen from glory, was a battleground, even if it is not at the centre of this tale. People live and die, suffer and find joy, at the edges of a story, too.

Gurçu's forces fought to subdue that wild land of mountains, ravines, rushing rivers, but supply lines were difficult, and the Jaddite rebels obdurate and savage. Their leader, a very big man with red hair and a full beard, was implacable, appallingly skilled, vicious in his own raids. Women and children sent to occupy that land with their men were killed, not just the men. Farms and barns were burned. People within them. These were settlers, not soldiers. Yes, they had been sent for a reason that had to do with conquest, but even so . . .

Skandir was what people named this man. He had been a lord of Trakesia, in the southern reaches of it, his family playing that role for centuries. He was a rebel now, unhoused, always on the move. Reprisals against Jaddite villages did not stop him. They just killed people. And that led others, especially the young, to set out to find Skandir and join his insurrection.

Asharites kept being encouraged to move down there, begin the process of converting those lands to the faith of the stars. Many died, or lived in a bowel-gripping fear of doing so. No one knew it, they could not know it, but Skandir's rebellion would continue for a long time, and Trakesia would never be quiescent, even after he died, many years after.

A khalif (or a king) could bribe and threaten his people, entice and thunder, send armies, but there were limits to these things, too, what they could achieve.

∽

King Émery of Ferrieres was young, ambitious, worldly, brave, and he hated the Esperañans more than he hated the followers of Ashar.

That last was an issue, given Folco d'Acorsi's mission to him.

It was likely, though not certain, they'd outpace the news of the High Patriarch's fleet. It could matter that Folco bring the tidings himself, have a chance to weigh the king's first response to it.

Émery's loathing of Esperaña was a known thing, there were no secrets as to that. For years the king had allowed the ships of the Majriti to use his ports as a return for attacks on Esperaña. He exchanged gifts and compliments with Gurçu in Asharias, ignoring the atrocity of what had happened in Sarantium.

The High Patriarch raged, but had not yet gone so far as to cast the king of Ferrieres—and his people—out from the rites of Jad. That was a threat held in reserve, but it was a real one.

Folco Cino d'Acorsi was carrying that threat. Act in certain ways, join and fund the fleet—or clerics could be withdrawn, including the high clerics at the royal court. Sanctuaries would be emptied of their holiness, retreats unsanctified in all of Émery's lands. No rites would be chanted at death, no blessings or intercessions invoked in childbirth or illness, no clerics' prayers before the sun disks.

The hope of light with the god after dying would be stripped away from all those living in Ferrieres under a treacherous, Jad-denying king.

Folco had licence to declare this. He carried a letter from Rhodias affirming it. He really didn't want to have to say it, show that letter. It was dangerous to be a messenger with these tidings, but the threat was prodigious. Émery would be part of the force headed for Tarouz in spring, his ports would close that year to the Asharites—or his country would face consequences that could break the Jaddite world. Or him.

HAMADI IBN HAYYAN, born in the small but important city of Aram on the wide plateau to the south of what had then been Sarantium, had joined the Osmanli court at Sarnica, the first major city occupied by them during their expansion, and then the army of Gurçu the Conqueror (not yet of that name) fifteen years ago, while still a young man, as Gurçu had been.

He was competent with a bow but not otherwise a soldier. His skills were otherwise, and became more useful once Asharias was theirs, in all its splendour.

He was a tall, pleasant-looking man. Gurçu was also very tall, of course. Hamadi had cultivated a slight stoop in the presence of the khalif until one day, when they were alone except for the mutes, Gurçu had said, quietly, "You need not stand like that. It might offend me—that you'd think I am so delicate as to care."

He didn't stoop, after that.

Of an age with the khalif, able to converse with him intelligently, ibn Hayyan became an adviser on dealings with the Jaddite world, those parts of it not targeted for invasion. As such, the failure, year after year, of assaults aimed at the Holy Jaddite Emperor's fortresses, with a view to breaking through to Obravic itself and taking it the way they'd taken Sarantium—those failures were not his.

Generals and supply train commanders were dismissed, sometimes executed. They blamed weather and distance, rivers in flood, insubordination in the ranks. None of these availed them, even though they were all true at times.

Ibn Hayyan accrued no blame for any of these disasters.

Nor for the problems in Trakesia, where Skandir and his rebels kept themselves hidden, surfaced to cause havoc and death, then disappeared again. Settlers sent down there were killed in numbers that made it increasingly hard to . . . well, to send settlers there.

No, none of these infuriating circumstances attached in any way to Hamadi ibn Hayyan. His was the task of improving life in Asharias, and of dealing with those Jaddites who *wanted* to deal with them, on terms of mutual benefit. He kept an eye on the Kindath, too. Useful for trade.

It was ibn Hayyan's task to consummate the rise to glory again in a vast city of palaces, domes, and gardens, marketplaces, massive walls, and the sea, a place where chariots had raced, long ago.

But another part of his duties was, indeed, to shape and affirm useful alliances in the west. Right now the important ones were with Seressa, where the truest god was profit, and with the rapidly rising power of Ferrieres, where an ambitious king wanted to crush the king and queen of Esperaña even more than Gurçu did, it seemed.

Opposing the enemy of a friend can seal a friendship, he'd told Gurçu before sailing, escorted by four ships, to the port of Marsena. From there he proceeded overland north to the court of King Émery in Orane.

He was a good horseman. Just about all of the Osmanli Asharites were. He was accompanied by gifts even more sumptuous than the usual, and proposals of a quite specific nature, with authority to go beyond these, if required.

He didn't travel secretly. There was no way to do that. But neither did he have the escort a senior courtier and official envoy normally would. Too large a party, if so, for speed. He did have a good number of guards.

There was a possibility he might be abducted or even assassinated on orders of the High Patriarch, if Scarsone Sardi (his name be accursed) learned ibn Hayyan was here, and found him. Hamadi didn't dismiss this, but he didn't indulge it as a fear. It had been unlikely he'd be found at sea, and once in Ferrieres he was in the lands of someone who *wanted* an alliance.

He was a man of generally philosophical disposition, and not especially young any more. He enjoyed his work, his rank, the things that came with rank and power in Asharias, including a capable wife and a number of concubines. He was properly devout, healthy, not unhappy to travel. He would have said his was a pleasing and rewarding life, on the eve of a disruption within and without that changed many things.

THE KING OF FERRIERES required the presence of the lord Folco d'Acorsi and his party immediately upon their arrival at his hunting lodge of Chervaux, west of Orane along a river in wooded, attractive country. He was, they were told, already in his reception room.

Messengers had brought advance word of their coming; their party had been seen some distance back along the road. They were escorted the last part of the way to Chervaux and the king.

Folco said, as they walked through the lodge, looking through tall windows at the river, that leaders liked doing this: to catch a visitor at a disadvantage, even one you might be happy to receive. More so if you weren't, of course. Draw conclusions from how they dealt with the speed of things. It did mean, he said, that you had been judged important: many waited days or weeks to be received. There were stories of people dying before being ushered into a royal presence.

Folco d'Acorsi was who he was, however, and had made clear in Orane, before heading on to the lodge, that he was representing the High Patriarch. They wouldn't make him wait. Émery of Ferrieres knew there were complexities to his current relationship with Rhodias.

So Lenia was still in dusty, stained, dark-brown riding trousers and a green, belted tunic when she entered the reception room with d'Acorsi and three of the others. He had said she should come with him, he hadn't said why. They all had mud on their boots. She removed her hat. Pushed a hand somewhat pointlessly through her hair. Saw Folco do the same, with what hair he had left.

It was a handsome, high-ceilinged room they entered, many courtiers present, the king on a massive oak chair most of the way along. This was a hunting lodge only by function and location. What it really seemed to be was another palace, decorated with the heads of creatures hunted in the woods here instead of portraits and statues and precious objects. Mostly stags and boars, she saw. There were two enormous stuffed bears mounted to stand erect, one on each side of the long room. She counted four fireplaces, all lit towards day's end. They were farther north than she'd ever been. It would be cold here, she thought, as autumn deepened, then winter came.

Approaching, bowing low, several steps behind Folco, she eyed the king for the first time, and suppressed a smile. King Émery of

Ferrieres was not, despite what the duchess of Macera had told her, a handsome man. It seemed obvious that Corinna Ripoli had been playing with Lenia. Malicious, trivial.

The king was short, his face pitted with scars from the pox. He was wide-eared and narrow-eyed, though the eyes were an arresting shade of blue. He had good hair, golden, worn long in back. He was not yet fat, that would come later in his life, along with the gout that made an angry monarch even more so.

The king of Ferrieres and the lord of Acorsi exchanged formal pleasantries. They spoke Émery's language. Lenia knew enough of it to follow—from time spent in Marsena, and because it was not so different from Batiaran—but the courtesies went on long enough for her attention to wander.

She was not deeply invested in what was happening here. Émery was going to agree, on some to-be-determined level, to support the fleet. He had to. The degree of commitment mattered, and so did the actual sending of payment and of men. A king could promise, and fail to follow through. That issue would not be addressed on this first visit. She cared—she wanted the attack to happen—but in truth, Ferrieres joining the siege of Tarouz did not rank high on the list of what she wanted from the world.

She was travelling with Folco for the experience of it, and because she had no better idea what to do before spring. She supposed, if she examined her feelings, she still wanted to kill Asharites.

And thinking so, she noticed a very tall man in the cluster of courtiers and emissaries behind and to the left of King Émery, and realized, from his clothing, that he was Asharite, from the east. Folco had warned her such a man might be here. Ferrieres and Asharias did have links, she'd known it from her times in Marsena.

She hated the idea of an emissary from Gurçu here, so close to the king. It was a hard thing to see.

HE NOTICED THE woman right away. Ibn Hayyan had an appreciation for women, but although this one was not unattractive at all,
might be appealing if properly attired, it was not her appearance that
drew his eye. It was the fact of her being one of four people with the
Batiaran warlord. Women could wield power, variously, and many had,
at courts, variously, but he had never seen one—dressed as a man just
now for riding, holding a leather hat—in a circumstance such as this.

Some would say it was another reflection of weakness in Jaddite
lands, her presence. He wasn't prepared to take that view. He was
curious. It was not an important question, but it nagged at him
already, like a toothache. Still, he knew what mattered here. His task
at this court, to which he had been sent to expand both trade and
operations against the Esperañans, had now changed—because this
man, d'Acorsi, had come. He needed to learn why.

The mud-stained woman with the unkempt brown hair could
wait, or be ignored. Hamadi concentrated on what the king and the
Batiaran were saying, how cordial the welcome was.

He was gratified to see that it was not especially so.

SHE WAS TOO unsettled by the very *public* presence of an Osmanli
Asharite in a place of honour. It became difficult to concentrate on
Folco and the king, though she knew she should. They were still offering pleasantries, questions about travel, and the health of family and
friends. It was possible that was all that would happen just now.

She knew about Ferrieres and its ties to the star-worshippers,
but this man standing where he was . . . he was like a slap in the
face, or spitting at someone's feet, or the two-fingered insult of the
Batiaran south.

Sarantium had been sacked less than five years ago! Lenia, who had
been Nadia then, remembered the celebrations in Almassar when
word came. A memory that burned. There had been fireworks, bells
ringing all day and into the summer night, people shouting and
singing in the dark.

They might not love Gurçu and the Osmanli tribes in the Majriti, but they knew who the truest enemy of all Asharites was: the Jaddites and their god.

The king of Ferrieres did not appear to regard this recent history as any impediment to cordial relations. The world had changed with the fall of Sarantium, Lenia Serrana thought, and some could carry on as if it hadn't, at all. It would please her, she thought, to kill the man in the blue silk robe.

"I am sorry, majesty. Would you say that again?"

Folco's tone had changed, enough to reclaim her attention.

King Émery was smiling. "I merely said your reputation as a wrestler precedes you, my lord, and it would please us to see you display it here. We are inclined towards such entertainments in the countryside."

Lenia caught her breath. It was very nearly an insult, even if couched otherwise. She took a step forward, nearer to Folco. Perhaps unwise, but she didn't think about it, just moved. It was noticed, even by the king. But that covered d'Acorsi's pause before he replied.

He did so with care, but you'd have to be a fool not to see that he was choosing his words.

"One would always wish to please the king of Ferrieres," he said, his voice quieter now. "And were I here in my own capacity I might seek to find a way to do so. But I am not, my lord."

Another deliberate pause, a controlling one—a man accustomed to courts, and not always friendly ones.

"In the unfortunate circumstance you have not yet been advised, your grace, the way a great king ought to have been by now, I should tell you that I am here as the formal representative of the High Patriarch of Jad, who has matters he wishes you to take in hand for the assurance of your own soul's path to light. Given this, I fear I'd be tarnishing the Patriarch, and the god's holy name, were I to offer an entertainment of the sort I did as a young man when I killed someone wrestling."

Killed. It had always been rumoured. She'd never heard of him saying so himself.

The king had paled, she saw. The smile was gone. Folco kept going. "For some time now I have only killed people with a purpose and under contract, as I am under contract now to Rhodias. Perhaps we might find a more private place to discuss that? After which, I'd greatly enjoy seeing what entertainments your court here can offer. For my own part, I am always happy to be diverted from the darkness of the world, especially since Sarantium was taken from us."

He was looking, Lenia saw, straight at the Osmanli envoy as he said those last words into what had become a silence. But she kept her eyes on the king, and she saw him flush. A young man still, and he was being shown up, at his own court. He'd erred, and would be realizing it. Batiara was known as the subtlest place in the world. Not the most powerful—the city-states were far too divided, fractured and fractious—but that would only *increase* the need for cleverness. Rafel had said that to her once.

King Émery cleared his throat. Folco was still staring at the Osmanli. Lenia couldn't see his face, but she could guess his expression. She'd been around him long enough now.

The king said, "We will be greatly pleased, of course, to hear what you have come to share with us."

"Thank you, majesty." Folco was too experienced not to turn back to the king, not to bow again, not to speak in a manner conveying gratitude. But he had just unsheathed a sword in words, Lenia thought.

And then . . . he wielded it. "Of course, whatever we have to say will not be relayed in the presence of a man at your court serving Gurçu the Destroyer."

He hadn't had to say that, she thought. He was still angry. This wasn't subtle.

Unexpectedly, the tall Asharite took a step forward, as she herself had done, and spoke, in quite passable Batiaran, addressing Folco.

"Grown men deal with the world as it is, my lord. They do not offer insult based on the world they wish were so. I am here because the great king of Ferrieres sees this clearly. The khalif in Asharias also does so, is open to trade and treaties with the people of Jad. That offends you?"

Another mistake, she thought. One did not speak that way to—

"Spiking the head of the Emperor of Sarantium and defiling his city does," Folco d'Acorsi said. "I had people who mattered to me die there, envoy. It occurs to me . . . I'll be happy to accede to the king's wish, after all. I'll wrestle you here, should you also be willing to offer him the requested amusement."

A sound in that large room. It was hard to say what it represented more, Lenia thought: apprehension or anticipation.

The envoy smiled, then ceased to do so.

"We are not all men of violence," he said. "Some of us find that the dignity of—"

"Were you," snapped d'Acorsi, "at the walls of Sarantium? You can lie, of course. We have no way of knowing. You are free to lie, are likely skilled at it. Were you there?"

He was, Lenia realized belatedly, not just angry, he was in a rage.

"Yes," the envoy said calmly, "I was there. I would be ashamed to deny so glorious a moment. Wars and sieges have winners and losers, my lord. I was with the grand khalif before those walls and when we broke through them. I played little role—I am not a man of war, as I said. My tasks began after. And continue. But will you blame me for celebrating the triumph of Ashar and my people? And then praying with humility and joy in that converted and renamed temple by the palace complex where Gurçu the Conqueror now dwells?"

He hadn't needed to say that last thing, either, Lenia thought. This was moving very quickly. She wished Rafel were here. She missed his presence. He'd have explained much to her, after.

"Majesty," Folco d'Acorsi said, in a cold voice, "I need to know, are you protecting this man?"

A hard silence in a crowded room.

King Émery cleared his throat again. "Of course we are!" he said. "He is an ambassador to our court. D'Acorsi, we are sorry to have jested about wrestling. Our good spirits at your arrival led us astray."

Prettily spoken, Lenia thought, but the set of Folco's broad shoulders still showed his fury. He really would not have been a man you'd have wanted to wrestle when he was young. Or today, in fact.

She saw him draw and release a slow breath. He had a task here, she thought. He would be reminding himself.

"Thank you, your grace," he said finally, in a tone closer to his usual, if not quite there. "You are right to remind me of these things. This is not the time to revisit the past. Might we retire to discuss the present matters I am sent to raise with you? I'd be grateful."

The king of Ferrieres signalled his agreement. Lenia could see relief on his face. She looked at the ambassador from Asharias again. He was still staring at Folco. It was impossible to read his expression.

She had a thought, though. Asked Folco, walking from the reception chamber, if she could be in the party that accompanied him to his meeting with the king.

He nodded acquiescence.

IN THE EVENT, it was only her. Gian and Leone, Folco's most trusted men, were tasked with something else, she didn't know what. She had no idea if it was usual or deeply not so for the king to closet himself with an envoy, however significant, so soon after the man's arrival. She guessed it was not. They were in their riding clothes, among other things, had not even been offered food or drink. Émery had two guards inside the room and two in the corridor. He was accompanied by three men, older, bearded, looking soberly concerned.

A much smaller room, down from the reception chamber, past more trophies of the hunt. A good many animals had died here, it seemed. Emery's father, grandfather . . . she didn't know how far back his line went, or this hunting lodge.

She did know enough to wander towards the windows overlooking the garden. Not right up against them, but she placed herself on that side of the room as the king and Folco took chairs by another fire. She'd been a guard herself, towards the end in Almassar. It had amused ibn Anash to have a woman do that for him. A mark of his distinctiveness. Vanity. Dhiyan ibn Anash had prided himself on being distinctive.

She'd checked the walls of this room when they entered, but there would have been no chance for someone to anticipate a meeting in this room and spy from an adjacent chamber. The garden windows were more likely.

And proved so. She would not deny that she felt pleasure in being right. Why would you deny that?

She wasn't listening to the discussion by the fire. It was not why she was here. She had a different role now, one she'd claimed. They were talking about Ferrieres and its arrangements with Gurçu, she caught that much. The first stages of conversation, a prelude. There was an art to exchanges such as this. She had no idea how much patience Folco had for it, as a fighting man. But he was also lord of a city-state. He'd be patient enough, she thought.

Then she heard the sound she'd been listening for. Two of the windows were slightly open: a scent came from late-blooming flowers planted beneath them. She saw a vineyard, beyond fruit trees. Western exposure, the sun setting now.

She didn't hesitate. No reason to, reasons not to. She pushed open the nearest of the open windows, leaned out. Having drawn a knife. Probably an offence, with the king here.

The spy was right there, crouched low so as not to be seen from the room. Where she'd guessed he might be. But . . . it wasn't the man she'd hoped for. The tall ambassador would have men here with him, of course; he'd not have done this himself.

Lenia could almost pity the one outside. She didn't.

"In Jad's name!" she exclaimed. "You will catch a chill, listening from there! Why don't you climb through the window, come by the fire . . . and the king? Surely you'll be welcome!"

The man stood quickly but didn't flee. He had no time, no chance. He was accosted, not gently, by Gian and Leone, who had—she now realized—been posted outside to watch for exactly this.

It wasn't as if, she later thought, the lord of Acorsi would miss dangers or possibilities that Lenia Serrana perceived. Still, she'd been right about a spy, there was that.

He wasn't Asharite, though. There was also that.

He had nothing to do, it turned out, with Asharias or the ambassador. His clothing and language said as much. As soon as Leone and the king's men from the corridor manhandled him into the room and pushed him, hard, to his knees, the man looked up at the king of Ferrieres and cried, "I claim the protection of a diplomat, your majesty!"

He said it in Esperañan. Calmly, in the circumstances.

She hadn't known there were diplomats from there at this court, given the tensions and conflict. She didn't understand much about such things. She was bitterly disappointed it hadn't been the Asharite ambassador himself, rising from his knees, blue silk robe muddy from the earth, bearded face shamed and afraid.

Following the counsel of his advisers, and taking note of a brief but undeniably acute observation by Folco Cino d'Acorsi, the king of Ferrieres declined to extend the asserted protection to the man who had crouched under his window to spy on him—or worse.

That last was d'Acorsi's comment. The Esperañan could easily have been there to assassinate. Had Folco's men not been outside, and a sharp-eyed woman of his company not seen this man beneath the window . . .

The king's guards had not been part of this. That mattered.

THE SPY WOULD not be executed. There were too many layers of relationships between courts and no formal state of war between Esperaña and Ferrieres.

Envoys spied. It was known. It was expected. But this had been extreme, and Folco d'Acorsi was right that creeping under a window where the king was meeting people carried a threat that could not be indulged.

The man's right hand was severed above the wrist. It was done in public, members of the court here in the countryside attending. An ice-cold letter was sent to Esperaña, to the king and queen, making clear that this punishment was regarded by King Émery as a lenient one, in the interests of harmony under Jad, but also demanding an apology.

The envoy and his attendants were formally expelled from Ferrieres, accompanied by armed men to the border. Unfortunately, on the way his wound festered, turned green, and a doctor in the party heard the crackling sound in the wound that augured ill. He attempted to sever the arm higher up but did so badly.

The ambassador from Esperaña to the court of King Émery died not far from the border of his own country. It hadn't been intended, but when does life unfold so as to offer only the things we intend? His body was carried the rest of the way to the border, where it was claimed by his countrymen. He was buried quietly in his home city, as there was embarrassment for the court in what he'd done and in the lenient punishment inflicted—it was seen to reflect badly on them.

No apology was sent, but no angry outcry was raised in Esperaña.

The envoy's name was Rabanez, Camilo Rabanez. He was from the city of Fezana originally, still unmarried, though there was apparently a child somewhere. He was ambitious, clever, good-natured, of a respectable if unremarkable family. Said to be brave. Men and women liked him, and some loved him. He had inherited unusual, memorable green eyes from his mother, and an easy laugh.

366   Guy Gavriel Kay

You can indeed die at the margins of a story, but you are as dead as if it were your own tale ending and never told.

⊗⊗

Lenia had expected the banquet to be a subdued affair, given what had happened, but she'd underestimated the young king of Ferrieres. For one thing, after the spy had been taken from the room, pending punishment and expulsion, Émery wasted little time coming to an agreement with Folco as to the fleet.

He might not have had a *great* deal of choice, but he committed his country with grace and an impressive simulation of enthusiasm. He would send ships, money, fighting men. His advisers would negotiate the precise share for Ferrieres of anything looted from Tarouz.

He also agreed that the ports of Ferrieres would be closed to Asharite galleys (though not merchant ships) immediately. He would send word south. It would not do to have war galleys taking on water and supplies here, then attacking Esperaña, when the king and queen there were expected to join in this holy war, come spring.

There was a great deal of wine at dinner, from vineyards nearby, and many courses of food—mostly game, of course. Three musicians played continuously. Perhaps deliberately, King Émery called for wrestling towards the end. Two younger courtiers stripped off their shirts and obliged, bodies glistening with oil and sweat in the lamplight and firelight. Attractive men. One vanquished the other, to applause, and a purse from the king. Folco also applauded, Lenia saw.

She left, as soon as she saw others beginning to do so. It wasn't especially late, but it had been a long day. She thought she'd ask if a hot bath could be provided in the chamber she'd been assigned. Folco was still at the table beside the king. He gave her a quick look as she rose. She didn't know what the look meant.

She was escorted by a servant with a lantern down the corridor, up a flight of stairs, then along another hallway towards her room.

There was a man outside her door. Behind him were two others, holding lights.

Lenia stopped. Her escort stopped. She had only the one, a servant, not a guard.

The man by her room bowed to her. He said, "My master means you no harm. He would be grateful for the opportunity to speak with you, my lady."

She didn't draw her knives. Not yet. She didn't have her sword, it had been taken away when they arrived. They hadn't searched her, she was only a woman. Folco had been allowed to keep his blade. Rank and stature. Folco wasn't here.

She said, "Your master is in my bedchamber?" She kept her voice level.

"He is, my lady. He wishes a private conversation."

Lenia shook her head. "Tell him to come out. If he has something to say to me, he can do it here."

"Here is . . . not private."

"It is as private as I'll accept. Quickly, or I'll summon the king's guards and report someone breaking into my chamber. You will be aware that another envoy is to have a hand severed in the morning. There are limits to an ambassador's protection, especially now. Call him out here."

It proved unnecessary. The door to her room was opened from inside. He'd been listening. She had stopped too far away to see, but the door had likely been ajar.

Hamadi ibn Hayyan stepped out, tall man in a handsome robe. A green one now; he'd changed for the banquet. It would not have been difficult for him to have a locked door opened. She hadn't seen him leave the hall. Ought to have been watching. A mistake?

She thought of pulling out one or both knives now. She thought of killing him.

He bowed as well, gravely. Spoke Asharic to his men. She understood it, of course. He said, "Give us distance. She will not harm me."

"You are too certain," she said in that language.

She thought he'd be startled. He wasn't, or not visibly. He waited for his men to withdraw a distance down the corridor. The servant escorting her also stepped back, as was proper.

Ibn Hayyan said, again in Asharic, "I am not a fighting man, as I have said. I suspect you could kill me."

She wasn't going to do that. Not yet. They both knew it. A part of her wished it were not so.

"Why do this? Why *my* chamber? What am I to you?"

"You are d'Acorsi's companion," he said simply. "Chosen despite being a woman. Perhaps because a woman, I do not know. But after this afternoon in the reception hall, I believe he will not converse with me."

"I'm to carry a message?"

Ibn Hayyan nodded. It was dark in the hallway now. The light from behind her wavered faintly on the wall. The servant holding it would be afraid, she thought.

"That, and I have another reason," the Asharite said.

"Which is?"

"First, will you hear me?"

"I'm listening," Lenia said.

What else was she going to say?

He said, "We have received indications that the High Patriarch of Jad intends an attack on Tarouz."

"Have you?" she said.

He smiled briefly. "Zariq ibn Tihon has written from Tarouz, asking for aid against such an attack."

She said nothing. She felt entirely out of her depth, but she had only to listen, she reminded herself. And relay this to Folco.

Ibn Hayyan said, "He will not receive any assistance. It has been decided. I have been sent a communication about this. The ibn Tihons offended the grand khalif, and Zariq will now lose his city—or save it by himself, if Ashar and the stars decree."

She was being given information of *huge* importance in this dark corridor of a hunting lodge in Ferrieres. Who was she to be hearing this? Lenia thought. How did life and chance do such a thing?

"Or Jad of the sun," she said.

Another brief smile. Her eyes were doing better in the darkness now. He had an earring in his left ear and many rings on his fingers. He said, "The grand khalif's request is simple. Do what you wish with Zariq ibn Tihon and his fighters and whatever treasures his city holds, if you can take it. He's skilled at war, especially at sea, even if he has outlived his usefulness. You may well fail. But . . . the people of Tarouz are blameless. It would be an act of cruelty to kill them for his sins, or his brother's."

"What sins?" she asked. "And why *outlived*?"

He hesitated for the first time. Then, as if ending a dialogue with himself, he said, "The brothers arranged for an assassination in the city of Abeneven, killing the khalif there for their own advancement, unsettling the Majriti, bringing no benefit to Asharias."

The woman who had been one of the instruments of that assassination was glad it was dark in that corridor.

A question rose within her and could not be supressed. Lenia said, "Was Gurçu the Destroyer generous or cruel at Sarantium?"

Hamadi ibn Hayyan looked surprised. He shook his head, but in wonder, not dismissal.

"You should know the answer, my lady. He killed those who fought him, as one must do when a city falls, to *cause* it to fall, if there has been no surrender. But his intent was, and remains, to rule there, not to destroy, whatever name you give him. Jaddites live in Asharias. More are coming all the time. Many have converted to the faith of Ashar, some have not. Those pay the taxes required and are allowed places of worship. Others arrive and leave, trading by sea or overland. This cannot be unknown to you. There are always deaths when a city is taken, but the grand khalif is a man of conquest, not savagery. So, to answer you, he was generous. And now asks that the worshippers of your sun god be the same to people in another place."

She was silent, thinking. Then said, "How did you intend to convey this? You could not know Folco d'Acorsi was coming here."

He smiled again. "We didn't know it would be him, but knew it was possible. We have eyes and ears in many places. Our people are in Rhodias. In Seressa. Seressa spies on the world and the world gathers there, as the phrase goes."

He seemed to have answers for everything. Whether they were true was another matter. He was courteous, eloquent. She still wanted to kill him. Perhaps *because* of that smooth courtesy.

He said, "You have my message for the lord of Acorsi. I'd be grateful if you conveyed it. I said I had another reason for being here, Lenia Serrana."

She waited. For some reason her heart began beating faster.

"Why," asked Hamadi ibn Hayyan of Asharias, "do I know you? Where have we met?"

She stared, in the faint light of a lamp behind her, and two behind him, farther off. She shook her head. "We have not met. I have never been in the east."

"I think we have. I believe I remember you from somewhere. And I've been west, in the year after the conquest, speaking to leaders in the Majriti for Gurçu, may the stars forever bless him and his line."

"Why would the Majriti have anything to do with me?" A reckless question.

"Because your Asharic is flawless, and you speak it with an accent from the west. I am going to guess you were taken, young. A hard fate. To what city?"

Lenia drew a breath again. "You understand I am closer to ending your life than answering your question."

She meant it. There was a strong impulse in her, a thrumming in the blood. She could *see* her hand moving to the knife in her boot, see it coming up, throwing—aiming for his eye. With a knife, that was one of the surest ways to kill, if you were certain you could hit there.

She tended to be certain she could, by now. She flexed the fingers of her right hand. She went that far. The thrumming was an imperative of sorts.

He exclaimed, "*Almassar!* That's where I saw you! In Almassar! In the house of Dhiyan ibn Anash! You were a guard for him. He was very proud of it!"

She stopped her fingers. She gazed bleakly at this man through the wavering not-quite-light. The servant, she thought, would see her kill him, his attendants would see it. She was part of Folco's company, on a mission that mattered, and . . .

"Proud? He *owned* me," she said. "He bought me and he owned me. He was also proud of his vineyards and library and his best horses. Other things he owned."

His turn to be silent. He was thinking about her words. It could be seen, even in the shadows. He said, "Ibn Anash died a year or so after, we heard. Did you kill him?"

A disturbingly acute man. He would be so, Lenia thought, to be as close as he evidently was to Gurçu. She could lie or tell truth.

She didn't owe him either.

"What were you doing at his house?" she said.

He accepted her deflection. He said, "I told you. In the year we claimed Asharias I was sent to the Majriti. I was tasked with making clear the grand khalif saw all Asharites as brothers, with himself in the role of eldest brother."

She said nothing.

He said, "I was also trying to draw men of distinction to Asharias. Scholars, judges. That was why I visited ibn Anash. To offer him a position as a judge, and a life of great comfort, if he'd help make our city greater, add to its lustre."

"It *was* great," she said. "It *had* lustre. It was the City of Cities."

"And needed to be made so again, under Ashar's stars. Surely you can see that?"

"You ask for too much," she said.

Staring at him, she found a memory. One that burned. Spoke it before she stopped herself.

"Hear me. When word came to Almassar that Sarantium had fallen, the man who owned my body, my life, summoned friends for a banquet, wine and music and celebration. He made me dance for his guests. I am not someone who dances. It was not a skill I had, or was ever taught. Nor was it a choice. They were laughing and drinking, his friends, and some reached for me, clutching at my body."

"He stopped them, surely?" said Hamadi ibn Hayyan.

She wanted to kill him, again. It was so strong a desire. She said, "He did. But only because it was disrespectful to *him*. Then later he summoned me to his bedchamber. With another woman, and one of the men from the stables. To amuse and excite him. But you are correct, he didn't let a friend tear off my garments when I danced. There is that, yes."

Hamadi ibn Hayyan was silent. Eventually, he said, "Your High Patriarch in Rhodias hated the Eastern Patriarch. Never liked the Emperor in Sarantium. No one in the west ever heeded their pleas. The lands where Jad is worshipped never sent any help to them, for years. And now . . . now the Patriarch feels shame, guilt. So he brings war to a city close to his shores."

"Can you blame him?"

"Given he refused aid of any kind? Perhaps I can."

"None of that concerns me."

"None of it concerned any of you! The kingdoms of Jad let Sarantium fall. A handful of men came to fight by choice, at their own expense. From towns and cities, farms. From a village of pirates in Sauradia! They died with honour. Our cannon that broke the walls? They were cast by a Jaddite master gunner who came to us.

Did you know that? And, now, *now* the warriors and kings and all the holy men of Jad mourn Sarantium."

She was silent.

"It is about shame," he repeated.

"Shame can move men to action."

He looked at her. He said, "I really do remember you. You stood by a door, guarding the room. You have a memorable look to you." She saw him smile a little, his teeth showing in darkness. "I don't, evidently."

She said nothing. She didn't remember him at all, it was true.

He said, "Where are you from?"

She was thinking about what he'd just said. The bitter truth of it. No force had ever gone east. They were too divided here, too greedy. Too afraid?

"A farm near Casiano," she said. She wasn't sure why she'd answered.

"And taken in a raid? A long way inland, if so."

"Yes."

"And young."

"Yes." She wasn't going to say more. Saying this much was . . . a great deal.

"I'm sorry," he said. "It happens to so many, of all faiths. They lose their roots, their childhood. The self they might have become in a different life. Perhaps the new self is stronger? I don't know."

Near-darkness, the strangeness of this conversation in a corridor. Fatigue, and . . . he was not what he'd seemed to be.

"I don't know either," she said. "I will give your message to the lord of Acorsi."

"Thank you," he said. "Good night, Lenia Serrana."

He turned and walked away. She watched him go, approaching his light-bearers, passing them, followed by them down the corridor then around a turning, and it was dark again in front of her.

"How much did you hear?" she asked, not turning around.

Folco d'Acorsi walked up, carrying the lamp. "You heard me?"

"I saw the light sway along the wall and guessed he was handing it to someone. You were kneeling? Rose as the servant backed away?"

"Yes," he said. "Exactly so. I'm impressed. I had an instinct and followed you as soon as I could get away."

"You were worried for me?"

A quiet laugh. "More about what you might do."

She looked at him beside her. A reassuring presence. If you were with him, not opposed.

"I did want to kill him," she said.

"I thought you might. I do too."

"Perhaps less so now, for me."

"Perhaps for me, as well. A little."

"How much did you hear?" she repeated. She really was tired. In her bones and heart. Hard things remembered.

"From when he said he knew you."

She nodded. So he'd have been here for her story of that night. Dancing, and after. His eye was on her, alert, and you could say gentle. She wasn't sure. Lamplight.

"You didn't hear his message for you," she said.

"Only when you mentioned it at the end."

She told him, as precisely as she could.

After she was done he said, "That is extremely useful. Also . . ." a hesitation, "you need not answer, but . . . *did* you kill that man in Almassar? Ibn Anash?"

It had become such a strange night.

She said, "I did."

"Will you tell me how?"

She told a story she had never told in full, not even to Rafel.

"There was civil war in Almassar. The city's khalif and his brother. A great deal of violence. Ibn Anash was allied with the khalif, a judge in his courts. I slept outside his room on nights when . . . when I wasn't required inside. And also after such . . . such times."

She drew a breath. Folco was silent.

She said, "One night I heard an intruder slip in through the garden window. He was skilled, mostly silent. But he didn't expect me to be there, and didn't see me in the dark. I killed him from behind as he approached the bedchamber door. And then . . ."

This was so difficult.

"And then you realized it was an opportunity?"

She nodded. There was pain, and the strangest sort of release, in telling. Trusting someone.

"I went inside and killed Dhiyan ibn Anash as he slept. Then I came back out and raised an alarm in the house. I told them I'd killed the assassin fleeing after he'd murdered the judge. He was there, he was dead, the window to the garden was open. I was believed. I was only a woman, a loyal slave, a guard."

"And then?"

"And then there was turmoil, in the house, in the city, and I used it to leave a week later, after we buried ibn Anash and burned the assassin. I went down to the harbour to Rafel ben Natan's ship."

"You knew him?"

"We had spoken in the market twice. He . . . he had a thoughtful face. I took a chance. I brought him some gems. I had watched them being hidden by the man who owned me. Rafel agreed to accept me on board, for those, and for what I had been taught, about killing men. I had been thinking I might run away without killing ibn Anash. That was just . . ."

"A moment claimed?"

"Yes. That. I stayed on the ship whenever we were in Almassar afterwards, disguised as a man in case someone came on board. There was a search for an escaped slave, of course, but it died down. There were greater concerns in a civil war than a woman slave who had run off."

They were entirely alone. D'Acorsi said, and she remembered it all her life: "My sister, and one other woman I knew, were like what I think you are, Lenia Serrana. In having this much courage. Life allows, or doesn't, the chance for people to grow into what they might become. They weren't permitted. Perhaps you have been, and still are. I believe that might be so. Thank you for sharing this."

"Sharing ibn Hayyan's message?" She attempted a wry smile. Failed.

"Partly that," he said. "Good night. We will talk in the morning."

He carried the lamp back up the corridor and entered a room not far away. She saw which room it was. It was dark, then, in the empty hallway. She had intended to ask for a bath, but was too exhausted now, unravelled by many thoughts.

She went to bed and dreamed of home, the farm, under two moons rising and crossing the night sky, of loss, and desires of many kinds.

Hamadi ibn Hayyan was not the formal ambassador from Asharias to the court of King Émery of Ferrieres. He was in the west to conduct diplomatic negotiations—trusted more than the man there who was not particularly happy about ibn Hayyan's arrival. He didn't reveal that, of course, or thought he wasn't revealing it.

That night, ibn Hayyan decided it was time for him to leave. The discussions as to lowered tariffs and their ongoing joint engagement against Esperaña's ambitious king and queen had largely been concluded and he anticipated no difficulties, though there might be a need for Émery to be cautious for a time now if, as appeared to be the case, a Jaddite fleet was indeed headed for Tarouz, and Ferrieres and Esperaña both were a part of it.

He was ready, though, suddenly. Ready to go home.

He'd spoken with a woman in a dark corridor and—to his very great surprise—he felt as if he was being, had already been, changed by that. Of course he knew of raids and slavery. He *owned* slaves.

But something had happened to him, or within him, just now. *Hear me*, she had said. And told him of a moment in her life. Made him hear it.

A story of being made to dance for Asharites when word of the fall of Sarantium had come. And then, after, that night . . .

You could know that hard things happened, and then . . . be made to confront them? See them differently? More clearly? Because of a person you met.

He took his leave of the court a few days later.

He was given sumptuous gifts—for Gurçu, for himself. He was given letters and documents. He travelled south to Marsena and took ship from there to Asharias. Escorted again by war galleys, but an uneventful voyage. He wrote poetry as they sailed east.

He had been an occasional poet, part of his link to deepening the culture of a newly Asharite city. But after that time he became much more of one. Hassan ibn Hayyan began the life course that led to his being acclaimed—years after, centuries, even—as among the greatest of the writers of verse in the Asharite world. Indeed, his gradual withdrawal from a formal role at the grand khalif's court towards a life of reflection and the pursuit of what excellence he was capable of in verse . . . this had its beginnings on that long sea journey home.

Or, more properly, a little earlier, with a conversation with a woman in the darkness of a hunting lodge in Ferrieres.

He wrote only one verse about that woman, Lenia Serrana—who had been called Nadia bint Dhiyan in Almassar (he was amazed he remembered). He'd have sent it to her but had no idea where she was. He could have tried to find her, but he didn't. He dreamed of her. With a feeling close to yearning. Over the years he became known as the poet of the night sky, of loss, and desire.

WE CAN BE CHANGED, sometimes greatly, by people who come only glancingly into our lives and move on, never knowing what they have done to us.

We can do this ourselves to others. And never know. Move past an encounter, away, leaving something significant behind for another. It is unsettling to think about. One can call it a sorrow, or a thing of beauty running through the turning of our days and nights, however many, however few, they are.

CHAPTER XIV

Rafel woke from a dream, and the words that woke him, that he had cried in his head, seemed to have been *"I had a brother!"* But they might also have been *I have*, and it was hard to remember now, to reach back into sleep's world and pluck words like flowers to try to hold as daylight and awareness of the world streamed in, through the shutters, into his mind.

He was in Seressa, autumn arriving. He had come back to supervise the building of their carrack, and had stayed. There were details to address every day, just about. He'd known that would be so. The ship was nearly done. He felt pride (and even love) as he watched it happen.

He was not living in the Kindath quarter. Seressa was relaxed about such things. He was staying with Guidanio Cerra and his daughter. Had met the man's parents, eaten dinner with them. Cerra's father, a tailor, was fitting him for new clothing. He liked Cerra quite a bit, as it happened. Had begun, at request, to call him Danio.

Port cities were often relaxed in this way. So many people coming and going, all kinds of people. Seressa was perhaps uniquely so, how-ever. It was unique in many ways. Rafel liked it, even as he was aware it was a dangerous place.

There was a humming here, a vibrancy. He had begun to think he could live here as easily as in Firenta. Or Marsena. Or Sorenica on the other coast, where Raina Vidal was—for now. She had spoken of Asharias. It might well be a better place to be a Kindath. He could go there, too. Travel with her, even. Or not.

You could have, Rafel thought, too many possibilities. But you could not—not properly—lament that this was so. Having no choices, or only one forced upon you, would always be worse. Some paths had closed for him. He could never go back to Almassar now. And Esperaña had been locked to his people since he was a child.

Paths. Sometimes they were decided for you, not by you. His wife, after it became clear they could not have a child and he would continue to be away much of the year, had divorced him, as was allowed in their faith, and had left Almassar.

She'd changed her name, taken a Jaddite one, and a ship to the coast of Esperaña. Eight years ago, that had been. She'd done it too quickly. Anger and speed, not enough preparation. He'd told her that. She wasn't inclined to listen to him by then.

He remembered, he always would, the day he learned what had happened to her, not long after she'd landed and gone inland to join her relatives in Aljais—the ones who had stayed, converted, taken on a Jaddite identity.

They had survived. She did not.

She was too new, a threat, seen as a danger by them. Her family. She'd been informed upon and had died.

Not a public burning. She didn't matter enough for that. She had probably had her throat slit, then an unmarked grave somewhere. He felt all of that, to this day, as a wound. And a source of guilt. He had nightmares about this, too.

Theirs had been an arranged marriage, of course; they had both been young. But she'd been a good person, his memories were affectionate, until some moments at the very end. If he could find a way, he thought, he'd kill her cousins in Aljais. Even now, all these years after.

You didn't *do* what they had done.

He'd had a brother. He'd had a wife.

Letters had come to him, mostly from Firenta, mostly related to his new business in the cloth trade. He had told people to write him care of Antenami Sardi, and those were being forwarded. He had begun to feel a genuine affection for young Sardi, the man whose life he had saved. There was a saying among the Kindath that if you did that—saved someone's life—you were responsible for all they did afterwards. He wondered what Antenami Sardi would be, would do.

Rafel's father had written the letter that mattered most. His parents had arrived in Marsena, the god and the moons be praised and sanctified. Relief brought him to tears, reading this, seeing his father's handwriting. He went to the Kindath quarter of Seressa, a long walk, many bridges, and walked into one of the houses of prayer, and he gave thanks, joining the moonrise invocations. He lit white and blue candles.

They were not certain why all of this had to happen, his father's letter said, but he understood Rafel must have good reasons to uproot them in this way (he did not write "again," which would have hurt, badly), and they were grateful for his continued devotion to them.

He was a good son, his father wrote. They had a place to live in the Kindath quarter of Marsena, Gaelle had arranged for that, and they saw the two children almost every day, which was a blessing. He understood that they would not want for resources to live, but he didn't want Rafel to concern himself greatly. Their needs, he wrote, were not extravagant. He did hope for enough funds to buy books, as he had not been able to bring very much of his library, in their haste. He missed his books. He ended with love from both of them, and added that Gaelle sent hers.

Gaelle sent hers.

That didn't sound like her. He doubted she'd done so, theirs was a different sort of relationship. He kept thinking about his father, who had lost his library twice now. Left it behind. Been taken from it.

A letter had come from Lenia in Macera. They'd been about to leave for Ferrieres when she sent it. Macera had been challenging, she wrote, but Folco had been successful in his purposes, as Rafel might (or might not, she added) learn from the Seressinis, who would doubtless keep abreast of all reports.

She was not certain what would follow their visit to King Émery in Orane. Possibly, she'd go with Folco back to Acorsi; possibly she'd leave him and come to Seressa or Firenta, wherever Rafel was. She'd find out where that was. She hoped the shipbuilding was proceeding, and his recovery as well. She wrote nothing about the night at her brother's ranch. What would she say? he thought. What would *he* say?

She suggested that they might have the *Silver Wake* moved around the coast to Seressa now. There would be an issue, she added, about finding a new captain for it, if Rafel's intention was eventually to sail in the new carrack himself. Elie could command the *Silver Wake*, but better perhaps that Elie become helmsman of the new one for Rafel, in which case they'd need someone for the *Wake*.

He smiled, reading all of that, because his own thoughts had been the same. He'd already written to Elie, and to Raina Vidal, asking if she had any way of helping them find a helmsman in Sorenica, though Seressa was a likelier place. It pleased him that he and Lenia were thinking the same way, even at a distance.

She signed her letter without any sentiments expressed at all and with just her initials. There had been a change, however. She was *LS* now, not *N*.

On the night she'd come to the *Silver Wake* she'd brought him gems of considerable worth to sell. Jewellery as a price paid for freedom. Later, he'd calculated and offered her a small owner's share of the ship for those, their value.

He hadn't had to do that. He'd done that. Can we always explain ourselves to ourselves? he'd wondered. Still did.

She'd written this most recent letter in Asharic, to make it harder to read for someone who might intercept it.

There had been other letters, as the days passed, from other people. And then . . .

And then he'd had a visitor. Yesterday. A man he didn't know, from Firenta, sent by Piero Sardi, with a note from Antenami. That visit had surely been the reason for what had come to him in his dreams last night. Receding now, the way so much receded from you.

"*We have found him,*" Antenami had written. "*Valli will explain. You will tell us what you want done.*"

A man named Piedona Valli, one of their spies, it seemed, met with Rafel at the small office he'd leased near the Arsenale. He sent away the two employees he'd hired, gave them each an errand to run. He listened alone to the man who'd come.

We have found him.

Sayash, his brother, his younger brother, was in Astarden in the north, among the merchants of diamonds and other jewels. He was alive. Astarden had always been a possibility. He had taken a Jaddite name.

He had also taken a Jaddite lover, and partner.

It was not a real surprise. How could Rafel not have imagined this might be what had happened? Not be the reason Sayash had left a wife and small children and his home and gone to a northern city? That sort of escape, or dying—those had been Rafel's thoughts when Sayash disappeared, and they had remained his best guesses.

Sayash's lover and partner, the Firentini spy said, was a man named Goffred Anders. He was a merchant from the north who had done business for years in Marsena, would likely have encountered Sayash ben Natan there, trading.

They were living quietly with three household servants and four employees in their business. Two of the servants were trained as guards, Piedona Valli said. Rafel had no idea how he'd learned that. Sayash and his partner had a house with a trading space attached on the ground level, alongside one of the canals. They owned it, were not leasing the property. A good neighbourhood, Valli added. Their business appeared to be prospering. They bought and sold raw gems, and cut and set them also. The house was large, well maintained and furnished. They dressed very well when they went out or dealt with clients in the trading rooms. Furs, and so forth.

They had not been approached or engaged, would not have known that Valli and another man were gathering information on them. The Sardis' men were, said Piedona Valli with some pride, discreet in pursuing their tasks. They could go back north, if for any reason that was desired by Signore ben Natan. His instructions were to do whatever Signore ben Natan requested in this matter. They were at his service.

You will tell us what you want done.

What you want done.

What you want.

༄

I was not accustomed to seeing Rafel ben Natan as unsettled as he was when we met that evening at the Arsenale.

He was a small, neat, composed man with a sense of humour I enjoyed (I can remember wishing I were so quick with a clever remark), but he also had the unrevealing look of a long-time merchant when he needed it. He was a Kindath, and had been a corsair. Such people didn't tend to show what they knew or were thinking.

We met at the main gates amid the noises and the continuous smells of the Arsenale. You could get used to these, people did. I never liked them, though. It had been a bright, breezy day. A feel of autumn in the wind off the lagoon. It was still mild as the sun set, still windy. Some clouds, but the stars and the blue moon were visible.

We did this once a week, to look in on his carrack, speak with the master or assistant master of the Arsenale, remind them (it needed doing, there were so many ships being built now) that this man had the favour of the duke. We went at day's end, when the Arsenale was at least somewhat quieter and after my tasks in the palace were done, before going somewhere to dine together.

The duke had assigned me to ben Natan. It wasn't a burden. We both respected the Kindath merchant, and Duke Ricci had decided he might be a useful man. In Seressa, a man with good instincts in trade, one who knew the world—including parts of it we might not understand as well as we wanted to—such a person would be someone to know, and try to bind to us. Being of his faith was a problem, but less so here than in most places. Clerics made fiery speeches at intervals; the council ignored them, mostly.

I had invited ben Natan to live in my home while the ship was being built. It was a blessing for me, in truth: another presence in the house in those months after my wife died, especially in the long twilights before the summer dark. He spoke of finding a house for himself, a small one. He had a large one in Firenta, was engaged now in the cloth trade—a matter of interest to us. We didn't much trust or like the Sardis (they didn't much trust or like us). They were no threat to our sea trade and tariffs, needed us for shipping and receiving some of their goods and materials, but they were encroaching, without subtlety, on our control of the banking world.

There were always threats of one sort or another.

The duke would want to bring Rafel ben Natan—and a fortune large enough to build a carrack with just one partner—more completely into our world and allegiance. The two of them did use a Seressini bank, at least.

But besides all this, I liked him. He was kind to my daughter at a time when it felt to me she needed kindness from as many people as possible. She was too young to know this, of course. It was my own feeling. I realized it then, not just looking back now.

He sang Kindath lullabies to her in the evenings, I remember. In Batiaran. I'd watch them together, take some solace, a slight easing of the heart, listening to him as he sang to my girl. It is likely ben Natan knew that. That he was singing to me as much as to her.

Who knows love?
Who says he knows love?
What is love, tell me.

"I know love,"
Says the littlest one.
"Love is like a tall oak tree."

"Why is love a tall oak tree?
Little one, tell me."

"Love is a tree
For the shelter it gives
In sunshine or in storm."

I forget much, but remember that song. Memory is like that.

He had no children of his own. I'd asked. His wife was also dead. He didn't tell me how.

At the Arsenale that windy evening I did ask what was disturbing him. It was obvious even by lantern light, in part because his mood was never obvious.

"I am dealing with difficult tidings, Danio. It isn't a matter of business. No effect on Seressa."

"It affects a friend of mine," I said.

He smiled at me. We moved inside the gates, fell into stride together. There were many people walking along the wide, newly cobblestoned landing between the lagoon and the shipworks. It was still busy at that hour. Carpenters, oar-makers, caulkers, makers of pulleys and sails and cannon. Blacksmith's forges. The smell of pitch.

"It'll be all right," he said. "Just something to address. A family matter."

Someone had reported a visitor from Firenta at his offices the day before.

"If I can assist in any way . . . ?" I said.

"I will ask you before anyone else. Thank you, Danio. Shall we go look at the ship?"

He hadn't named it yet. It was considered bad luck in Seressa to name a ship before it was ready to be launched. My understanding was that the Kindath were cautious about invoking bad fortune, too.

People came to the Arsenale in the evenings to promenade, be seen, peer inside to where ships were taking shape or at the almost-finished ones already moored on the lagoon. Prostitutes were busy here every night, taking men back to rooms not far away. It was all-hours-noisy because ships were our life.

We had two armed escorts as we walked. I was there as the duke's adviser. It was proper to display status when I went abroad in that role. I was hardly expert in shipbuilding. It was more about my presence, representing the duke and the council, walking with a Kindath man.

We live in a world defined by symbols. I wonder how it could be otherwise. We were both well-dressed that night, though not formally, both coming from our work. Expensive clothing also sent a message. My father had made what we both wore. He liked ben Natan, and my mother seemed slightly infatuated with him, wearing jewellery and scent when we came to them for dinner, which was amusing enough, even for her son.

My guards didn't do their job very well that night. There have been many times when I've thought I was about to die. That night was one of them.

༺ঔৈ༻

They walked towards the ship. It was far enough along in construction that it was already on the water, moored among others, including foreign merchants' ships arriving to trade, a long way down, towards where the lagoon opened out to the sea.

Rafel liked approaching his ship, the walk along this expensively cobblestoned landing. The three masts were now up. What he felt when he looked at the carrack was disturbingly close to love. All day, however, his mind had been on his brother and Gaelle and the children, on the ways life and love twisted on you. How memories needed to be revisited, with the arrival of new information. How you suddenly understood your own life—or your brother's—in a different way.

That is what he'd been thinking about when he saw a tongue of flame on his ship, far off. He blinked, stared.

There were many people here, moving in a gathering darkness lit by torches. Talking, laughing. But he was the one with eyes only on that ship, and he was the one who saw the fire.

It was windy. He began to run.

There was always a risk of fire here, they *used* fires all through the Arsenale, how else cast the great and small cannon and all the other elements of metal for a ship? There was also, undeniably, the danger of deliberately set fires. Why let business rivals smoothly build their galley or caravel? And many of the ships under construction here were for owners not from Seressa. Possible rivals. The Arsenale guards were supposed to protect these with even more ferocious attention; the city would lose too much revenue if they didn't. And some of the ships under construction now were for the High Patriarch's war, for Tarouz.

As his was. For that war.

"*Fire!*" he heard himself scream. "*Fire! Fire!*"

He kept on screaming it as he ran. The one word, over and over. People reacted. They would always react to that cry. One ship burning, one forge igniting, and so much could burn in a wind off the sea. He pointed as he ran. He stumbled, kept his balance.

Wasn't this what the Arsenale's guards were *here* for, in the name of whatever they deemed holy in Seressa? There would be firefighting equipment and men, he thought desperately, still screaming, still running. He saw another lick of orange in the dark on his ship. Other people were shouting now.

Then he saw something else, even as his cry was picked up, perhaps *because* it was picked up: a man, more shadow than anything else, appeared on the carrack's deck, climbed up on the rail, stood a moment, then leaped out and a long way down, into the lagoon.

Rafel saw it because he was looking right there, running through the lurid darkness, pushing people aside, swearing, twisting to get by them. It could be a workman escaping flames, but there was no great fire yet, you could try to put it out, you *should* do that if you were a workman amid an accidental fire. It could, therefore, be someone trying to *create* a conflagration and flee, now that an alarm was raised. Hoping the fire you'd set became unstoppable before others arrived to fight it, while you swam away in the night.

No one else seemed to have seen the man, the splash where he hit black water. Sometimes busyness was the best screen for what you didn't want seen. Chaos could conceal you.

He had used that truth in his time. It was a thing he *knew.* Had he not been here now, tonight, had it not been their ship, flickers of flame might have become a blast of wind-borne fire before anyone . . .

Still might. Fire was the destroyer, the enemy, in every city in the world.

Cerra and his escorts were running with him. One of them, a younger man, passed Rafel, raising the alarm as he went. Rafel ran on, still shouting. He had no way to get to the man in the water, he thought, no way to know which way he'd swim and surface. They needed to reach the carrack, and pray for the arrival of guards and those who fought fires.

He had no weapon beyond the sort of knife one used at meals. He did draw that blade, fatuously.

And then, because sometimes the moons could bless you, or curse you, with what might or might not be a gift, Rafel saw a shape in the water. Someone swimming just ahead. It should not have happened. It happened. You could succeed or fail, live or die, because of moments like that.

You could surface alive, or drown, or be killed in a lagoon.

He changed course, angled to the water, dove in without breaking stride or pausing to consider what he was doing. Not like him. At all. He would never have done it if he'd been thinking. He was holding his knife, there was that.

They threw a jewelled ring into the sea here, Rafel ben Natan knew. Absurd thought just now. But the dukes of Seressa did wed the sea that way, every year. The sea from which their wealth and power came. All their gifts.

The night water was colder than expected. Cloudy, black, there was seaweed. His clothing was heavy, he was wearing boots. He was not a good swimmer. He was a fool.

He had tried to live a life *not* shaped by folly. And a single moment . . .

But he had done his dive at the right place, it seemed. The moons and the god were choosing to be kind. Or he was meant to die tonight in Seressa.

He did intercept the man who had leaped from his ship. It was not possible that this was anyone else in the lagoon waters at night. People didn't do that. The man was swimming steadily and well, relying on darkness to hide him. It ought to have worked. He was barechested, which meant he had *intended* to leap into the water from the fire he set, or had been prepared to do so. He would be a fighter, a guard, an assassin. Rafel was none of these things. Or, well, yes, he was the last. Indirectly. Even so . . .

He stabbed immediately as the angle of his flat dive and swimming strokes brought him into the path of the other man. Surprise was all he had. No tunic blocked his blade. He couldn't see clearly in the water but he aimed for the chest and he thought he struck there.

Not a good enough knife, not a deep enough blow. The man turned swiftly, grappled for Rafel, and pulled them both under the surface.

Dark and cold, the lagoon. The swimmer twisted Rafel's wrist hard. His hand splayed open, the knife fell, lost in black water. Not like a ring, not a wedding symbol. The man shifted position, and then he had Rafel from behind, a thick forearm at his windpipe.

You didn't even have to choke a man underwater, Rafel thought, just be younger, better at swimming, at holding your breath. *I am such a fool,* he thought. He writhed, squirmed, got enough purchase to grope with his good hand for the other man's eyes, trying to gouge at them. But his arms were heavy in the sea and the other man was stronger, agile. A better swimmer, yes, and . . .

And the arm at his throat fell back.

Then the man's whole body did. Pulled away from behind. Someone else was here, someone had the arsonist. Desperate for air, Rafel thrust towards the surface. He broke water, gasping. His wrist hurt, he wondered if it was broken. With his good hand he clawed seaweed from his eyes. He couldn't seem to breathe properly yet, was still fighting for air, in the air.

Who was it? Who had saved him? Cerra? Could Danio have done this? He wiped at his eyes and face again. The Arsenale dock was not far away. You could drown so near to land.

Frenzied movement along the walkway, people running towards where his ship was on fire—with the risk of that fire spreading. That was the terror. He saw Cerra at the edge of the lagoon, kneeling, reaching out a hand, shouting for Rafel to come to him. The two escorts were not there. Had they run on ahead, or had one of them . . . ?

He heard a splash. From the blackness of the Seressini lagoon two shapes emerged beside him. One was unconscious, limp. The other was a stranger, long-haired, full-bearded, gripping the other from behind.

"He isn't dead, I don't think," this man said. He spoke Batiaran with an accent, one Rafel didn't know, though he felt he should. "Better if he lives. We'll want to know who sent him, won't we?"

YOU COULDN'T CONTROL everything, Rafel was thinking, sitting on the cobblestones outside the Arsenale, water puddling about him, his heart beating crazily fast, still.

Someone had evidently thrown a cloak over him. His wrist was still painful, but he didn't think it was broken. He was shivering. He had tried to keep control of his life as much as a man could, he thought. Had wanted to do so, perhaps because so much control had been ripped away when he was young. No decisions you could make on that strand, edge of another sea, if you were a child. Wanting to wasn't enough. He had never stopped thinking about his father's face, by that other sea.

He looked down at the lagoon water puddling around him. You just *couldn't* though, he was thinking, you couldn't control some things. Perhaps most things. Even your own impulses. Maybe you had to somehow learn not to be terrified of this? Accept it. Hope or trust.

Hope and trust were hard. They could be misplaced, that was the eternal problem. But they could save or change your life. Or something entirely unexpected might, something not about control. Nor about trust.

Danio Cerra was speaking urgently to him, crouching down. Rafel forced himself to look at the man's face, try to focus on his words, the way someone's spectacles could help them see writing, read it. The duke of Seressa used those. So did Piero Sardi.

His mind was still scattered, like birds above a battlefield or at sea when cannon boomed. Swallows. Swallows were seen as good luck by mariners. Perhaps because they meant you were close to land. Sometimes being close to land was bad, though, wasn't it? Rocks. Enemies?

This was terrible. He needed to rein in his runaway thoughts. He forced them back to where he was. He looked to his right, down the Arsenale walkway. His wrist hurt.

Danio was still talking. "Listen to me! They have the fire under control! They do, Rafel. It is all right. You saw it in time."

"And this one will live to talk," said the voice he'd heard in the water.

Looking a long way up he saw the man who'd saved his life. Shirtless, scarred, with long red hair and a red beard, standing above the unconscious arsonist. He didn't know this man at all.

Danio stood up. He cleared his throat. He said to the big man, very quietly, "There is danger in your being here, my lord. I will not say your name because of that, but I believe I know who you are."

"I'm not here to hide," the red-bearded man said. Thick eyebrows, a long, lean face. "I am here to speak with your duke, and your council if need be. Seressa is treacherous and deals with Sarantium under its false name, but I believe you will not betray me if I tell you why I am here."

"We betray too easily," Guidanio Cerra said. The big man smiled at that, thinly.

Rafel pushed himself upright, still dripping. The man had said Sarantium, not Asharias. The High Patriarch was like that, never said the other name. He looked at his friend. Cerra's expression was strained.

"How do you know me?" the red-bearded man said to Guidanio.

A short silence. "I was well taught, years ago. Geography, other things. I knew your name before the fall of the city. And I am an adviser to Duke Ricci. We learn what we can about . . . some people."

"Of course you do," said this tall man. He smiled coldly again. There was malice, even rage in it, Rafel thought. The man turned his head away and spat into the water. Rafel didn't know him at all, didn't know why he was so angry. The arsonist lay at their feet, not moving.

"Do we know who this is?" he asked, gesturing, his first words. "Who sent him?"

"We are about to," said the big man. "My men are coming with them now." He looked at Rafel closely for the first time. He said, "My name is Skandir. I used to be Ban Rasca Tripon of Trakesia. I no longer use that name. I am lord of nothing now. I fight Osmanli Asharites in the east, in Jad's holy name. It is all I do."

And Rafel knew the name. Both names. Everyone did.

He bowed. With respect, and a measure of awe. Then he looked to his right, to where this man was pointing, to see a cluster of men leading others towards them. And in the second group, stumbling as he was pushed along, was someone he recognized.

And so Rafel finally understood what this attack on his ship had been about, and the folly of men, their endless capacity for it, was brought home to him again. Again. He wanted to weep for it, even if he was not a man—had not been a boy—inclined to do that.

He'd been watchful as a child, kept his counsel, shielded his grief, seeing his father's. He hadn't changed in these things. Remembered, still, looking back from the deck of a ship taking them away from what had been home. A place where music could be heard almost every evening—from a garden down a laneway behind your house, from a square the other way—and you would know, even as a child, who was playing a stringed instrument so beautifully, and be made easier, more secure in the world, listening as night fell.

He hadn't expected to be known so quickly, it was not his intention. But it was good, perhaps: the young-looking man had just said he was an adviser to Duke Ricci, and the duke was why he had come here. A dive into the lagoon after a fleeing fire-setter might turn out to be the best thing he could have done. Jad was with you or he was not.

He did want to find a sanctuary tonight. He'd missed the sundown invocations, had to make up for that.

Plans needed to change all the time. If you were a rebel engaging a colossal force you did that or you died. Or people died fighting with you, for you, brave and young, and trusting. That had happened too often. He'd buried so many young men. What he was doing—Rasca Tripon, called Skandir—was warring with a small number of fighters at any given time against the might of Gurçu the Destroyer. That war had death embedded in it, written against his name. He was not going to live a long time, he knew it.

But this young man by the Seressa Arsenale who had recognized him had a look he knew, even by torchlight: because he'd been royalty once, and in many courts besides his own. He saw intelligence, and an inward calm, even on a night such as this one had become.

He had the first thing himself, not the second.

He was all rage, the endless burning of it. There was no calm in him, except in battle or planning for it. Then, he was precise, inventive, deadly. Between engagements with the Asharites he felt as if he might choke to death sometimes on his fury.

Sarantium was fallen, and they had let it happen. The Sanctuary of Jad's Holy Wisdom, a thousand years old in glory, was profaned by infidels now—turned into one of their temples. A black bile rose in him even thinking of these things. He would wake in the nights, stalk through darkness, long-striding, heedless of where he was going, where he was.

You didn't deserve Jad's mercy, continuing life under his sun, if you had permitted this to happen. None of them did. Unless they fought back. He was fighting back. For the god, for his own soul, and a hope of light after he died.

He *had* fought for the City, had taken two hundred men all the way from Trakesia northeast through lands by then under Osmanli control. Had harried and chafed and killed behind Gurçu's army as it besieged the triple walls. An army, however mighty, could be harassed. It needed weapons and supplies and food. He'd gone after their supply wagons, arms being brought up, digging equipment, cannonballs, fodder for horses. He'd burned horses. He'd killed courtesans being brought to service the leaders of Gurçu's great force as the siege went on.

He'd done things no man could be proud remembering, except that in a dark way he was. He had done it for the City and the god. To be counted as having been present.

And after . . . after they had failed, when the great walls broke, he'd fled back to Trakesia and stayed on this chosen path of a life. The short, violent life he expected to live. He made endless war down there, on Asharite settlers—farmers and villagers and their children. War on blacksmiths and artisans and tax-gatherers, and on Gurçu's soldiers whenever he could assemble the numbers and find the ground to make it possible.

He was a name of terror to the Osmanli Asharites. Had shaped a fearful resistance among them to come settle in Trakesia. His Trakesia.

He had not been taken. Nearly so, yes. Nearly killed, yes. Wounded, many times. A legend began growing among the enemy that the red-bearded giant *could* not be killed. That Skandir was a demon sent by the sun god against them, not even human. He didn't mind that. It was useful. The wounds he did mind, of course. They could keep you out of the saddle, and a bad one could kill you.

He'd been lucky with one that ought to have done that (he was not, after all, a demon sent by Jad). Someone in his company that summer knew a healer in a nearby hamlet, and they went to her at night. She cleaned and dressed the sword wound in his side. Did it discreetly, as he'd been discreet, two men only for escort to her cottage.

She was young and skilled and clever and he thought her beautiful, but you *would* think that of a woman who saved your life. She was a pagan, not a believer in Jad, but he didn't care about that.

He had no room in his life for love, none at all, but was still young enough to feel desire. And one evening, when he came back, bringing two of his wounded men, she admitted she felt the same thing for him. They spent that night together. And then others, whenever he was nearby and could make his way to her. She became an island of peace, a benison, a haven in a life otherwise entirely without such things. He said he was placing her at risk. She said that risk was hers to choose.

This would continue, in fact, for many years after the time of this story. Rasca Tripon, called Skandir, would live much longer than he'd ever expected to and die not at war but with two women beside a bed where he lay, holding his large, scarred hands, and with prayers spoken by clerics afterwards, and candles for his soul.

On the long waterfront by the Seressa Arsenale, he watched eight of his men leading four Seressinis towards him. The four were not bound, but they were gripped, each of them, by the arm, tightly, and he knew there would be knives against their ribs.

Ilija was in charge there. His brother Itanios had stayed back to guard their small ship, docked on the far side of the carrack that had been set on fire. Fortune's wheel, turning, had placed them there.

Itanios had the fire out, Skandir could see, glancing down the way. The two brothers had been with him from the start. They had come to him from the farthest south of Trakesia, a land so deadly houses were built on stilts for security, could only be entered from trap doors below, which made you easy to kill. You didn't want a feud with such people. You did want them beside you in a war.

Stopping a fire which, out of control, could have run raging down and through the Arsenale should earn them goodwill here, if there was goodwill to be found in Seressa for him.

They'd been watching a group of men earlier—foolish men, it needed to be said—gathered too close to where the carrack was docked, eyeing it. Ilija had pointed them out. He said he'd seen them talking to an official of the Arsenale, then that man had walked over and called the carpenters and shipwrights off the carrack, saying they'd worked enough on a summer's evening, could have the rest of the night off.

That, even a stranger to this city knew, was not normal. Seressa's Arsenale was famed for working all day and night, building and building ships.

Skandir and his men had kept on watching; some on the cobble-stoned dock now, on his orders, others from their own ship, while readying the cargo for sale tomorrow morning. It was a real cargo: wine from Candaria, olive oil, and the true blue—the lapis lazuli painters' shade from the east—that was worth more than gold. He'd stolen that last from a party of Dubravae merchants coming overland through Sauradia. Hadn't killed them. He didn't kill Jaddites, not normally, but he did always need money. Without it you couldn't make war for Jad against infidels.

"You can call it a tax," he'd told those merchants. He always said that. Dubrava had refused him funds; he'd been there asking. He knew they were in a difficult situation, but if they refused him . . . well, he'd take. In the god's name.

That was not why he was in Seressa, but trading was a thing he might as well do, he'd thought, as long as he was coming here. This city had dealt steadily with Asharias almost from the time of Sarantium's fall. They had warehouses there, factors living with their families, merchant parties going back and forth overland with passes, preferred tariff rates. They lived for profit more than faith. The world knew it. But . . .

But something was happening now, it seemed, and he was prepared to see what that meant to the duke here. The acting duke.

So he had come to Seressa, and they'd seen a man walk alone, not hurrying, up the long gangplank onto the now-empty carrack. A big ship. Expensive. It should have been watched closely by the guards. It didn't appear as if it was.

He'd made changes in his plans. You did that.

∽

"Why did you go into the water?" I asked Skandir.

I don't know why that was the question that came to me first, as we watched his men bring four Seressinis this way. To us, clearly. To me, as the duke's man here. I recognized who they were escorting, and my heart faltered. This was very large, added to a deliberate fire in the Arsenale, and the presence of the man beside me.

This man beside me had been lord of a goodly portion of Trakesia not so long ago. All Jaddite lords there had been declared dispossessed by Gurçu, fugitives to be hunted down, prices on their heads.

He had not yet been hunted down. He had done the hunting, instead. Reprisals had been vicious but had also spurred more young men to join Skandir. Trakesia, land of the Ancients, was a place of hard men and women. My teacher had taught me that.

And the hardest of all of those was beside me tonight, without warning. Lean to the point of gaunt, but muscled in his arms and scarred chest. His hands bore scars too, I saw.

He looked down at me as I asked my question. I am of more than average height, but he towered over all of us, still wet from the lagoon.

"I don't know," he said frankly. "The man had done something evil. Was fleeing that. And then this one jumped in after him." He looked at Rafel, grinned suddenly.

Rafel shook his head slowly. He wasn't himself yet, was visibly shaken. "Thank you. You saved my life."

I remembered I needed to say this, too, for Seressa. I was not thinking clearly yet either.

"Thank you," I added. Then I turned to one of my two men, now back with us, and said what I ought to have said immediately. "Find the duke. He'll still be in the palace. Tell him it is extremely important he come here right now."

He paled a little. "You want me to tell the—"

"I do, yes. I said that. Take a boat. It's faster."

I didn't need to say that last, not to a Seressini. He went off, running for the gates.

Rafel walked the other way along the landing, and bent, and came back carrying Skandir's dark tunic and his sword. The big man pulled the tunic on over his head.

"I ought to have taken mine off," Rafel said. "Not experienced at this."

"Who is?" Skandir said, pushing long, wet hair from his eyes. "It's the boots that become a problem."

"Yes," Rafel said. "Will you want new ones?"

"Boots dry," the other man said. Rafel extended the sword and sword belt to him. Skandir took them, too.

"Naked without this," he said, buckling it on.

Rafel said nothing. Neither did I. What was there to say? A life unimaginably far from either of ours, I thought. Rafel had been exiled from his home; this man was pushing back with everything he had against losing his. Against conquest, invasion, erasure. Were these two things images of each other, reversed, as in a mirror? I'd never had a thought like that before.

He turned to me. "Do you know these people mine are bringing?"

"I do," I said, returning to the moment, to this night. "Unfortunately."

He raised an eyebrow. "Ah. Men of rank?"

"One of them is a member of the Council of Twelve," I said.

They were close to us now. I saw fury in the eyes and posture of that one, and something else, too.

"These are the ones who sent the fire-starter on board. We saw him standing among them. The one lying here," Skandir said, loudly enough for them to hear. "They sent him on board right after the work crew was told to leave. Looks like they bribed the Arsenale officer down that way. Probably the guards, too."

"*That is a lie!*" cried Branco Ciotto, newest, youngest member of our council, held tightly, and with a knife against his ribs.

"Oh dear," said Skandir. "Well. That is a mistake. You are not permitted to say that to me. Ilija, pain, but don't kill him."

The knife went into Ciotto's side. He yelped. I felt like doing so.

"I'll have you flayed and burned!" Branco roared.

"Not if you're dead," the big man said.

He seemed unnaturally calm. But how would I know what was natural for him?

He added, "Speak again, unless to a question asked, and you will be killed. I'm not known for patience. This man at my feet and the three with you and the officer and guards by the carrack . . . none of them are going to be willing to die under questioning, risking their families, to protect you. You must know this."

I swallowed. He was right, but . . . I needed to take control of this moment. I was the adviser to the duke of Seressa. This man had no status here at all. He was, arguably, someone I should arrest and detain, given our dealings with Asharias—where he was possibly the most hated man alive.

He seemed to recognize something—in my posture, my face? Skandir looked at me and said, "We can wait for your duke. You make the decisions in the meantime. My men and I are at your service. Your name is? Your position?"

I told him. He nodded. "Young for a ducal adviser."

"How old were you when you became Ban Rasca?" I asked. Perhaps reckless, but I was so on edge that night. "How old when you went to war?"

He grinned. "Younger. Then perhaps a little older. Shall we wait?"

I wanted to—this affair was a matter for Duke Ricci, in all its aspects—but it would be a while yet before he arrived. I needed to do *some* things.

"Do you know which officer you saw with Signore Ciotto?" I said it to Skandir's men.

"I'll know him to see. Missing a finger on his left hand," the one named Ilija said.

That made it easy enough. I had my other escort summon a dozen of the Arsenale guards and the night commander. The night commander ought to have been here already. Likely afraid. Likely hiding. I told my man to choose guards from by the gated entrance. I was now concerned about those at the far end. Or some of them. Surely just some? Perhaps, with luck, just the one?

Finally, I turned to Branco Ciotto.

A man I knew, about my own age, placed on the council through his father's influence—which was considerable. One of the aspects tonight that required the duke. I looked past him to the others being held. Another man I knew, also about my own age.

"Tazio," I said, "what have you done? What have you allowed?"

Skandir heard my tone, and nodded. His fighter released Ciotto's cousin. A decent person, as far as anything I had ever seen or heard.

"Allowed?" he said. He swallowed hard. "*Allowed*, Cerra?" He was close to tears, I saw.

"Keep your mouth shut, cousin! My father will be here soon!"

"Really? Why?" I asked. "Why to both things, if you were merely at the Arsenale to enjoy a summer night. You sent a man hurrying to your father? Rescue again?"

Ciotto's look was murderous.

"We chased someone running off when we rounded up these four, Captain." It was another of Skandir's men.

"And caught him?"

"We did. Didn't get far."

"Good. Alive?" the big man asked. He really was calm, as if this were an evening among friends by the lagoon. It helped me.

"A bit the worse for wear. He tried to fight."

"Alive?" Skandir repeated

"Possibly," said the other man. "Probably, I'd reckon."

"Where is he?" I asked it. This was my encounter to control, I reminded myself.

The man called Ilija jerked his head backwards. "Bit of a way towards the carrack. He didn't get far, as our man just said."

About a dozen of the Arsenale guards came clattering up. Haste was good, I thought. I said, "Two of you go and bring someone they'll show you. We need him alive. Others, get me more torches and make a ring around us. We'll want space here and more light."

"Shall . . . shall we use my quarters, Signore Cerra?"

It was the night commander finally joining us, walking quickly, despite his bulk. His round, bearded face was a painting of apprehension. With cause. With multiple causes.

"No. Here for now. Torches and a ring of guards."

I don't know why I insisted on that. Maybe just to insist on something? I was still young that night.

Rafel stepped forward. "Were you," he said quietly to Branco Ciotto, "really going to burn my ship, risk all the others here, the whole Arsenale, because Folco d'Acorsi made you make restitution for abducting me this spring? Are you *really* that stupid?"

I'd forgotten about that.

I'm ashamed to say it. I hadn't been there, but had been told. Had had no notion up to that moment why this fire had been set. Now I knew. And yes, it did seem Branco was that stupid. That enveloped in pride and power.

Decisive moments in a life, lives, the affairs of city-states and empires, can happen because someone is a fool. Twenty years have passed since that night. I've seen it happen many more times by now.

⊷

Rafel had watched Ciotto being led this way and the mystery of why someone would set fire to the ship had disappeared. So had the flames by now, down the way. He had Skandir and his men to thank for that. Seressa did.

But he himself, it seemed, had been the target of this. And for the most petty, stupid, vindictive reason. A kind of hatred? The old kind?

"I have nothing to say to you," Ciotto said. "You are not worth my words."

"As a Kindath?" Rafel said. He was slow to anger, but right now he was enraged, and knew it. Needed to keep control.

"Not worth my words," Ciotto repeated sullenly.

"Am I?" the man named Skandir said then, quietly. "Am I worth your words? If I ask the same question?"

A wiser man would be careful, Rafel thought, after a warning and a knife.

A wiser man would not be here, bleeding and restrained, having caused a fire in one of the most dangerous places in Seressa for such a thing. Ciotto was, Rafel reminded himself, a member of the council here. In a way, that made the Council of Twelve feel *less* intimidating, even if they could torture and kill people, and cut off their hands and other things. But if one of them could be this foolish . . .

He'd even come to the Arsenale to watch!

Ciotto looked down and away, then at Guidanio Cerra. "I do not answer questions from uncouth men, or Kindath, both of them dripping and stinking of the lagoon. My father will come, and the duke, and we will discuss this matter as civilized people. I rely upon you for—"

What he had been about to rely upon Guidanio Cerra for was never known, though could be guessed at, Rafel thought afterwards.

Afterwards meaning late that same night, back in Cerra's home, remembering the moment when the man called Skandir killed Branco Ciotto with a straight sword thrust, standing on the new cobblestones of the Seressa Arsenale, not far from the lagoon's edge, under a blue moon and many stars on a summer night.

Ciotto made no sound. He fell. A small sound then.

"I did caution him," Skandir said mildly.

Rafel felt as if his mind had gone blank. Empty, like a corner of an artist's canvas not yet painted, waiting for an image to arrive. A ship, a tree, a man, a horse, clouds. Clarity.

The big man bent and cleaned his blade on Ciotto's overtunic. It was a big sword; he had used it like a small one, an easy thrust. In and out. A man alive, breathing, dead. Alive. Dead. Skandir sheathed his sword.

Rafel looked at Guidanio Cerra, whose face was now bone-white. His own face was probably the same. It felt that way. The bulky commander of the Arsenale reached out a hand a little desperately, gripping the arm of the guard beside him for support. Rafel wondered if the commander was about to fall down.

Extreme and sudden violence could do that to you, he thought. And death. Death could do that. An arrogant man had been speaking contemptuous words—and now he was lying without breath on dark stones darkened further by his blood.

"Oh, Jad," said Guidanio Cerra. "Oh, fuck."

"I cautioned him," said Skandir again.

"He is . . . he was . . ." Cerra could scarcely speak.

"He was a member of the council? I heard that. But think. This is better. Were you going to hold a trial of one of the Twelve of Seressa? For burning the ship of a Kindath? Try a man who has, it appears, a wealthy father? Wealthy fathers rule here, do they not?"

He was, Rafel realized, not disturbed at all. One might say he was almost amused, diverted. But also . . . thinking, analyzing.

Skandir added, "You'll get Ciotto's men, including the one I fished from the water, to give evidence, and the bribed guards. I'm certain the commander will wish to address that last, for his own reasons. I imagine the duke will want to hear from him."

The commander made a small, involuntary sound. Skandir smiled thinly. He went on.

"There will be no doubt of the crime. One that could have had your shipyard in flames in this wind. You know this. Your duke will arrive and be grateful I have simplified this for him, solved it—whatever he says aloud. He will likely have me brought to the palace. Under guard—I'm a dangerous man. And there we will talk about what I came here to talk about, before being forced to save a ship and perhaps the Arsenale of Seressa. I think," he concluded, with some satisfaction, "it is a good solution I have found, for everyone. You couldn't have executed him, but he needed to be executed."

Executed, Rafel thought.

As if from a distance, while they all looked down at a foolish, dead young man, he heard Guidanio Cerra ask, softly, "What did you come here to talk about?"

Then he heard Ban Rasca Tripon, called Skandir, answer, also quietly.

⤜⤛

Duke Ricci of Seressa was not unduly disturbed by his title of acting duke, even after years of it. Time would do what it did, if he survived. But . . . it would be a lie to say he didn't care at all. True, he had all the powers and almost all the respect he would have had if Lucino Conti, still formally duke, were not still alive, however incapacitated. But *almost* was still something. It was a space. A hesitation in someone's speech, a tone, a beat before certain members of the Council of Twelve acceded to his plans. A flicker on some faces.

No faces flickering just now. He was sitting alone finally, in the quite comfortable private chamber in the Arsenale of the commander there. He would rise soon and head back to the palace, not home. It was late enough that he'd snatch some sleep on the cot he had there before dealing with many things in the morning—mostly to do with tonight.

He had elected to address some of this evening's matters here. More specifically, he had decided quickly (he was good at quick decisions, he had to be) not to bring Rasca Tripon to the palace. There was a chance that some there, seeing the man, would bring pressure on Ricci not to let him out. He wouldn't listen to this, but it would require a response, and he wasn't prepared to deal with that on top of all else. There were more important things right now, however unexpected this man's presence in Seressa was.

He was enjoying the relative quiet, the late-night calm, although work had already resumed in the Arsenale after the fire threat. Hammering, saws and files rasping, men shouting, swearing. It occurred to him that some men spent a lot of time swearing. Ricci took another sip of wine. The commander had good wine. Fine glassware, too.

It had taken him some time to process what he found after he'd responded to Guidanio Cerra's message and taken a swift boat to the Arsenale. Cerra would not have been urgent if urgency had not been called for. He'd seen where to tell the boatman to pull in. There were torches in a ring.

What greeted him was word of a fire, a deliberate one, put out due to Jad's great mercy, and—it appeared—through the intervention of Rasca Tripon, calling himself Skandir, rejecting his name and the royal title of Ban.

What that man was doing here was the second question that came to him.

The first had been addressing the reality of a dead member of the Council of Twelve. Dead meaning killed. Sword to the chest. Blood pooling around his body on the cobblestones.

He understood why Cerra had wanted to stay where they were, waiting for him. He had now arrived, however, and this was *far* too public. He ordered everyone involved to be removed to the commander's compound near the gates.

Cerra had looked pale but composed, which was good. Ricci was used to making assessments of those in his service—who might rise higher there, or not. The Kindath man that he rather liked, ben Natan, was tense and angry. It had been his ship set on fire. The man might be permitted fury. He was also dripping wet, for some reason to be discovered. Ricci was, he realized, angry himself. He needed to determine where to direct it, and do so carefully. This was, it might be said, a flammable situation.

He allowed himself the word but not any sort of smile.

The man named Skandir was also wet. He did smile briefly at the duke, but contented himself with waiting in silence until they were away from people and their watching eyes and about-to-bewagging tongues. He did bow to Ricci, who, surprising himself a little, bowed back.

This man was a legend, and braver than any of them, he thought. Probably be dead soon, all things considered, but until then . . . you could offer him a bow.

The currently dead man he had carried to the commander's compound to be placed, covered respectfully, on a wooden table in the courtyard there.

Oh, bloody Jad in the fucking night, he had thought, seeing who it was.

He was not a man inclined to swearing.

This was not a circumstance inclining one towards normal patterns of response.

Which made it, Ricci thought, even more important to preserve what calm he could. He did so, in a series of quick, acutely focused interrogations and decisions in the commander's reception chamber. The commander was not a part of these. He waited in the courtyard where the dead man was, until the end, when he was summoned and dismissed immediately from his position, with further discipline to be determined by the council. He had required assistance in walking from what had been his own chambers.

You thought you knew what your life was, how it was unfolding, how your later years might be and . . . a fire started. That might apply to himself, too, Ricci thought sourly. Branco Ciotto was dead. Murdered? Executed? How did one want to present this? How *could* one present it? Ricci confirmed that a doctor had arrived to see to the unconscious arsonist. He wanted that man alive.

He then spoke with Cerra, with Skandir present. Also, the small, neat (if wet, still) Kindath whose ship had been the target here.

Duke Ricci forgot very little. He did remember Folco d'Acorsi telling him about Ciotto abducting Rafel ben Natan in the street (not far from here) in spring. Just before the first council discussions about the High Patriarch's fleet and the commitment expected of Seressa. Ricci had said nothing about the incident then. A foolish one, chasing information Ciotto had not really needed. Better to let it go, he'd decided. D'Acorsi had done him a favour, he judged.

Now, it seemed, Skandir also had. A greater one.

Which led to that first question he'd asked of the red-bearded man. "Why are you here?" He needed to know.

"Because there is a fleet going in spring against the Asharites."

Entirely unexpected. Ricci drew a breath. He said, "Just to Tarouz. You'll know that."

"I know that. You do not have the courage to go east. None of you."

Ricci let that pass. "And why does this bring you to Seressa?"

Skandir gazed down at him. Very blue eyes. "Because I will be with that army, that fleet."

Again, not expected. The duke said, "Why? That is not, as I understand things, where you wage war."

Skandir hesitated for the first time. Then said, quietly, "Because I do not want anything done, ever, in any war for Jad against them, without my being a part of it."

Ricci was silent. There was loss embedded here, and a towering rage. Grief, and a purity of faith and will that he didn't think he himself had, or ever would.

You did not, he decided in that moment, imprison such a man. Especially if he might have just saved your Arsenale, and many, many ships moored outside it. Whatever the angry fathers of dead, reckless, *stupid* young men might say or demand. Whatever Gurçu the Destroyer might offer, to be given this man to kill.

He nodded, once. "I understand," he said finally, and he felt he almost did.

His own life, his ways of dealing with the world, they'd never be the same as those of this one. But, he thought, he could at least recognize—and honour—what he'd just heard, and what he knew of the last many years. He was also moved, though that wasn't helpful at all.

Brisk became the night's watchword.

He told Cerra to arrange for Ricci himself to purchase Skandir's ship's cargo and to have it offloaded before morning. He undertook to transfer a fair sum for it to Skandir's bank, wherever that was. It turned out to be with a merchant he used as an agent in Dubrava, one Djivo, not fully a banker, but lending money to other merchants there and holding it for some. A man Rasca Tripon trusted, it seemed, though he had no love for Dubrava. Neither did Ricci, as it happened; they were rivals, if not deadly ones.

"Will you trust me as to the amount?"

"I know what the cargo is worth, pretty much," the big man said. "I'm not concerned."

Not really a reply as to trust. Ricci wasn't sure what he'd expected. This was Seressa, after all.

"You should leave as soon as the cargo is off your ship. I regard you as having done us a good turn. I have no intention of subjecting you to interrogation or detention."

"Or handing me to the Asharites?"

"We wouldn't do that."

Skandir smiled at him. Not a pleasant smile this time.

"We wouldn't," Ricci repeated. He smiled back. "We might kill you ourselves, of course."

"Of course. So, on the whole, better I leave?"

"On the whole."

"And the fleet? The attack?"

"I undertake to ensure you know what is being planned and how you might join it. This campaign might falter yet. Too many princes and powers."

"Yes. But I think it will happen. Greed, only a short distance to travel. A way to assuage your Patriarch. Claim a holy blessing for oneself."

Your Patriarch. Skandir would follow the eastern rites of Jad, the darker, suffering incarnation of the god. He'd still be mourning the

Eastern Patriarch at Sarantium. There was no Eastern Patriarch any more. It occurred to Ricci he'd have enjoyed talking at length with this man had there been more leisure, had life allowed.

"Can I get messages to you through this Djivo?"

"Andrij Djivo, yes. He's an honest merchant."

"Rare."

Another thin smile.

"I'll arrange to have a proper ship by spring," said Skandir. "Not my usual, the sea, you're right."

Someone cleared his throat.

"You would be an honoured guest upon mine, with however many men you choose to bring," said Rafel ben Natan. They all turned to him.

"That carrack is for the battle fleet?" Skandir asked.

"It is," said ben Natan. "And a merchant vessel after, if we survive."

"So I just saved the ship that might carry me to war against the infidels?"

"If you like to think of it that way."

"I do. Very much. I accept."

Two other men, two such very different men, exchanged a brief smile.

Ricci reminded himself to find out why they were wet. He was a man who was happiest when he sorted things out himself, by gathering information, then thinking. He didn't have his notebook with him. He regretted that.

Skandir left with his men. He wanted to find a sanctuary of the god, he said. Ricci dispatched someone to guide him to the one at the Arsenale. The two men exchanged a final nod. No more than that. What more would there be?

Tasks and decisions. He had the cousin, Tazio Ciotto, brought in. A man he'd had his eye on, in fact, for future service. Tazio could be tortured and executed for what had happened here. Ricci didn't intend to do that. He had enough power, or could claim it, to make a decision himself. He ordered Tazio—deeply unhappy about tonight, close to tears—exiled.

Immediately, he said. Out of the city by sunrise. No goods to be taken with him. Money was allowed. He could have some personal property follow him. Tazio was unmarried, which was good. Lived with his wealthy cousin. He told the man, who was kneeling by then, to be sure Guidanio Cerra knew where he was. There were ways, Duke Ricci added, whereby Tazio Ciotto might work his way back into the good graces of his beloved city. They would tell him what those might be.

A clever man, a decent-seeming one, and in his debt? That was a resource, very possibly. Even a weapon. You needed those. The world was not gentle.

The other Ciotto men he ordered tortured tonight in the rooms below the palace. Confessions to be recorded, signed if they could still do so after, witnessed, and, depending on what they said, they would be executed or sent to the galleys for two years. There was always a shortage of men for the Seressini galleys. You *could* survive two years on one. Some did. This limited mercy would apply if the confessions were deemed adequate, and useful. There would be no pursuit of their families if so, he decided.

Confessions would be needed to show to the dead man's father and the council. They mattered.

The actual arsonist, when he revived, would also be tortured for his confession. Mercy was not available in this case. He'd been *seen* setting fire to a ship. In Seressa? A public death, burning in the square before the palace. Appropriate, no one would say otherwise.

The corrupted guard or guards and the supervisor who had ordered the workers off the ship? They'd have to confess to being bribed and would also die. Theirs had been a blow against the state. It was treachery, in fact.

A bad night. There would be ripples from it.

He made another decision, sitting alone for just a little longer, thinking about the man he'd met tonight, whom he'd almost certainly never see again. A reproach in his very existence to all of them, Ricci thought. When the accounting was made for Skandir's goods, and forwarded via bank documents to the man, Djivo, in Dubrava, two thousand serales would be added to the sum as a separate entry. His own money, but not to be stated as such. Skandir would see there was a surplus, looking at the papers. He might think it was state funds, he might not. It didn't matter.

You could hear, see, register a reproach and ignore it, or you could try, in however small a way, to respond. Endless war, rebellion, flight, return to battlefields, a life lived entirely that way . . . this required money.

You could spend what you had accumulated on paintings, a ship, jewels for a wife or mistress, on expanding your palazzo, on a quiet property you dreamed of on one of the offshore islands, on candles and eternal prayers for your dead and then yourself, or, some of it, on this.

⌇

I'm not certain why I'm now remembering moments from that year. It is not the time in the course of my emergence into the man I seem to be where my most powerful memories lie, with sorrows embedded and vivid people who still haunt my dreams. One in particular, but not just one.

I thought, a little earlier today, that I was remembering that time twenty years ago because I'd been put in mind of Lenia Serrana by someone I have just now met. A woman who might end up—later this evening, in fact—accepting a role to serve Seressa. Taken from the Daughters of Jad retreat where I brought Lenia on a spring day all those years ago. I could wonder about myself, I suppose, about how strong women . . .

As I sit here now in my handsome new home, preparing to go out, escorted by Duso and my guards, to the palace to assist the duke tonight at council—the Council of Twelve on which I now sit—Rafel ben Natan is in my mind, as well. For himself, not reminding me of anyone else, not by some association.

I think he is a man who could have been, had our lives unfolded differently, a friend, for all the divisions faiths are supposed to sow between people. They need not. They can, but need not.

I've had friends over the years. One must count himself fortunate, the saying goes, if one has had that. I do count myself fortunate, even if some losses are hard, and wine steers you in other directions on damp, windy nights in Seressa. But no one is without their losses.

And another step, another stage in my own still-emerging life *did* take place after Rafel ben Natan and I finally arrived home, deeply shaken by what had happened at the Arsenale.

He went up to change his wet clothing. I had lamps lit, wine poured, in my small reception room. I dismissed the servant to bed, telling him I'd close up myself. Everyone else was asleep, even Duso, who would be angry in the morning to learn I had been in danger and he not there. I hadn't really been in peril, I would say. That wouldn't mollify him, and it might not be true.

While waiting for ben Natan to come back down, I tried to count the number of men who would now die because of what had happened. I couldn't. It depended on how many of the Arsenale guards turned out to be implicated. Tazio Ciotto would live, I was happy to know that. He would write to me later. Or not. Perhaps he would not. How could one be sure?

In fact, he did do that, and I replied, on behalf of the duke. Tazio would shortly afterwards undertake certain tasks in Rhodias in the service of Seressa, at some risk. And then would do so again, in Dubrava. He was permitted to come home. We came to know each other well. I liked him. He died in the last plague, four years ago. The longer we live, the more people leave us. We light candles.

We were both tired. I could see it in ben Natan when he joined me, feel it in myself. I handed him a glass. We were silent, then Rafel spoke.

"If he truly did this because Folco d'Acorsi shamed him over a Kindath, the stupidity of it is disturbing to me. I'll need more wine, Danio."

He wasn't a man who drank much. The duke had taught me to observe that about people.

"Stupidity and youth and arrogance," I said.

"He's no younger than you. Older, probably."

"A year or two, I think." I shrugged. I stood and refilled his glass and my own. "I'm a tailor's son," I said. "Where would arrogance emerge?"

"Perhaps the better for it."

"Perhaps." I wasn't going to debate the point that night. Too many things lay tangled there. But a thought came to me and I spoke it. A small hinge in a life, but a real one.

I said, "Rafel, you were relying on us, on Seressa, to protect the carrack. We failed. You will need insurance, once it is finished. You need it now."

He nodded. "I know. We do." We. It was Lenia's ship, too.

I said, glass in hand, late at night, "Will you let me arrange for that? And pay for it? In exchange for whatever return you think fair when it becomes a merchant ship, after the fleet?"

"If it survives."

"If it survives."

"You have . . . the resources for that, Danio? It will be expensive, since it is going to war first."

"I believe I do. I can obtain funds."

"And you want to put those into a carrack owned by a Kindath and a woman?"

I said, and meant it, "I can think of nowhere I'd rather put them."

He looked at me a long moment. Then smiled. "Let us do that, then. I'll do some numbers and make you a proposal."

What I didn't think through, not being any true business person then (a disgrace for a Seressini, really), was that he and Lenia could easily pay for insurance themselves. He did it for me. I didn't see it then. As the duke's adviser I was able to get better terms than most would have, but even so . . .

He did it for me.

Most of my own money came to me with my second wife, after Duke Ricci arranged that marriage some years after the events of that time. But I made a start, a real start, with the interest in the ship that Rafel and Lenia offered me for covering the insurance, then further investments in it with the profits we made. He was extremely good at what he did as a merchant, Rafel ben Natan, and I reaped the benefit of that.

I wish he'd chosen to live in Seressa. Lenia, too. I wish she had. For different reasons, perhaps. Dreams, I have found, can carry you down paths daylight doesn't allow.

Neither of them did. Neither ever made Seressa their home.

I've only really known this one place to live. My city. Other people, for different reasons, seem to never really have a home, even if they settle somewhere. That becomes a place they live. Not the same thing. They go through their lives as if adrift on all the seas of the world.

Maybe *home* for some is always the one they lost.

⚭

Rafel found himself pausing in the doorway, lamp in hand, on his way back upstairs. Beside the door hung a small painting of Jad as Warrior, shown in the sky above Rhodias, the city identifiable from its buildings and the river. The first piece of art he'd ever bought, Cerra had told him. He looked back at the man with whom he'd shared this night. Young but not *so* young, he thought. He was in this small, handsome house, whether he owned it or was leasing it with assistance from the duke. Probably the latter. Property was expensive here. Cerra was already bound closely to the most powerful man in

Seressa. He'd be all right, Rafel thought. He deserved to be all right, though that seldom mattered, what you deserved in life.

A thought came to him and he spoke it before he could stop himself.

"I may have made a mistake, it occurs to me. Inviting Skandir to come on our ship in the spring."

Danio looked at him. He said, "I thought of that. Because of Lenia, you mean?"

Rafel was astonished. He hadn't been sure he'd even be able to explain the thought, if he'd even want to, had already been regretting his words, and Cerra had . . .

"Yes," he said.

"She has the same desire he does, you think? You're afraid she might go with him, after? A life spent at war?"

Rafel looked away and then back to him. "I do, suddenly. A bitter, hard, short life, I fear. Perhaps he would refuse a woman in his company."

"Or she isn't so completely driven by the one thing now?"

"Perhaps. I don't know."

Cerra nodded again. Said nothing more. A kindness.

"Good night, Danio," he said, and went up with the lamp and along the dark hallway to his room.

He sat at the desk they'd had brought in for him, set the lamp down, took ink and paper, and wrote out the instructions he would hand to Piero Sardi's man in the morning, concerning what he wanted done about his brother. He found himself close to tears. Some memories, returning, can do that.

⚬⚬

He hadn't known where he even was at first. He seemed to be looking down at his own dead body on the walkway between the Arsenale and the water.

Dead body.

That was it. That was where he was. He'd been speaking of someone annoying him, a person standing in his path, and . . .

A mistake. He'd made so many of those.

He didn't expect to be welcomed to light by the god. His father would have candles lit, but only for the public display of it. His father had never respected him. Never cared for him, in truth. Had seen him as a tool, an instrument, had made clear he was only that for want of any other son. The Council of Twelve, such a lofty position! Money and persuasion used. Bribes and threats. And there he'd been, too young, not knowing nearly enough about anything, whispered about mockingly, no least clue what to do, except what he was told to do. No desire to be there, either. He hated his father.

Power was always said to be mostly about information, so he'd tried for that in spring with the Kindath merchant. That hadn't succeeded at all, had humiliated him. He couldn't stop his father from doing that, but he'd made it the point of his life not to let anyone else, ever.

Perhaps a foolish thing to make the point of your life.

He felt very sorry for himself. He was dead. Wasn't it still a sad thing, even if you'd never done much good with your days? He thought it was. He wondered if you could weep in this strange, drifting, muffled space. If you could curse men and the god.

He didn't curse the god.

He still, somehow, had hopes for understanding. Forgiveness. Light. You had to hope for that, didn't you? Didn't you?

And maybe that someone left behind—surely there was someone?— would remember him with regret, kindness. Light a candle, meaning it. Speak the prayers, meaning them.

You had to hope. What else was there?

CHAPTER XV

If a story begins with a single ship sailing at night along a coast, preparing to put a small boat ashore to set in motion a plot built around death, there is at least an arc, even a circle, if it turns towards an ending with many ships headed for that same coast, somewhat farther east, with many deaths intended.

A tale-teller might not always say this, not remind listeners of that beginning in the dark, but some might. This one has, just here. Arcs and circles, a story drawing nearer to its end. Harbours, havens, a hope for grace, an awareness it does not always come. Is there enough candlelight?

The Middle Sea divided and it linked in that time; it had always done so, really. So much went in all directions across and along it. Violence was only one of these things, but it was one.

LENIA KNEW WHO the big man boarding the *Silver Light* was. She wouldn't have, by sight, but they had come here to meet him, and the men accompanying him. They were at the docks in Megarium, on the eastern coast of the Seressini Sea. Both Rafel and Guidanio Cerra had seemed anxious when she was told about this task, and who he was.

Lenia had said, "You fear I'll go off with him after? Skandir?"

Neither had said a word.

It might have been kinder to reassure that she wouldn't, but she couldn't honestly do that.

"We'll see," was what she'd said. "Let's survive Tarouz first?"

It was no certainty. The city would be very well defended, had a narrow, guarded harbour entrance, and a famed commander ruling it. Folco d'Acorsi was not a man of the sea. He had some with him who were, or were supposed to be. He had been closeted with them in Seressa almost daily before they sailed.

He and the High Patriarch had wanted three hundred war galleys and ships. They had a little over half that number, if Esperaña and Ferrieres came through as promised. A large fleet but no one would say it was certainly enough, especially given divisions emerging before they even set out.

The Esperañans had made clear their ships would accept commands only from their own commander, a man named Querida de Carvajal. He had agreed, by way of letters, to consult with d'Acorsi but reserved the right to make his own decisions in any battle, based on the safety of his men and his ships.

It was not ideal.

It was never going to be ideal, Folco had told her earlier, riding from Acorsi to Seressa in end-of-winter rains. Seressa was where the Batiaran fleet was to gather. The ships from Ferrieres would assemble in Marsena. They'd join up at the tip of Batiara and go south together. King Émery had formally placed his fleet under Folco's command, there was that blessing. It was unknown if there were private instructions given to his own commanders as to avoiding extreme conditions of risk. There probably were.

No one wanted to lose ships. Men could be replaced, casualties were expected, it was war. Galleys and ships, however, were ruinously expensive to lose in large numbers, especially given the tensions between Esperaña and Ferrieres, which might easily become open war soon. No one trusted anyone else.

This, too, was not ideal.

She had embraced Rafel briskly before departure, standing on the dock across from the Arsenale. They hadn't said much. It was a loud, crowded, public moment as sixty ships and galleys prepared to make their way out to the lagoon and down the coast. They'd stood amid cheering people and in the presence of the duke of Seressa and the members of the Council of Twelve, including the newest, replacing one who had recently died. Killed here at the Arsenale, in fact.

"I will do what I can to send messages," was the last thing she said.

"I will rely on that. Be as safe as this allows. Come back."

She'd boarded their huge, splendid carrack, named *Silver Light* to pair with the name of their smaller ship. That was around the coastline on the western side, for use in the way merchant craft were normally used. They'd decided not to bring it here. Their business was mostly going to be out of Firenta for the present. They were cloth merchants now. Trade would continue, with some limitations. They might even be able to take advantage of those, he had said. The world was not about to stop for this attack.

Still, at the prow later, as Elie guided their ship out into the Seressini Sea among so many others, Lenia had had an image of the world pausing. Taking a breath, holding it. Surely something like this fleet *meant* something, as far off as Asharias and Esperaña? Even in the north? Or not. Maybe it didn't.

At Megarium a few days later she watched the man named Skandir bring seventy fighters on board. Hard men. Accustomed to war, she thought, looking at them. Not a large number, but they'd know how to fight.

The tall man stopped in front of her on the deck. He bowed.

"We are grateful for passage," he said. "Your partner was generous to offer."

"You saved his life, I am told."

"Perhaps. He was still generous. As are you."

She was going to say she'd not really had a choice, but didn't. "The lord of Acorsi has written you what he wants us to do?"

"He has. It suits me. It is acceptable to you?"

"Of course," she said. "I'll come with you."

He hesitated. "That is unexpected. Have you ever been in a battle, signora?"

"I've killed," she said.

"Not the same."

"I know it isn't. I won't slow you down, you may trust in that."

"How do you kill?" he asked. A military question.

"Knives, small sword. Poison, I suppose, although that won't apply."

He smiled.

She hesitated. "Rafel, my partner, and Guidanio Cerra, the duke's adviser, both fear that if we survive this I will want to cross to the east and fight in your ranks."

He looked down on her. At least he didn't smile at this. "Is that so? You have reasons?"

"I do."

He nodded, as if he'd heard such things before. He said, "We can sail, I suppose. All my men are on board."

She was being dismissed. As to this.

A part of her wanted to cause this man to lose that certainty, break from it, or be broken, but standing in a north wind blowing, she saw that Elie was visibly impatient to cast off and make use of it.

She nodded to him. He shouted commands. They sailed out of the harbour and continued south, crossing back towards the west coast of that narrow sea. Elie was trying not to smile as they went, Lenia saw. He liked this ship. He had hand-picked their crew in Seressa, especially those who would man the cannon. The *Silver Light* was very heavily armed.

They overhauled the rest of the Batiaran fleet just before Remigio. They all took on water and provisions there and a number of additional fighting men, and they carried on.

⚬⚭⚬

Rafel had been dreaming of his brother almost every night as autumn came. Often the same moment from their childhood. He didn't like it, didn't want it, couldn't stop the memory from coming in his sleep.

They'd been thirteen and six. About that. He'd been taking Sayash to see fireflies in a wood not far from their Kindath quarter outside Almassar. His brother was proud and excited to be with him, to be allowed out so late.

It wasn't even night, only twilight; he had promised their parents he'd have the little one back by full dark. You could see the fireflies at this hour among the trees without difficulty. Sayash refused his older brother's hand as they walked, even when the ground became challenging. Normally he liked holding hands, but this was an *adventure*, a mark of his being older now.

It wasn't especially far, and the summer night was mild. They came within sight of the trees and Rafel pointed to them.

"Just there," he said.

"Who are those people?" Sayash asked.

Those people were Asharites, young but older than them, from the city. Probably coming for the same reason. Six of them, he saw. He thought about turning back. In his dreams, he wondered why he hadn't.

They walked forward, following the others. One of those looked back, saw the two of them. Alerted his companions.

A different sort of diversion. They were too close, a mistake. He was the older one, responsible for his brother. But there wasn't anything like routine violence against Kindath at that time. They lived outside the walls but went into the city often, an accepted part of Almassar. Usually.

But young men in a group, outside the walls, unobserved, at twilight, that could be different. He wondered, after, if they'd been drinking wine. Asharites weren't supposed to, many did.

"Fuck off, brats!" the one who'd seen them said.

Rafel stopped. And he did take his brother's hand then.

There was no one else around. More people would come out later, in the darkness. They were early because Sayash was so young. Rafel didn't know, never knew, why these others were there so early.

He said, another mistake, "We won't be near you. It's a big wood."

"Are you fucking *arguing?*" another of the men snapped, raising his voice.

Rafel shook his head. "I wouldn't do that. I'm just showing my brother the fireflies, then we'll go home."

"He *is* arguing!" the first one said.

And three of them started towards the two of them.

They could have run. The others would be faster, but might not bother chasing them, that wasn't why they'd come here.

And in that moment Sayash said, "I've never seen the fireflies. Please may we?"

"*I've never seen the fireflies,*" the nearest one mocked. "If you're dead you never will, either. Fuck yourself and fuck off."

He came close, and gestured at Sayash, faking a punch at the boy.

"Don't hit him," Rafel said. And stepped in front of his brother.

"Very well," said the man in front of them, and clubbed Rafel, hard, on the side of his head.

He went down, not crying out, but in pain, and fear.

"*You fuck off!*" cried his six-year-old brother. "You can't *do* that!" And Sayash stepped beside his older brother's fallen body and then in front of him and bunched his small hands in fists, looking a long way up at the man who'd knocked Rafel down.

He had never heard his little brother swear before.

They could have died there. No one would have seen what happened, no one would have known who did it, and no court in

Almassar would have done anything but chastise the older boys, in any case. He really had, Rafel realized later that night, expected both of them to be killed.

But—such a strange feeling just then—he was so very proud of his brother.

The biggest of the six in front of them began laughing. "Sarid," he said, "leave them. Fuck off, like the little warrior told you. It is beneath our dignity to fight children. Come on."

And Sayash ben Natan, small fists bunched and lifted, looking up at them at twilight, said, "I still want to see the fireflies."

"Because you never have, I heard," said the biggest one, still amused. "Wait a bit, then you can go in. Don't come anywhere near us."

Rafel sat up. His jaw hurt but he was all right. He heard his brother say, "All right then. We won't."

They did go into the wood a few moments later, after the others had gone ahead.

Sayash took his hand on the way. Rafel could feel his brother trembling. His own heart was full.

They saw the fireflies together. They walked home after, together.

Brother,

I express the wish this letter finds you well, but the contents may not bring comfort. I can report that your wife, parents, and children are healthy and all are currently in Marsena. I am aware that had you felt any interest in this, you'd have been able to find out. Perhaps you have, secretly?

In any case, it doesn't matter. Here is what does. You will do a number of things immediately—in order to let Gaelle divorce you and be free to go on with her life unencumbered with doubts as to whether her husband is alive or merely a man who has abandoned her and his children.

It will not please me to intervene further, especially thinking of our parents, so I urge you to do the following.

You will send a letter to the Elder Teacher at Marsena's central house of prayer declaring you renounce your marriage and Gaelle is free.

You will write our parents at the same time, informing them you are alive but have elected to begin a new life in an unspecified location. You can say whatever else you wish to say to them. It is not my concern. These letters can be given to the man bringing you this one. He will take them to me.

I will not reveal where you are living.

You will deposit to your wife's name the sum of five thousand serales in the Sardi Bank in Astarden, to be credited to the branch in Marsena. Instructions can be given that the originating bank be kept private. I will undertake with Piero Sardi, whom I know, that this happens.

This sum is for your children, who remain—as they have always been—your responsibility. That is what pains me in all of this. I do not care who you love, how you live. I will always want you to have a good life. You ought to have known this of me, brother. I had thought you were dead. I imagine you hoped I'd think so, that we all would.

Five thousand serales is a large sum but I am informed that you have, by the grace of the sisters and the god, done well in your business, and can arrange for it.

If these things are done I will wish you only health and a long life.

The man who brings you this letter will wait three days for your replies and a confirmation of the bank deposit. If no answers are sent I will act as I judge necessary. The decision is yours, but freedom is one of the many things that carry a price.

Rafel

IN WINTRY WEATHER, Piedona Valli arrived back in Seressa bearing confirmation of a bank deposit and two letters for Marsena. Rafel was aware that Valli had travelled north and back in bad weather. He knew Piero would take care of his agents, but he offered the man a dinner in a good tavern and a night with one of the more celebrated prostitutes in Seressa, and the offers were gratefully accepted.

He opened the letters. They were not addressed to him, of course. He did not care. He saw that his brother had written what he'd required—to the house of prayer and to their parents. He decided to take them to Marsena himself, after the fleet sailed in spring. He wanted to see his mother and father, and Gaelle, and these were not letters to be delivered by a stranger.

Sayash had written nothing to him.

He was not surprised. There was heartache, but there had been for a long time.

⚬

Three high clerics from Rhodias were assigned by the High Patriarch to accompany his great fleet. Two had volunteered, pious warriors of Jad, keen to kill and burn infidels in the god's holy name. The third was less enthused, but Scarsone Sardi had reasons for wanting him out of Rhodias for a time, to do with the man's mistress, a poet with magnificent auburn hair.

Count Anselmi di Vigano had stepped forward to pay for and lead a company. A surprise. He was young enough, physically capable, but had never shown any intense level of piety, or an interest in war. A sophisticated, worldly sort of man. Paying for a dictionary in three languages.

Because di Vigano went, and only because of that, Kurafi ibn Rusad found himself on board a ship carrying him back to the Majriti that spring.

The count, to whose household he belonged, had insisted that ibn Rusad accompany him. He wanted a translator.

Kurafi was unsure how he felt about this. He didn't like the sea. He had, for obvious reasons, terrible memories of his last voyage. No one would *seize* him in the midst of a war fleet, but he couldn't see anything good for him in this. He'd be seen by the mariners and soldiers as one of the enemy. He wasn't going to be able to escape, was much more likely to be killed in some engagement with the ships of Zariq ibn Tihon.

Nonetheless, lacking a choice in the matter, he rolled up and brought his manuscript with him. If anyone searched his belongings it was unlikely to be seen as suspicious that a scholar should bring what he was writing. He hoped.

It had progressed, that work on the nature of exile, once he had begun it again after his earlier papers were burned. He hadn't taken it as far as he might have wished, but there really were considerable distractions in Rhodias at night, and he did have his work every day with the other translators. Arsenius Kallinikos, who had unaccountably burned Kurafi's draft, then killed himself, had been replaced. Scholars who had fled Sarantium were plentiful in Rhodias. He thought about Kallinikos more than he'd expected to. He wondered what the other man had seen in his words that led him to destroy them.

The new man was not much more pleasant than the dead one. Ibn Rusad had begun to wonder if all Sarantine scholars were bitter men. They weren't the *only* exiles in the world, he'd wanted to say. He didn't, in the interests of harmony. He'd decided to try to be a more thoughtful man.

Mature beyond his years, he imagined someone being moved to say. He didn't die at Tarouz. Could have, though.

～

It was not his world, the sea.

Folco d'Acorsi had been on ships many times, on both coasts of Batiara, but never, as it happened, out of sight of land and never in a sea fight. He did not for a moment regret accepting the role of commander. He had been part of proposing this, after all; the contract was the most generous of a long career; and this *was* a response to Sarantium. He funded his city's growth with his fees. Paid for his army. For diamonds, too.

But with all of that, he was deeply unhappy about being so dependent on others.

He would lead the land armies once they came ashore, if they did, and that was part of his planning, but Tarouz was widely known to have a formidable fleet and many cannon defending its harbour and walls. That meant he needed leaders who knew what they were doing at sea on a level—or near to it, at least—of his own skill on land. Hence, unhappiness, because he wasn't sure they did. There was a great deal at stake. You didn't want to be the commander who lost a holy war.

Batiara's force he mostly trusted. He had picked their naval leaders himself and had spent a winter with them in Seressa. Ferrieres, after his visit to King Émery, he felt more or less confident in. Also, Lenia Serrana, who had been in his company there, had spoken with the envoy of Gurçu at night in a corridor, and they'd learned that no help would be sent from the east for Zariq ibn Tihon and his city.

Hugely important. The envoy's only request had been that they not kill too many if they took the city. Looting was expected, understood. Folco was perhaps more willing to accede to this than might have been presumed, for his own reasons.

He could control the Batiarans if they breached the walls or there was a surrender, and he knew Ferrieres *wanted* to keep good relations with Gurçu, for afterwards. Esperaña was a worry. They'd been the prime target of the ibn Tihon brothers: raids for slaves and goods and the burning of towns and farms to instill terror. Esperaña had also attacked the Majriti whenever they could. For slaves and goods and the burning of towns and farms to instill terror.

Their commander had written to Rhodias that he would take note of d'Acorsi's communications, treat them as requests, but make his own decisions. That was the only way his king and queen would participate in this campaign, he informed the High Patriarch. Querida de Carvajal was not, apparently, a man anyone had ever called brave, or wise, but he wasn't known, as best Folco could determine, to be vicious.

Scarsone Sardi had not been pleased, but Esperaña had to be in this fleet. It was the first conjoined Jaddite effort since Sarantium had fallen. The Patriarch needed to take Tarouz, and he needed it to be an effort of the nations that worshipped the god of the sun. *That* was what would make this important.

He'd accepted the Esperañan conditions, told Folco to make the best of it, do what he could. Said he trusted his commander.

It was good to be trusted. It was bad to not be in control of your own force.

LENIA WATCHED AS Folco d'Acorsi was rowed across from his galley to her ship. The seas were choppy; there was no harbour at the southern tip of Batiara. They were anchored in open sea, a safe distance from the rocky shore. The fleet from Ferrieres, meeting them here, had not yet come. There was a saying that people from Ferrieres were always late since there was always more wine to drink. It was less funny to her just now.

Elie had the rope ladder lowered as Folco's boat pulled up. There was a need to keep ships properly apart. Collisions had been known to happen, especially with this many gathered. She watched d'Acorsi climb up. He had a bad back, she knew. There was no outward sign of it.

He came on deck, saluted her, nodded to Elie, faced the man whose seventy fighters she was carrying to Tarouz. Neither spoke for a moment, standing on her ship, two ferociously formidable men sizing each other up, one enormously tall, the other stocky and muscled, neither young.

Folco said, "Well met, Ban Rasca."

And the other man, as he apparently always did, shook his head. "Just Skandir. I am lord of nothing."

"I would, in another circumstance, suggest that the Jaddite world sees you yet as properly ruling much of Trakesia, fighting against invasion, but I have no desire to debate it. I am happy to call you whatever you like, and happier you are with us." He turned to Lenia, said briskly, "Can you carry another hundred and fifty men?"

She blinked. "Not easily."

"Nothing about this is easy. My mercenaries will be in the way in a naval fight. It was always so and has become clearer to me. Some will stay on the galleys, to be used as best they can be, but I plan to be with the party that is put ashore. I have spoken with the man I'll leave in command on my galley."

"Less a hundred and fifty men for him?" Skandir said.

"We are devising other movements, ship to ship. Balancing. Can you do it?"

"No," said Elie. "Forgive me." This was really his ship right now, Lenia thought. "That is too many. We can manage a hundred. Otherwise if we run into winds or a storm while crossing we are in real danger." They all looked at him. Unlike Elie to speak this way, especially to this man, but he was the one true mariner here.

"And what will fewer than two hundred of us do ashore?" Skandir was asking as a soldier.

"I have thoughts as to that," Folco said. "Would you like to hear them? If, that is, Signora Serrana and her captain say one hundred of mine can be managed. I am not ordering it."

"Of course you are," she said. "We are going to say no to you, my lord?"

Folco smiled. "Your captain already did."

"He proposed an adjustment. Men have been crowded on ships before. If he says we can do one hundred, we can. We'll need food and water brought from other ships."

"We can do that, before we break away east."

"Break away east?" she said.

Folco nodded. "I told you, I have thoughts as to what might happen once we've crossed."

He smiled again, she would later remember.

In the event, remarkably, events fell out much as he explained that they might, in a cabin below to her and Skandir. He'd had decades of commanding men, planning campaigns, sieges. This was different, but some things did not change. And that included the role fear could be made to play.

He had six Asharites with him, from Seressa, as interpreters and messengers. He'd had a winter to think about all of this.

When they came back up on deck, it was because Elie had had someone run down to tell Folco that the fleet from Ferrieres had arrived. It was an inspiring sight, Lenia thought, seeing them approach from the west on a bright spring day.

The weather remained good. A gift of Jad, the clerics said, leading prayers. One had come across with Folco's hundred. Other men had been shifted from ship to ship to galley. Water was brought to the *Silver Light*, and food. They were crowded, but not impossibly so, as long as the winds stayed calm enough.

They crossed. Open sea. Towards Tarouz.

ॐ

Khalif Nisim ibn Zukar of Abeneven, once vizier there but, as of some little time ago, reigning in the palace and enjoying, by all accounts, widespread support in his city, would regard that spring as a time when he learned a great deal.

About warfare, among other things. He did not see himself as a warrior, had no intentions in that regard, but a city needed to be defended, and you could learn elements of how to do that from an assault on another city. One in which you played a role. He did not, unfortunately for him, live long enough for these lessons to signify greatly in his life, or for Abeneven, but they were real, nonetheless.

His decision to accept the invitation of the Jaddite warlord d'Acorsi to participate in the attack on Tarouz was more about a letter he'd received from someone else as winter ended—a letter from Asharias.

By the great benevolence of Ashar and the holy stars, it appeared that he, ibn Zukar, had the favour of Gurçu the Conqueror. Approval was expressed for his having assumed the role of khalif here, and gifts were sent to him, accompanying the letter.

Gifts!

In the same letter that affirmed support for him was a single sentence that mattered, very much. *"We are displeased with our servant Zariq ibn Tihon in Tarouz, and have not acceded to his request for aid from us."*

If ever there was an invitation to participate in the ouster of ibn Tihon (the surviving one), that would be it, surely! Indeed, it might be argued, Nisim told his bewitching concubine, that the letter contained an *instruction*, not just information.

He wrestled with this. Caution had defined his life until the day the last khalif had been assassinated and ibn Zukar had moved more boldly than he'd ever thought he could. A bold man could reap death—or glory and power and a dark-haired, dark-eyed, scented concubine of astonishing skills in the privacy of the dark.

When a second letter came from the warlord of Acorsi, he was ready. He was, ibn Zukar told himself, acceding to the desires of Gurçu, not those of a Batiaran mercenary.

He confirmed first, as a prudent man should, that the djannis, the soldiers from Asharias posted here, had also received a communication from the grand khalif, and had a similar understanding of current matters.

They had, it seemed. Zariq ibn Tihon had lost the favour of Asharias. It was not a thing that could really be survived. There were not many of them here—they were a symbol of Gurçu's attention, the grand khalif keeping track of events in the Majriti—but the djannis mattered.

Also, he needed to explain to all the military men exactly how this move towards Tarouz was to be handled. It was not to be kept secret, he said. There would be spies for Tarouz here. They were not to be impeded when they hurried out to carry swift word. Their carrying word was, he explained, the point of this.

There was some disappointment expressed by his commanders, but this was alleviated when he explained what he thought might very possibly happen now. As to this, they expressed pleasure.

The warlord from Batiara had offered his thoughts and plans on this. Nisim, clever in the way of prudent men, also had thoughts about the safety of his own city, and the Esperañan part of the Jaddite fleet that would be coming past them on the way to Tarouz. He needed to be careful about his own harbour, fleet, walls. He was.

He sent two thousand men in the direction of Tarouz, on the road along the coast; some on horseback but most on foot. Only a portion of Abeneven's forces, but not a trivial one, and he had word spread through the city—for the spies to hear—that it was a larger force than it was.

The Jaddite warlord had promised ibn Zukar rewards if Tarouz fell and he had done these things, but the great reward, the truest one, would be if the countenance of Gurçu might shine upon him.

A vista of life's richness felt as if it might be opening before him. He thought, for the first time, of having a child. An heir.

A STORY CAN *travel in this way, to this place—to the point where thousands of men (and one woman) and well over a hundred ships and war galleys are crossing the sea. The storyteller—speaking in a marketplace, writing in a quiet room—might conjure anticipation of battle on the waves, fleets colliding, deciding the fate of a city and those within it, and of other cities, too, perhaps affecting the balance of the world . . .*

It is also true that the balancing of people's lives, however trivial they might be within a grander tapestry, can matter just as much in a certain kind of history. Most lives are trivial, after all, in the reckoning of the world, if not for those living them. These stories can also be told, however. Perhaps they need to also be told.

᳇

Seven days after the fleet left Seressa, Rafel ben Natan rode west, escorted, to Firenta.

He had been restless and fearful, those last days in Seressa. Guidanio Cerra had tried to ease his fears, but Cerra had his own concerns. Rafel made his decision to leave, and didn't linger.

He was not likely to be calmed readily, in any case. Their carrack, a good part of their fortune, was with that fleet, and so was Lenia. It was remarkable, and unsettling, and he wanted her to be as safe as the world allowed.

He'd tried to concentrate on business affairs, revising and defining their place in a shifting world of trade. Also, there were the letters he had received from the north, from his brother.

He had already decided to take those to Marsena himself. It was tempting to let the Sardis' man do it, but he was not a coward, Rafel told himself. A fleet was going to war; he could deliver tidings to a woman and to his parents.

On what sort of scale, Rafel thought, did one place two such things for measurement? And yet . . . how did one live, if not by trying to do so? Your own griefs were still griefs.

You could lose a brother to death, or in other ways.

He thought of his mother and father, forced to leave Almassar (by him!), and he knew it did need to be himself carrying them word of Sayash.

Gaelle he was uncertain about.

In Firenta he requested a visit with Piero Sardi, grateful beyond words for the random chances of life that made this possible for a Kindath. It was not normal, and he must never let himself forget that.

His gratitude was not just about the opportunities that knowing the Sardis offered, but also because he was genuinely impressed with the man. Piero was not someone to elicit affection. Rafel doubted he cared, had ever given it a thought. Perhaps when young? With a mistress? Perhaps.

If he'd been a man like Piero, or the duke of Seressa, he'd have probably written these thoughts down as a note. Maybe he should start doing that? Lenia would laugh at him.

He really wanted her back safely. He really wasn't certain she wanted to come back.

His hope? That her brother would draw her here. Keep her from going east to endless war with Ban Rasca Tripon—if they both survived this invasion.

Bad thoughts. He pushed them from his mind as he arrived at the Sardi palazzo. He was known by now, a guard accompanied him upstairs to the room where Piero always was. Antenami was there, too. The younger man rose quickly and came over. Rafel embraced him, and then smiled at the father, who had put down his glasses and looked up from his papers. Piero nodded back at him, then he also rose. Rafel bowed to him.

It was chilly, but Piero led him out on the terrace again. Rafel declined an offered cloak, then regretted he'd done so. Above the river that sliced through Firenta, exposed to the wind out here, he felt the cold. Sardi wasn't wearing a cloak, though. Men, Rafel thought wryly, could be endlessly strange in their silent duels. Or endlessly predictable.

When he left, not long after, they had come to an agreement about a matter he brought up. Which meant there was nothing to delay his going to Marsena. He cast about for reasons to linger and found none that were not obviously about avoiding sorrow. He even considered riding south to visit Carlo Serrana on his ranch. He'd be welcome, he knew, could tell them what Lenia was doing.

Except they'd know it, from her. She'd have written her brother.

He rode west instead, to where the *Silver Wake* was docked at Basiggio, the nearest commercial harbour for Firenta. Elie was with the new carrack, headed for war. Rafel might as well learn how their new man handled the smaller ship. An added reason for doing this.

He really was uneasy, however. Nothing seemed to be assuaging that.

The new captain, once they left port and started north along and then around the curve of the coastline, seemed capable, and mild-mannered. Elie had picked the man himself. He was not a Kindath, there weren't many of those with nautical experience in Batiara, but he had a calm look to him behind a heavy black beard, and showed no obvious disinclination to serve one of the moon-worshippers. He'd not have taken the job if he'd felt that.

The mariners were on alert but they didn't expect Asharite raiders so far north, especially not this spring, and there wouldn't have been any, in any case, once they crossed into Ferrieres waters towards Marsena.

On deck, wrapped in a warm cloak, with nothing to prove by not wearing one, Rafel considered what he'd just agreed to with Piero Sardi. It didn't take away any of their options with Seressa, but it did place them somewhere between the two great city-states. He had decided that could be a good thing. He might one day be forced to choose, but that wasn't now.

He stood on the *Silver Wake*'s familiar deck at night. His ship for so many years now, he knew the way it moved, the way it sounded. He *had* made a way in the world, Rafel ben Natan thought. He was still doing so. He looked up at the fierce hard diamonds of the stars in the fierce hard blackness of the sky.

His usual thought, seeing the glittering arc of them, perhaps everyone's usual thought, was to feel how small mortals were beneath that sweep of majesty. Not tonight. He felt anxious, sorrowful, but also determined. You could make something of your days, however they'd begun.

He'd set something significant in motion. Or, it might be. He was going to Marsena to open an office and warehouse for the new textile business he was doing out of Firenta. That office could handle raw cloth coming from the south—the Majriti and below it, along the caravan routes. And also from Esperaña, finished and raw, if there was peace between Esperaña and Ferrieres. Esperaña might even, he had told Piero Sardi, provide an alternative to Seressa one day and fabrics from the east. Again, if there was enough peace for ships to sail. Even if there was no true harmony, goods would still need to flow. The laws of war and commerce were different laws, and trade was a river.

He had undertaken to pay the Sardis twenty percent of what he made, in exchange for being able to call himself their partner in Marsena.

"Twenty is past generous, ben Natan," Piero Sardi had said, seemingly impervious to the wind on his terrace, "if all I do is lend my name and deposit payments from you."

"Your name is potent, my lord. You know it. It is protection and enhancement. I am happy if it feels generous to you. Also"—he smiled—"I might hope for you to use my warehouse and agents, perhaps my ships, to handle goods of your own, and I'll charge fees for that."

Piero offered a rare smile.

"Do you plan to live there?" he'd asked, abruptly. "In Marsena? It is safe for your people?"

Such a clever man, Rafel thought again, on a ship headed that way in the dark.

HIS PARENTS CRIED when he told them Sayash was alive but had changed his name and was not coming back from a new life he'd made.

Of course they did. Rafel did not, although he was close to doing so, seeing them weep. He had too much anger. He hoped they couldn't see it, but had a feeling they did. He said he had promised not to reveal where his brother was in exchange for sums paid to Gaelle for the children. How had he found him? He had been helped by friends in Batiara. Yes, Sayash was well, healthy by report. Yes, it was wrong for Sayash to have done it in this fashion. It was very wrong, regarding the two children, by any measure you could bring to bear, he agreed with his father putting it that way.

Yes, he would be going to Gaelle's house now, a little farther into the Kindath quarter, to speak with her before turning to his business affairs. Yes, of course he would greet the children, he had indeed heard they grew more wonderful every day. He offered the opinion that having their grandparents nearby now played a role in that. He kissed them both.

GAELLE WANTED TO go to bed together first. She was like that. There was a girl in the house now, helping to care for the children. Sayash's money had been deposited to Gaelle's name, and the bank had sent a note. Which meant she had resources. Also that she knew her husband was alive.

Afterwards, lying spent in her bed, as she always left him, Rafel heard her say, beside him, unclothed, one leg resting on his, head on his shoulder, long dark hair spread out, "Who is she, Rafel?"

"*What?*" he said, genuinely startled.

"Please. We have been lovers for long enough and often enough. You do know how to please me, and I am not shy about my ability to address your needs. But even so, today . . ."

She let the silence linger. He couldn't see her face, because of how she was lying, but he could imagine her smiling. He liked the scent of her, always had. She must be, he thought, entangled in many different feelings.

So he told her.

She listened in silence until he was done.

"This is the woman I saw with you last spring? In the street at night?"

"Yes." It was difficult, but also a strange relief to be speaking of Lenia.

"Your business partner, then. And a Jaddite. Is that wise, Rafel?"

"I am certain it is not."

"And she . . . feels the same way about you?"

"I don't think so, no. I don't think she can."

"Why?"

So he told her. About Lenia Serrana, who had been called Nadia bint Dhiyan when he'd let her come aboard the *Silver Wake* years ago.

"She wants to kill Asharites? That is her purpose in life?"

"I think, and perhaps die fighting them."

Gaelle sighed. "Not a good place to put your heart, my dear."

"No," he said. She never called him *my dear*.

"You'd be wiser proposing to me. It even accords with our laws, if your brother abandons me, as he has."

"I know, Gaelle. Would you have me?"

"No," she said cheerfully.

He shifted to be able to look at her. "Because?"

"Because I am happier with my freedom, now that I need not fear for money. Between what Sayash has finally sent, and what I know you will give us, at need. I prefer to be alone, except for the times when I prefer not to be. It suits me, it is what I want from life. Tell me, Sayash is with a man, isn't he?"

He hadn't intended to talk about this. He wasn't sure why, but . . .

"Tell me," she repeated.

"Yes," he said. "You guessed? Before?"

"We were married many years, Rafel. He was dead, or with a man somewhere. Astarden?"

He hesitated again.

"I have no desire to contact him, or punish him. None. I wish him happiness, a good life, while cursing him for leaving two children without a father, and forcing you to do whatever you did to give us money he ought to have sent long ago. That will have been hard for you. Not giving us money . . . his not doing so."

"Not so hard," he said, which wasn't entirely the truth. "I think he was ashamed about leaving, Gaelle."

"Of course he was! He wanted us all to think him dead. Easier that way. But he needn't have felt shame with me, and marriages do end. The shame was leaving a brother to care for his family."

He had bitter words close to his tongue. Didn't say them.

She saw him holding back, and smiled. "You've cared for us very well, Rafel. If I wished to wed again, any man alive, it would be you. Please know that. I mean it."

And hearing those words, only then—not before in Seressa, learning the tidings, or with his parents—he wept.

"Oh, my dear," Gaelle said.

She was not by nature a tender person. And so when she drew his head to her breast and wrapped her arms around him it was as if tears were somehow permitted, perhaps even required, in this one place, for this time. Her bed, mid-afternoon, the world what it was. He wept for her, for the children, for his parents. For himself.

For his brother, who was gone. Alive, held in memory, but gone. Like fireflies.

It lasted some time. At the end, Gaelle kissed the top of his head and said, crisply, "Very well. Good. Now we need to think of ways to keep this woman of yours from killing herself at war. She does at least like you, no?"

"She likes me," he said. "I'm not sure how much it matters, given what has happened in her life."

"Tell me more. Including when you met."

So he told her.

LATER, THEY DRESSED and went downstairs and he had a sweet, cool drink with the two boys, who had always found him amusing. He made them both laugh again, pretending his drink was scalding hot, burning his tongue and even his fingers on the cup. They were clever and affectionate. He thought it was better than he'd even imagined it might be, that the two of them had their grandparents here now.

He'd done a good thing, he told himself. Gaelle said the same when he left to deal with matters of business for himself and the Sardis, and Lenia.

He found a well-located space recently available to purchase as offices and a warehouse, by the port. The Sardi name helped ensure it would be theirs, no attempt to avoid a Kindath buyer. His own skills made the price not unreasonable, although they did try.

He hired four people over the next several days, not rushing this. He had a sign made: *Firentini Merchant Offices.* Firenta, stated so baldly, generally meant the Sardis, and people would know that, but it also now meant, here, right now, Rafel ben Natan and Lenia Serrana.

He stayed two weeks, spent the nights at his parents' home, made time during the days to help his father buy books to restore some of the library left behind. The ones they couldn't find he noted down. Guidanio Cerra's cousin owned a bookshop in Seressa. He'd place orders there he told his father, and have them sent. He took a genuine pleasure in doing this.

He visited Gaelle and the children, and they came to his parents for meals several times. In the afternoons, when he could get away, he and Gaelle made love.

Afterwards, on each occasion, her busy, agile mind turned again to Lenia. She was overflowing with suggestions, none of which seemed to apply at all, be helpful in any way. It was a side of her he'd never seen before. People could surprise you, even after years.

And then one thought did, unexpectedly, seem somewhat useful to him.

It made him even more fearful, thinking about it, wondering where she was, how that assault by sea and land was proceeding. They'd be there by now, he thought. They'd be fighting, perhaps a siege had begun. Perhaps it was over? For good or ill, for living or dying. If there was fighting, Lenia would not be staying behind. She had not gone to Tarouz to stay behind. It was difficult, Rafel thought, to have your heart no longer be entirely your own, lodged in your breast where it had always been.

To have part of it be somewhere far away, in a place of war.

∾

One day in that same spring, Raina Vidal was sitting at the writing desk she used to review correspondence and instruct her agents and advisers. A servant came in. She was informed by this person that someone had arrived, was at the door.

She preferred open windows this time of year. The springtime air was good—in her own view, if not her physician's—for staving off the headaches from which she suffered. So she'd heard horses, a carriage creaking up the hill, then coming to a stop. She couldn't tell who this was, of course, so when the name was given to her, hesitantly, it precipitated shock, and anger. And perhaps, yes, the immediate beginnings of a headache.

How not? Truly, in the world of the goddesses and the god, how not?

The door to this room was usually open. So a short while later the person who had arrived simply walked in and stood just inside that door, looking at Raina.

"I'm back," Tamir said. And then, of course, began to cry.

Raina was not entirely certain she'd be able to refrain from doing the same, for different reasons.

She moved from her desk to one of the chairs by the fire. Tamir, once seated opposite her, had drained a glass of wine quickly and gestured for a second, but was letting that sit on the small table beside her chair. She was extremely pale. Probably frightened.

Raina didn't really mind that, if she was honest with herself.

"It is all so unfair, I am *aggrieved*, Raina!"

"The duke has sent you away?"

It seemed obvious.

Tamir stared, her magnificent eyes wide. "They . . . they wrote to you?"

"I assure you your arrival comes as a complete surprise."

Tamir swallowed. Looked as if she'd cry again, but didn't. She might have decided it would have no useful effect on her sister-in-law.

"Yes," she said. "It is humiliating!"

It was more than that, Raina thought, depending on how the finances she'd been disbursing by agreement into Tamir's accounts had been handled at the ducal court. She drew a breath. It was early for her but she signalled her steward for wine. Tamir used that as an excuse to drain half her second glass.

Raina looked at her. No real reason to prolong this. It felt as if she knew this entire story. She said, "You slept with someone at the court."

"*Raina!*" her sister-in-law exclaimed. And then, of course, did commence to cry.

Raina waited, not too long. She said, "Tamir, did you sleep with someone at the court?"

The other woman looked up, a handkerchief to her eyes. Lovely, wide-set blue eyes. "*Only one!*" she cried. "And only once! We agreed on that!"

Raina nodded briskly. It was all so predictable. "Only once. I see. You agreed on that. And was he a courtier? Handsome and charming, and he sought you out, ardently?"

Tamir lowered her head, handkerchief in hand. She had such a beautifully long neck, Raina thought. She went on. "And did he, perhaps, after your one encounter, beg of you an item of intimate clothing, to remember the moment by? The shining moment he would never forget?"

She was being slightly cruel. She didn't care.

Tamir looked up, fear in her expression. The fear of someone seen too clearly. But it was such an *old* court story.

Raina said, "And was that intimate garment produced a little later by Duke Ersani when he confronted you, and after you denied the encounter?"

"Raina! How was I to know that the—"

"How anticipate enemies? At a court where you'd just arrived, and been swiftly elevated? How, indeed? Tamir, you are as foolish as a small child or a drunken soldier. Did you never consider that someone at Ersani's court—a would-be new wife, or a rejected mistress, or another woman who *desired* to be his mistress—might wish the Kindath woman disgraced and gone?"

Her sister-in-law, she saw, had not, in fact, considered this. It was arriving as thunder in a clear blue sky for her.

Raina went on, remorselessly, "And there is more! You shamed a powerful, proud man, since the duke's enemies will now happily share the story of his new mistress wasting no time finding a young lover! His new Kindath mistress."

"I changed my faith," Tamir said.

"You did, didn't you. And how do you feel about that now?"

Another silence. Then, "Raina, I have nowhere to go."

Said with dignity, to be fair. She didn't want to be fair!

Raina got up and crossed to the window, her back to her returned sister-in-law, the tall, exquisite woman her husband's brother had wed in joy, so many years ago. She remembered the wedding. They had danced together, she and Tamir, dark and fair, to delight and applause.

Both men were dead. It was only the two of them, and she didn't *want* it to be the two of them! Tamir had money of her own now, that was the agreement! Raina to be free of her, Tamir to have resources to build a life in Casiano!

She needed to have someone check that bank account. There *should* be no way for anyone to have accessed the very considerable sum there, but . . .

She looked out and down, towards the harbour of this small, lovely city where Kindath had found a place to dwell, a home, for hundreds of years. There had been tragedies, a great burning of people and property once, long ago, but that had led unexpectedly to guilt, contrition, and the High Patriarch of the day declaring Sorenica a city forever open to the Kindath. That decree had never been rescinded.

It was a city where she could see herself staying. A place to bring people from Esperaña and elsewhere as a first stop or a destination in their journeys towards as much safety as was available. To stay or move on, that would be a choice for each person, each family. It was not hers to make for them. Following her husband's course, she was simply doing what she could to take them from peril. Give them chances, choices.

Their lives were their own. Everyone's life ought to be, Raina Vidal thought. One reason she knew she would never marry again.

It was a bright day. No wind up here, but she could see the waves were choppy beyond the harbour, far off. Whitecaps in sunlight. With spring arrived there would normally be much activity there, but a war fleet had sailed for Tarouz.

Until they knew what happened there, merchant ships would be extremely careful about leaving their ports. This was affecting the price of goods, all goods. She'd been making decisions based on that just now.

Then her sister-in-law had arrived, and—

Sometimes the decisions of our lives, decisions affecting many lives in some cases, are made after reflection, conversation, correspondence, sleepless nights, the weighing of disparate elements amid doubt and uncertainty.

Sometimes they come in a moment at a window, looking out on a springtime day.

She had been thinking about Asharias, had had two visits here with a man quietly (that was the phrase he used) acting in the interests of the grand khalif.

Standing there that day, Raina Vidal abruptly realized that she would, after all, go east. Tamir had not shaped this decision. To say that would be to give her far too much importance. But Raina knew she was not going to abandon her sister-in-law to what the world might do to her, and one of those things could well be revenge from Casiano. Duke Ersani—she had met the man—was clever, proud, and vain, and the people of the south in Batiara were known to remember slights.

Not that they forgot them elsewhere, but . . .

No, what she realized, again, in that moment by the window, weighing the possibility of revenge sought against Tamir, and against *her*, was that for their people, being among the Asharites might not be a *good* thing, but the lands where Jad was worshipped were too often worse.

You could know some things, Raina Vidal thought, and then there might come a moment when the knowing entered into you more deeply, like an arrow. That applied, she supposed, to love, but love wasn't the issue just now.

She looked out a little longer. It truly was beautiful, Sorenica in spring light. Tamir was blessedly silent behind her. Raina realized she didn't seem to have a headache after all. She felt, in fact, astonishingly clear in her mind.

She turned back to her sister-in-law. Her anger seemed to have also passed. She managed a smile.

"We will deal with this, Tamir. But we will have many things to do."

Tamir looked up at her from where she sat by the fire.

"Thank you," she said. "Thank you, Raina."

WHEN RAINA VIDAL, long named the queen of the Kindath, finally passed from life many years later, in her house in Asharias overlooking the strait and its dolphins, she was surrounded by a great many people mourning her loss. There was even a representative of the grand khalif attending, for it had been reported in the palace complex that the lady was near to her end.

This was the new khalif by then. Gurçu had died some years ago, and then so had the son who succeeded him. Many things had changed, but not the edict that allowed the Kindath to dwell in the lands of the Osmanli Asharites—in the City of Cities and anywhere else they chose. They paid a tax to do so, but it was not usually an unreasonable one.

This, it was widely known, had much to do with the lady who was dying that day. A great many of her people had travelled east after she came to Asharias, often with her aid in making the long journey.

She died in a wide bed with tall glass doors before it, open that day to her terrace, the evening light, and a sight of the sea. It was not received medical wisdom among the Asharites to have windows open for those who were ill, but her preferences in this matter were well known, even if the lady could barely speak her wishes towards the end.

It was believed that she was not in great pain, that the arts of the physicians were equal to easing that, at least. Indeed, the khalif had sent one of his own doctors to her when it became known she was dying.

Outside the handsome house, a large crowd of her own people had gathered, to honour her and mourn. Prayers were chanted and blessings offered in many languages, and it was possible that she could hear these from where she lay, her grey hair spread out on a pillow. There were tears, outside and inside the room, but the person who held her hand at the end, held it tightly, with a long, complex love, and awareness of loss, was her sister-in-law, Tamir. And though she could not speak to say it, so no one knew, that was all right for Raina Vidal. It was.

SHE WAS NOT in her bed. The house was gone. Everything seemed to be gone. There was a space in which she seemed to be hovering. There was, she realized, no longer any pain.

She saw the two moons, the sun, bright stars—all visible at once, in the same sky! It was wondrous. But then, even as she looked, awed and afraid, she heard a voice she knew, and the words it spoke were, "Be welcome, dear heart!"

And this voice, this so-much-remembered voice, was that of the man she had loved, and lost long ago to flames. And Raina began to weep then *in this strange, suspended space. She didn't feel, she had never felt, that she had lived such a pure or virtuous life. Not so as to deserve . . .*

But now there came other voices to her. Known ones—even her mother and father—and some not known at all, speaking under the sun, moons, stars here, all shining at once, but gently. And each voice was saying sweet, healing, welcoming words. To her. To her, Raina. It became a choir, a warmth of sound washing over her, through her, through what she was, now that she was dead, now that she was here.

Be welcome. Dear heart.

CHAPTER XVI

He was predator, never prey. He attacked, he didn't brace for an assault. Zariq ibn Tihon in his city of Tarouz was aware that people had begun streaming out through the landward gates in late winter. Not a disaster, fewer mouths to feed if this became a siege, but it sent a bad message.

Problem was, Tarouz was better situated to withstand an attack from the sea than it was to endure a siege. They *could* be starved out if the Jaddites came and held together long enough.

By then he had confirmed the name of the warlord leading the force coming to destroy him. It was not good news. He missed his brother like death. But death had found Ziyar—at the hands of this same man. And now Folco Cino d'Acorsi—may he rot for eternity, his body devoured by animals, his soul tormented—seemed intent on making it both of them he killed.

A new sensation, with that. Zariq couldn't remember being *afraid*, not since they'd been captured as boys, before they'd seized the ship that had taken them, killed the crew, and he and his brother had set a course for lives that led them here.

Led him here alone now. And dealing with fears that could not be shown.

The worst of those was Asharias. Gurçu had written nothing to him. And Zariq had no idea what word he'd sent to the djannis here, or elsewhere. Elsewhere being, in particular, Abeneven, where the ibn Tihons had made a move for power that had not turned out well at all.

There came a rumour, as winter turned to spring and wildflowers bloomed outside the walls, tidings ridden this way from his spies in Abeneven. He didn't believe it, but he was afraid it might be true, and knew that people in Tarouz would *think* that it was true. He was aware this story was in the city, not just his palace.

It was not entirely about what he himself believed now.

He really had not thought the new khalif there would be so bold. A pallid counter of money, an adjuster of tariffs. But the word sent was specific: Abeneven appeared ready to send a force overland to meet the Jaddite fleet here.

He consulted with Farai, the only one of his commanders he trusted entirely, both as to loyalty and skill. Farai was confident he could best the infidels at sea: they would not know the waters here, whereas the two of them knew this part of the sea like they knew their dreams. Zariq did not share the nature of his dreams. Some were of the island where he'd been born.

If their galley commanders stayed confident and bold, Zariq said, they could smash the Jaddites so badly on the water the infidels would lose heart, will, their precarious unity. This was, he said, a gathering of men who hated each other. The Esperañans might not even join the rest. Could one really imagine Ferrieres and Esperaña fighting beside each other?

Not in the world as they knew it, Farai agreed.

Their mariners and their soldiers and the citizens needed to be reminded of this every day, Zariq said. That any attack could be ended by a single decisive encounter on the waters of the harbour or outside it, depending on wind and seas.

People continued to go out and in through the landward gates. The markets stayed open. The idea was to keep life as normal as possible, reduce panic. Some who went out did not come back, however. Some left with laden carts. He was trying to decide when he should forbid this, execute a few of those showing such cowardice and treachery.

He had the state of the walls checked yet again, and the munitions for the cannon that guarded the harbour. The granaries and cisterns were full, it was confirmed. He had his red beard shaved.

Then the fleet of the Jaddites was sighted by one of his small, quick scouting ships. They are coming, the captain said breathlessly, having run up the hill to the palace.

Of course they are, Zariq wanted to scream at him. *Where else would they be going?*

Their numbers were not terrible, however. He had feared many hundreds of ships and galleys. There were not many more than a hundred, the captain said, as best he could judge, having had to turn quickly to outrace them here. To bring word, he said, perspiring. To the khalif.

The Jaddites would not be far behind him, he said.

No, he had not seen any banners from Esperaña.

That was good.

Zariq had the gates closed. It could not be delayed any more. No one to go in or out. Of course people always had ways to enter and leave a city, any city, but they could also be executed if seen doing so. He expected to have to do that a few times.

Another messenger, on horseback from the west. He reported, also breathlessly, that an army had indeed set out from Abeneven. The rumours had been true. It was not overlarge, he said, but nor was it unduly small. It was of . . . middling size, he said. Zariq wanted to kill him. What did "not overlarge" mean? he asked, as calmly as he could manage. There were a number of people in his throne room at the time; it was important he seem calm.

The man suggested it might be three thousand.

Djannis? Zariq asked.

Some, yes, the messenger said.

Zariq thought about Gurçu, whose best warriors the djannis were. It was easier, he reflected bitterly, for a new khalif in Abeneven to be bold if he had licence—or even instructions—from Asharias.

He missed his brother all day and every night. At meals, at prayer, lying awake. He regretted the assassination of the khalif in Abeneven with increasing fervour. The Kindath merchant, the woman, the man he'd placed with them to do the killing—he wished them all dead. The assassin was dead, mind you, the other two had told him that, in Marsena.

He wished those two were dead.

Within his city, word began to spread about the overland force now coming, and also, even worse, that Gurçu had sent word that Zariq ibn Tihon no longer reposed in his favour. Zariq had three people decapitated in the palace square for saying this. It wasn't certain they'd been the ones doing so, but that didn't matter. It was not to be said.

But it would continue to be. He was certain of that. You could not stop people whispering.

Two mornings after this he woke to a knocking at his bedchamber door. He was sleeping alone; he hadn't had any of his women with him at night for some time. He snapped a command, and the door was opened by a guard. It was Farai who had come. His posture told a story even before he cleared his throat and reported.

Half their ships had slipped away in the night, and the Jaddite fleet would very likely come in sight today. The sun was rising.

He had many thoughts, did Zariq ibn Tihon. They chased each other in his mind. He'd been dreaming when the knocking came. He couldn't remember the dream now.

"Why did you not stop them? From fleeing?"

"How, khalif? Attacking our own ships in the harbour? Chasing them west?" Farai was angry too, and unhappy.

Zariq had no good answer to this. Only rage, and this new, unfamiliar feeling: fear. Such desertion had always been possible, though. A majority of the ships he commanded were those of corsairs, and the ibn Tihons' control over these men was entirely due to their own self-interest. For years Tarouz had been a haven for them, a marketplace for taken goods and slaves, somewhere safe to repair galleys, and with large enough numbers of them gathered to launch attacks on cities and guarded merchant ships with one of the brothers, attacks they could never have dared do alone or in small, mistrustful numbers.

Loyalty to him would not be a dominant feeling for any of the corsairs. Nor would religious zeal against infidels. And all this was made worse by his brother being gone. Zariq had made these men wealthy with his planning; Ziyar had made them feared.

They feared the Jaddites more now.

Their departure also meant something else.

Farai said it. He was, in no possible way, a cowardly man.

"Lord, I do not think I can defeat them at sea with the ships we have left. Even with the fortress cannon. And . . ." He hesitated, said it: "And if there should be instructions from the grand khalif as to what our ships from Asharias are to do . . ."

He left it for Zariq to complete the thought. Which he did. Had done for many days and nights in his mind.

He said, "Do not venture out of the bay. Make them come in to you, under the cannon, not knowing the rocks and tides. Use what we know and they don't. Hurt them badly before the siege that will now come."

"Yes, khalif," said Farai. He bowed and left. He had much to do.

Zariq lingered a few moments in his bedchamber. He was the khalif of Tarouz, he reminded himself, the representative of Gurçu the Conqueror here. Although he was, as of this morning, not certain to be the first thing for long, and hadn't been the second, it seemed clear, for some time.

He did not want to die.

There were always ways out of a city. And he had, as a preparing sort of man, prepared for this, too, even to shaving his beard. Farai could not be part of this planning, for many reasons. One (only one) being that he was needed to engage the infidels in the harbour, delay the siege, kill as many of them as he could, create a chaos of sunken ships and drowned men.

He summoned a messenger. Sent him to a man he knew, a soldier, not a djanni, someone who could, indeed, be a part of this next stage in his life—being from the island where Zariq and Ziyar had been born under different names and into a different faith, in a fishing village by the sea.

Alone in his room he assembled some things in a pack he could carry. He prepared a sword carefully, sheathed it, belted it on. He hid a dagger on his body. He put on a nondescript hat. And then, without hesitation or any glance back at the luxury here, the glorious life he had created from as near to nothing as could be imagined, Zariq ibn Tihon left through an inner door, and went quickly down a hidden staircase behind a panel on the other side.

You always want a hidden staircase, he'd told his brother once. The world was too unpredictable not to have one.

Ziyar had laughed, he remembered.

THE FIRST CLASHES of the assault on Tarouz took place elsewhere. At Abeneven, in fact.

This happened because Folco d'Acorsi was extremely good at warfare, and because he did not like the king and queen of Esperaña or, more precisely, their ambition to dominate the Jaddite world.

He had been extremely careful not to let the High Patriarch, or anyone else, discern his own twist on this invasion. Some things a leader kept to himself. Or he did, in any event.

The plan had been born of a realization that Querida de Carvajal, commander of the Esperañan fleet, was not entirely a fool but was a man defined by ambition and greed. Folco had, accordingly, set something in motion. He'd sent the man, quite properly, a copy of the letter concerning the Asharite force from Abeneven that would be going east to join the assault on Tarouz. He said he *believed* it might be as large as five thousand men.

This was almost true.

A subsequent communication conveyed the results of a newer exchange with the khalif in Abeneven, reporting that his marching soldiers were going to turn back, not carry on to Tarouz.

The khalif (Folco wrote to Carvajal) was worried about his own city. It was a prudent concern. He would only allow his forces be seen marching out, before they turned back home. This marching forth would help the invasion—it would cause Zariq ibn Tihon's spies to report that an army from Abeneven was coming, causing useful panic in Tarouz.

This subsequent letter, however, about the marching army turning back, was sent, by design, just a little too late to reach Querida de Carvajal before he arrived at the waters by Abeneven. It shouldn't matter, of course. If the Esperañan commander was acting properly he'd sail straight past that city to join the assault at Tarouz.

That marching out had been all Folco really needed from Abeneven's soldiers. He didn't want them at Tarouz, with a claim to a share of any spoils. Panic could win wars—if it lay with the other side. But, of course, if the army of Abeneven was, in fact, back in the city, and their fleet was prepared (he'd sent the khalif a note suggesting they might want to be), then Querida de Carvajal's personal ambitions might be . . . unwise.

It remained the case, in brief, that the Jaddite world could not be called united at this time. Folco d'Acorsi, commanding an attack force, saw himself as anticipating a possible betrayal, even treachery, not betraying anyone himself. If the Esperañan did what he and his monarchs had agreed to do, nothing at all unfortunate would happen to his ships and men.

Querida de Carvajal did not do that.

IT HAD SEEMED a good plan to him, a *very* good one. *Almost compelled by circumstances*, he could see himself saying modestly to his king and queen when he returned home to be celebrated. Count Querida de Carvajal sounded suitable as a title.

Why would glorious Esperaña, why would a Carvajal, scion of a family that had been (somewhat) prominent for hundreds of years, accept merely a portion—a widely divided portion—of the spoils from Tarouz? Why, especially, he thought, when Tarouz was going to be ferociously defended by many ships and galleys, *and* when he'd be passing an equally treasure-laden city along the coast on his way there?

And that other city had just sent a large part of its forces east, he had been usefully advised by the overly admired Batiaran who had been—foolishly—given command of this fleet by the High Patriarch, who was also from Batiara, of course. That divided, fractious, puffed-up collection of city-states would be ripe, soon, for being plucked itself by the might of Esperaña.

He tested phrases in his mind that he might deploy at court in the ceremony they would hold to honour him. He set soldiers ashore, just west of the city of Abeneven.

Tarouz would fall or not to the blustering d'Acorsi, busily telling an Esperañan aristocrat what to do in letter after letter. Carvajal and his ships and men would take a different city, wreak the havoc the Asharites deserved, a burning and a slaughter on a huge scale, long to be remembered. There were probably Kindath there, too. More tinder for the fires, he thought. Though burning needed to wait upon looting, of course. It was harder, he'd reminded his men, to sack homes, palaces, religious buildings when they were on fire. And if you wanted women or boys for a conqueror's pleasure (he wasn't a man to judge in that regard!) it was easier if there were places to find and have them that were also not burning!

And all this while serving in a holy war, for the good of one's soul when it came before Jad in judgment. And sharing the spoils with, well, with no one! It was glorious.

Getting soldiers ashore was a little more troublesome than he liked; there were rocks, and no really good landing places west of the city. But he reminded his officers that most of the army of Abeneven had gone to Tarouz—one *more* contingent to share in the spoils there. And d'Acorsi had ordered that there could be no burning, no killing of people in the city. An agreement made. One being honoured by the Patriarch. The *shame* of it, Querida de Carvajal thought.

Whereas here it was all for them, with the city's soldiers gone, as poor Folco had obligingly told him. And *he* had made no such disreputable agreement on behalf of his king and queen as to the treatment of Jad-mocking infidels. For the riches that lay ahead of them they could endure some losses in choppy seas, damage to a few ships hitting rocks farther out than they ought to have been. It wasn't as if you never took losses in a conquest, was it?

He put ashore two thousand men. It took time, which he didn't like, and there was some unpleasantness: screaming men in the sea, unable to swim, but Carvajal didn't linger for them, he was in a hurry. He wanted to reach Abeneven from the sea now, surprise whatever fleet was in its harbour (along with merchant ships to be plucked). The soldiers put ashore would march east and be upon the city before any notice came, and they knew how to scale landward walls, bring down the gates of an unprepared city with most of its army away. No one would see them arrive at this lonely place on the coast.

No one should have seen them. No one should have been anywhere near here. Carvajal waited for the last of the small craft to return from ferrying men, and gave the signal for his thirty ships to carry on as soon as these were made fast. He had captains capable of assembling the troops on the beach into order and getting them to the city. They didn't need him for this.

Unfortunately for those capable captains and their men, three thousand Asharite soldiers were waiting just inland from that strand, having watched the ships as they approached, then waited to attack until they'd offloaded their men and moved on.

The Jaddite soldiers were still wet, still struggling to organize themselves. Many were sitting on the stones eating their rations after the challenging exercise of getting ashore. Most elected to at least have a drink from their flask. They'd earned it, was the general view.

(Not far away, a year before, a small merchant ship called the *Silver Wake* had put people ashore in the night.)

Their footing on the strand was terrible, the surprise extreme. The soldiers and their leaders were, on the whole, brave men, or brave enough, not strangers to combat, but they had no chance to arrange themselves—and nowhere to retreat, with the sea behind them, and their ships gone.

It was very bad, what happened on that shore west of Abeneven. More than half of the Esperañans died there, or were wounded in such a way that death came not long after. The rest were captured. Those worth ransoming were eventually ransomed. Most were not worth anything and were enslaved into the war galleys of Abeneven, or sold to corsairs.

The Jaddites' own ships, which might have been able to defend them with cannon fire, and have the small boats carry at least some of the soldiers off the beach to safety, had moved east, with a good wind. The commander of the Asharite land force had instructed his soldiers to use swords and arrows, to avoid the sounds of guns or mobile cannon that might have caused the Esperañan ships to hear them and turn back.

They did not, accordingly, turn back.

Carvajal's thirty ships carried on, the fresh wind and the afternoon sun behind them on a spring day. They ran straight into a doubled fleet: the ships of Abeneven and the corsairs from Tarouz who had headed west when they fled that city. The Asharites knew this coastline exceptionally well; they had tucked themselves out of sight behind a curve of the shoreline, close to the city.

They came out, sixty ships of varying size, only when it was too late for the Esperañans to turn with the wind, form a proper line of battle, do anything an experienced commander could do to stop a slaughter. The only exception was a handful of ships, to the north in the Esperañan fleet. Those few did get away, and eventually home.

The rest of the fleet was lost that day, offshore from Abeneven. They were struck by cannon. There were fire arrows. They were rammed, they were boarded. Querida de Carvajal fought well, it was agreed, even by the Asharites. His galley sank four ships before it was rammed by two others, and taken. He yielded his sword on his own deck, stood tall, wounded in three places, as he surrendered. His heart was ashes.

The Asharites had been like ravening beasts, he would say after being ransomed, when he was interrogated back home as to the disaster that had befallen the invasion force of the king and queen on land and at sea, at a city that was *not* the one they had been instructed to take.

He was executed, by judicial order. Because he had rank he was permitted beheading rather than hanging or burning. His head and body were returned to his family for burial. They were not, after all, barbarians in Esperaña, or ravening beasts.

There was private bitterness among his people that they'd paid a ruinously large ransom to the khalif of Abeneven, only to have Querida killed at home.

Some time later, a salt-stained envelope was delivered to that family in the city of Seria, where they lived along the coast, and where their elder son had learned ships and the sea. It was addressed to him. They opened the letter, read it, did not understand it at all. They sent it north to the court, since they were being careful, still, to exercise caution in all matters. (A rumour had begun, somehow, since his death, that the Carvajal family had Kindath or Asharite blood, going back to conquered Al-Rassan, hundreds of years ago. It was not a safe rumour, given a disgraced and executed son.)

It was not even permitted to light a candle to the memory of someone executed by order of the court, but Querida de Carvajal had

had a younger brother and a sister die before him, and his mother elected to light, from that time on, one large yellow candle in their private sanctuary for all of her lost children, and so mourned her shining, beloved older son that way until she died.

At the court of the king and queen, the letter, associated with recent, terrible failure, was read by someone attached to the army, and was also not understood by him. It told of some force of Asharites that would not, in fact, proceed to join the siege of Tarouz, but would be turning back home. Commander Carvajal was simply being advised as to this, the letter said, though it was not something that would impact anything the Esperañan fleet was to do. More details would be offered, if desired, when all the Jaddites came together at Tarouz. It was signed with expressions of goodwill by Folco Cino d'Acorsi, the Batiaran, in his role as supreme commander of the High Patriarch's forces.

It seemed an inconsequential document, had obviously never been received, but it was filed, as such things were in a properly organized administration, among thousands of other papers at a warehouse assigned to such things.

The result of Carvajal's catastrophic error, the loss of so many ships and men (especially the ships) rippled for some time, delaying and undermining Esperañan ambitions in other Jaddite countries.

It could be said to have been, ultimately, a principal consequence of the campaign against Tarouz that year.

FOLCO D'ACORSI NEVER spoke of that letter sent strategically late. Its remarkable results did give him private satisfaction. He had, again, judged someone rightly, even with limited information. It was important to be able to do that. And had he been wrong, the Esperañans would simply have joined the rest of them—as they were supposed to do.

He hadn't been wrong, however. He prayed to holy Jad for the souls of those lost at Abeneven, as he always did for all who died in his wars. He also prayed for his own soul, for shelter with the god when he should end his days, despite his many sins.

Coming ashore in a small bay east of Tarouz in one of the many small craft going back and forth from the *Silver Light*, his thoughts were, however, as they absolutely had to be, on this moment, and what he wanted to do.

He wasn't in control of everything that might unfold, one never was on campaign: there were enemies, there were uncertainties in your ranks, there was weather, sickness, ambition, greed, rage, fear . . .

But your task as a commander was to assert as much control as circumstances allowed, and be ready to make changes. One thing that had already occurred was that half of Zariq ibn Tihon's fleet had fled. They'd gone west, it was reported.

It was both astonishing and not entirely unexpected. Too many of those ships and galleys belonged to corsairs. With a massed invasion fleet coming, they were facing a savage battle. They might triumph, yes, but . . . what would *they* win, these raiders? They could find shelter elsewhere, couldn't they? Other cities where they could take on water and food, make repairs, buy slaves for their oars, offer what they had to trade.

Just as mercenary leaders in Batiara, including himself, would avoid a major battle whenever they could, so would pirates on the Middle Sea, Folco thought. If you had somehow captured a good ship for yourself, you never wanted to risk it—unless you could take a better one, and then you might have two, be moving up in the world. And trained, experienced fighting men on a corsair galley were worth—well, they were your access to any wealth you hoped to claim.

As long as Zariq and Ziyar ibn Tihon had dominated this coastline, they were men, and Tarouz was a city, to bind yourself to. Ziyar was dead. Zariq was facing an invasion. He needed them more than they needed or feared him now. And massed ships of the Jaddite world were not what pirates became pirates to deal with.

Still, they might have stayed, Folco thought. The city was well defended, the harbour notoriously difficult to penetrate with its many cannon guarding it from towers. There had been nothing foreordained about victory in and around this harbour. Now, there might be. Jad might have blessed them already.

He'd have to leave that to the naval commanders he'd selected, and the ones chosen by Ferrieres. Esperaña had not yet appeared. They didn't yet know why, although he had an idea he shared with no one.

They would all come to know why, not long after, and those Asharite corsairs fleeing west from here would be a part of that story.

Folco d'Acorsi waded ashore with not quite two hundred men by the ruins of a city of the Ancients. In a different time, he might have paused here in Axartes, lingered to explore the ruins, think about time, the weight of centuries, crumbling of honey-coloured stone, palaces and mosaic floors. The evidence of a great, long-ago fire.

He did think about such things, but not on campaign.

One immediate distraction was Lenia Serrana, and he was working to not let her be so. If she wanted to be part of the land force, that was her choice—in one way. He could have forbidden her to come ashore. It was her ship, but he was commander.

He hadn't ordered her to stay on board. Some people's griefs he could honour, even against his instincts about a battlefield. And he had seen her being capable several times now.

Rasca Tripon was also with him as they began moving through the ruins along a dusty road towards Tarouz, clearly visible in the distance. Their boots made footprints in the dust. There was birdsong. There were probably wolves and other wild creatures here; he didn't see any.

He hadn't been the one to agree to Skandir joining this campaign, but he didn't regret it, or resist. He was pleased to meet the man, salute him. And happy not to be fighting against him. He could acknowledge who might be dangerous, if arrayed against you. He'd been forced to learn that, young, by one other commander. Only the one, but a life's lesson, and still with him.

He ordered Gian and a group of others to the front, to watch for an ambush. Skandir had already sent five of his men to the back, to warn of any attack from behind. Folco hadn't called for that, but it was all right. It was the proper thing to do. These were men who lived by fighting in this way: limited numbers, endlessly alert, in enemy lands.

Lenia stayed close to him. Folco had an odd feeling she was doing that to protect *him*, which was amusing in a way. He said nothing to her. Put his mind to their task.

His purpose was to get to the landward gates quickly and assess what he found there. If Zariq had the city walls fully manned, archers and guns visible, he'd stay out of range, wait for the sea attack to resolve—he had reason to believe they'd win that battle now, if his commanders knew what they were doing. Not a certainty, but surely a fair chance?

It might already be different on the landward side, too. There were many things they might find when they reached the city, which is why he wanted to get there.

But also . . .

He had a thought, as they moved through the ruins of a city sacked long ago. An unexpected idea, sudden and compelling, and so he was intensely alert as they went west, wet from wading ashore. He knew that Gian would also be watchful. He assumed the same about Skandir, who had his seventy men just behind Folco's on the road.

But it was Lenia Serrana who noticed something first, and called it out, pointing.

His personal guard, Folco thought wryly. He looked. He saw what she had seen. He called a halt.

He was about to order men over that way, up a ridge to their left, towards what remained of what would have been a temple to some pagan deity, but before he could do so, a dozen men emerged from behind a crumbled wall, moving past a row of columns supporting nothing now.

It would be well over a thousand years old, Folco thought, that temple. He ought to have known or remembered exactly how old, and also the name of the pagan god or goddess it was dedicated to. He'd been taught about the Ancients and their enemies at school as a boy, by a teacher he'd loved.

Wrong moment for such memories.

The men who approached, waving at them, were dressed like corsairs or fishermen, some with a sailor's kerchief tied around their heads in the fashion of eastern men at sea. They had that colouring, too, he saw, as they approached, smiling. They'd be from the islands, most likely. They had swords, he saw a few guns. The leader gestured to him in an elaborate salute. Then he stopped some distance before reaching Folco, because he was caused to stop by a number of d'Acorsi's men arrayed in front of them. He bowed. Folco nodded. Waited.

That leader, a good-sized man of about his own age, smiled again. He appeared to have blue eyes, hard to be sure at this distance. It was very quiet. The birds, only a thread of wind. He wondered what that would mean for the fight in the harbour.

The man spoke then, in Trakesian, a tumble of urgent words. Folco waited until he was done. He turned to Skandir, whose language this was.

Skandir's face was unreadable. "He says their small ship was broken on rocks east of here as they tried to land at sunrise. They made their way here and hid, hoping more of us would come. They wish to be taken back to sea, any craft we have, to join the fight for the harbour."

Folco looked at the leader of these dozen men. He said, quietly, "Why were you landing? Answer in my tongue. Trakesians will know Batiaran."

The leader looked rueful. "I speak it badly, lord. We are all from islands near Candaria. We heard of the great war for holy Jad. We come to join it. Thirty of us. The others I fear are dead at sea. The rocks."

"That is not what I asked. Why were you coming ashore if you wanted to fight with the fleet?"

The man looked down. Took a steadying breath. "Lord, I admit to you . . . we hoped to find people fleeing the city with goods. We are very poor, lord, only fishermen. We thought we might find treasure to bring home to our wives and children, then turn back to join the sea battling when it began. We are brave fighters, lord!"

"You come from the east?"

"Yes, lord! We need to board a ship, to fight for Jad!"

"No tracks coming this way," Skandir's man Itanios said softly.

"I know," Folco said.

He saw that Gian had come back towards them.

"Boot marks in the dust to the west," Gian said. "Along this road, then they veer towards that temple. I think they are actually the fleeing people he says he came to rob."

"Might be," Folco said. "Someone check the temple for carts or goods."

Two men went that way.

The leader of the twelve men looked uncertain, seeing this.

"My lord," he said, still in Batiaran, an eastern accent, "in the name of holy suffering Jad, as we worship him in the east, we have brothers and friends who have died this day! Let us fight in their names!"

"I think," Folco said, "that you are lying. I think you fled Tarouz yourselves, and are corsairs, and know to speak Trakesian because you were born there."

"Corsairs? It is not true, lord!" the big leader cried.

"A good sword," Skandir said, again very softly. Folco nodded.

"How do you come to have a blade like that?" he asked. Behind the twelve men, he saw one of his own emerge from the ruined temple and shake his head. No carts or goods up there.

"It was my father's!" the leader cried. "Jad shelter his soul in light. He defeated a raid on our island when I was a child. He claimed the corsair's sword."

Folco was about to reply when Lenia Serrana stepped forward, to stand between the two groups of men. He was irritated, she had no place doing that, and she—

"Hello, Zariq," she said. "This is a surprise."

"ABANDONING THE PEOPLE you rule?" Lenia added, mockingly. She felt something rising within her, dangerously near to joy.

"What is this?" said the man she addressed.

Behind her Folco and the others stayed silent now. She said, "You have been unlucky, though I doubt it would have worked, not with these men. You wanted to be put on a small ship you could seize in the night? Sail away unnoticed? Didn't you begin that way all those years ago? Seizing a ship. Isn't that your story, Zariq?"

Silence. A large number of men waiting on her.

"Why do I say you are unlucky?" she continued, as if in a calm conversation with him. "Because I am here and I know you, ibn Tihon. We have met twice. A courtyard in Almassar, a tavern in Marsena. Shaving your beard, changing clothing, they are not enough, Zariq. As it happens, I even know the hilt of your sword. You ought to have taken one from a guard when you fled the palace. A mistake. Like Ziyar's raid in Sorenica. Killed him, that mistake. This one will kill you."

Behind her, Folco spoke. "You are certain?"

"I am certain," she said, not turning around.

"Then this is a gift of the god," Skandir said. "We will pray and give thanks."

"After," said Folco. Lenia looked back. He was smiling, it was not a pleasant smile. He nodded at her. Said to Zariq ibn Tihon, "Why did you do this? No loyalty at all to the people you rule?"

Zariq was staring at him. His eyes were very blue, the eyes of the Jaddite fisherman he had indeed been when young and taken in the raid that set him on the path to glory and power, and now here among the ruins.

"The fleet is half gone," he said, finally. "The city will not hold when we lose the harbour. The djannis are loyal to Asharias, not to me. If I wished to continue to fight on, to live, to do anything at all, it had to be elsewhere."

"Leaving your city to be burned, its people savaged and killed?"

"You would not kill them with me gone," Zariq ibn Tihon said. "They will surrender, open the gates."

"Are you so sure," Skandir said quietly, "that I do not want Asharite blood?"

"I am," Zariq said, with impressive composure. "You speak Trakesian. I believe I know you. Your enemy is in the east. Not the people of the Majriti."

"My enemy today, just now," said the man who had been Ban Rasca Tripon, "is you."

"Then fight me," Zariq said. "The two of us. If I kill you, I leave with my men. No ship, but we walk on. If you kill me, you have your trophy to display, slain in combat. Two men from Trakesian lands, met in a far place."

"Done!" said Skandir.

"No," said Folco d'Acorsi in the same moment.

Lenia looked back again at the two of them. They were staring at each other now. Not hostility, something else, she didn't have a word for it.

"Do not deny me this, d'Acorsi," said Skandir. His voice could go very soft.

"I cannot let him leave," Folco said. "Under any circumstances. This man is the treasure the Patriarch will demand if we do not kill people in the city."

"Then you can kill people in the city."

"No," said Folco. "We have undertaken not to do that. We take everything we can carry if we get inside Tarouz, but if they surrender I will not have innocent people assaulted and murdered."

"Innocent people," Skandir said bitterly. "They are worshippers of—"

"*Innocent people*," Folco repeated. "We will fight the djannis, if they do not surrender."

"And if they do? They go home? To make war on me and my own people again in the east?"

Folco hesitated for the first time. "No. No, you are right. Gurçu's infantry we will deal with, regardless. For you. We will send the ones who survive to the galleys. For you," he repeated.

Skandir was rigid still, Lenia saw. A fury, a bleak rage. "Thank you so much," he said bitterly.

"They will die there," Folco said.

"We have not taken the city," Gian said. "With great respect, my lords."

He so rarely spoke, she thought.

"You will now," said Zariq ibn Tihon. "Let me fight him, for my life and the lives of these men."

"D'Acorsi, I need this," Skandir said. "If you honour me at all, let me have it. I have been battling Asharites since before the City of Cities fell, while you made money in petty wars in Batiara and bought paintings and built sanctuaries and pretty gardens. You owe me this. You *all* owe me this."

Folco's face was grim.

"Just kill him then," he said. "Use a bow."

"No. In combat. Me slaying Gurçu's man."

Folco looked at him a long time. Then he finally nodded his head, once. Lenia hadn't thought he would. There was reason to what Skandir said, but . . . that wasn't entirely why he was agreeing. Something about men, she decided. And maybe also about Sarantium's fall, the guilt of it, even here, now, where they were, amid what remained of another city set on fire long ago.

HE WASN'T CERTAIN why he'd agreed to this. Partly a feeling Skandir really was owed this fight. Respect, awareness of what the man was doing every day. But partly a strange, dark, undeniable excitement at the idea of single combat. There were so many legends, so many songs and stories, and here was another about to happen in these ruins. It occurred to him suddenly that the idea of *a fair fight* had an appeal, in a world where so little was ever fair, especially in war, but not only there.

He made another decision, as they formed a wide circle around two men. Two very big men. Skandir the taller, Zariq broader of shoulder, muscled. Ibn Tihon had been fighting battles for longer than Ban Rasca Tripon of Trakesia had. He had been at war on sea and land since he was a boy. He'd know how to do this, Folco thought. Skandir could easily come to his end in the dust of Axartes, far from his home.

Folco d'Acorsi decided that if that happened—if Skandir died now—he was not letting Zariq ibn Tihon go free, whatever he'd just promised. He'd seek his peace with Jad for that, beg absolution from the Patriarch, if he himself survived. This was, he reminded himself, a holy war. What was proper changed in those, didn't it?

He had lost control of the moment, however. He didn't like it, but his heart was still pounding, something primal taking him as he watched two men begin circling each other, in order for one of them to die.

The sun would matter, he thought, and the terrain. They'd both know that.

Lenia, I don't like this! This is bad.
  Oh, child. I know it is.
  I'm afraid.
  So am I.
  But can't we—

Hush, Leora. Please. For a moment. I need to think.

And thinking, watching, a memory came to her, driven hard, like a crossbow bolt. A moment in Marsena, a tavern there, the last time she'd seen this man. Something his brother had said, drunken, threatening violence and death, before she and Rafel had been paid and had gone out into the darkness, safely.

But she was certain of something now, and knew why she had felt so afraid. The feeling had come before the knowing.

Oh, Leora, they are going to hate me so much.

What? Why? You? Why would they—

Because I'm a woman, and this is a dance for men.

A dance? I don't understand.

Later. If we can. Wait now.

If we can, she thought. There was a circle, many men deep, most of those gathered here. She stood in the front row, next to Folco. About forty of his men were watching from up on the slope towards the temple. They had taken Zariq's people with them, and disarmed them. A number of others stood with their backs to all this, on watch. Gian was one of those.

Her own need was to address the two men circling each other inside the circle. They hadn't yet drawn their swords, were examining the ground. What would doing this be like? Lenia thought. What *could* such a moment be like?

She looked at Zariq, his blue eyes when he faced her, his muscled back when they circled the other way. He wore a leather vest over a dark-blue tunic. The vest mattered. She didn't see his knife, knew he carried one. Probably two. Knew it as surely as she knew her own true name.

They circled one more time. Stopped. Drew swords at last. Zariq right in front of her, Skandir, tall and lean, across from him, facing her and Folco.

Pray for me, she said to the small child in a sanctuary near Rhodias.

And then she moved. Light-footed, quick and decisive, as she'd been trained.

Two steps forward, right-hand knife drawn from her belt—and she stabbed Zariq ibn Tihon with it in the back of his right shoulder, high up, hard and deep, slicing into muscle, ripping upwards. She pulled the blade immediately, plunged it straight back into him as he shouted in surprise and pain. She stabbed down, right at the top of that shoulder.

His sword fell into the dust.

Zariq started to turn around, swearing. He moved his left hand downwards. There was shouting all around. Skandir was roaring in fury. She stabbed Zariq a third time, left shoulder now, angled around the leather vest, deep, hard, ripping upwards again. Pulled the knife out, plunged it once more into that shoulder, again on the top, driving down.

He howled. Both arms hung limp by his sides, useless. He wouldn't be able to lift them. She knew it. She knew how to do this. The man who'd owned her had arranged for her to be taught.

There was so much noise now, in what had been a silent place among ghosts.

She stood in front of Zariq ibn Tihon. "For my father and mother," Lenia Serrana said quietly. "And for my brother. And for me."

He would have killed her if he could have. He couldn't. He couldn't kill her.

Skandir, however . . .

The big man surged forward, red-faced, sword levelled at her.

"*Woman, what have you done?*" he cried.

She turned to him. She didn't step back. She would *not* retreat. She felt shaky though, almost sick. It was one thing to do something in the moment, movement and training and instinct, but . . .

She said, trying not to let her voice show how she was feeling, "Have I spoiled a fair fight, my lord?"

She became aware that Folco was beside her. He wouldn't let her be killed, she thought.

"*Yes!*" Skandir snapped. "*I am shamed by this! D'Acorsi is!*"

"I'll decide if I'm shamed," Folco said. His voice was a miracle of calm. "Lenia, what did you see?"

Relief, hearing that question. So much of it, washing over her.

She looked from one man to the other. The shouting died down. "He uses poison on his blades," she said. "It will be on the sword. And on the knife he will have intended to throw at you. He needs only to draw blood to kill. His brother told us once." She looked up at Skandir. "Fair fight, my lord?"

She could be bitter too, she thought. She could be enraged in ways she would not explain to these men, or even to the child who spoke to her.

Silence in the ruins. You could hear the birds again. The world busily carrying on above them, past them, around whatever they did, men and women, wherever they were.

She saw the moment when the big, red-bearded man accepted what she'd said. His shoulders eased. His posture changed.

"Where's the dagger?" he asked calmly.

"Left boot. He was reaching for it. No one touch the sword."

FOLCO CAME AROUND in front of the maimed corsair, careful to step over the fallen blade. He did not doubt for an instant that Lenia Serrana was correct about the poison. It explained many things, including why a man disguised as a fisherman was carrying such a good blade. Zariq had not expected to encounter people who would know about such things. Just mariners, and a small ship to board—and seize. Or, if not, he'd have carried on walking east as far as he needed to, to find a fishing village, a fishing boat. He'd started life that way. Bad luck, Folco thought; the man could have escaped.

"What did you expect," Skandir was saying to Zariq, "if I died of a poisoned scratch? That he'd let you go?" He was calm again. It hadn't taken long.

The wounded man, arms at his sides, said, "He wasn't going to let me go if I killed you. I saw it in him."

"Really?" Folco said. "So you just wanted a death to carry across with you?"

Zariq looked away, upwards at the bright sky and then back down. "I have been doing this as long as you have. You command a force for your Patriarch. You will be expected to bring me to him. Kill me cleanly now. Warrior to warrior. Do not carry me back alive to be shamed."

"You are dead already of those wounds, if we don't treat them."

"Then don't treat them."

"If so," said Skandir, "you will be known to have died of a woman's blade. More shame that way, oh warrior of Ashar."

Ibn Tihon winced.

It *would* shame his memory, Folco thought, that would be eating at him now. Why Skandir had said it. But there was—another thought came swiftly—something more to this. And with that realization, he knew what needed to be done here. He had, indeed, been doing this sort of thing, dealing with death, for a long time.

He met Skandir's gaze and was a little surprised to see the big man nod.

"Not her," Skandir said quietly.

"No," he said. "But for her sake, not his."

"Not for his at all," Skandir said.

"What are you saying?" Lenia asked.

He said, "I have a thought, Ban Rasca." The old name, deliberately. His idea might be a mistake, might not be. You could so easily make mistakes, Folco thought. "Let him die here, my lord, but let it be you. I have a reason."

He expected more questions, but there were none, from the man, or the woman. *I have a reason* seemed to have been enough to . . .

Skandir said nothing to the Asharite either. He did not curse or pray. He just stepped forward, a long stride, and he drove his sword straight through the leather vest Zariq ibn Tihon wore, and he killed him in the sunlight of Axartes, where so many had died already, long ago.

LENIA MADE HERSELF watch as the Asharites were killed, up the slope. She hadn't seen Folco signal for this, but he must have done so. They *could* have released them, she thought. Let them wander east through the desert or along the coast, try to live, find a future, days and nights. But they were not simply people who lived in Tarouz, they were fighters. Possibly djannis, even; they'd all looked as if they might be Jaddites, and the djannis were almost always children from Sauradia, Trakesia, the eastern islands, taken in raids, changing faith, as so many did.

The boundaries of belief, she thought, could be hard as iron or permeable as air.

They would let merchants and artisans and farmers live if they took Tarouz. Not the soldiers. This was, after all, a war for vengeance. Hard as iron.

I don't like this, Lenia, she heard. *The killing.*

I know, child. Look away?

It was over, in any case. Folco's men were well trained and the prisoners had been disarmed. They had done this sort of thing before. Skandir, she thought, would never have taken prisoners. Ransoming was not what he did. Rafel, she remembered, was afraid she'd choose that life, away to the east.

Does this honour Jad?

I don't know, Leora. I'm not . . . clear on such things.

I will pray for all of their souls.

Even the Asharites?

Even them, Leora Sacchetti said firmly inside her head.

Skandir, beside her, was looking down at the man he'd killed. He smiled, that thin, hard smile. "A ruin among the ruins," he said.

Folco looked at him. "He isn't a ruin. He's just dead."

"We're going to cut off his head now, d'Acorsi. What will that make him?"

"Dead, still. But this man and his brother changed the Middle Sea and the lands around, west and east. We can kill him and still remember that." He looked up the slope towards the temple and the fallen pillars.

"Ah, so we do what? Honour him?"

Folco shook his head. "No. But he isn't a ruin. Nor will you be if Gurçu kills you."

Blunt, Lenia thought.

"As you like," said Skandir, with a shrug. "It doesn't matter. It is just a word." He gestured to one of his men.

That man, Ilija his name was, came over, drew a sword, and decapitated Zariq ibn Tihon where he lay.

It looked as if he'd done this before. Lenia didn't want to think about that. The severed head was placed, dripping, in a heavy canvas bag. There was a great deal of blood in the dirt by the body. The bag was tied up. A man was named by Skandir to carry it. He seemed happy, proud to be doing so.

The fallen sword was picked up, carefully, by a different fighter, gloved, and carried down to the sea. Lenia watched him do that. It was thrown into the water, in a flat, spinning arc. Might have been a trophy. Not now. Who knew if sea water would erase that poison. Probably, she thought, over time. She hoped it would never be found.

An idea, with that. She put on her own leather gloves, went over to the headless corpse, stepping around blood.

"Lenia, you need not."

It was Folco, who really seemed to notice everything. She ignored him this time. Someone *would* come here, to despoil the corpses left in the dust—if they arrived before the animals did. Always a race.

She pulled off the dead man's left boot, grunting with the effort. A sheathed knife was indeed strapped to his calf. She drew it free, cautiously.

Someone said, "Let me."

It was Gian, she saw, looking up.

He had followed her in Seressa—it seemed so long ago—on a foggy night. He had followed her to her brother's ranch, guarding her. He almost never spoke. He was an immensely reassuring man. She let him take the blade and walk away to hurl it, as well, into the sea. She drew off her gloves and discarded them.

Her brother's ranch, she thought. A memory connected to nothing here. Carlito. He'd be there now. She could picture it.

Not a time to be weak, she told herself.

They left that place. Walking west, her mind turned to what Folco had said, just before Zariq was killed by Skandir: *I have a reason.*

She fell in stride with him.

He glanced over, spoke first. "That was well done. Likely you saved Ban Rasca's life. Were you afraid?"

"Among a crowd of men stupidly hungry to see that fight, be able to tell of it all their lives, you mean?"

He grimaced. "Some truth, but Lenia, it was not entirely folly. Skandir could have ensured no one else among us died if he won. Without it, ibn Tihon and his men fight us. They die, yes, but so might a number of our men."

She looked at him. "And *that* was your reason for agreeing?"

A wry face. "Probably not my principal reason. He would never have hurt you, Lenia. You know that."

"Skandir? Maybe not," she said. "But a woman spoiled men's chance to see glory. I killed the songs. The single combat in the ruins of Axartes!"

He walked on a few strides. "You are angry."

"I am angry. So tell me honestly, why did you want *him* to do the killing?"

He looked at her again. "Two reasons. But you'll know them both."

She swore. "I might, but I deserve an answer from you."

If he smiled now, she thought, she would . . . she would swear again, she decided.

He didn't smile. He said, "One: I did it for you. Same as in Sorenica. You are a merchant, will be travelling, or might be, your choice. It is not safe for you to be known as the person who killed—and shamed—the khalif of Tarouz."

She nodded. Had guessed this, yes. "And the second reason?"

"The Patriarch. You saw how he reacted when we brought him Ziyar's body. You were there, Lenia. This is *his* war. If we succeed, and return to Rhodias, I promise you Scarsone Sardi will send a reward to the one who killed Zariq ibn Tihon. And Skandir needs all the money he can get. He is fighting every day, Lenia."

She stared at him. "You were thinking of this? In the ruins? Right then?"

"It is what I do, Lenia."

She thought about it. "And if the Patriarch doesn't bring it up, you'll make the point yourself? In the palace. When you tell the story."

"I will. But you aren't in the story, unless you want to be. Not that story."

They walked on. She said, "I don't need to be. I don't want to be."

"I thought as much," said Folco d'Acorsi.

She'd never known a man like him in her life, Lenia thought.

She never would. There are such people. We sometimes meet them. Walk beside them for a time, for many years, or just along a dusty path towards a city at the edge of a desert, at the edge of the sea.

෨෨

Three things of decisive importance happened that day, in what became known as the War for Tarouz.

The first had to do with Elie ben Hafai, captain of the *Silver Light*, and what he did, coming back from ferrying almost two hundred people—including the supreme commander of the fleet—to a strand east of the city.

The battle for the harbour had just begun as he was doing this. He'd sheered away from the fleet earlier, on orders, looking for a place to beach a landing party. The winds were light. He had advisers as to rocky places here. He didn't entirely trust them, or their charts. He didn't entirely trust anyone but himself at sea. He'd taken the wheel coming in, though a captain shouldn't normally do that. He didn't care.

He was manning it again, coming back out past the pine-treed bluff that hid the harbour of Tarouz on this side. They could hear cannon and guns and the shouts and screams of men. War at sea was loud. He still had fighting men on board, and exceptionally good cannon, and those who knew how to aim and fire them.

Both those last were because of the fire at the Arsenale of Seressa.

The city had felt (rightly, in Elie's view) deeply contrite about the breakdown in security. Especially for a ship being built for the Patriarch's fleet, with the duke himself supervising at a distance. They'd undertaken to give Rafel and Lenia, and pay for, the very newest, most expensive cannon, fourteen of them, six each to port and starboard, firing through gunports cut in the hull of the gun deck, and two great guns, carefully balanced, fore and aft. The gunports were elegantly designed: the new cannon, on tracks higher off the gun deck than usual, could be rolled out and back smoothly, then the ports closed tightly with shutters and bolts when not in use.

Rafel, the owner who was not coming to war, had accepted this gesture with all proper expressions of gratitude. And as a result, Elie ben Hafai had command of this . . . gift.

Sailing back out, trying to judge when and where to come around the bluff and join the fight, he . . . well, he would later say it had been a miracle. That it was not him. It was the moon sisters being good to an unworthy mariner.

He had been looking ahead, mostly. Towards where the bluff ended. But he glanced, for whatever reason, to his left, to port—and he saw, through the canopy of pines, what he saw.

Only a glimpse, but enough. Enough.

He screamed for the sails to be taken in on all three masts. His mariners leaped to obey. His heart was pounding. He'd later say it had been like a wild creature in his chest. He was not given to such turns of phrase. Or to a pounding heart.

But what he'd seen was the glint of sunlight off the massive cannon mounted—six of them, it later emerged—on the tower-fortress guarding the eastern side of Tarouz harbour.

And he knew two things. One, he was *behind* them. Those cannon faced out, they could be swivelled, and angled up and down of course. They could not be turned around.

Two, Elie ben Hafai knew, because he'd been testing them all along, from the moment the *Silver Light* sailed, how far his own glorious cannon could reach, and how high they could be tilted through the tall gunports . . . *and they could reach that far.* Over the trees to the tower.

Over the trees to the tower.

He had two sails raised, tested his ability to turn about quickly in this beautifully sheltered place before they'd round the bluff to where there was battle at sea. He did that so as to be able to keep both sides of his ship firing and reloading and cooling down, *and* use the single guns fore and aft. Elevation was an issue. They had to fire *over* the trees.

He knew how to do that, with an almost empty ship, ready for whatever treasures they took from Tarouz, if they took Tarouz.

That fortress beyond the pines had no defence against him. None. There had never been ships' cannon that could do what he was about to do. The world had changed, the world of war, at any rate. And he was the man bringing the new thing here. Each time he had the guns on either side fire, he had every mariner on board move carefully to the opposite side, canting the *Silver Light* that way, giving him that much more elevation. In higher seas it would have been terribly dangerous.

The seas were gentle in this bay, and Elie ben Hafai knew exactly what he was doing with his gift, the miracle given him.

He destroyed that tower. He did more. The Asharite cannon up there beyond the trees had a great deal of gunpowder to fire them. Powder that could, as every seaman knew, easily ignite into a blaze. Or an explosion.

Both things happened that day, because of what Elie had seen with that glance to his left. Because of what he did.

The cannonballs of the *Silver Light* cleared the pines. They found their range and smashed into the fortifications and the artillery of the tower. Over and again, without surcease. Starboard, port, fore, and aft, as the ship turned.

The inferno they caused brought the tower crashing down in lurid, upthrust sheets of flame. Fire caught the Asharite ships towards the back of their fleet, the ones nearest to the harbour docks, where none of the Jaddite fleet would yet be. These caught fire in turn, sails first, then wood. Elie kept sending cannonballs that way. Once the tower fell, he had his gunners elevate their aim a little more and they began firing into the harbour itself. He couldn't see it, but he knew what was there, whose ships.

They could hear the screaming of wounded and dying men, even above the sounds of the full engagement. He was not a violent man, Elie ben Hafai, not warlike by nature, or angry, but he was here for a war, and he took pride in his work, and what he did that day was completely decisive in that sea battle by Tarouz.

Many of the ships' commanders of the Asharite fleet farther out panicked, seeing what was happening behind them by the harbour. Farai Alfasi did not. He would have been a prize, taken alive for the Patriarch. He was not. He rammed a Seressini galley with his, boarded it ahead of all his men, died sword in hand, choosing death, screaming defiance, fighting a great many men.

The guns of the harbour fortress on the western side were hit with a rain of fire from the Jaddite fleet. Ships were freed to do that because of the panic and death and burning that Elie had caused.

That western fortress, too, blew up, in flames. Which ended things at sea, really. The flight of the corsairs before sunrise had gone a long way to deciding this battle. Elie ben Hafai did the rest, one ship behind the pine trees, in the quiet of the bay beyond the bluff.

THEY WOULD SHOWER him with glory and gifts, after. Rhodias, Seressa (what had happened spoke to the magnificence of *their* cannon!), the king of Ferrieres, whose ships were scarcely harmed in that fight. Even the Holy Jaddite Emperor far to the north in Obravic learned the name Elie ben Hafai. He hadn't given much to this war in the Majriti—his true enemy, his danger, was Gurçu, threatening an army every spring—but he had given something. He'd needed to be *present* in a holy war.

He didn't have a great deal of money to spare, was busily repairing his own fortresses, but he sent the Kindath mariner a necklace of heavy silver with an enormous lapis lazuli pendant. The emperor, an eccentric man, as many of his dynasty had been, had suggested this himself. The colours of the Kindath, he'd said. He thought it suitable.

Elie had been offered a command in the fleet of Seressa, a house there, other honours. He'd declined the command. He would have had to embrace the faith of Jad to take it. Many changed their religion, of course—his two brothers had become Asharite in the Majriti after their family fled Esperaña—but he had decided he would not, back then, and he wasn't a changeable sort of man. He liked his work. He loved Rafel ben Natan, with whom he'd grown up in Almassar. He loved his new ship (and would love the others they were able to build as their business grew). He realized he even loved Lenia Serrana. That was *something* of a change, but he didn't see it that way. People could grow on you.

He accepted the house in Seressa's Kindath quarter. He saw much of the world in time, as a mariner does. He went east as far as Khatib on the grain and spice run many times, and he was twice in Asharias itself, that had been Sarantium.

He wandered that city, looking at the glories of it. He saw the dolphins in the strait. He went into Emperor Valerius's thousand-year-old Sanctuary of Jad's Holy Wisdom, now the Temple of Ashar's Stars. He thought it was handsome. There were silver stars suspended from chains overhead. He walked through the ruins of the fabled Hippodrome. He thought he might have enjoyed seeing chariots race there among a vast, roaring crowd, cheering for one of the teams, wagering on it. There were statues and pillars and monuments to charioteers of long ago, almost all of them fallen.

He experienced some danger in Asharias on his second visit, but he escaped it, survived, did the quiet thing he'd come to do: bringing Kindath families at the request of Dona Raina Vidal, still (always) the queen of his people.

His knees began to bother him as the years went by, and one shoulder, legacies of a life on the waves. When he retired from ships and the sea, it was to a ranch near Bischio, in Batiara. This surprised people: he had the house in Seressa, another he'd bought in a small town near Marsena with a Kindath community, but it was to the ranch that he went for his last years, having visited there many times all along.

He settled happily into quarters they built for him near the main house. He told stories on the porches at sunset in summer, by a fire inside in colder months, and listened to others' tales. He laughed easily and often. He hadn't been like that. We can change. He went into Bischio for Kindath festivals and holidays. Told stories there, too.

He watched the children of the ranch grow up, then he watched them marry, have their own children, begin to take responsibility for their father's ranch and horses. He loved them, as well, was loved by them.

He never married. That part of life seemed to have not been for him, even young.

When he died he was buried on the ranch, among those they'd lost, in the small graveyard to the south of the last pasture. A long way from Esperaña, from the Kindath quarter by the walls of Almassar, from the sea. But honoured and mourned. A good life, by almost any measure there might ever be.

∾

The next thing that happened at Tarouz happened on the landward side, on the dusty path approaching the city from the east.

Skandir caught up with Folco d'Acorsi and the woman beside him. With no preamble he said, "We need to halt, d'Acorsi, before we reach the gates."

Folco glanced at him. He lifted a hand overhead. One of the men up front with Gian, looking back at their commander, always, relayed that signal and they stopped. The wind blew.

They were close, but not yet at the walls.

"Why so?" Folco asked.

To their right, towards the sea, explosions and cannon fire were continuing steadily, and the harbour and the ships within it appeared to be on fire, thick black smoke rising. They didn't know why, how this had happened so quickly. It was unexpected, and extremely good.

Skandir said, looking that way, "I think we have the city now. They'll be panicked. They'll want to surrender, and pray for mercy from us."

"You know those are my instructions."

"And your inclinations?"

"Not yours?" Folco asked.

"We have discussed this. Not usually. But hear me. If your plan is to have the people in Tarouz walk out, you understand the djannis in there will know they are doomed. That we will kill them."

"That would be my inclination as to the djannis, yes."

Lenia, standing beside them, listening, was thinking about the decapitated man, his head in a sack now, his men slain, unarmed, behind them. She had spent years wanting to kill Asharites. Had done so.

"There will have been hundreds of them in there," Skandir said. "Some are on their galleys, for boarding our ships in the fight, but I'd wager four or five hundred are still inside."

"They'll want to keep the gates locked?"

"I don't think they can close the city. Not now. Not with what is happening in the harbour. Not if we tell people they can leave. The people of Tarouz will know what happens in cities that do not surrender. And we'll remind them, in any case."

"Yes," said Folco. "We will. So . . . ?"

"So the djannis are going to come out to us. You have archers, so do I. So will they. And if I am right, if there are four or five hundred of them . . ."

"And the djannis are worth fearing."

"The djannis are worth fearing. I have fought them and won, but with terrain chosen, and deception, and good fortune. And many losses. We'd be outnumbered here, and in flat, open country. I would rather . . ."

"You would rather wait for better numbers."

"No commander likes having men killed without cause. I don't have enough fighters to ever do that."

"None of us do." Folco nodded. He looked away, past the city, to the west. "I agree with you. Which is why I asked the commander from Ferrieres to put three ships' worth of fighters ashore on the western side. I believe I see them now. Do you?"

Skandir looked. Lenia Serrana looked.

A dust cloud on the far side of Tarouz.

The big man from Trakesia was grinning, she saw, as he watched it. A cold smile, she thought. "You make me wish," he said, "that I could bring you back to Sauradia, to join in my fight, d'Acorsi."

Folco looked at him. "I am honoured by that. Thank you. It is not my world, not my life. I need to be in Acorsi to sustain my people, let my son grow up to follow me. Also, my wife would cross the water and find and kill us both."

Skandir smiled again. "I have heard she is formidable."

"You have," said Folco, "no idea." He smiled back, briefly. "But I will make a vow to Jad now. For the rest of my days, and yours, every year I will send a sum to you, enough to be of help. And you will always have my prayers, Ban Rasca."

"Both matter," said Skandir. He didn't offer his usual correction as to the name.

Folco turned back west. The dust cloud was larger already. It began to resolve itself into men coming towards them.

"Look," said Lenia. She shivered, couldn't help it.

The gates of Tarouz were opening.

"Jad grant us light at the end of our days. We will slaughter them now," Skandir said.

They watched the djannis of the city, the ones sent from Asharias, march out in their distinctive hats and coats.

"They know we will, I think," said Folco d'Acorsi quietly. "They will not hide."

Lenia thought she heard respect, perhaps even sorrow. She hadn't heard it in Skandir's voice. Different worlds, different battles. Different men.

And that opening of the gates, and what followed, was the second thing that decided the War for Tarouz.

The djannis, marching briskly out, turned west towards the men from Ferrieres and were pincered by Folco's and Skandir's force coming up behind them. They'd had to turn one way or the other, Lenia thought. They chose the larger enemy army.

She was not in the midst of that fight. Had been given a flat, unconditional order by Folco. Gian was with her. They were in a group of twenty sent up a small rise to watch—and cut off any djannis who tried to escape that way. There would be another group doing the same among the men from Ferrieres. Folco had, evidently, also arranged for that.

And it did happen. About ten men did come running away. They'd try to get south, then turn east, most likely. A dream of getting home to Asharias, eventually. But Folco had them posted to stop that flight. So there was fighting on that slope. She was in a war, against Asharites.

All through the skirmish Lenia was aware that Gian never left her side. Guarding her. Because she knew how to kill, but this was different. A battle was not the same as what she'd been trained to do.

She did kill two men in that engagement at the edge of the larger fight. Did that mainly because those she stabbed with her sword were fighting Gian when she did so. She was entirely certain he saved her life there, twice. He would have wanted to be with d'Acorsi in the larger battle. He wasn't. He had been ordered to protect her. She was torn between being unhappy about this, and feeling desperately grateful. The gratitude was a revelation, something new.

It was over quite soon. Not just their small fight. The Jaddite army left no one alive that afternoon. Almost two hundred of their own force were killed or wounded. A brutal toll. The djannis of Asharias were formidable, and brave. And they died there.

Blood and hacked limbs, terrible screaming and the moans of dying men, outside the city's walls in the sunlight.

So quick, Lenia found herself thinking. She seemed to be trembling. Couldn't quite stop. She was dripping with sweat, had blood on her face and boots. Death could be so swift.

But also, there came to her a different thought: how swiftly something that had existed as a possibility for one's own life could be gone. Entirely gone.

They had feared she'd choose a battlefield existence. Go east with Skandir to his endless war. She'd said it to him herself, when he first boarded her ship. He hadn't replied.

A door hadn't closed here, Lenia thought. It had just never opened. This, she realized, on a rise of land outside Tarouz . . . this was not her world. Perhaps some woman could play a role in Sauradia, fighting beside him, but it would not be her.

Also, she thought suddenly, making herself smile inwardly—something none of the men around her would have understood—Skandir and his rebels *lived* on horseback.

But that made her think again of Carlo. Carlito, who was alive and in the world, had a place in the world. She so much wanted to see him again. There were people she needed to see again. To say many things. She didn't want to die killing Asharites any more. She had thought that was so for a long time.

Something had changed.

I'm all right with living, Lenia thought.

Folco was coming over this way, she saw, up the shallow slope. Bloodstained. She couldn't tell if he was wounded. She didn't think it was his own blood, not mostly.

"Is it over?" she asked as he stopped in front of her.

"If I can keep control here now," he said.

THERE HAD BEEN a massacre in the small city of Barignan when it fell to an army under his overall control. He still felt it as a stain against his name, a sin for which to atone every time he prayed.

This did not happen at Tarouz. In part because of that guilt Folco d'Acorsi carried.

And this was the third thing that defined that war.

Speakers of Asharic who accompanied the fleet and the army it put ashore were sent into Tarouz, guarded, carrying a clear message. People would be permitted to leave, unharmed. They could take nothing but food and clothing. Anyone found carrying items of value out of the city would be killed where they stood. But also, any Jaddite soldiers abusing them would be executed, by order of the commander, Folco Cino d'Acorsi.

Tarouz would be sacked completely, the messengers said, to the walls of houses and shops and temples and the palace. To the guns and ropes on any ships left unburned. The ships and galleys, too, of course, if they were sound enough to take north. Many were. They became spoils, part of what was divided. Ships were genuinely valuable.

But the people would be allowed to leave. They could go find a place—a village, another city, somewhere with water in the desert, perhaps wherever their family came from—to wait for the Jaddites to do what they'd sailed here to do. And then they could come back if they wished, although there were going to be fires, and they'd need to rebuild from ashes.

Or, they could move on with their lives, settle somewhere else, begin again.

People were always having to do that for one reason or another.

IN SARANTIUM WHEN it fell there had been famine and death through a long siege, and all those left fighting by the walls when Gurçu the Destroyer broke through were killed, including the last Emperor and the Eastern Patriarch, and soldiers and lords, and clerics with weapons.

But the people remaining alive in the city were not slaughtered, nor was there a ransacking, or widespread fires. Gurçu had always intended to occupy the City of Cities, make it his, have people return, or come there for the first time. He had done that, and was still doing it.

The Jaddites at Tarouz never intended to stay.

There was no way they could settle and defend this city. Make it some harbinger of conquest in the Majriti. This had been a different sort of assault with a different goal. An Asharite they'd brought with them was proposed as regent, in anticipation of people returning, and as a gesture of goodwill—to ensure co-operation, as a very large number of people began to go out through the landward gates, and the looting of the city started.

The man proposed was a diplomat of sorts, suggested by a nobleman from Rhodias who had employed him. He was apparently named Kurafi ibn Rusad. He'd been a captive in Rhodias, working on some scholarly task. He was released in Tarouz, on condition he stay and deal with the aftermath there when they left.

Kurafi agreed. Of course he did. It was freedom. But he departed from Tarouz not long after the Jaddite ships sailed with all the treasures of the city. A promise extorted by infidels was not a promise a star-worshipper was required to keep. That was known, it was a teaching. He went all the way west, to home. Overland at first, then taking a boat for the last part of the journey to Almassar.

He wrote his book there (he had wisely brought his notes with him). It was about his travails: being captured and enslaved, the pain of exile. He revised it carefully. He came to feel he had been excessive in early versions in describing his physical hardships. The pain of exile was real, even if you were not starved or beaten. He modified this. He went on to write other books. He was not, he had told himself when leaving Tarouz, a public figure. He wanted to be a writer, a thinker.

Over time, he became one. Kurafi ibn Rusad died with a body of work that was not inconsequential. He never forgot his time in Rhodias. He was buried with honour in Almassar.

We can grow, sometimes.

There were about a hundred deaths in and around Tarouz in the days after the Jaddites took the city. Half of them were residents trying to carry out items of value (or sometimes just of importance to them). Others were Jaddite soldiers who chose to believe their commander was not serious about executing them for abusing Asharites in what was, after all, a holy war blessed by the High Patriarch himself.

They were wrong.

After some were executed in a very public manner, matters proceeded in a disciplined fashion, surprisingly, given how many contingents were represented there. It helped that King Émery of Ferrieres, for reasons not entirely understood, had ordered his commanders to defer to the Batiaran, d'Acorsi, on pain of their own demise on return, should word come of their failure to do so.

The king didn't know, no one ever knew, the role Folco had played in blunting the ambitions of Esperaña—with a fleet and soldiers destroyed at Abeneven.

As to that, however, the Asharites of the Majriti would come to tell the story of that spring's war in their own way. An invading force sailing from Esperaña had been destroyed at Abeneven, on land and at sea, while Tarouz, the city of two renegade corsairs—servants who had lost the trust of the grand khalif—had been allowed by him to be sacked by a ragged collection of infidels.

It was even said in the months and years that followed that Gurçu had *ordered* the Jaddite commander not to harm people there, and the man and his force, fearing the wrath of the Conqueror, had complied.

The sack of Tarouz brought a staggering amount of wealth back north. It had become a genuinely prosperous city under the ibn Tihon brothers. All that was taken was itemized and accounted for as it was loaded onto the ships, distributed carefully, supervised by those assigned to this task. Armies need such people, too. Sometimes they are honest. Sometimes they are fearful enough to be so.

Those who had sent substantial forces, or sums, reaped very large gains. The Trakesian rebel against Asharias, Skandir—the warrior who had slain Zariq ibn Tihon—was richly rewarded by the Patriarch.

He was already back east by then, fighting in Sauradia. He was always fighting. His monies went to a man named Djivo in Dubrava. Not really a banker (his family would be, later) but trusted by other merchants, apparently, for holding or advancing sums, after and before voyages. Djivo never told anyone about this service he performed for Skandir. Men came from the east, discreetly, and were given sums by him at intervals. His younger son did learn of it, much later. He would once encounter Skandir, while on his own journey.

The two owners of the *Silver Light* kept a generous portion of what came back to Seressa on their carrack. The captain of that ship, the Kindath Elie ben Hafai, was a hero of the war, among other things.

Folco Cino d'Acorsi became the favoured military commander for the Patriarchal forces in Batiara in the years that immediately followed. For a time the only commander. His wife, the lady Caterina, made it clear that she was extremely pleased to see him when he returned to Acorsi from that war in Tarouz. She wore a green diamond about her throat to welcome him, and all through their first night together in her chamber.

They had not accomplished a slaughter in Tarouz, but over time the High Patriarch Scarsone Sardi came to believe this was a good thing for both his soul and his legacy. He had assembled a mighty fleet, taken vengeance for Sarantium, and had done it while showing the world the mercy of Jad.

Wars continued, of course. So did trade. So did all the affairs of men and women living out their lives everywhere, and always.

☙

In Seressa they told her Rafel had left for Firenta some time ago. Guidanio Cerra, clearly happy to see her, and now a partner in the ship and its revenues, agreed to supervise the unloading of what they'd brought back, deal with any issues, and keep records. She knew Rafel would want records. She left the ship, and Elie, who was being feted in Seressa, and went overland, by horse, to Firenta.

Danio insisted on making her a gift of what he said was a very good, extremely gentle horse. She named it Earthquake, which amused her, though would probably not make anyone else laugh. She had an escort, of course.

Folco had been still in Rhodias. Having brought there, among other things, the head of Zariq ibn Tihon.

She didn't hurry west, didn't want to deal with changing or adding horses or anything like that. She concentrated on trying to develop a cordial relationship with Earthquake.

In Firenta, she went to the house the Sardis had given her, from the time she'd saved Antenami Sardi's life. She called on the Sardis, father and son. Antenami greeted her with delight. She went to his home for a cheerful meal with several extremely good wines. She told him a little about the war. He wanted to talk about horses. She let him, a little. He was a happy sort of man, she'd decided. She liked him. She wondered what he'd be like as a lover. Idle thought. Unusual for her.

They'd already told her Rafel wasn't in Firenta. Antenami thought he might be in Marsena. She understood he had opened an office and a warehouse there for their business. A note had been waiting for her about that, in their office in Seressa, signed with his initial only, as usual. She'd started doing that with her own letters to people when she'd first seen it, copying him.

She spent another day in Firenta, then, feeling restless, pushed on to the coast, to Basiggio, where the *Silver Wake* was now docked. If it wasn't there, he'd have taken it to Marsena.

New escorts. From the Sardis now, four of them. The ones from Seressa went home.

She wasn't, she decided, as unhappy on a horse as she once had been. Carlito would approve, she thought.

On the way, a familiar voice.

Hello?

Oddly tentative.

Leora! Hello! Are you all right?

I . . . yes. I am.

It is good there? At the retreat?

A silence. Then, *Everyone is so much older than me.*

Lenia reminded herself this was, at one and the same time, a very small child and someone beyond anyone she knew, or expected to ever know. And away from home, she thought.

It can be hard, being in a new place, she said.

Yes.

Lenia thought for a moment.

Is anyone there . . . not kind?

The right question.

Well, the one who is closest to my age. But she's four years older! And she gets angry because I can read and she can't! They ask me to read aloud in the refectory, when we dine.

Oh, Lenia thought.

Oh, she said. She was riding through low country, nearing the coast. It was summer. Hot now, a shimmer at midday. *Leora, people can be unkind if they are envious. Most children your age can't read. Do you think she wants to know how?*

I have no idea.

She could almost hear the sniff of disdain. She was careful not to let amusement show.

I have a suggestion, if you want it.

Yes, please.

Ask if she'd like to learn. Say you'll teach her. Is there time you have, when that can happen?

Yes. Because we're the youngest. We have time without tasks.

Then try that. See what happens, if she accepts. If it doesn't help, I have other ideas.

A silence.

I love you, Lenia.

And suddenly, on the road, on a horse, a summer day, she seemed to be fighting tears. This child.

I love you, Leora Sacchetti. I think everyone will love you in time.

Will you . . . can you come see me here? Someday?

I can. I will. It is a promise. More than once. I'll be there. And I'm here. Like this. Always, child.

I won't always be a child.

I know. I'm waiting to see what you become.

Are you . . . Lenia, are you all right?

I'm looking for someone. But I'm all right.

I'd bet a copper coin I know who!

Leora!

Laughter, then the child was gone.

The ship, their small ship, was in Basiggio's harbour. She gave up. Had no idea where her partner was, what he was doing now. Was irritated not to have had a letter explaining this.

She went to where, she decided, she ought to have gone first. Not chasing someone fruitlessly across the width of Batiara. On a horse.

༄

Carlo Serrana was walking back from observing someone new training a colt to a light saddle, having it go in circles around him, controlled by tension on a long rope, getting it used to the idea of commands. Man and horse were both doing well.

He saw a single rider approaching his gate. It was late in the day.

He clenched his fists for self-control. Opened them. He told himself not to cry. He failed in this.

He went over and opened the main gate, waited there. His sister rode through, quite proudly, he thought, on a good horse. She had no escort. Had probably left them in Bischio.

"Much better," he said.

"I know!" Lenia said, dismounting.

He saw that she was weeping too, and also smiling, and then he was holding her tightly in his arms, and she was holding him.

"Oh, Carlito," she said, "I'm so happy to be back."

He cleared his throat, then had to do it a second time before he could speak. "You have ruined my life," he said. "My wife and my children call me Carlito now, all the time! If any of my men ever do so—they have been told this—they will be tied to a horse and dragged around the ranch."

She laughed as she cried, head against his chest, her dark hair. His arms were around her. Around her, in the world. Here.

"That seems proper," Lenia said.

SHE LIFTED HER head. Wiped at her eyes. Her brother looked, she thought, entirely wonderful.

"We heard it went well at Tarouz."

"It did," she said. "Jad was watching over us."

"I prayed for you. I don't usually pray."

"Neither do I. Thank you."

Someone was walking up, she saw, the sun behind him. The man she'd seen training a horse as she'd come along the road.

The man was Rafel. Her heart thudded, hard.

He said, "He told me I can call him Carlito."

"I didn't," said her brother. "But I like him."

"Good," Lenia said. She found it impossible to say more, suddenly.

Carlo looked from one to the other of them, grinned widely, then took her horse and led it away. "I'll tell Anni we have another for this evening's meal," he said. "She'll be very happy. So will the children."

They watched him lead her horse towards the stables.

"I named him Earthquake," she said.

"I see."

A silence.

"You came here," she said. "I was looking for you everywhere."

It was a foolish thing to say, he clearly *had* come here, he *was* here. She thought he'd raise his eyebrows, or chide her.

"It was where I wanted to be," Rafel said, quietly. "Waiting."

"You were waiting for me?"

Also an absurd thing to say. Why else would he be at her brother's ranch?

"I was," was all he said, still looking at her.

She read the world, a home in the world, in his eyes.

"You don't have to wait any more," she said. "I'm here."

And stepped forward to where he was, where he stood, so that they were in the same space on the earth, or as near as could be to that, as near as was allowed.

∽

Sunlight and summer for an ending. Inland, not waves at sea, not a coastline, no moons or stars. A journey has been taken.

In some places, times, the writer of a story might use ink, inkstone, brush to shape her telling. There are other ways, other times. A tale can be spoken, or sung—in a castle hall, a sun-bright marketplace, a tavern filled with singers listening to the oldest one. Or there might be pages to be turned, slowly or quickly, by a fire or a river, or before sleep comes at night.

Sometimes the tale offered is of the lives and deaths of those deemed powerful. And sometimes it is about men and women trying as best they can to live, shape lives, despite the loss of a home, roots, origins, a sense of where they might belong. That loss never goes away but it can, with great good fortune, become one thing among others. Because there are sometimes grace, mercy, kindness, friendship, love . . .

We may be marked by how we begin, but there is not only that.

Children yet to be born, or very young in this story, will grow up to live through their own days and nights. Some will become important in their world, most will not. Most cannot be. But in what is given to us, the ink and brush put to paper, words offered, words we read . . . there might come a thought, a shared one, about this back and forth, the music made between the singer and the listener. Hands, minds, touching across space and years. Stories are, as much as anything else, an act of love. They begin, they trace or weave their path for us, with us. They end. This one has, my loves.

ACKNOWLEDGEMENTS

All the Seas of the World was substantially written during a pandemic year. I have had many discussions about this with other people working on their art, or finding it difficult to do so. I don't think there's a direct presence in the novel, but we all live and work, by definition, in a context. Sometimes that is personal, immediate, sometimes it is wider. It would feel a presumption to add a dedication for this book to those who died (and those who loved them), but it is true to say that they were in mind as I worked.

I do know that themes of exile have been in my novels before, and are obviously present here. There were, as always, writers and books that sparked my thinking on this and other themes, and it is proper (as always, for me) to acknowledge some of them, with the hope that this will be of interest to readers who might want to explore the background for themselves. These are never meant to be comprehensive bibliographies, only signposts.

Many years ago, my father-in-law gave me a book he'd had recommended to him. "This is probably more your sort of thing than mine," he said. I didn't read it for some time, but when I did, *A Man of Three Worlds*, by Mercedes García-Arenal and Gerard Wiegers, immediately led me to take notes—it is very much a part of the origin story of this novel. I have long been interested in the fluidity of religion, identity, and place in Renaissance times, and the story of Samuel Pallache fed straight into that and gave me my first thoughts of the figure who would become Rafel ben Natan. Sometimes, of course, people's fluidity was forced, necessary, not a choice. That's part of this book.

Another character—a supporting one, but important to me—emerged from Cecil Roth's *Doña Gracia*, and the remarkable woman it chronicles. She's the inspiration for my own Raina Vidal.

There is no "real person" behind Lenia Serrana, only an awareness through all my reading of how much raiding, piracy, capturing and enslaving people were elements of life (mostly coastal life, but not exclusively) of the time. Among other books, Jacques Heers's *The Barbary Corsairs*, David Abulafia's *The Great Sea*, Gillian Hutchinson's *Medieval Ships and Shipping*, Lincoln Paine's *The Sea and Civilization*, Roger Crowley's *Empires of the Sea* . . . all these were helpful in steeping myself again in awareness of this, and other maritime aspects of the time I was drawing upon.

Allen James Fromherz's *The Near West* was highly useful, as was the great Natalie Zemon Davis's *Trickster Travels*, which gave rise to a captured scholar and his story here. Michael Brett and Elizabeth Fontress's *The Berbers*, Robert Irwin's *Ibn Khaldun*, and Jane S. Gerber's *The Jews of Spain* were key parts of my reading, as was Lauro Martines (a historian I greatly admire) with *April Blood*, about the Pazzi Conspiracy. *The Last Storytellers*, by Richard Hamilton, started me down a path to using marketplace storytelling early in the novel, and *Renaissance Woman*, by Ramie Targoff, about the remarkable life of Vittoria Colonna, reaffirmed my engagement with thinking about the lives of women in this time: both the limitations and the occasional possibilities.

I enjoyed Massimo Montanari's *Medieval Tastes* (food!) and Valentina Fornaciai's *Toilette, Perfumes and Make-up at the Medici*

Court: I always love "daily life" works of research. Same, in a very different context, with *Firearms*, by Kenneth Chase.

On a more personal level, my thanks are owed again to the editors I work with, who show a real generosity in responding so strongly to novels that never fall neatly into a category: Nicole Winstanley and Lara Hinchberger, Oliver Johnson, Jessica Wade, and my long-time copy editor Catherine Marjoribanks. I am grateful to all of them for their commitment to the work. The same applies to my agents. It is a pleasure to thank John Silbersack, Jonny Geller, and Jerry Kalajian. I've worked with them all for years, reaped the benefit of their engagement with my writing.

Martin Springett adapted his earlier maps of my near-Europe to fit the needs of this story, and did so with his customary skill and patience: he's a dear friend. So are Deborah Meghnagi and Alec Lynch, who created and continue to maintain brightweavings.com, the authorized website on my work. My brother Rex remains my first, sharp, very careful reader. It's a role he appears to enjoy—because he keeps taking it on. My appreciation is extreme, and my love.

That same appreciation and love, always, belong to my wife and my sons. I build what I build upon the ground they offer me.

One more acknowledgement that was to go here now sadly becomes the dedication for this book. My mother was a reader in manuscript of everything I ever published, including *All the Seas of the World*. I'm very glad that this was so. She is dearly missed, always will be.

GUY GAVRIEL KAY is the internationally bestselling author of fourteen previous novels, including the Fionavar Tapestry series, *Tigana*, and most recently, *A Brightness Long Ago*, *Children of Earth and Sky*, and *River of Stars*. He has been awarded the International Goliardos Prize for his work in the literature of the fantastic and won the World Fantasy Award for *Ysabel* in 2008. In 2014, he was named to the Order of Canada, the country's highest civilian honour. His works have been translated into more than thirty languages.

A NOTE ABOUT THE TYPE

The body of *All the Seas of the World* has been set in Adobe Garamond. Designed for the Adobe Corporation by Robert Slimbach, the fonts are based on types first cut by Claude Garamond (c.1480–1561). Garamond was a pupil of Geoffrey Tory and is believed to have followed classic Venetian type models, although he did introduce a number of important differences, and it is to him that we owe the letterforms we now know as "old style." Garamond gave his characters a sense of movement and elegance that ultimately won him an international reputation and the patronage of Frances I of France.